THE LONDON CHEQUE

THE LONDON CHEQUE

ALLEN LONGSTREET

THE LONDON CHEQUE

ALDEN LONGSTREET

I often wish I could forget that dreaded summer. Those of us living in the sleepy village of Catrine had mused the darkness of night was too afraid to show its face around the evil residing there. We figured the same was true of the sun, for neither did it choose to appear. Our village was enshrouded beneath a blanket of clouds, casting it in a perpetual grey which never seemed to end.

—from the diary of Catherine Mcleod
October 12th, 1979

"Of all the things you choose in life, you don't get to choose what your nightmares are. You don't pick them; they pick you."

—John Irving

CHAPTER 1
THE MAN WITH NO SKIN

Catrine
1964

The story began at the quiet end of Blackwood Avenue, in a lonely room, damp and dark. Its walls were made of old brick, lit by a dingy halide light, the kind that were slow to warm up when switched on. Then there was the smell—stinging formaldehyde and antiseptic that filled the nose to the point of discomfort.

A single surgical table straddled the centre of the room, and lying on its cold, metallic surface was a man. He had chain-link restraints strapped across his neck and ankles, like iron snakes coiling and constricting tighter with each slithering pulse. Each panicked breath was followed by a deluge of excruciating cries. He pleaded to the heavens to be freed—moaning and shouting for someone, anyone, to help him.

But the most unfathomable part of this naked, helpless man was that he had no skin.

From the collarbone down, all that could be seen were striations of bloody muscle and bone. Tiny remnants of the skin he once had hung in pieces like the thin, wilted leaves of a plant. The edges of the surgical table bore the evidence of his flaying; an abstract spattering of blood now decorated its gleaming surface.

Another man appeared out of the darkness. Tall and well-built, he wore a raggedy excuse for a surgical gown. He approached and curiously watched the man with no skin writhe in pain, shaking against his chains, veins bulging along his temples. Soon, the message within his cries shifted. He begged to be killed, to be put out of his misery. The man in the surgical gown did not respond; he simply raised a scalpel and sank it into the flesh of his victim's neck. The man with no skin's gurgled screams echoed throughout the cavernous room, amplifying with each reverberation, continuing with no end in sight.

But the room, the man with no skin, and the man who had skinned him were *not* at the quiet end of Blackwood Avenue. They existed in Arun Khan's mind, a young lad just shy of thirteen, in the small bedroom of his family's home. He was having a nightmare, and the man with no skin's screams were so vivid and terrifying that Arun shot up in his bed and wailed at the top of his lungs, exhausting all of his air as he slowly pulled back to reality, barrelling into the realisation that he wasn't in *that* room; he was in *his* room. Safe and sound.

His screaming stopped and he began to blubber. His mum barged in and rushed to his side.

"Arun, it's okay. You're all right." She cradled his head to her chest, smoothing his dark hair with her hand. "It's okay, you're awake now."

He continued crying, unable to get the horrific images out of his head.

As his mum embraced him, she flinched. "You're drenched in sweat. Take that off." She helped peel the sticky t-shirt off his back and then fetched a new one from the dresser, watched as he put it on, still panting heavily.

"What happened? Why did you scream like that?"

Arun didn't know how to explain what he had just dreamt about. He figured his mother might think the Devil had cursed his dreams. Either way, he'd have to tell the truth. He wouldn't be able to escape her prying stare. Bengali mothers were gifted with an unrivalled persistence. He choked on the words before he could get them out and looked up at her solemnly.

"I had a dream about a man with no skin."

Margaret Brown sat at the same rickety wooden desk she had for the past sixteen years, struggling to keep her attention on the woman in front of her. Mrs. Young was a local widow in Cumnock who, ever since her husband passed, consistently found some trivial issue to bestow upon the police station and, more specifically, Margaret.

Mrs. Young often incorporated elements of old complaints into new ones. For example, Liam Smith's boy, Ian, had trampled over her blooming heathers, and he wore a red shirt. He was *always* wearing a red shirt when he reappeared in new accusations. Other times it was the *same* bed of plants ruined twice. Did Mrs. Young replant that quickly? Or perhaps she was beginning to exhibit a touch of dementia.

"Ye listening to me?"

Mrs. Young's droning finally broke through Margaret's thoughts.

"I apologise. I'm feeling a bit off today."

"Well, it is yer job to listen to me, isn't it?" she retorted.

Margaret pressed her lips together to keep from saying something that'd ruin this miserable hen's day.

"Aye." She gave a curt nod.

"It was that Derek Scott lad—Mr. Scott's boy. He cut through my garden and ruined my bluebells! One of these days I'll be quick enough to catch him."

That won't be happening anytime soon, Margaret thought, and fought against cracking a smile.

As Mrs. Young continued her rant, Margaret's eyes wandered across the station walls. They settled on the framed black and white photos of the handful of detectives that had served throughout the years. She found herself revisiting them often. The insecurities she normally kept at bay suddenly surfaced, eddying in her gut. It wasn't that Margaret was unsuccessful; she had a comfortable job at a fair wage. She simply wondered what her police work had amounted to. The lack of an adequate answer to that thought was what haunted her the most. The past sixteen years had been filled with a slew of traffic tickets, domestic quarrels amongst East Ayrshire's poorest and least educated, and complaints from the likes of Mrs. Young that were so paltry she often daydreamed about cutting her own life short just to avoid having to listen to another.

"Nothing more than a bampot," spat Mrs. Young. She pushed the chair haphazardly toward Margaret's desk before stomping out of the station, grumbling insults under her breath.

Maybe one day I'll leave this shite town, Margaret thought.

As Margaret gathered Mrs. Young's complaint paperwork, a commotion arose from behind her.

"I swear it! Get your hands off me, ye coward!"

Margaret rounded the corner to see her sergeant, Stu, pushing a scruffy-looking lad toward the station exit.

"Don't come back again, ye hear?"

"You'll regret not listening to me!" shrieked the lad as he was shoved out the door.

Stu let out an aggravated huff as he returned, nodding at Margaret, who lingered at the threshold.

"What was that about?"

"That Colin Clark lad, the homeless one. He's messed in the head from drugs, can't believe a word he says."

"Well, what did he have to say?" asked Margaret.

"Nothing but shite."

Margaret shifted her weight from one foot to another. The tiniest shred of curiosity, dormant deep within her, urged her to press Stu to elaborate. A decade ago? Maybe. After sixteen years in this station, whatever measly flame of gusto that remained had been almost entirely snuffed out by the rest of the department. All of whom preferred the Margaret that kept her opinions to herself—not the one that asked questions. She unconsciously chewed at the inside of her cheek.

Stu clocked her muted behaviour and sighed.

"What's the matter?"

"Never mind," said Margaret, as she retired to her desk. The loud creak of the chair sent a shockwave through her nerves like razorblades, causing her to shudder.

Stu began the walk to his office and paused after a few steps. He turned back to lean against the open doorframe to the main floor.

"Margaret."

She gave an expectant raise of her brow.

"If it does turn out to be important, I'll let ye know."

Margaret mustered a tepid smile as Stu left. She finished Mrs. Young's complaint paperwork and neatly filed it away.

Although Margaret's days, and years for that matter, were filled with such endless mundanity, she still met the ordinary with an extraordinary persistence; a quality she knew of herself but wondered if others registered. When she'd taken her oath long ago on a wintry morning in Cumnock, she had meant the words she uttered. Her actions, however small, were a service, and she clung to that belief with a fierce grip. She closed her eyes and saw the glowing pride on Stu's face when he handed her the police badge. A smile tugged at her lips; then, she opened her eyes and went back to her mindless work.

She swivelled in the desk chair and faced the rest of the station. The faded white walls, the chipped eggshell paint that peeled back from the skirting boards, and the jarring ring of the rotary phones were more family to her than the handful of faces she interacted with daily. She had grown to accept that fact. What truly bothered her was that her position held no real value in the community. After all this time, she had yet to do anything meaningful for the people she'd sworn to serve.

That ate away at her soul.

Margaret wouldn't call herself pious, but she was a member of the local kirk. In a quick moment, she closed her eyes and asked God for something: *Please, Lord, even if it's just for a little while, let my life be worth living. Amen.*

She felt a bit better after that, pleased by her wee prayer. She ruffled out a newspaper to look through in her downtime.

Little did Margaret know; in less than twenty-four hours her prayer would be answered. Those words would come to haunt her in the coming weeks. For no one knew, especially someone as demure as Margaret, what horror the answered prayer would summon. In the aftermath of these events, some asked how God could have allowed it all to happen. Others conjectured that the Lord himself knew a devil walked among the people of East Ayrshire, and from the very beginning, He was pulling at the strings of His children from the heavens, directing them down the paths of their fates in order to eradicate such an insidious evil.

Margaret Brown was one of those children, at the end of one of His strings.

"You're sure you don't mind?" asked Aniqa.

Elaine crossed her arms as she stood in the doorway.

"Of course not." She ducked her head with a slight nod. "These two couldn't be happier."

Elaine's son, Craig, stared up at Aniqa, beaming.

"I wish you'd have tests more often, Ms. Khan," he said.

Arun and Craig snickered, bouncing on the balls of their feet, brimming with excitement to spend a long weekend together. Aniqa crouched, pulling Arun into a half-hug with her free arm, and giving him a kiss atop his head.

"I'll be back Sunday night," she said.

The lads fixed their gazes on Elaine, silently pleading for the magic words.

She pursed her lips and raised her brows playfully at the rambunctious duo.

"Well, go on." She gave a lackadaisical wave of her hand.

"Behave!" shouted Aniqa as Arun and Craig darted into the house, disappearing around a corner.

A muffled response came from inside: "I will, Mum!"

"He's a good lad, that one," said Elaine. "I'm praying one of these days he rubs off on Craig."

"Even if he does, I can't imagine they'll get any better as teenagers."

Elaine snorted. "Aye, they'll give us a run for our money. And they're growing like weeds, won't be long till they've got lassies hanging from their arms and want nothin' to do with us."

Aniqa produced a lukewarm smile—that last part stung.

"I suppose you're right," she said. "Thanks again for taking him. I really appreciate it."

"I've said it a hundred times; Arun's a joy to have around. One extra night doesn't make a difference."

"You're a lifesaver, Elaine."

"Aye. Damn right I am," she said with a wink, fishing out a crumpled box of cigarettes from her trouser pockets, then lighting one between pinched lips.

"Well, I'd better get going."

"Good luck on your test," said Elaine with a puff of smoke. "I'll have Arun ring ye after dinner."

The two said their goodbyes and Aniqa headed to her car. She cranked the ignition of the old Ford Anglia, its engine chugging cantankerously as it roared to life. *About time for an oil change,* she thought. She'd bought it at a used lot in Cumnock a few years back, and since then it had never left her stranded.

As she snaked through the narrow streets of the village centre, she passed the site where the Catrine Mill had been demolished by fire the previous year. It had taken the demolition crew months to fully clean it up, but even now there were flecks of ash and pale fragments of rubble mixed in among the dirt, feeling more like an open grave than an empty lot. She'd heard stories from locals over the years of what Catrine was like in its heyday. The birthplace of one of the first cotton mills in Scotland in 1787, it became a centre of cotton manufacture for the next 150 years. But the demolition of the Catrine Mill marked the end of it. Aniqa found it upsetting to only be able to witness the *end* of the village's legacy without having experienced the good times. There was an unspoken solemnity shared amongst the townspeople—an air of death everyone refused to face, because in doing so they would have to acknowledge the truth; that their beloved Catrine was haemorrhaging jobs and population at an alarming rate. Nevertheless, those born and raised here still went about their business, clinging to their dying village as if it were a loved one who had long gone cold. That was part of the reason Aniqa had come to Catrine from London. She felt those around her were kindred spirits. Living mirrors of sorts, reflecting back the particular pain knowable only from great loss. Besides that, it was safe, quiet, and the people were proud of their village. They had warmly welcomed her in with open arms. After the ultimatum her mother had given her, stumbling across Catrine by chance was like seeing the hazy image of an oasis materialise on the Sahara.

She felt indebted to the village and its people. And to this day, arriving in Catrine had been the first time she hadn't felt alone since leaving Bangladesh as a teenager.

Narrow streets eventually gave way to the rolling green hills of the Scottish countryside. A twinge of uneasiness prodded her gut. No matter how short the time or the distance, she hated leaving Arun. She glanced at the rearview and watched Catrine get swallowed up by a thick, deliberate fog, and for a moment, it appeared as if the entire village and all its inhabitants had vanished.

CHAPTER 2
THE DESCENT

One week earlier

Silence filled Albert Reid's study. The room was dimly lit by the handful of candles interspersed throughout the space, rivulets of wax slipping down their yellow-white bodies, and a persistent morning fog licked the sole window of the room with its moist tongue.

The chimes of the grandfather clock rose in a crescendo as the minute hand reached the top of the hour. Al glanced at its silvery face—08:00.

He rose to his feet, put on his coat, and headed for the door.

It was time to begin the day.

He began each morning precisely at eight, first spending time with his art. To him, art was the single most important thing to his happiness.

This act was reflective of the rhythmic punctuality present in Albert Reid's life. His days were a series of rotating routines, each so similar that even the keenest observer would struggle to discover inconsistencies between them. This quality was something the people in Al's life noticed and found quite intriguing, yet no one questioned its origin.

Al was candid in the display of his routines. He went about them day after day, never tiring. For although he had no family in Catrine, his life felt full. He had Kissinger Grounds, the orphanage he'd founded, Elder Louise and Deacons Angela and Gillian, the people he employed at his restaurant, TLC, and many friendly faces among the townsfolk. For the first time in his life, he truly felt at peace. The rough seas of the past had finally calmed.

How long will it last?

A nagging feeling in his gut accompanied the thought. He shrugged it off, shimmying along the tight space between his car and the house as he snaked up his drive. When he reached the door to his shed and held the weighty padlock in his palm, a realisation struck him.

He'd forgotten his key ring.

An amused chuckle escaped his lips.

First time in years, he thought. He was about to pivot back down the drive toward the house when he felt two competing sensations pull at his spirit. Superstition tugged at one side, warning him to not break habit. Compulsiveness heaved in the other direction, chastising him for the added delay circling back would cause.

Al yielded to the latter. Anyhow, his closest neighbour had no clear view of this side of his house. He reached up onto his tiptoes and slipped his fingers into the inner overhang of the shed's roof eaves, gently tracing them along until he found what he was looking for.

The padlock emitted a soft *click-click-click* as he inserted the spare key. With one turn, it popped open, and he was in his shed.

What Al didn't realise at the time was that he shouldn't have scoffed at superstition. Because one of the orphans had been watching him from a distance.

Present day

Craig kicked the football to Arun. He stared at it a moment before kicking it back.

"What's up with ye today?"

"Nothing," said Arun. "I'm fine."

"Sure."

Craig knew better. Arun wouldn't tell him even if there were something bothering him.

They continued kicking the football back and forth, occasionally running manoeuvres around to tease the other. A game of *who-can-keep-it-the-longest* before the other could steal it away.

Craig ducked left and with a swift kick, he stole the ball from Arun. His brown hair whirled as he spun around to show off, then began dribbling the ball closely to entice Arun to steal it back.

"Bet you can't take it from me," he taunted.

Craig's pale, freckled skin flushed red from the heat of the game. He was a few inches taller than most their age, and he'd been the first of their grade to develop some muscles. Arun, on the other hand, had yet to fill in his frame with anything other than skin and bones, and he was a little on the shorter side. But the lack of height made him a nimble runner—it was his biggest asset on the football field. He bolted for the ball and saw the shock flood Craig's eyes as he realised he was a goner; he pivoted and dribbled the ball down the field, but Arun overtook him in a matter of seconds and stole the ball back.

He didn't taunt Craig for having so easily lost the bet. Instead, a smug smile bloomed across his face. That was the biggest difference between the two of them. Where Arun was shy and reserved, Craig was dominant and outgoing.

They were too young to realise it at the time, but that was what made them such a great pair.

Arun wondered the time. They had been playing for a while, so he assumed it was after midday, but he couldn't be certain. The clouds seemed to be resting for a while, having fallen wearily from the sky. The breeze, intermittent at best, would clear away some of the mist, but its denseness would quickly return, eclipsing visibility of the world around them.

Just two lads kicking the ball within an endless band of grey.

I'm glad I'm with Craig this weekend, he thought. After his nightmare, the last thing he wanted was to be alone. He still couldn't make sense of it, nor did he have the courage to try. He just focused on the football in front of him. The hollow *thump* it made as they kicked had a cadence that Arun found soothing. Back and forth, back and forth. *Thump-thump, thump-thump.* In the background of that rhythm, he heard a new sound—the rustling of grass. He looked up as Craig kicked the ball to him; it rolled past his feet.

Two lads approached. They stopped just inside the perimeter of fog.

"Mind if we play?" asked the taller one.

"Who are you?" blurted Craig.

"I'm James," said the taller one. "He's Gavin."

Beneath Craig's deadpan expression was a layer of distrust. This didn't surprise Arun. Craig was a sceptic.

"Where ye live?" asked Craig.

James and Gavin shot sidelong glances at each other before Gavin's gaze fell towards his feet.

"Kissinger Grounds," said James, a nervous timbre to his tone. Before James finished his answer, Craig headed toward Arun, shielding him from the lads' gazes.

"They're orphans," whispered Craig.

Arun stared back at him blankly.

The lack of response like a telepathic, *"So?"* in Craig's head.

"Mate, ye know, from school. Kissinger kids are just…a bit off."

He remained silent.

"Let's just go home," said Craig.

"You can play with us," shouted Arun, peering around Craig's shoulder.

James lit up with a broad smile. "Aye! Two on two?"

Gavin seemed pleased, but his reaction was far more muted. As the lads took their places, Craig cast a disappointed look in Arun's direction. He ignored it, because deep down, Arun sympathised with the orphans from Kissinger. Everyone treated them as if they were less than, purely on the basis that they were orphans. They weren't weird; they were just viewed as different.

It's not their fault they don't know their parents, thought Arun.

He felt strongly about this because oftentimes he felt like an orphan, too. An orphan to this country. An orphan to Catrine. There wasn't a single boy in his grade that had darker skin than he. He'd been born and raised in Scotland, but despite this fact, deep down he couldn't shake the notion that he, too, was different.

Out of place.

Three knocks sounded at the door downstairs.

Right on time as always, Al thought.

He descended the spiral staircase to the door, opened it, and saw the postman already walking away.

"Thank you, Brian!"

"See ye tomorrow, Al!" said the postman with a wave.

Al walked down his long gravel drive to retrieve the mail. He sifted through it quickly and noticed the last piece was weightier than the rest. He paused on it for a moment, fixating on its red wax seal. He opened it with a gilded paper knife and pulled out a folded letter.

I will be visiting two weeks from today.

Al stared at the words for a few moments longer, then crumpled the letter, tossing it in the rubbish. He put on his coat and headed for the door to begin the day's errands.

Arun, Craig, and the two Kissinger lads, James and Gavin, had been playing for hours. Craig was spent and his stomach began to growl; he kept studying Arun's behaviour to see if he was showing signs of tiring.

Arun *was* growing tired from an afternoon's worth of football, but he was purposely masking his fatigue. He felt bad cutting the day short, because James and Gavin were still just as enthralled as when Arun had first invited them to play. The fog had finally cleared, but the sky remained overcast. They were playing at an open field along Mill Street, just a stone's throw away from where the Catrine Mill had burnt down. Abutting the field was the River Ayr which coiled along the town's edge, separating them from an expanse of rolling green hills, speckled with little cottages and farmhouses as far as the eye could see.

Arun finally met Craig's eyes. The internal plea of *let's go* was so clearly written on his face he could no longer ignore him. He stopped running for a moment to catch his breath.

"What's the time, Craig?"

Craig glanced at his wristwatch. "Four."

James and Gavin followed suit and stopped.

Craig casually crept toward Arun. "You ready?" he asked, voice low.

Arun nodded.

James caught wind of this interaction and hastily jumped forward. "You guys want to go somewhere else?"

"Nae," said Craig. "I'm starving. Think we're heading home."

James knew it wasn't often lads outside of Kissinger would want to hang out with them, and he wanted to cherish this rarity. His eyes darted along the grassy ground, thinking.

"We could get ice cream," said James. Gavin stood meekly at his side.

Arun and Craig stopped, looked to each other for confirmation. "Let's just go home, Mum's probably cooking something," whispered Craig. Arun silently agreed, and they began to walk away. "No thanks," replied Craig over his shoulder.

"For free!" blurted James. "My treat."

Arun stopped, grabbed Craig by the arm.

"It's free."

"So is me mum's dinner," whispered Craig.

"Come on," Arun pressed. "The ice cream will cool us off."

Craig dithered.

Arun changed his angle a bit. "It's not like we'll ever hang out with them again. Just this once."

"Alright," said Craig, sighing. "We'll go."

Arun was pleased, primarily because he was craving a sweet frozen treat, but the other being that he didn't want to be rude to James and Gavin. They were constantly shit on by the other kids at school. It made Arun feel good to know he had the power to change that, even if it be just for a day. The lads headed toward the village centre, and Craig left the worn leather football behind.

The four boys sat on an old wooden bench, lapping away at their dripping ice cream cones. In between licks, James carried on about an action film coming out next week, bogging them all down with needless details—descriptions of the main character's weapons, how the weapons worked, how the evil king's powers affected his enemies, and so on.

Gavin sat beside them quietly; neither Craig nor Arun had heard him utter a word since they met.

"So?" said James.

"So, what?" asked Arun.

"Do you guys want to go see that film next weekend?"

Craig kicked Arun in the ankle. A warning of sorts—that by all means necessary he was to avoid agreeing to James' proposition. James nervously darted his gaze between the two, but he soon settled on Arun. He remembered that it was *Arun* who had allowed he and Gavin to play football. Craig probably couldn't have cared less.

Arun suddenly felt queasy. The look in James' eyes reminded him of a stray cat he had once befriended years ago by leaving food in the garden. Even after being fed, the cat would mosey around day after day, when it knew Arun would be outside. And now, James' silent pleading was sewn of the same cloth as the cat's lingering—a cry for attention, affection, or anything of the sort.

"Sure," said Arun vacantly.

Craig stomped on his foot lightly enough for him not to yelp, but hard enough for Arun to fight off a grimace. James was over the moon, peppering the lads with more gratuitous details about the film. That was when Arun noticed that Gavin had cracked a small smile at the news, but it slipped away just as quickly as it had arrived.

He knows Craig doesn't like them, thought Arun.

Gavin caught Arun studying him out of the corner of his eye. He didn't care what anyone else thought. Kissinger kids were weird because they lived in an orphanage. It had become a part of his identity. He acknowledged that he would never be cool. It made him sad, but he would rather face his reality and accept it, rather than concoct the many performances his older brother did to convince someone, anyone, of the contrary.

Arun sat cornered between James' now-bubbly demeanour and Craig's glowering side-eye. He didn't know whether he'd done the right thing, but it felt that way, despite Craig's obvious disapproval.

Craig had long been ready to leave. He glanced at his wristwatch—it was getting close to six. His mother would be expecting them to come home soon to shower and wear something nicer than pyjamas. His parents were hosting a party tonight. He also needed to grab the football on the way back. The thoughts of what he needed to do bombarded him, and every second that passed, he grew more restless.

Arun noticed this change in Craig but stayed silent. He saw James fixating on Craig's body language as well.

James was proud that he had kept Arun and Craig around for as long as he had. Despite this, a sinking feeling arose in his gut; he hadn't a single idea left entertaining enough to keep his new friends around. "Want to play some more football?" he asked.

"Nae," said Craig. "We're heading home." He threw the last bit of his dripping cone into the grass and stood.

Arun followed, shooting an apologetic look towards James. "Thanks for the ice cream," he said.

James looked over at Gavin, helpless. He dropped his head, staring defeatedly at his melting cone, the sticky cream sliding down his hand. It crushed James that a potential evening of hanging out with these lads had been shot down. And they'd likely never get to hang out with them again, especially if they ran into them around more of their *normal* friends.

Gavin didn't care to impress Craig nor Arun. He didn't even really care for their friendship, but what hurt him more than anything was to see how badly his brother did care. Disillusioned or not, he hated seeing James wear his heart on his sleeve, time and time again, only for the callous boys outside of Kissinger to rip it off and throw it in the dirt without a second thought.

Though two years younger than James, Gavin was a silent observer, taking in the details of the world around him and hardly saying a word about his observations, or anything else for that matter. As Craig and Arun walked away, and while watching the downward spiral his brother was sliding down yet again, Gavin wracked his brain and combed through his memories, searching for something that would keep the two lads around a little longer, for the sake of his brother's happiness.

"I have a secret key!" he blurted.

Craig and Arun paused, and James stared at him with his mouth agape.

"What secret key?" asked James.

Gavin was visibly trembling with all eyes on him; he could see Craig wasn't interested. He stammered before getting the words out.

"I know where Al keeps a secret key to a hidden door."

James' eyes widened. "Are you serious?"

Gavin nodded, silent.

"Al as in, the owner of your orphanage?" asked Arun.

"Aye," said Gavin. "He's like a dad to me and James. To all of us at the Grounds, really."

This new information had wholly captured Arun's attention, and even Craig held just the slightest bit of curiosity to hear more. "So, where's the door lead to?" he asked.

Gavin opened his mouth to answer Craig's question, but then realised he may have dug himself a hole he wouldn't be able to get out of.

"To Al's…art."

"Art?" asked Arun.

Craig was already rolling his eyes. "Piss off," he said. "We're leaving, now."

Gavin scrambled to his feet, wedging himself between Arun and Craig. "It'll be cool, I swear it!" he said.

Craig elbowed Arun. "Let's go home. *Now.*"

Arun glanced back at James and Gavin. Both donned that same look. Like stray cats that had been abandoned, looking for anyone to care for them. "I mean, why not?" Arun said.

Craig snorted. "I can't believe you right now. Me mum's party is at seven and here ye are wanting to dick around for some art."

James took Arun's indecisiveness to his advantage. "Al spends whole mornings with his art. It must be cool if he spends that long in there."

"How do you even know he keeps his art in there anyhow?" Craig fired back.

The lads fell silent until all eyes settled on Gavin. He timidly glanced around at them.

"Well, a week ago I saw him go into his shed. A few days later, I asked one of the Deacons what Al does in there and that's the answer she gave me."

"And we're going to trust the word of some loser orphans?" said Craig, baulking.

"Why not just check it out, really quick?" said Arun.

James and Gavin echoed Arun, and now all eyes were on Craig. The pressure was on.

"Fine," he huffed. "Ten minutes tops. We need to be home for the party soon."

They headed away from the village centre, led by Gavin, who was internally pleading that his memory wouldn't fail him.

The four lads stood silently in front of Al's house. It sat across the southern banks of River Ayr, tucked away at the very end of Holm Farm Road. Its face was more ornate than the ageing farmhouses it shared the street with—the windowpanes and finishes were black, and the colour of the house was a dark bluish grey.

Gavin's steps were measured. He quietly led them up Al's drive, sneaking around his parked car, and closing in on the attached shed at the back corner of the house.

They were met with a plain wooden door.

"You said it was red," said Craig.

"That door is on the inside," Gavin assured them.

Silence fell over the boys, and no one moved a muscle.

"Where's the key?" asked Arun.

Gavin pointed up to the shed's roof eaves. *Help*, he mouthed to his brother.

James came to his aid and hoisted Gavin onto his shoulders.

Gavin reached up, slipping his fingers along the inside of the eaves.

Arun glanced at his surroundings to check if anyone was watching them.

"You think this is going to be worth it?" asked Craig in a whisper.

"I don't know," Arun answered.

"Sure hope so." Craig grumbled something else under his breath, annoyed to see Arun didn't pay him much attention. "What's with ye today?"

He looked up at Craig. "What's wrong with being nice once in a while?"

Craig shook his head. He was counting the passing minutes, neurotically glancing down at his watch. He just wanted to be home. "We've already been nice enough today, mate. I don't see what it is about these Kissinger freaks that makes you care so much about them—"

"I got it!" exclaimed Gavin in a strained whisper.

There was a massive piece of Craig that wished Gavin hadn't found the key.

The whole scenario piqued Arun's interest because he tended to stick to the ordinary, never straying away for adventures. This was the first time the roles had been reversed. Usually, it was Arun that had to talk Craig out of a mischievous idea that might have gotten them into trouble.

Gavin waved an enthusiastic hand for them to follow. They all kept peering over their shoulders, constantly checking if they'd been seen. Gavin fiddled with the key, then inserted it into the padlock. A sharp *click* echoed in an otherwise quiet night.

Gavin gingerly pulled on the shed door, opening it steadily so as to not allow the old wood the opportunity to groan or creak. Once their eyes adjusted to the dim light inside, they were shocked at what they saw:

Nothing.

"I swear it's here," said Gavin shakily.

"Where's the red door?" asked Arun.

"When I peeked in that day, I saw it. There's no chance it was just my imagination."

Panic rose in Gavin's chest, because what met them inside the shed was nothing out of the ordinary. Hanging from nails encircling the walls were a myriad of tools—hammers, garden shears, axes. In the corner was a jug of petrol and a few canisters of paint.

"Look at this," said James.

He pointed toward the top left corner of the shed, where the roof met the back wall. In the faint light spilling in, the lads squinted, barely able to discern what had caught James' eye.

It was an opening. Just a mere sliver of a gap, maybe a fraction of an inch thick.

James gave the wall a big push. The wooden wall seemed to rock slightly but didn't budge.

"Help me," he said to the rest of them.

Gavin and Arun gave it a shot. The wall seemed to move again.

"We shouldn't force it," said Craig, standing with his arms crossed behind them as they gave the door another shove. A large part of him wanted to stomp off and not look back. But he couldn't leave Arun. He knew if he went home without Arun, his mum would be livid. Especially since Ms. Khan had left him in her care.

For a moment, Arun wondered if Craig was right. Maybe this door wasn't meant to be opened. Just as doubt creeped in, though, he heard something shift.

"That's it!" yelped James.

Gavin held a finger up, shushing him. "Let's try to slide it, not push."

With one great big heave, James, Gavin, and Arun struggled to slide the wood door open. It was rather heavy, and James helped hold it fully open while the rest of them walked in. When the door slid closed behind them, the only light that remained was what slipped through the wooden slats. They stood in a tiny hallway, and a few feet ahead was a bright red door.

Their approach was slow and measured.

"What kind of person keeps their art locked away?" asked Craig.

"Maybe Al likes to be left alone when he's making art," suggested James.

The suspicion that *something* wasn't right here kept nagging at Craig's gut.

Gavin outstretched a trembling hand. "Should we do this?"

"No," blurted Craig.

"We'll go in and come right back out," said James.

With James' approval, Gavin grabbed the knob to the red door. Its worn metal spindle squeaked as it caught the latch, and then the door popped open.

A stone stairwell faced them. The first few steps were visible in the dim light sneaking in through the wooden slats, but the rest were obscured by an impenetrable darkness.

"Go on," said James.

Gavin walked in first, and the rest followed in, one by one.

Craig was last, and he kept what seemed like a permanent scowl aimed at the Kissinger boys. "Let's make this quick," he said.

"Where does this go?" asked Arun.

"I'm not sure," said James. "Can you guys relax? You're making me nervous."

As they made the descent, no one said a word. Though he was the one who'd asked the question, James felt on edge. Neither he nor Gavin had ever strayed this close to Al's residence. Not that they were barred from visiting, but Al visited the Grounds daily, so there was no reason to.

Arun, on the other hand, was full of curiosity. Though once his feet hit the floor, his curiosity fizzled out far more quickly than it had arisen. This place felt familiar to him, but he couldn't put his finger on why.

"Whoa!" shouted James. "This is so cool!"

"More like creepy," muttered Craig.

The four slowly crept down the hall, inspecting it as they went.

"Can someone find a light switch?" asked Gavin.

Arun's eyes wandered across all the worn brick that surrounded them. He didn't realise it, but he was already the farthest down the length of the hall. As the echoing voices of the other boys softened, he heard a new sound—one that made his brow furrow.

"Guys. Do you hear that?"

The others turned to him.

"Hear what?" asked James.

Arun hushed them and held up a finger. "It's water."

"Water?" blurted Craig.

Arun waved them to come closer.

The three boys quietly listened. Gavin was still a length behind them searching for the light switch.

"You're right," said James. "It sounds like the river running."

"How is that possible?" asked Craig. "We're in a bloody basement."

James shrugged.

Arun was still trying to locate the source. Double doors framed the end of the hall, and it seemed like the sound was coming from that direction. Suddenly, an electric hum buzzed throughout the space. "I found the switch!" shouted Gavin, his voice echoing wildly through the cavernous hall. James and Craig pushed forward and noticed the sound of gurgling water growing louder as they approached the double doors.

But Arun hadn't followed. He was rooted where he stood, hypnotised by the light hanging above his head. It gyrated ever so subtly from its own weight, misbalanced on a thick cord attached to the ceiling. He watched as its luminance gradually increased, slowly growing brighter. When the connection clicked in his mind, a wave of nausea swept through him.

A halide light.

The ones that take a while to warm up.

His memory catapulted him back to the damp, dimly lit room, the surgical table, and the man with no skin. Before fear fully petrified him, the *thud* of someone hitting the floor pulled him away from this realisation.

James had tripped a foot shy of the double doors. He brushed himself off and stood up.

Craig leaned down to inspect something just off the ground. "It's a string. You must have tripped over it."

"A string?" asked James, shooting Craig a look.

"See?" Craig pulled at the string between his forefinger and thumb. Hardly visible, it spanned the width of the hallway. On one side it appeared as if the string had more thread that crawled up the basement wall and into the ceiling.

Al was so wholly dumbstruck by the first ring of the bell that he could hardly process the reality that it had rung a second time. It reverberated, jingling until it came to a halt. The bell was directly behind him in the study, connected by a string that ran into the floor beneath.

Someone was in his basement. If whoever had made it down there went too far, there would be no unseeing what they would find. He leapt to his feet, grabbed his keys, and headed downstairs, knowing what he'd be forced to do if they made the discovery before he could get to them in time.

"Guys," said Arun. The others turned to him. "I've seen this place before," he stammered.

"What do you mean?" asked Craig, clearly unnerved by Arun's tone.

"I had a nightmare about it. We shouldn't be here."

"A nightmare?" repeated Gavin.

"Don't be a wimp. Dreams are just dreams," James said, and he turned around to face the double doors.

Craig approached Arun and leaned into him. "What was your nightmare about?"

Arun just stared back at Craig, frozen in fear.

"Maybe Arun's right," said Gavin meekly. "We should leave."

James paused for a moment, but he didn't listen to his brother. He used both hands and grabbed the handles to the double doors. "They're cold," he said.

"What?" asked Gavin.

"The door handles. They're freezing."

"Guys, let's go. Something feels off," said Craig.

Just as Craig finished his sentence, James swung open the double doors. Immediately, they were hit with a blast of frigid air that filled the hall.

James couldn't process what he saw. "Are you seeing what I'm seeing?"

The three approached James' side, shivering in the cold.

Arun's jaw dropped.

The room was comprised of four windowless walls that were coated by thick frost. A deep, droning hum filled the space, and Arun's eyes darted around until he located its source—it came from a rectangular grated vent fan on the ceiling. *This place is a gigantic freezer,* he thought. Where the floor should have been, there was water, along with a wooden dock that bisected the room into equal halves. But none of these details were of much importance to the lads. What grabbed their attention was what was *in* the water. All except Craig crept along the walkway to test whether their eyes were fooling them.

On both sides of the dock, perfectly circular blocks of ice floated on the water's surface. They mimicked the appearance of massive lily pads. Atop those blocks of ice, and what the boys' minds refused to process, were children.

Frozen children.

"They're ice sculptures," said James, trembling wildly from a mixture of fear and the cold.

"Guys," said Craig. "Screw this, let's go!"

Gavin retreated to Craig's side.

James' words probed Arun's thoughts, and he noticed each of the ice blocks were connected to the dock by a thick, frosted rope. He reeled in one slowly, frost stinging his fingers. This child, like the others, sat cross-legged with their back upright. The eyes were closed, and they almost looked…peaceful. Arun ran out of rope, and the ice block rested against the dock, bumping against it from the fluctuations of the lapping water. He swallowed at the rock in his throat. Upon closer inspection, this child was a girl, and the skin on her arms and face was a lighter shade of blue than that of her lips. Her hair was frozen solid and matted in frost.

"She's real," uttered Arun.

"Nae…" said James. "It's not possible. Gavin *said* it was art. It's just art." James began to tear up. He hiccupped as he let out a few cries and continued rambling, attempting any way possible to rationalise what Arun had just said.

"*Art*," whispered Arun, stretching out his hand.

"What are ye doing?" shouted Craig. "We need to leave. Now!"

Craig was right, but Arun wanted to make sense of what he saw on the frozen girl's arms. Just below both shoulders were decorative protrusions that had been peeled back and flayed into intricate slices, carefully sculpted into little petals.

Like a frozen orchid made from skin.

"Art," he said again vacantly. With nausea overtaking him, he slowly spun around and spotted similar flaying on the arms of the other frozen children. Though he shivered violently, Arun was in a trance, stuck between the physical world and a dreamlike state. Gavin huddled by Craig's side, and Craig turned around to pull Arun closer to the group. James stood closest to the double doors, and his muffled sobs came to an unsettling halt.

When they arrived at James' side, they saw the hallway was empty.

"Listen," said Gavin. "The door."

In the absence of their cries, they heard it squeak open. Gavin and James trembled where they stood, while Arun looked up at Craig for answers, lacking the courage to find a way out of the situation.

Craig's mind flashed to the frozen children and his fight or flight response kicked in. "We have to get out of here," he said. "Is there another way?" He scoured the hall for a door, a stairwell, anything, assisted by James and Gavin in the panicked effort.

Arun had stayed behind, and a thought arrived with a shiver. *We need to close the doors to the frozen room.* His arms didn't span wide enough to close each side of the double doors at the same time, so he grabbed one side and began to pull it closed. Just as it budged, Arun heard heavy footsteps lumber down the hallway, and he turned around, hairs bristling on his neck.

"Al," said James, his tone betraying his sorrow.

Al didn't answer; his gaze slowly drifted toward the wide-open double doors, eyes bulging as he saw them.

"Run!" shouted Craig. He charged toward the stairwell, and before he could reach it, Al ran to it and locked the gate up top. Craig punched and kicked at Al's back and legs. "Let us out!" he yelled. The moment the gate was under lock and key, Al whipped around and struck Craig with a tremendous blow to the face. Craig fell limply, skidding down the stone steps.

"No!" cried Arun. He ran to Craig's side and shook him. Out cold but still breathing. He craned his neck around to see Al looming over him, staring down with icy blue eyes. Sweat dripped off his short, sandy-brown hair.

He didn't look like the man from Arun's nightmare.

Al pointed a finger at Craig. "Unless you want to end up like him, I suggest you stay quiet."

"Al," said Gavin. "What is this place?"

James burst into tears again. "Those kids. Did you do that to them?"

Al stared silently back at James.

"*Did* you?" cried James.

Al strode toward them; Gavin and Arun flattened themselves against opposite walls while James sobbed in his hands. Al stopped at a seemingly ordinary section of the basement wall. He felt around with his hands for a few moments, then gave the wall a push—and it popped open. Arun stared at the false wall in disbelief as Al pushed it open farther. He turned to face them.

"Look. I'm not going to hurt you, but I need you to stay in here for a while."

After what they had seen in the frozen room, Al's promise didn't seem likely. When they didn't react, Al's expression turned dark. "If you don't come into this room right now, you'll end up like your friend."

The lads all glanced at Craig's unconscious body.

"Or worse," said Al, nodding in the direction of the frozen room.

Gavin gulped. He slunk closer to Al, looked over his shoulder, and cast a remorseful glance at James and Arun. As Gavin walked past Al into the room, his head barely came up to his waist. When Arun saw Al's height magnified like that, he knew they didn't stand a chance physically against the man.

James followed in his brother's footsteps just a moment later. "I'm sorry. I'm so sorry," he groaned endlessly as he sobbed. When he disappeared behind the false wall, Arun's gaze drifted back to meet Al's. He caught a glimmer of smugness in his eyes.

He knows he won, Arun thought.

He stared back at Al sternly, trying his hardest to exude defiance.

"My friend goes in first," said Arun, almost spitting out the words.

They held each other's gaze for a few moments, with Al breaking away first. He walked over to Craig's limp body and slung him over his shoulder.

"Follow me," he said, mimicking the same trying tone Arun had used moments prior.

The way Craig's limbs flopped limply around as he was carried made Arun queasy. What was even worse than watching Craig get knocked out cold was the knowledge that if he hadn't pressed to continue hanging out with the Kissinger lads, none of this would have happened in the first place.

When they made it into the room, Al laid Craig on the ground, slipped out, and closed the door behind him. Arun ran his hands along the brick wall, trying to discern where the edge of the false wall began, but it was completely smooth. He then turned to the Kissinger lads. Gavin met his eyes; Arun hadn't known him long, but he could see that he was silently pleading for answers.

In the far corner of the room, a soft groan caught his attention. He whipped around and saw a tuft of blonde hair slip out from beneath a blanket. A girl's head rose, and she rubbed her eyes groggily. Once she processed them in her peripheral, she violently flinched awake, gaze darting around with a look of pure terror scrawled across her baby face.

"Who is she?" asked Arun.

Gavin shrugged his shoulders.

"How did you get down here? Did *he*—?" asked the girl. She flicked her gaze frantically between Arun and Gavin.

Neither answered.

Then Arun's attention fell on James. He knelt with his hands cupping his face, and he emitted the most guttural cries Arun had ever heard in his life. Arun didn't mirror his sadness, though. Only two thoughts plagued him.

Will Craig wake up?

Will my mum be able to survive without me?

That last thought was accompanied by a sinking feeling that burrowed down to the deepest reaches of his gut. He was the only family she had left.

Arun pored through his memories for anything that might be able to ease this helpless feeling. He'd only met his grandmother once, when she was on her deathbed, paying her a single visit in the hospital before she passed away. He remembered giving his grandmother a hug, and the rest of the visit, which probably lasted under five minutes, Aniqa and his grandmother spoke in Bangla—a tongue Aniqa never cared to teach him.

But as they left the hospital room, he had craned his neck around to take a final look at his grandmother, since he knew this was both the first and last time he would ever get to see her.

"Allāha āpanāra sāthē thākuna," she had said.

He remembered that his mother didn't respond to the statement, nor did she acknowledge anything had been said at all. He also remembered how his grandmother's eyes were fixed on him. That was when he realised those words were meant for him, not his mother. He uttered them under his breath, the whole way back from the hospital, just so he wouldn't forget.

And now, surrounded by the damp brick of the basement with no way out, he chose an arbitrary corner of the room and knelt.

He wasn't sure if he faced east, but he hoped God still heard him. *"Allāha āpanāra sāthē thākuna,"* he said, over and over, unsure of its meaning. Though the longer he said it, the more he felt comforted.

A feeling he suspected he'd have no acquaintance with in the days to come.

Elaine Robertson glanced at the two plates of the now-tepid food she had cooked as she headed for the front door. Her husband, George, trailed her through the kitchen. Behind them, a dozen or so partygoers sipped on their drinks; some were munching on the bowls of crisps laid out on the coffee table. A few of the guests were couples. They shot each other sidelong glances; the interpretations of those glances clear as day: *should we go?* The discomfort of their hosts the most likely cause; housed within those same glances were bits of worry, for perhaps if they were to leave prematurely, Elaine's distress would worsen.

She opened the front door and scanned the neighbourhood. It was still bright as day, and all was quiet.

"Craig! Arun!" she shouted.

"Elaine…" said George. He gently rubbed her back. "They've probably just got caught up with their friends. I bet they'll be home soon."

She shook George's hand off her back and continued to look out on the street. Despite her husband's optimism, she knew it wasn't like Craig and Arun to miss dinner. She had this sinking feeling that something wasn't right, and as a mother, thoughts raced endlessly through her mind, the next appearing just as quickly as the current dissipated.

How long should I wait to call the police?

To call Aniqa?

What if something bad has happened?

"We don't want to worry everyone," said George.

Elaine took the last gulp of her wine and turned back inside. She feigned a smile for the guests and shakily uncorked another bottle.

Al entered his study with a ferocious rage and knocked a row of books off a shelf. He spun around like a cyclone and tore everything in his path down to the floor—glass ornaments, a coffee mug, photos—he groaned and yelled at the top of his lungs. But once there was nothing left to tear down, he fell silent for a moment, catching his breath. He looked at the mess strewn about at his feet.

His lower lip trembled, and from the depths of his gut he emitted a long, guttural cry. He hadn't cried that way in decades.

Not since…

He drew in a sharp breath to snap himself out of the memory. He continued to sob, and then collapsed into his desk chair. Without even stopping a moment, he opened the desk drawer and pulled out a knife. He put the tip to his forearm and sliced just forcefully enough to cut across the width of his arm. Blood pitter-pattered on the floor, and he continued to moan as tears dripped off his cheeks. He would mend his arm in a few moments, but first, he wanted to savour the pain. In those few, fleeting seconds, he could feel…*something*.

Because most days he fought to feel anything at all.

CHAPTER 3
THE REUNION

Colin Clark sat cross-legged behind a wooden bench along the River Ayr, beneath the waning shadow of an old, looming oak tree. He rocked his legs out of nervous habit, took a swig of whisky from his flask. He grimaced as the liquid slid down his throat and settled in his stomach; sadly, it was one of the only forms of nourishment he'd had all day. Being homeless in Catrine wasn't a much gloomier story than it was to fare well in this sad, small town. But it was a story Colin had been living for close to a year since he'd left his family's home. Addiction and joblessness had plagued his mum and pa for as long as he could remember, and to top it off, his father was an abusive prick that couldn't even put down the bottle long enough to stand up and give his children a hug when they'd arrive home from school.

And look at me now, he thought, taking another swig from his flask.

He resented the fact he'd become an alcoholic, but it was one of the few things left in this world that would ease the pain he felt every single day. Being homeless had chipped away the boy he used to be until the point where old friends wouldn't recognise him out in town anymore. At a certain point, even he had a hard time recognising the man he'd become in the mirror. He smelled so foul he couldn't even enjoy a drink at the local pubs—they'd kick him out a few moments after he'd walk in. Now nineteen, he felt worthless, and even among the bushes he'd become so familiar with, he didn't feel at home.

Despite the dismal darkness of his day to day, he'd been given the gift of a newfound purpose. A year ago, the Kilmarnock courts had sentenced him to forty hours of community service for a fight outside a pub that had soured quickly. In the heat of the tussle, he'd accidentally hit an officer. Though unintentional, the courts didn't see him in the same light as they saw an average person, so he didn't receive a simple slap on the wrist.

Looking back on his sentence now, he wasn't sure if it was a fluke or serendipity, but to the credit of whomever was calling the shots behind the curtains of this universe, he was thankful. He spent all forty hours volunteering at Kissinger Grounds, and it was there he stumbled upon his new purpose. Most of his time was spent with Elder Louise and Deacons Angela and Gillian, but for a mere hour every day, he was in the presence of Albert Reid.

After having lived the entirety of his short life surrounded by imperfection, the perfection that was Al so starkly contrasted everything he'd known that it left him more bewildered than impressed. *How could someone be so perfect?* he remembered thinking after his first week working the Grounds. Louise, Angela, and Gillian adored him. When he'd mention Al's name in passing in town to the few folks who didn't ignore him, they all said similar versions of the same praise:

"You should feel lucky working for Mr. Reid. He's a great man."

"He's doing God's work."

"He's the best thing to ever happen to this town."

The longer he tried, the more he struggled to find a single person in Catrine willing to speak ill of the man. He outright failed. No one disliked Al. On its face, their love for him seemed completely reasonable. He'd founded one of the largest orphanages in Ayrshire. He owned a historic church that the Kirk of Scotland marvelled at, which the majority of the religious in Catrine attended every Sunday, and he ran TLC, the town's most popular restaurant that was such a success, Al attracted the talents of a head chef from Glasgow to help him run the operation.

But Colin couldn't shake the feeling that someone couldn't be that perfect. He had to have flaws—or at least—*a* flaw. As time volunteering passed, he failed time and time again. He never once saw him raise his voice to Elder Louise or the two deacons, nor to any of the orphans. Al was always glowing. Happy to be alive. Happy to be in Catrine. The only thing he observed that he found even the slightest bit peculiar was that Al often checked his pocket watch. Every fifteen minutes or so, he'd pull it out to take a quick glance. He also arrived at the Grounds at the exact same time every day. But as Colin's community service at the Grounds came to an end, that was the furthest extent of his discoveries.

He then found himself reunited with his lone acquaintance while homeless. Time.

Besides being free and clear from the Scottish justice system, what he also brought away from his service at the Grounds was that itch…the tiny, unyielding fragment of curiosity that he couldn't rid himself of.

That there was something more to Albert Reid.

Something that couldn't be seen.

From that moment on, learning about Al became an obsession.

Colin began to watch Al from a distance. What started as one day of studying his routine turned into two, then two to three, and before he knew it, he had watched him for an entire week. Again, the only thing he gleaned from his following of Al was that the man did the same thing every day. His schedule was so regimented it sometimes made Colin feel nauseated.

Weeks turned into months. The longer he watched Al from afar, the more he doubted his intentions. Maybe he really was the great man he seemed to be. Al poured his life into this town. *Do I really need more of an explanation?* he thought. In the months he watched him, he only discovered two new things about Al.

The first was that once a month, he went to the Bank of Scotland in Cumnock and drove immediately back to Catrine.

The second was that there was one evening where Al broke his routine. Instead of his house going dark as normal, he hopped into his second vehicle—a black cargo van—and disappeared for a few hours. When he returned, he lugged a bunch of supplies into his shed. They ranged from pieces of plywood to cans of paint. But there was one item that had caught Colin's eye; a long, wooden crate covered with a tarp. The heaviness of the object was evident in how Al had to hoist it down from the van, then drag it along the ground into his shed.

It was the same shed where Al spent his weekday mornings. Colin always wondered what he did in there. *Perhaps some woodwork?* he mused. It was a fair size, attached to the back corner of his house. Easily large enough to have some sort of workshop.

But nothing else happened. Al just locked up his shed and went back inside.

Colin did, however, scribble down the date of this occurrence in his little black notebook.

Nothing else happened in the weeks that followed.

Until yesterday, when he was riding the bus from Catrine to Ayr to visit an old friend. As they cut through the dense morning, Colin's wandering eyes fell onto the gentleman sitting in front of him. He was reading the daily paper, and the headline read:

Search continues for girl who went missing from family's home.

He discreetly peered closer, over the man's shoulder, and caught the first few lines of the editorial.

Authorities are still looking for Fiona Campbell, twelve, who disappeared from her family's home in Cathkin sometime on the night of June 8th without a trace…

Reading the date caused something to click internally. With sweaty hands, he shakily pulled out his notebook and quickly flipped to the most recent pages. The night Al disappeared in his van—*June 8th*. A sickly feeling sunk into the centre of his chest, and the longer he spent on the bus, the more he felt its glass and metal frame crushing in around him. His breath shallowed; he wiped the sweat off his brow with the sleeve of his jacket. Some of the passengers cast worried looks. Half of them wondered if he was having a panic attack, and the other half thought he might be tweaking on drugs. As more eyes fell on him, he tried to steady his breathing. Less than half the trip to Ayr remained.

Once he arrived in Ayr, he used one of the last remaining pounds in his pocket to purchase the same paper the man on the bus had been reading. In the hours that followed he read the article about the missing girl a dozen times over. Fiona Campbell had gone missing from her own bedroom, as if she'd disappeared into thin air. No signs of forced entry, nothing disturbed. The family, the neighbours, and everyone close to Fiona had been cleared from being suspects.

Colin was so frantic from his discovery that he scrapped his plans and hopped on the next bus back to Catrine. And as he compared the date in the newspaper to the date in his notebook, he could only focus on one thought.

Albert Reid had kidnapped before, and he would surely kidnap again.

And that's what had led Colin here, crouched behind a bench, hidden by shrubbery. For a few hours ago, something had happened. Al broke his routine again. He hadn't driven anywhere in his van, but he *had* gone into his shed. It was the first time Colin had seen him enter it at night since June 8th, when he saw him bring in all the supplies, along with the suspiciously shaped wooden crate.

This was where Colin waited. *Something's off*, he thought. He'd stay up all night if necessary—to capture the evidence he desperately needed to prove his theory.

I've got you, you bastard. I've got you.

Aniqa sat cross-legged on the bed of the threadbare hotel room she stayed at every weekend when she attended university. The smell of cigarettes clung so strongly to the fabric she'd almost become comforted by its presence. Every whiff of lingering tobacco was reminder that her time here was yet another iteration of working toward her goal.

A physics degree.

By now she'd become glassy-eyed, mind foggy. She was nearly three hours into the solving of a complex circuit. What remained for her to do was much worse—a challenge to solve one of Schrodinger's equations. When she felt as she did now, intellect barely hanging on by a thread, she imagined what her father would do.

Would he give up?

No, she'd answer the thought.

Half-eaten scotch pie sat on the edge of the bed—its formerly warm, crumbly edges were now stiff as a board. The room was quiet apart from the soft scratching emanating from the tip of Aniqa's pencil and the ticking of the wall clock. She was so fixated on the problem set that its ticking hadn't surfaced the subtle sensation that something was missing from the evening.

Suddenly, the room telephone rang, jarring her from her work.

She looked up at the clock—twenty-two minutes past midnight. An odd feeling crept through her skin as the phone continued to ring.

Why hadn't Arun called?

She slowly picked up the phone.

"Hello?"

"I'm sorry, Aniqa," said Elaine, sniffling. "The boys never came home for dinner."

Anger washed over her. *Why did she wait so long to tell me?* Having exhausted most of her logic on physics, she fought to use the little bit she had left for this moment.

"Have you called the police?"

"Aye, but they can't do anything till morning," she said. "George told me to relax, said they were probably at a friend's house. We called every neighbour in the phone book and nothing. We searched all over, Aniqa. I'm so sorry."

Elaine erupted into tears. Aniqa was more nauseated than anything; her hand shook as she held the hard, smooth plastic of the phone pressed to her ear.

"I'm coming home," she said into the receiver. "It's not your fault, Elaine. See you soon."

She hung up and packed her things. A thousand thoughts bombarded her. *Where could they be? What if someone took them? What if they're dead?*

That thought struck at her core. Arun was the only family she had left. He was her whole world. Aniqa headed for the door, and she knew exactly where she was going. If the police department couldn't do anything about her son's disappearance until morning, then she damn well would be the first face they saw when they arrived.

Colin's hands trembled wildly as he watched Al leave his house, taking furtive glances in each direction before he walked around to his drive. Colin was hiding less than twenty feet away at the river's edge, struggling to hold onto a 35mm camera between sweaty palms. His heart pounded in his chest, and he knew his moment had arrived.

This is it, he thought. *Now or never.*

Al fiddled with the padlock on the shed door. Colin realised something was different about Al—his hair. He had donned a wig full of black locks that fell just past his shoulders. The terrifying thought crossed his mind that perhaps no one would be able to recognise Al within the photo because of that difference. *I must get a photo of his face, then*, he thought. Once the shed doors were open, Al disappeared inside.

Now!

He popped out from the shrubbery and quietly sped up Al's drive. He held the edge of the shed door with a wavering hand and cracked it open. Stagnant air filled his nostrils; a musty amalgam of dust, wood varnish, and spilt motor oil. As his eyes adjusted to the faint light slipping through the narrow slats, he saw something materialise at the end of the landing.

A red door.

He tiptoed toward it and gingerly pulled it open, praying that it wouldn't creak. He stood atop the edge of a stone staircase that was half-obscured by shadow. He slunk down the steps, holding his 35mm in one hand, and supporting himself against the basement wall with the other. When he lifted his foot and placed it down to find he had reached the bottom, he turned to see a long hallway illuminated by hanging overhead lights, casting everything in a dingy yellow glow. Al was halfway down the hall, turned away from him.

I need to get his face…

"Hey!"

The moment Al whipped around, Colin pressed the shutter button with a trembling index finger—a bright white flash ripped through the dimly lit basement.

Al broke out in a sprint toward Colin, who turned to run back up the stairs as fast as he could. He knew his life was in grave danger, but the only thought that crossed his mind as he ran was the preservation of the photo. As he reached the top of the stairs and made it to the mouth of the shed, he turned and saw Al gaining on him. In a panic, he threw the camera with all his might, and it disappeared into the night, followed by a tinny shattering sound as it landed.

It seemed to land far enough away, he thought.

His next thought was to scream.

Sadly, all these thoughts were slowed from the alcohol he had been drinking in the hours before catching Al. The moment he screamed Al tackled him to the ground. They writhed together as Colin fought to free himself, but he was much smaller than Al in both height and weight. He tried to scream again but was punched clean in the face before he could. The pain was excruciating, and he saw specks of light in his vision. A second later, he felt a pinch. Al had stuck a needle in his neck. Whatever it was, his limbs began to go numb.

Al disappeared for a few minutes, and the rest of Colin's sensations began to fade. He heard Al cursing under his breath every few moments, and assumed he was searching for the camera. He prayed that if tonight was his last night on this earth, that the camera would stay far away from the grips of this evil man.

Now Colin's body was completely numb, and he felt himself slipping closer to unconsciousness. Al had returned, and he began dragging him by his ankles. All he could see were the faint stars trying to shine through the half-dark night and the distant tops of trees. Tears slipped down his cheeks as he realised this was the last view he would ever get of the sky.

For he knew wherever Al was bringing him, there wasn't a chance in Hell he'd get out alive.

As he was dragged into the shed, just before his vision turned black, he had one last coherent thought.

I failed.

Arun sat in the corner of the dank, dark basement room. He had stopped praying hours ago; now he wondered if he'd be able to sleep at all tonight. There were no beds, no pillows, and no windows—no way to discern the time of day. He gulped at the thought of what his mum was going through at this very moment. He was certain Mrs. Robertson had called her by now. He also wondered if the police knew about their disappearance yet. *Would they start looking right away?*

James was still crying in his own corner of the room, but his eyes had dried. It was like he had no tears left to cry, yet going through the motion of it was an act of comfort. Gavin sat next to him. Silent, uncertain. Craig was awake now, and his eyes hadn't left Arun for a second. Arun averted his gaze, but every minute or so he'd drift back and face his glare. Each look conveyed the same message: *This is all your fault. You should have listened to me.*

The part that bothered him the most was the fact that Craig was right. It *was* his fault. If they had left James and Gavin at any point in the afternoon, they would be at Craig's house playing games or watching late night TV. But no, they were here. The only reason he'd agreed to all James' suggestions was because he felt bad for them.

Because he knew the feeling of being an outsider.

Suddenly, a sound cut through his thoughts: *the stairs.*

The others heard the footsteps too. Craig didn't flinch, but James and Gavin huddled closer together in anticipation of what was to come. Arun followed Craig's lead. The last thing he wanted to show Al was fear.

"Don't worry," said the blonde girl flatly. "This is when he brings food."

The wall across from him came to life, and its edge appeared from the seemingly smooth surface as it was pushed open. Al threw two baskets and a bundle of blankets on the floor, exiting just as quickly as he'd entered. Arun kept his eyes fixated on the precise portion of the false wall the edgeless door had disappeared into. He stood and began to run his hands along it, attempting to feel where its boundaries lay. *There must be a way to open this door from the inside.* As elaborately as this basement lair was constructed, he figured that Al wouldn't allow for the possibility of being trapped within his own contraption. There had to be a touch point that would pop the edge open.

What felt like half an hour passed with no success in popping open the basement wall. But Arun was determined. His curiosity had grown because beyond the wall, he could hear echoed groans, along with the occasional scream.

James kept asking, "What do you think is going on out there?"

No one cared to answer him.

For none of them knew, nor wanted to know—outside of Arun—what horrible act was causing such screams.

Arun focused his attention on the other side of what he believed to be the door. He closed his eyes every few seconds to imagine how wide it was. If the door only popped open from one point on the other side, the *opposite* side would get it to open from where the boys were being held. He ran his hands up and down, pushing every few seconds.

He pushed, and the wall gave slightly.

"Guys. It budged."

Craig jumped to his side. "The edge!" he exclaimed.

"I need your help. Push."

A few seconds later, both James and Gavin were at their sides.

"On the count of three," said Craig.

"One, two, three!"

They all pushed simultaneously. Its weight was unbelievable, but their combined effort caused it to begin to slide open. The gap to the hallway could finally be seen.

"Harder!" groaned Arun. They gave it their all, and the gap became large enough for them to slip out. Craig sprinted to the stairwell gate, nearly barrelling into it before coming to a stop. James and Gavin were right behind him. Craig shook the iron gate, kicking it with all his strength.

"It's locked!" he said, defeated.

Arun wasn't concerned with the stairs. There wasn't a chance that Al would leave it unlocked for even a moment. What entranced him were the distant cries and groans that echoed off the basement walls. Their eerie familiarity piqued his curiosity. As he wandered down an adjacent hall, the sounds grew louder. He passed a series of open, door-less rooms. Each one looked identical to the last, and they all shared something in common—a single, dust-covered halide light hung from the ceiling. Arun's stomach sank. Now, the groans sounded as if they were right next to him. At the end of the hall, there was one archway opening to a room. He cautiously approached it, and the moment his eyes reached the opening, he felt faint.

The man with no skin.

Al stood over him with a scalpel, wearing the tattered, makeshift surgical gown and a wig made of long, black hair. Arun's heart pounded as the man with no skin cried out for Al to kill him. The red muscle and bone were just as vivid as he remembered from his dream.

After seeing it with his waking eyes, his soul deflated.

He wondered what kind of fate he would have being down here.

Will I end up like the man with no skin?

The thought sent chills down his spine.

Suddenly, the screams stopped. Silence filled the basement. He trudged listlessly back toward the room they were being kept in and passed Craig, James, and Gavin still fiddling with the metal stairwell gate. Craig clocked the look on Arun's face and followed him back into the room.

"Arun. What happened?"

He didn't care to respond.

"What happened to the screams?"

"The man. He's dead," said Arun. There wasn't the tiniest inflection of hope left in his voice. His statement crushed Craig, for the same thought Arun had had when he saw the man with no skin on the surgical table had crossed his own mind. *Are we going to be killed too?* He pushed the thought away the moment it entered, because he didn't want to imagine that possibility.

One by one, Gavin and James re-entered the room.

They had failed at opening the gate, and all four boys fell silent. Not a word exchanged.

The only sound that could be heard was vociferous chewing from the blonde girl who ignored them, eating the food Al had left in the baskets. In the hours that were to come, all the boys were forced to come to grips with the reality of their situation, each in their own way.

None of them were leaving the basement any time soon.

Darkness filled Margaret Brown's room. The thick curtains blocked out the faint light of the Scottish morning. Her husband's periodic snores cut through the space, but after fifteen years of marriage, she slept through his raucous breathing with ease.

The phone on her bedside table rang.

Its trill vibrato pulled her from her sleep. A phone call in the middle of the night was so foreign that she wasn't sure if she was still dreaming or if it really *was* ringing. After the third ring, her husband grumbled her name incoherently. She leaned sideways, propped herself up in bed by her elbow, and picked up the phone.

"Hello," she said.

There was a half-second pause, and she was about to hang up, thinking it might have been local kids up late making a summer night prank call. Before she did, Stuart's voice sprang from the receiver.

"Margaret. Two lads from Catrine have gone missing."

The words that followed were hazy, so dreamlike in fact, that after she hung up with Stu, she wondered if she had awoken to begin with. Never in the village's history had anything like this occurred. She returned to her original position in bed, with her back facing away from the bedroom door—she always faced away from it as she fell asleep. After all these years, it had become more of an unconscious reflex than a bona fide routine. But now, promptly after that phone call, she could feel the pair of eyes boring into the back of her head more intensely than usual.

"Help me."

An icy shiver slid down her spine. She hadn't heard her voice in years.

"Why did you leave me?"

Margaret flinched on hearing her a second time. She knew from experience that once she spoke, Margaret would be forced to acknowledge her presence.

She slowly rolled over in bed and saw the little girl. She sat with her knees tucked against her chest, arms wrapped around them, back pressed against the bedroom door. The little girl stared up at Margaret with wide, vacant eyes, unblinking. The tears that filled them shimmered with an ethereal glow not of this world.

Then, the sky fell.

It was the loudest rain Margaret had heard in months; the thrumming droplets on the roof a fitting background noise to the current of worry that swept through her mind.

Eventually Margaret rolled back over, turning her back to the girl, and the rain pulled her to sleep again, persisting long into the night and with the same intensity. To the residents of East Ayrshire that were still awake at such a late hour, it was simply a downpour.

Yet its presence held far greater significance.

Although God's plan was righteous and perfect, the Lord cried for Catrine that night.

He wept because the only soul who knew the truth of Albert Reid's wickedness had been murdered.

CHAPTER 4
THE BLACK RABBIT

Kensington Palace
1934

Duke Leon of Albemarle meandered through the farthest reaches of the palace grounds. The light of an early summer sun was just beginning to peek over the horizon. Moist air filled his lungs, fresh and invigorating. Dewdrops clung to the blades of grass and dampened his shoes and socks the longer he walked.

He deliberately slowed his traipse between the trees because this time was his only solitude. As the youngest of the Queen's children, there was hardly a single moment in the day where he was alone. This was why he awoke before the rest of his family. All was quiet on the grounds, and he savoured every moment of this peace. His only companions were the chatty birds that consistently welcomed the new day with endless conversation, and John, the lone guardsman who watched the eastern side of the grounds, which housed the Palace Gardens. They always exchanged a few words in the morning when Duke Leon went out the door and again when he returned around an hour later.

While John had a family of his own, over the past few years of these morning run-ins, he'd developed a soft spot for Duke Leon. Leon knew this, and although he wasn't technically breaking any rules, he would ask John to not mention these trips to his mother.

Duke Leon arrived at the spot where the gardens met the corner of the gate. A ten-foot wall separated the palace grounds from the public. A perimeter of foliage had been deliberately planted to give the royal family more privacy. He craned his head skyward—the treetops coalesced into a canopy that swayed gently with the breath of the wind and shaded everything below its cradle of green.

Before he could even kneel, the snuffling began.

The two rabbits were overjoyed at Duke Leon's presence, and he let them out of their large wooden cage. They hopped around his feet and frolicked in the grass together. He sat and from his pocket pulled a drawstring leather pouch stuffed tight with vegetable scraps he'd grabbed from the chefs—carrots, radishes, and lettuce. They too were clued in about his trips to his rabbits. They simply gave him the leftovers without question.

Although he despised much about his life here, he thoroughly enjoyed the privileges of being a duke. Although most of his cousins weren't intelligent enough to capitalise on these privileges, he'd caught on from an early age. He was barely thirteen, and while the rest of his family often wouldn't spare him a passing glance, he received the acknowledgement and respect he craved from the residents of the palace of non-royal blood. The servants, the cooks, and the guardsmen. Though young, Leon was still a duke, and they would not dare upset one of the Queen's children.

He used this knowledge to his advantage but made certain not to put a foul taste in the mouths of the non-royals who treated him so well. He displayed kindness and charm in their presence. His mother and her like oftentimes treated them as if they weren't human at all. So, when Duke Leon treated them well, the effect was magnified.

This too he took note of.

He smiled as his rabbits continued snuffling. Their teeth chomped down on the vegetables in quick little bites, eating right out of his palm. He'd had these rabbits for close to two years now. Though there were a few pets living in the palace, he knew his mother wouldn't approve of rabbits. All it took to make it happen was a little bit of creativity—

he had offered one of his friends from church the opportunity to stay overnight at the palace in exchange for buying the animals. He waited until the Queen was on a state trip to execute the exchange. His friend brought the two rabbits, Duke Leon gave him the money, and he spent a whole night feigning interest in this acquaintance as he gawked at the luxury Duke Leon called home.

Since then, he had taken good care of Midnight and Snowball. Both had been named simply to correspond with the colour of their fur. These past few weeks he had noticed that Midnight was eating more. After she finished her food, Duke Leon sat quietly and watched her hop back into her crate. She began pulling out bits of her own hair and forged the beginnings of a makeshift nest. This piqued Duke Leon's interest. He continued to feed Snowball until Midnight finished the nest. He scooted next to her and gently fondled her belly. As he rubbed his fingers across, he felt marble-like protrusions beneath the skin.

Is she pregnant? he wondered.

Over the next hour his visit with his rabbits progressed as normal, but he told himself he would make a trip in the late evening to check on Midnight's condition.

Duke Leon awoke sluggishly in bed. He had intended to read for a few hours but had unintentionally taken a nap somewhere along the way. He stared out of the large windows that looked out onto the gardens— judging by where the sun hung in the sky it was late afternoon. He threw off his covers and headed for the door. The truth was that his bedroom bored him greatly. Its gilded skirting boards and mouldings matched the rest of the palace's lavish design. Thick, ornate wallpaper covered the walls like a luxurious skin that protected the palace's insides. Most of the great rooms bore elaborate murals that looked more suited to the Vatican than someone's home. As the Queen still lived here part time, she'd certainly added her touch. Sitting rooms, hallways, and a good portion of the staterooms were all a deep rose-red. Duke Leon saw this colour so frequently that he requested his room be painted a calming mint green. Though a stark contrast to the rest of the palace, he was able to convince one of the servants to do his bidding when his mother was away.

As he wandered the long, high-ceilinged halls that connected the various parts of the palace together, he was confronted with another reality of life at Kensington Palace.

The quiet.

The Queen commanded a quiet house. He often caught himself wondering what it would be like if the house was livelier. He would hear the shuffling footsteps of the department of the Lord Steward or the occasional playing of the piano by Princess Theodora more frequently than he would the distinct tenor of another human's voice.

Duke Leon had every possible physical need and want met at his whim. But he always felt as if there was something missing. He wondered if the others residing in the palace felt this way.

After navigating a few more hallways, he arrived at Prince Alfred's salon, his most beloved room in the palace. The wallpaper was a dark onyx soothing to the eyes, and for much of the year, the fireplace burned with fresh cut timber in the chilly evenings. There were no sofas, chaises, or anything designed for two. Duke Leon adored how his father had designed this space with no one else in mind but himself. All that existed were the study desk, the desk chair, and an armchair, the last of which was constructed so extravagantly—with gilded fixtures and plush cushioning—that it was quite literally fit for a king. This was where Duke Leon liked to sit and peruse new books. The crackling firewood would cut through the quiet of the palace with such delightful consistency that it brought him great joy. So much so, that the times he arrived at the salon to faded coals, he'd wander the halls until he found an unassuming servant who could stoke the fire.

Duke Leon disliked the quiet.

For the longer he was in its presence, the louder his mind grew. Sometimes the flurry of thoughts became so loud he wondered if there was something queer about him. But he didn't fret this trait too much, for there was always someone nearby to restore his comfort, and within moments they could breathe life back into the fire whose sound he relished.

Despite his age, Duke Leon was a voracious reader who read at a level far beyond his years. The royal family praised this characteristic a few times a year when his private tutors would deliver their reports. But he didn't see his exceptional reading skills as anything out of the ordinary. In his short life he'd only seen the walls of this palace and a handful of others across the kingdom. He needed books to explore the world outside the one he knew. A world of strict conformity, repetition, and, oftentimes, isolation. Duke Leon craved to be a part of the real world, and he knew that when that day came, he'd be far better suited than his peers to craft a successful life. Because there was one lesson he had learned from his mother that always stuck with him.

When royals talk, people listen.

After an hour of reading, something crept through the crackling of the firewood.

Voices.

The longer Duke Leon listened, the more he realised whoever the voices belonged to must have been cross about something, because their whispers were strained.

Duke Leon closed his book and shelved it. He left the salon and walked through the great room. Its carved, white ceilings were so high, and the space so large, that he imagined it could make the most powerful men in the world still feel small. He paused, trying to discern the direction from which the whispers came. The cavernous spaces of the palace made it difficult to pinpoint—everything echoed. He began down a hall that led to the northern wing of the palace.

As the whispers grew louder, he slowed his gait to a tiptoe.

They were coming from Apartment 1.

Princess Edith, he thought as he recognised one of the voices. *But who was with her?*

He closed in on the door, which stood ajar; but the opening was so small only a tiny sliver of the room inside was visible. Duke Leon stood with his body shielded by the door and steadied his breath.

The conversation was now clear.

"By no means are you to speak of this again."

Mother, Leon thought.

"Mother, what we've done is wrong. It eats at me every hour of the day and every hour of my sleepless nights."

Duke Leon shifted position to where his eye lined up with the miniscule crack between the door and its frame. He could see Princess Edith with her back to him, and Queen Eleanor was standing across from her.

"You will not shame this family solely on the account of a delusional fixation on what you presume to be dignity—"

"I just want him to know!" cried Princess Edith.

"I forbid it," said Queen Eleanor.

"It's not fair to him. You've seen how he's a bit at odds with the other children. He doesn't know his place in this palace because he doesn't know who he is."

A sinking feeling grew within Duke Leon's gut as he processed the description she gave. He watched as Queen Eleanor bridged the gap between her and Princess Edith.

"I *forbid* it. I expect you to ensure that letters like these stop. For good this time. As precocious as the boy is it's just a matter of time before he goes rummaging where he shouldn't, and you know just as well as I do that if he discovers who his father really is, everything we worked to hide will come to light."

"One day he's going to wonder why he is a Duke and not a Prince. What then, Mother?"

The Queen froze. She sighed and cast a patronising smile, then ambled toward the sitting room fireplace. Its flames had died down, but a small fire remained. She turned to Princess Edith, deliberately holding her gaze, and tossed the letter in. It caused a momentary burst of flame as it quickly engulfed the new piece of fuel.

"As long as these never reach the boy's hands," said Queen Eleanor. She glanced down at the fire, then faced Princess Edith. "And as long as *you* retire this idiotic notion that the boy must know who he really is, everything will be fine."

"I worry about him, Mother."

Queen Eleanor placed a gentle hand on Princess Edith's cheek.

"I know you do, my rebellious one. You're better for it."

Princess Edith embraced Queen Eleanor. While they held each other, Duke Leon studied his mother's face. It floored him how, as she embraced her own daughter, her expression was still stony, unflinching.

"Now, I expect you to put an end to this. We shan't discuss this again. Understood?"

"Understood."

The realisation hit Duke Leon that this rendezvous was ending. He darted from the door and hastily returned to the salon. He picked up his book, sat in the chair, and flicked through it to find his page. He continued to digest the conversation between the Queen and Princess Edith, but now, all his motions felt uncertain—as if he were still Duke Leon of Albemarle, but wearing a different skin.

For the first time in his young life, the crackling fire couldn't stifle his thoughts.

After Duke Leon took his nightly bath, he prepared himself for dinner.

He looked at his appearance in the mirror. He was going on fourteen next June, and already a bit taller than most his age, with sandy-blond hair that seemed to darken a shade every year. His complexion was as white as alabaster, and his features were a bit sunken, especially beneath his eyes. Almost as if he had lived another long, hard life before he became Duke Leon.

Although this tired look bothered him occasionally, he didn't think much about it. He was decently handsome, but what he coveted most was his late father Alfred's beard and burly figure. He hoped he would thicken up in the years to come and sprout facial hair.

The dinner bell rang throughout the palace.

It was time.

He quickly slicked back his hair with a comb and carelessly tossed it on the armoire before leaving. Typically, dinner wasn't such an occasion. The royals would often be served in their respective apartments' sitting areas, and only on Sundays would they eat together. But today was Queen Eleanor's last night before she returned to Buckingham Palace.

Mother…he flashed back to the cryptic conversation. From the moment he left the door of Princess Edith's apartment, he had attempted to fight a phrase from repeating endlessly, like an intrusive echo that he was petrified would become a curse.

"You know just as well as I do that if he discovers who his father really is, everything we worked to hide will come to light."

In the hours after his spying, he performed mental acrobatics to rationalise what he heard.

Whose father?

Maybe it is William they are talking about, or Lysander.

But they are both princes and…

"One day he's going to wonder why he is a Duke and not a Prince."

Princess Edith's voice ripped through his thoughts. The acid in his stomach curdled as he ran into the conclusion he kept trying to avoid.

They were talking about me.

This truth, if it were true, caused him to question everything.

Mother was married to Prince Alfred. If Alfred wasn't his father, then who was?

As he listlessly traversed the halls to the grand dining room, he was caught in a maelstrom of negative thoughts. That uncertainty trickled into his appearance in the final steps to the dining room. He nervously smoothed his dress shirt and tightened the belt to his trousers just before he entered.

Everyone was present except for Queen Eleanor.

There was an empty seat next to Princess Theodora. She gave him a warm smile as they met eyes; he took it as a signal to join her. Sitting to Theodora's left were her two children—Eugenie and Lysander. Princess Maud sat next to the empty seat at the head of the table that was Mother's, and her four children, Catherine, Caroline, Charlotte, and William sat in a line at her side.

Duke Leon adjusted the silverware in front of him ever so slightly. Although it had already been perfectly placed by the servants, doing anything other than sitting allowed his mind to avoid the voices of Queen Eleanor and Princess Edith that echoed endlessly in his head. The growing chatter of the other children helped cut through the mental noise as well.

A hand rested gingerly on his shoulder.

"Turn to me, Leon," said Theodora.

He obliged and faced his aunt. She fixed the one side of his shirt collar that sprang awry and smoothed its edges with her hands. She cast another warm smile, just as she had when he first entered the room.

Princess Theodora had an angelic face, and a thin, pointed nose. Her lips were also slender, but blush-coloured, like the rounds of her cheeks. Her skin was porcelain-white like his own, and even after a summer spent across the kingdom's holiday homes, she remained fair. She had curly brown hair that would alternate between being pinned up or let down where it flowed past her shoulders. Duke Leon's favourite feature of

Princess Theodora was her eyes. They were a golden brown that almost resembled jarred honey. He would get lost in them when they spoke, and he couldn't help but feel the energy they gave off—innocence, gentleness. These qualities were why Duke Leon was so fond of Princess Theodora.

She bestowed upon him a sense of calm that he couldn't replicate elsewhere.

Memories of the other royal children treating him as if he didn't belong were interspersed with flashes of the Queen's conversation with Princess Edith. He sat petrified in his seat while he connected memories to this new information. Fitting puzzle pieces in new positions he hadn't been able to before. He glanced around at his cousins' faces, one by one. Many of them gave him the odd look he was familiar with by now, never able to decipher its meaning.

Maybe they all know something I don't, he thought.

"Leon, dear," said Theodora with a brush of her hand on his forearm. "Are you all right?"

Duke Leon broke his trance and met her gaze, returning a halfhearted nod.

"I'm fine."

Queen Eleanor entered the room. The servants froze and stood along the walls, allowing her clear passage to the head of the table. The children hushed their chatter, and she cast smiles in the direction of her children and grandchildren as greeting.

The Queen wore a red gown that had accents of lace around its edges. Though stockier than her daughter Maud, she achieved an hourglass figure with the assistance of a tightly strung corset. Leon often wondered if she ever took a good breath. Her skin was fair, hair auburn, and she had eyes that were icy blue like his own. Her manner commanded the attention of every room she set foot in; it was a phenomenon that Leon had become numb to. To him, Queen Eleanor was his mother. The more time he spent with her, the more her power lost its gravitas.

They were served mutton, potatoes au gratin, and courgettes since they were in season. All perfectly seasoned and delectable as usual. Leon reminisced over the summer days when he'd find an excuse to escape the palace when Mother wasn't around, just to eat street food from the neighbourhoods around Kensington. An undulating dichotomy existed within Leon: one side enjoyed the lavish comforts of his royal life, and the other fantasised about living as one of the common folk.

As he picked at his food, the conversation grew dull. Queen Eleanor had already inquired about how Eugenie and Lysander had enjoyed their recent stint in Baden-Baden—just as she always did. She then focused her chitchatting between her sister Theodora and daughters Maud and Edith. What always intrigued Leon the most was that the topics at hand never drifted from the banality of everyday life.

It was as if family conversations were a carefully rehearsed orchestra, and Queen Eleanor was the conductor. Though she didn't need a baton, for just with deliberate glances and subtle fluctuations in her tone she could direct the dialogue of those around her, never overtly stifling their expression, but never fully handing over the reins either.

Minutes slipped by, and once Leon completely lost interest in his surroundings, he found himself in a trance.

That got his attention—the quiet.

The chatter of the Queen, his sisters, and his cousins was unintelligible. His eyes fixed on each of their mouths as their lips smacked closed and opened, yet the sound had almost entirely disappeared. His heart skipped in his chest.

Have I gone deaf? he thought.

Leon swivelled his head and studied each of his cousins, one by one. They were all on their best behaviour in front of the Queen. Backs straight, hands in lap when they weren't holding utensils, and calm demeanours. The many similarities between the six of them unnerved Leon. The youngest few of the group almost resembled porcelain dolls. Alabaster skin, button noses, and rose-coloured lips. His eyes met William's. He stared back at Leon with a look of confusion, shooting a sidelong glance to Eugenie, as if silently saying, *"Take a look at this creep."* She cast a critical look at Leon, then she and William met eyes again. They chuckled; each laugh they emitted seem to amplify the next to be more animated. But to Leon, the laughs were completely silent. Just gaping mouths pushing out noiseless air. The children restrained themselves the moment Queen Eleanor cast quizzical glances, though they didn't return to their food until meeting Leon's deadpan stare one final time with looks of distaste.

I must be going mad, thought Leon.

He shut his eyes and held them tightly closed, praying that when they opened, sound would return. He couldn't handle the quiet this long. When he opened them, his eyes bulged at what he saw. There were strings attached to the wrists of everyone seated at the table, save for the Queen. He watched in disbelief as his cousins ate; they picked up their forks, secured a scoop of food, and brought it to their mouths. The strings rose and fell buoyantly with their motions. His eyes followed the strings—they seemed to disappear into the ceilings high above them. Everyone at the table looked like marionette dolls, with every move orchestrated by flicks and pulls of the fingers of someone up above.

He looked down at his own hands. To his horror, he discovered that he too was attached to a pair of strings.

He flinched violently in his seat.

All eyes suddenly fixed on him.

"Leon, what has you vexed?" asked Queen Eleanor.

Panting, he fought to shake his hands to rid himself of the strings. He opened and shut his eyes a few more times in a futile attempt to make them disappear, yet they remained. Leon was now deeply in the grip of panic, and he felt like the weight of an elephant sat on his chest. With sweaty palms he grabbed the dinner knife and held it upright—all those seated around the table gasped in shock.

He slashed at the string, and the moment the blade went through, it disappeared. Leon glanced around at his wide-eyed family.

All the strings were gone.

His heavy breathing calmed, and his eyes returned to the knife, quickly realising how this must have looked to everyone else—he dropped it and it clanged against the table.

"What on earth has come over you, Leon?" spat the Queen.

Now it was *her* chest that rose and fell with each rapid breath. Queen Eleanor's corset fought to contain the irritability she felt as she witnessed this spectacle. The grandchildren eagerly awaited to see how this would play out, and Theodora flicked concerned glances between the two.

Leon, on the other hand, was overcome by the mounting pressure of the quiet—combined with the unanswered question that hung in the air like a thick, putrid smoke, which everyone knew was present and couldn't take a breath until it dissipated. He heard the echoes of the Queen and Princess Edith's conversation bouncing around his mind like an angry wasp caught in a glass. Feelings of doubt, isolation, and fear brimmed to the point where stomach acid licked at his insides—a bile that wouldn't settle. He knew if he didn't spit out the words which were the root of his tumult, he'd spew his dinner all over the mahogany table.

"Who is my real father?" asked Leon.

A pin drop could have been heard in the dining room. No one let out a breath. It even seemed as if the ambient noise of the servants and chefs in the galley came to an unsettling halt. Queen Eleanor's eyes fell on Leon as he stared back at her. As if two invisible beams connected their gazes, and neither could break the link between them.

"Your father is Prince Alfred of Lancaster," said Queen Eleanor.

"Then why am *I* Duke Leon of Albemarle?"

Queen Eleanor winced. The others at the table were preoccupied by the fact this specific question had even been asked at all. When Queen Eleanor gave an answer, no one dared invalidate the sufficiency of that answer by asking another question. Princess Edith stared intently at Leon; her flushed cheeks and the tapping of her leg beneath the table giving away how riddled she was with unease.

Don't let her win, Leon, she thought.

Much to her chagrin, Queen Eleanor had to produce a response.

"Your father named you after the honour of your great-grandfather whom he adored dearly. But rest assured that by blood you're a Lancaster."

Leon opened his mouth, nearly spitting out what he'd overheard in Princess Edith's apartment, but Queen Eleanor cut him off with a swift finger in the air.

"Ah tut-tut!" she uttered an ascending flutter of sounds to mask what might come out of Leon's mouth. She cast a commanding yet compassionate stare, attempting to convey to the rest of the table that she didn't want to stifle the boy's curiosity, she simply wanted to contain it elsewhere.

"Let's speak more of this after dinner, Leon," said Queen Eleanor.

With that, dinner resumed, though now the table was devoid of conversation. The only sounds were the tapping and scraping of utensils against the fine china.

Queen Eleanor shovelled a large bite of mutton into her mouth and chomped down, casting a smile in the direction of each of her family members. She exuded grace and composure, but most outside of the grandchildren knew this was a veil that covered her true emotions. Meanwhile, Princess Edith feigned a smile at the Queen when they met eyes, but the moment she moved on, she deflated. Leon caught this subtle change in Princess Edith's disposition but shoved it aside.

He swallowed a mouthful of lukewarm potatoes and wondered how the coming conversation with his mother would go.

Duke Leon's steps to Queen Eleanor's chambers were measured. Despite her instructions to meet there after dinner, he still felt like he was intruding. A nervous pit formed deep within his gut—he was smart enough to know he'd spoken out of turn, but too naïve to know the true impact of his words.

He arrived at the door to the Queen's chamber. He didn't know whether to knock or simply enter. Duke Leon could count on one hand the number of times he'd been in this room alone with his mother, for he didn't like the way the space made him feel.

Insignificant.

Even when she gave him a departing embrace, it felt the same; like he was a visitor in his own mother's arms. He pushed at the door, but it hardly budged. Made of solid wood, its monstrous height nearly crawled up to the ceilings. Duke Leon had to lean at an angle and push all his weight through his shoulder to get enough momentum for it to slide open. Once the gap was large enough to slide through, he found himself standing in the middle of the Queen's sitting room.

Not a sound could be heard besides the crackling of the fireplace, and in an instant, his most beloved comfort transformed into the contrary. For he knew Queen Eleanor was nestled somewhere in a corner of this room, eyeing him from a distance, waiting to be discovered. She need not announce her presence. Their silence was like a delicate dance—the first to break it was the first to lose their power.

Queen Eleanor made certain that she seldom cast herself in that kind of pitiful light. She knew a lot could be learnt from listening to someone speak unprovoked. *Was the tenor of their voice loud and confident, or was it quivering and submissive?* These were the types of considerations that ran through Queen Eleanor's mind when anyone visited her in her quarters, whether they were heads of state or lowly servants.

All would repeatedly relinquish valuable information regarding their temperament through speaking unprovoked. She was the queen on the chessboard, and through silence alone she'd force their hand.

"Mother?" said Leon, voice echoing lightly against the cavernous ceilings.

A moment passed.

"I'm in my study," said Queen Eleanor.

He instinctively turned to the left, slowly meandering through the sitting room, and began down a long hall dimly lit by candlelight. He loathed this hall. He was forced to look down at his feet as he walked to avoid making eye contact with the oversized portraits of late royals whom he had never had the chance to meet. Before long the hallway spilled out to the study. The room's walls were lined with bookshelves that seemed to disappear into the darkness of the ceilings. While Leon enjoyed the smell of leather-bound books, he much preferred them as company in the setting of Prince Alfred's study. Here, they were mixed with the faint scent of orange blossom perfume; an odour Leon had become averse to from his mother's perpetual use.

His reluctant eyes slowly rose from his feet to meet his surroundings. Queen Eleanor rested on the chaise closest to the fireplace; her white skin beamed with unnatural brightness, and her frost-coloured eyes flickered in the firelight. She had retired her formal gown from dinner and donned the same colour pyjamas. Leon had never seen her look so…casual. The Queen closed the book on her lap and set it aside. She cast a smile at Leon and ran her fingers across the luxurious materials she wore, then stared into the shifting flames of the fire.

"Would you like to know the answer to your question?" she asked without turning to him.

Leon swallowed hard.

"Yes."

She turned to him, and her smile grew. The firelight divided her face into perfect halves—one glowing white and the other cast in indiscernible shadow.

"Then ask it."

He mulled over his words.

"Who is my real father?"

Seconds passed—no answer.

"Do you hear that?" asked Queen Eleanor. She glanced around as if she were tuning into a frequency too faint for Leon to hear.

"Hear what?"

She turned, fixed on him with a steely gaze.

"The silence."

She stood and bridged the gap between them. Within a second only a foot separated the two; she looked down at him patronisingly, and her figure eclipsed him from the firelight, casting him completely in shadow. Leon pondered what his mother meant by those two words…*the silence*. He also ignored the sense of nausea that came along with the reminder of what the quiet had always meant to him.

"What do you m—"

Queen Eleanor struck Leon across the face so forcefully the sound from the clap against his cheek seemed to echo off the farthest reaches of her chambers. A singeing pain radiated across his jawline, numbing the left side of his face. Then, the blood rushed in. Heat permeated the inflamed skin, then a quick-rhythmed throbbing accompanied it. Leon wanted to take a full breath, but he was too focused on how the air that had formed his question was completely knocked out of him. Tears leaked from his eyes. Partly out of humiliation and partly from the pain of the blow.

"How dare you question out of turn like that in front of the family!"

Leon just stood there, frozen, face still downcast.

Queen Eleanor took a sharp breath and gently raised Leon's chin with her forefinger and thumb. "Prince Alfred of Lancaster is your father."

"But—"

Queen Eleanor raised her hand but stopped at the height of what would be the beginning of another strike. Leon winced in anticipation, yet the blow never came.

"And *I* am your mother." She roughly grabbed his wrist, squeezing it tightly. "Look at me."

Leon slowly opened his eyes. The one that had been hit wouldn't fully open—it was swelling, pushing the skin beneath his eye up into an unnatural squint.

"That question will forever be laid to rest here, in this room. It dies here, and it dies now."

She paused, searching for any remaining ember of rebellion in Leon's demeanour.

"Do you understand?"

He nodded.

Queen Eleanor let go of his wrist; it fell limply to his side.

"Say it."

He held back a sigh of defeat, but nonetheless uttered the words under his breath.

"I understand."

She returned to her chaise and opened her book where she had left off. The sting of Leon's cheek hadn't begun to fade, yet Queen Eleanor's display of anger had. It was instantly replaced with a chilling air of nonchalance.

"You are dismissed," she said, turning a page of her book.

Leon slinked back the way he came, head down. He imagined the faces of his royal ancestors casting scornful glances as he passed. As he exited the Queen's chambers, he fought against two undulating urges; vomit to rid himself of the bubbling nausea, or cry to eliminate the rock in his throat. He took a sharp breath and chose to satisfy neither. He feared the types of rumours that would spread if any of the servants saw him in such condition returning from the Queen's chambers. They were a chatty bunch. He equally feared the repercussions if word did get back to Queen Eleanor that he was spotted crying. He shook off the thought and continued through the labyrinth of halls that led back to his bedroom.

Once he arrived, he shimmied out of his dinner clothes and sat on the edge of his bed.

There it was again. The acquaintance he tried to avoid, yet persistently made itself known—the quiet.

In a flurry, all the evening's events replayed in his mind. The hushed voices of Princess Edith and the Queen, the crowded dining table with the horrific sight of his family's arms being guided by the imaginary marionette strings, and the thunderous slap from his mother in her chambers.

This recollection appeared so vividly to Duke Leon that it very well could have been projected on the bedroom wall in front of him, and it never seemed to end. Queen Eleanor's forceful blow would loop back to the conversation in Princess Edith's apartment, then to the question at dinner, the marionette strings, the slap, and then the cycle repeated.

This sequence of imagery built up a level of stress within Duke Leon that he had never experienced before. He shut his eyes as the pressure built, like a pot whose lid was about to pop off. His fists began to clench, brow furrowed, and he erupted into a roaring scream. He leapt from the bed and slammed his fist into the wall mirror. It shattered; large shards fell to the floor in a cascade of tinny echoes.

Duke Leon looked down at his knuckles. He had sustained cuts from the glass, and as he stared, droplets of blood dripped along his fingers, falling to the floor.

He smiled.

The nausea was gone. The rock within his throat dissipated. The endless loop of tonight's incidents came to a screeching halt. He wasn't sure what relief his punch and the sight of his own blood brought him, but he knew the sensation was valid.

No pain, no shame, and no guilt.

The question of his place in the royal family was a mere afterthought. The ache of his jaw had become numb. All his worries had faded. As the flow of blood slowed, the turbulent waters of Duke Leon's mind became still.

After sneaking into the servant quarters to bandage his hand, he returned to his bedroom. He let out a sigh of relief—he hadn't been caught. Now, though, his eyes fell to the pile of glass shards that sat in front of what was formerly the mirror.

What now? he thought.

He glanced around the room, searching for something, anything that could be a way out. Then he saw it. The drawstring leather pouch he carried the vegetable scraps in. He glanced quickly at the clock on the wall—ten o'clock. It was just past the normal time he fed the rabbits. He grabbed the pouch, shoving it in his pocket. When he turned, he faced the pile of shards once again. He needed to leave no evidence of his outburst, but he also wouldn't dare mix the rabbits' food with broken glass. He settled for a pillowcase, sliding it off, and carefully began collecting the jagged pieces of the mirror.

Once he was pleased with the clean-up, he hid the broken mirror frame in his closet and left the bedroom. A quick trip to the kitchen resulted in exactly what he expected—the small handful of veggie scraps the chefs left out for him when they finished for the night and retired to their quarters.

He tiptoed through the halls that led to the eastern entrance of the palace. With a gentle slip of his hand, he leaned back and put all his weight on his heels to move the gargantuan door. Once the night guardsman caught sight of Duke Leon, he hurried to his aid by widening the gap for him to pass through. He was careful not to clang the pillowcase of shards against the door, or move too quickly, because the last thing he wanted was to give himself away.

"Good evening, Duke," said John.

Damnit, he thought. *John normally guards during the mornings. He's not supposed to see me twice in one day.*

"Good evening." He meekly greeted John and kept on down the palace steps.

John was disappointed by the halfhearted greeting and tried again to be pleasant as Duke Leon shrank away as he headed into the gardens.

"Are they getting big these days?"

"Yep!" called Duke Leon. His voice was a fraction of its normal volume as he became completely obscured by the shrubbery.

Duke Leon wandered the familiar path to his beloved corner of the gardens. The summer night was temperate, slightly sticky and carried with it the subtle smell of hydrangea. When he neared the cage, he heard the squeaks of the rabbits. He knelt and set the shard-filled pillowcase to the side, pulled the knapsack from his pocket, and retrieved the vegetables.

Snowball came hopping out the moment he opened the cage and rummaged through the veggies that rested in his palm. But Midnight never emerged. Duke Leon's brow furrowed; there had never been a time when both rabbits weren't excited for a meal. He set the vegetables on the grass to let Snowball continue eating, and scooted towards the cage.

In the dim glow cast by the palace lights in the distance, he could hardly see Midnight inside. She lay on her side, her breathing rapid and laboured. He gently slid his hands under her body and pulled her out of the cage, struggling against his grip. He laid her on the grass in front of the cage, and she assumed her previous position. With every second that passed, her breathing intensified.

Then suddenly, her tiny body contracted all at once.

Duke Leon watched in shock as a tiny, fleshy rabbit slipped out of Midnight. *She was pregnant*, he thought.

The baby rabbit was the length of his palm, and as the feet of a second baby began to emerge, he noticed something that made his breath hitch.

The first baby rabbit wasn't moving at all. He gingerly poked at its skin—cold as ice. Panic parched his mouth, and he shakily tried to massage its skin with his fingers.

Nothing.

Midnight contracted again and the second baby slid all the way out.

It lay near its mother's feet and upon inspection, Duke Leon feared the worst. His heart pounded as he tried to palpate the chests of these two stillborn baby rabbits with his fingers.

Nothing.

He locked eyes with Snowball, who had finished his food and sat upright, watching the birth of his children. Duke Leon turned back to Midnight. She was still splayed out on her side, panting. The stillborns now lay parallel to each other, inches from their mum. Duke Leon took a moment to rest his trembling hands in his lap.

A minute or so passed, and the birthing appeared to be over.

Suddenly, Midnight whimpered and let out a bizarre screech. Her whole body contracted, and Duke Leon sprung back into action and readied himself for the delivery. What began to emerge wasn't grey and fleshy like the other two babies. No feet were visible, and the more that slipped out, his horror amplified. A mangled, knotty black ball of flesh plopped onto the grass.

He cupped his hands and scooped it off the ground.

A bloody, deformed rabbit foetus rested on his palms. He glanced down at the two stillborns on the ground. Yes, they were dead, but they were also perfectly formed. Normal. He returned his gaze to the gnarled, malformed baby rabbit in his palm.

The longer he stared, the more wildly his mind began to wander.

What if this one was the runt of the litter?

Perhaps the other two starved it of nutrients.

Did it even have a fighting chance?

Was it destined to be defective?

Was it cursed?

A new sensation slid over Duke Leon. Its arrival caused a chill to sink to the centre of his chest, and he felt as if he couldn't breathe. An emptiness he had never felt before ate away at his insides the same way a black hole slides through the universe undetected.

By engulfing all the light.

He glanced at Midnight. Her breathing had finally calmed, there was just a gentle rise and fall of her black fur. Midnight held his stare for what seemed like an eternity. She lay there, sitting in front of three stillborns, one of which was severely deformed, like she hadn't a care in the world.

What have you done? You just brought death into the world.

The emptiness began to expand within his gut, and the longer he stared into the beady onyx eyes of Midnight, the more she appeared at ease.

Nonchalant. As if *nothing had even happened.*

Duke Leon's pulse pounded in his throat. He leaned over, grabbed the pillowcase, and from it pulled out a long shard of the mirror. He grabbed Midnight with his left hand and dragged her across the grass, pinning her down. She writhed and squirmed, but she couldn't escape his death grip on her throat. He took the shard with his right hand, his own blood dripping along the edges from its sharpness, and he cut into Midnight just above the chest.

Heat danced along his skin, and he began to see spots of light in his vision.

Small popping sounds emanated from Midnight's chest as he slid the shard down the entire length of her gut. Blood and entrails seeped out onto the grass below. She was still writhing, but the blood loss caused her to fade quickly. Within thirty seconds, Midnight froze.

She was dead.

Duke Leon's chest heaved up and down, adrenaline coursing through his veins. He stood up and grabbed Midnight's lifeless body, walked a few steps toward the farthest corner of the garden, and chucked her corpse over the palace gate. He did the same with the pillowcase. He returned to the cage, guided Snowball back into it, and picked up the three stillborn baby rabbits. It didn't take long to find soil that had been freshly tilled in the spring soft enough to dig a makeshift grave with his hands.

He gently laid the three to rest, covering them with the soil.

His next stop was the garden fountains to rinse his hands. Blood still slipped from the fresh wounds. At the same time, the rush he felt was so intoxicating, he didn't care. Plus, he knew if he were gone too long, John the Guardsman would likely come looking for him to make sure he was safe. He headed back to the eastern entrance and John came into view. As the lights of the palace walls grew brighter, Duke Leon glanced down at his hands—they were clean, but another rivulet of red trickled down his palm. He shoved them deep into his pockets.

Duke Leon saw John studying him as he approached, and he walked past farther away and more quickly than normal, not even bothering to make small talk.

"Are you all right?" John asked.

"Mhmm."

Then he ran into another problem.

The door.

The young Duke nearly faceplanted into the palace doors, without even attempting to open them. *What would John think?* Especially when he'd gone to great lengths earlier to open it for himself on the way out.

"Do you mind?" he asked.

John sprang to assist him. "Not at all, Your Grace."

Duke Leon tried to act oblivious, but was sure John could see through him, because he caught John glancing at his pocket—at the blood he could feel seeping out—but didn't wait a second to allow John's mind to wander any further.

"I cut myself," he announced meekly.

"Let me see it," said John, "I'll mend it for you."

"I have bandages in my room. Goodnight, John."

He could see John wasn't buying his story. He'd have to be careful around him in the future.

Duke Leon slipped through the crack in the palace doors and raced to his bedroom. When he made it safe and sound, he bandaged his hand for the second time and slipped into his pyjamas. He lay in bed and drifted off to sleep much quicker than usual. He remembered one fleeting thought before he met the blackness of slumber.

The emptiness is gone.

CHAPTER 5
THE PRAYER

Aniqa stood frozen at the foot of the mosque steps, rooted to the grey brick pavement, eyes fixed on the entrance that lay fifty feet ahead. The only barrier separating her from it was a long set of shallow stairs.

A pinprick of cold touched her forehead. She readjusted her loosely fitted *hijab* to protect more of her hairline from the falling snowflakes. Suddenly, the busy streets of London and the never-ending sounds of the city fell to the wayside. Everything became a muted hush. It was as if the chaos in Aniqa's life came to a screeching halt—all to channel her focus.

The mosque.

Why am I here? she thought.

Someone softly tugged at her hand. Instinctively, she looked down.

Arun. He stared at her with his inquisitive black eyes.

She smiled warmly at him, but he didn't return it. He tugged at her hand again, nodded in the direction of the mosque.

"Let's go," he said.

Aniqa knew she had to walk up these stairs, but her feet felt heavy, as if they had calcified into the cement.

Arun noticed the shift in his mother's disposition.

"Come on." There was a wise air about his countenance that took Aniqa aback. As if he could see the unseen.

See the darkness that was within her.

"You can do this."

She hesitantly followed Arun as he guided her up the steps. Her pulse quickened as she neared the mosque doors. Though the air was frigid with the chill of snow, she felt as if she were walking through flames. Her body flushed with heat; the edge of the *hijab* fabric became damp with sweat.

Arun struggled with the weight of the tall, wooden doors. She aided him reluctantly. Because even though she had never stepped foot in this mosque before, she knew precisely what awaited her.

She and Arun slipped inside. The doors slammed behind them.

As far as the eye could see, the entire span of the massive room was filled with women. Hundreds, if not thousands of them, side-by-side. They all knelt, praying, and each wore a full, black *niqab*. The draping fabric of each woman's garment coalesced into an endless black sheet that eclipsed the intricate designs of the mosque carpet entirely. Only a narrow walkway was free of the women, just wide enough for Arun and her to pass.

Arun tugged at her hand again, nodding toward the walkway.

As they began down the path, the moment she and Arun passed a row of women, they would rise from their prayer. Each step caused another row to do the same, a consistent rippling of women bringing their faces up from the floor.

When they reached the end of the walkway, all the women were kneeling upright.

Aniqa turned to face them. Thousands of familiar dark eyes stared at her from behind the narrow slits in the *niqabs*.

All the women pulled down their face veils at the same time.

Her breath hitched as she realised—

They were all…Aniqa.

Thousands of her knelt perfectly still. She stared at their blank expressions. Each woman combined to form a room full of mirrors— reflecting her own emotions. Pain, guilt, regret. The longer she held the gazes of the copies, the more a sinking feeling eddied within her gut. The sensation quickly struck a nerve, and adrenaline coursed through her body.

Panic.

I shouldn't be here, she thought.

Arun tugged at her hand.

"Love, we need to leave. Now."

He tugged at her hand again. This time, forcefully.

"Turn around," he said.

"Arun, let's go." She pulled him and he jerked her arm back. The wind left her chest from the shock of her young son's unnatural strength. He held her wrist with a death-grip and planted his feet.

"*No*," he said, voice deeper.

Aniqa's heart was in her throat. Something had shifted in Arun because he glowered at her. Such an innocent boy now brimmed with disgust and resentment.

"I am your mother," she said. "Come along."

She yanked him again, but he didn't budge, as if he had the strength of three grown men. His grip was so tight she felt the bones in her wrist crushing under the pressure.

"Let go of me!" she shouted. "Ow!"

"Turn around." Arun's voice dropped another octave.

She pulled and pulled but her effort was futile.

"No! Let go!" She slipped as she tried to escape her son's grip. "*Let me go*!"

"Turn around."

Sweat dripped down her forehead as waves of panic crashed over her.

"Turn around," commanded Arun, voice so thick it sounded inhuman. "Turn around. Turn around. Turn around." He began chanting the words. "Turn a-round! Turn a-round!"

"No! Please, no!" cried Aniqa.

The countless Aniqas in the mosque started to chant with Arun.

"Turn a-round! Turn a-round! Turn a-round!"

Thousands of her own voice echoed off the cavernous ceilings of the mosque. They grew louder until the Aniqas and Arun were shouting at the top of their lungs.

"Turn a-round! Turn a-round! Turn a-round!"

"No, please!" she cried, exasperated. "*Please*, let me go."

She had collapsed at her son's feet, still facing the mosque's exit.

"Turn a-round! Turn a-round! Turn a-round! Turn a-round!"

She sobbed, bombarded by the cacophony of shouts that only grew shriller.

"Okay! *Stop!*"

The mosque fell silent.

Aniqa trembled as she rose to her feet, and Arun loosened his grip on her wrist.

She slowly turned around, and there it was.

The thing she had desperately fought to avoid.

A plain wooden coffin.

Her choking cries swelled because she knew this was the coffin that she'd never had the courage to face. Arun's disposition softened at her side. She laid her hand on the top of the coffin, brushing its rough texture.

A loud knock came from inside, and Aniqa's hand recoiled.

She looked down at Arun; he smiled as if nothing out of the ordinary had happened.

Three louder knocks came from inside the coffin.

Aniqa took a step back, and a moment later Arun's hand shot back up to grab her wrist.

"No," he said. "Stay."

More knocks came from inside the coffin—each set of three was more forceful than the set before.

"Let me go," she pleaded, whimpering.

The knocks became so strong the coffin lid was shaking.

Arun nodded toward the coffin. "Open it."

"No, no, no." She shook her head. "I can't."

"Open it!" he bellowed, the inhuman tone resurfacing.

The thousands of Aniqas began to echo Arun.

"Open it! Open it!"

The chanting commands were intercut with flurries of loud knocks becoming impossibly faster and stronger.

"Please, no!" she cried, exhausted from the torment.

"Open it!" yelled Arun, over and over.

Aniqa extended a trembling hand to the coffin lid that reverberated with near-constant knocks. Sobbing, she struggled to lift the lid, with the chants of "Open it!" ringing in her ears.

She lifted it but turned her head away and shut her eyes to avoid what was inside at all costs.

"Look!" the chants shifted instantaneously.

"Look! Look! Look!"

Aniqa groaned in agony. She painstakingly turned to face what lay in the coffin, the lid still knocking wildly around in her grip.

"Look!"

She opened her eyes.

Aniqa jolted awake as a female police officer knocked on her driver-side window. She caught her breath, releasing her death-grip on the steering wheel.

Thank God, she thought, letting out a sigh; she was awake and in her car.

"Everything all right? You were sleeping with your car running."

"What time is it?" asked Aniqa, disoriented.

"Half-past seven. You're in the car park of the Cumnock station."

"Right," she said.

Aniqa grabbed her handbag and turned off her car. She popped open the door, and the officer was quick to assist in opening it fully. When Aniqa stepped out, she was able to take a good look at the officer—she wasn't much taller than Aniqa, but their physiques were exact opposites. Where Aniqa was thin and angular, the officer was portly with a broad bosom and a kind face. Her brown eyes were round and attentive.

"Can I help ye with something?"

Aniqa came to, though a part of her still felt as if this reality was but a dream.

"I'm Aniqa Khan. My son and his friend went missing."

The officer's face blanched.

"I'm Officer Brown," she said, giving Aniqa a firm handshake. "We're going to find your son, Ms. Khan. Don't ye worry."

Aniqa caught a tinge of uncertainty in Officer Brown's voice, as if it weren't a promise, and the words served more to convince herself that she was capable.

"Thank you, Officer Brown."

"Ye can call me Margaret," she said, smiling. She placed a hesitant hand atop the small of Aniqa's back, ushering her towards the station.

Aniqa surveyed the modest police station. Moments like these reminded her of how rural East Ayrshire really was. Catrine was so small it didn't even have a police station, and the closest was here in Cumnock. But even so, its boxy, blue-and-silver exterior was more reminiscent of a small office park than the home of a police force that covered a fair number of small villages.

The slam of a car door caught Aniqa's attention. Elaine and George Robertson hurried toward the station. Even from a distance, Elaine was a dishevelled mess. She puffed on the dwindling end of a cigarette, flicking it aside before she reached the station steps. Aniqa clocked the fiery look in her eyes and immediately felt sympathy towards Margaret—because she hadn't a clue about the storm that was shortly to be unleashed on her. Before Margaret had a chance to open the station doors, Elaine wedged herself between them.

"I'd like to speak to your sergeant," said Elaine.

"He's on his way in now."

"Yer telling me that a full *twelve* hours after our lads went missing is the best this department can do? Where's the urgency?"

George tried to pull Elaine back as she inched closer to Margaret.

"Mrs. Robertson." Margaret eyed Elaine. "We're just over two dozen officers that cover an area of 200 square miles. I've been with this department for nearly seventeen years, and we've never dealt with something like this. I'm going to help ye, but first you both need to come inside to fill out some paperwork."

Elaine opened her mouth to respond but Aniqa placed a cautionary hand on her forearm. Margaret caught the gesture and met Elaine's gaze once again.

"Please, come inside," said Margaret softly.

Elaine acquiesced; George and Aniqa followed her into the station.

Margaret brought them into a stuffy office and slapped a stack of paperwork on the table. Very run-of-the-mill stuff—age, height, weight, colouring, ethnicity, and the last place they were known to be seen. Aniqa filled this out quickly while Elaine detailed to Margaret her last interactions with the lads.

"I made them lunch around one in the afternoon, and then they went out to play. They were supposed to come home for dinner at six."

Then came a line of questioning from Margaret that went on for quite some time.

Margaret: "Who did the boys go play with?"

Elaine: "Each other."

Margaret: "Did they have any mates that might have gone with them?"

Aniqa: "Not that I know of. Craig and Arun are inseparable."

Elaine: "Officer, my son isn't the most well-liked at school. I highly doubt any of the neighbourhood lads were jumping at the chance to join them."

Margaret: "Anything helps."

Elaine relented and began naming the lads that lived along her street. The questioning continued, and as Elaine droned on about the details, Aniqa felt herself slip into a trance while studying Margaret. How she never wavered—not even once—throughout the interview. Whatever tinge of uncertainty Aniqa had noticed earlier had disappeared entirely. Margaret never let her eyes drift from Elaine. She spoke clearly and confidently, breezing through the minutiae masterfully.

Perhaps this is where her confidence lies, Aniqa thought. *In the little things.*

That thought gave her a sudden qualm.

Detailed paperwork won't be what brings my son home safely.

She grimaced at the thought.

Two knocks came at the door. From where Aniqa sat, she saw a middle-aged man with a bushy grey handlebar moustache waiting outside. Margaret glanced quickly over her shoulder. "That's my sergeant," she said, with relief.

He lumbered in, extending a hand across the table. "Stu Simpson, pleasure."

He gave Elaine's hand a shake first, then turned to Aniqa. His hand felt far too smooth for a man of his age.

Must be all the time spent at his desk, Aniqa thought.

"I wish we were meeting under better circumstances," he said; the words seemed to sap the room of oxygen, and the two mothers shifted uncomfortably in their seats. Margaret slid the paperwork over to Stu, and he rifled through them quickly, then gave the papers' bottom edge three taps against the desk.

"I see Margaret's had you fill out the necessary paperwork." Stu smoothed out the wiry wisps of his moustache with his forefinger and thumb, then let out a titter. "I'd say it's all standard procedure, but in reality, this is a first for our department."

There was a long, uncomfortable pause.

No one else shared in his amusement. Stu's gaze flicked uncertainly between Aniqa and Elaine before continuing.

"Anyhow, the only thing I can do is go off the book. Most council areas wouldn't allow a missing child's case until twenty-four hours after they've gone missing—"

"Ye got no bollocks!" shouted Elaine. "If that's the book you've got to go by, I say it belongs in the rubbish."

Stu took a breath, steeling his nerves before meeting Elaine's scowl again.

"—As I was saying, we are filing the paperwork *now* given the fact that two lads who are unrelated disappeared together."

"Should've been sooner," spat Elaine.

Aniqa watched Stu's brow furrow as he chewed on his lower lip.

"I think what my sergeant is trying to say is that our department hasn't seen something like this—well frankly, ever—and we're doing what we can to put our best foot forward."

Margaret's words seemed to settle the friction in the air.

"That's right," said Stu. He eyed George, Elaine, and Aniqa, then let out a sigh. "Look. I'm a father too. I'm all for getting the ball rolling, and that's what we've done here. I know you're worried, but truth be told, in ninety-nine percent of these cases, the kids have just run off with some friends. You remember what it was like," he said, shooting a cheeky glance toward George. "Summer break—lads will be lads. Might just be off having an adventure."

Elaine slammed her fist against the desk. Even Aniqa thought his comment just added insult to injury.

"Sergeant, I can assure you our sons aren't those kinds of lads," Aniqa said.

"Especially hers," added Elaine. "If the two of them wound up in some trouble I'd bet it was Craig's idea, but even so, this clearly isn't just some summer adventure."

Elaine's voice became droning static in the background of Aniqa's thoughts. Her attention wandered back to Margaret, whose gaze pivoted between Stuart and Elaine. The way she looked at her sergeant intrigued Aniqa. There seemed to be the subtlest hint of protest in her stare.

Elaine stood and gave her chair a frustrated shove, sending it juddering across the laminate floor until it smacked against the desk. The commotion drew Aniqa from her daze. Elaine let the sergeant have it a few more times, ensuring she got the last word of vitriol out before Stuart could respond. She pulled Aniqa into a quick hug.

"I'm so sorry, Aniqa. Truly sorry." Elaine's voice trembled as she spoke. "I'll call you later in the day. You know our door is always open."

Then, Elaine and George left.

Aniqa awkwardly sat across from Stuart, who didn't utter a word.

Margaret took the opportunity to speak in place of her superior. "Now that the clerical side of things is over, we need to take a look inside your home."

"My home?"

"The Robertsons' as well, but since Elaine was too cross to let us get a word in, she'll find that out when I arrive at her door."

"I'm still confused," muttered Aniqa as she crossed her arms. "Why would you need to search my house—I'm not a suspect, right?"

"Not in my eyes, at least. But both houses might turn up details that will help the investigation. Journals, sketchbooks, bikes or toys; all things that may point to their whereabouts."

Aniqa gave a slight nod. Ready to be away from the station's stale air, she headed to the door. After a few steps, a pit in her stomach formed. All of this just was too much for her to bear. Like Arun and Craig weren't really missing, and this was just a nightmare she'd soon wake from.

Margaret saw her discomfort and began escorting her out of the station. "Look, I'm right there with ye that the lads aren't off on some summer adventure. But if my sergeant *is* right, there might be something in your house or the Robertsons' that tells us of their plans."

"We won't find anything," said Aniqa as they ambled down the station steps and were enveloped by the misty grey day.

A tiny sigh escaped Margaret's lips. "With all due respect, Ms. Khan, this is just the way we have to do things. I can tell it's not much comfort to ye the fact the department has never dealt with a missing child case, but we still collectively have a lot of experience under our belts. The standard investigative framework has merit, and you've got to trust me that I'll see to it that not a single stone in East Ayrshire remains unturned."

There it was again, thought Aniqa. *That tinge of uncertainty.*

Aniqa mustered a polite nod. "Thank you."

They split up and went to their respective vehicles. Aniqa popped open her door, and just before she slipped in, called out: "Margaret!"

Margaret rolled down her window. "What?"

"You can call me Aniqa."

Elder Louise's pulpit robe flitted at its edges as she whizzed between the tables of the canteen. She was a delicate woman in her early sixties who had dedicated her entire life to the Lord. She had a thin, pointed nose, and faded auburn hair that had long lost its ability to overpower the grey sneaking between the few strands of colour that remained.

Some of the orphans craned their necks to see where she was headed off to in such a hurry.

She exited the canteen and crossed the well-manicured church courtyard, followed the roundabout lined with flowers encircling a stone fountain, and entered the Deacon's quarters.

Angela swept the sitting area, humming a church hymn whose notes were riddled with a noticeable nervousness. She was the newest addition to the kirk—mid-thirties, straw-coloured hair, and freckles dotting her pale skin. Gillian sat at her desk thumbing through paperwork. She was slightly younger than Louise, with a rounder face, and salt and pepper hair.

"Any sign of the lads?"

Gillian looked up from behind her glasses, resting at the end of her nose. She gave a troubled shake of her head.

Angela's trembling hums buzzed throughout the background of Elder Louise's thoughts. "Quit it," said Louise. "That humming's making us more unsettled than the quiet."

Angela sheepishly fiddled with the broomstick. "We called Al," blurted Angela.

Louise turned to her, wide-eyed. "And?"

"He said he'd speak with us in person."

The answer only made Louise more unnerved. She began to pace, and only a few seconds passed before Gillian reached out over her desk to grab her forearm.

"Louise. The time."

The gentle smile on Gillian's face quickly faded. With it came another reminder that this morning's discovery had soured the regularity they were accustomed to.

That's why I feel so odd, she thought.

Louise glanced up at the clock—08:00.

She whipped around to face Angela. "But he's not due for another five hours."

Both Angela and Gillian fell silent. Louise glanced between the two, desperate for one of them to answer the question burning a hole in her psyche.

"He's on his way now," murmured Angela.

Louise's heart sank. She checked the clock again to ensure her vision hadn't lied. The air in the Deacon's quarters suddenly became stifling; she tugged at the collar of her pulpit robe and drew in a deep breath, only to realise that each inhalation was more strained than the one before.

"I need some air," she said and quickly exited the quarters.

The freshness of outside eased her breathing, and the chill of the morning air cooled her hot skin. The night's fog hadn't yet burned off—its moisture yet another familiar comfort that accompanied the light of a new day. These sensations were a brief respite from the reality that faced her.

The time.

She fought to keep herself grounded. To not give into her nerves and start pacing again—a habit her mother had chastised her for in youth. Louise didn't fear the time. She feared the significance of it. Al's early arrival was the true fear, and the news that might come along with it. In her entire tenure at the kirk and the Grounds, Al had never broken his routine. Not once.

Elder Louise closed her eyes to take a moment of prayer. She prayed for the lads' safety. She prayed for them to turn up at the Grounds. She asked the Lord to watch over them, wherever they may be. She attempted to visualise positive outcomes—simple scenarios with simple explanations.

They were just playing a prank with some of their friends.

What friends? she thought. *Their only friends are each other.*

Her eyes snapped open.

Al stood a length away from her in front of the fountain. He didn't have to summon her—she knew to join him. With every approaching step, she tried to shed the bits of nervousness that lingered in her appearance. "Al," she said.

"Elder Louise."

Al's figure loomed over her small frame. This never intimidated Elder Louise because she also looked up to him as a person. He was a rather handsome man, with dark brown hair that was often slicked back. But his most distinguishing features were his eyes. They were a piercing blue grey. The droning gurgle of the fountain water pulled her away from her thoughts.

"Where are the lads?" she asked.

"I was hoping you could tell me."

Elder Louise choked back a snort. "We waited, just as you instructed. Angela, Gillian, and I took turns searching the Grounds throughout the night, but no sign of them anywhere. Nor did they show up this morning. I'd be lying if I said I wasn't worried that something serious has happened—"

"I agree," said Al, cutting her off. His countenance stiffened, and a troubled look flickered across his eyes. "This isn't like them. They've hardly ever caused trouble."

"Aye. They're the most well-behaved out of the lot."

"Very well then." Al stroked his stubbled chin. "I'm afraid we have no other choice but to call the police and file a report."

Elder Louise gave a curt nod. "Right away then." She clenched her trembling hands and flinched back in motion towards the churchyard path.

"Louise," called Al. She turned back before he continued. "When you call, make no mention of the fact we waited the night. It won't look good for us, so just tell them when you checked the beds this morning, they were gone."

"Understood."

Elder Louise made her way back to the Deacon's quarters. The sound of the fountain trailed off in the distance, and part of her wished she could have stayed near its gurgling waters to help stifle her racing thoughts.

When she entered, she passed a wide-eyed Angela and Gillian, then retreated to her bedroom. She knelt, opened her bible, and began to pray.

It was a seemingly endless prayer, all directed towards the wellbeing of James and Gavin.

"Amen."

After she finished, she rose to her feet, alleviating the pain the knotty wooden boards inflicted on her old knees, and headed to the kitchen. There, she picked up the phone and began dialling.

Within three rings, someone answered:

"Cumnock Police."

In the depths of Al's basement, the mental state of some of the children was deteriorating.

James coped by pacing the length of the room, back and forth, muttering to himself. "Al won't hurt us; he'll be down here any minute and bring us back to the Grounds. I know he's going to let us go."

"None of us are going anywhere," said the blonde girl flatly, who had informed them earlier her name was Fiona.

"How do you know?" countered James.

"Because I've been down here what feels like a week."

Gavin sat in the corner of the room, silent. He hadn't spoken a word since last night. Sometimes, Arun would catch Gavin's timid eyes looking at him. But only for a second, because the moment after he noticed, Gavin would turn away.

Arun knew why. The two sharing a gaze was like looking at a mirror. An intense pang of sorrow and regret. Gavin for mentioning Al's art, and Arun for having agreed to go.

Then, there was Craig. He sat against the wall, opposite Arun, and he had ignored him since he awoke. He went to great lengths to avoid his gaze entirely.

This is all my fault, thought Arun.

Guilt bubbled up, causing a sour stomach that was impossible to settle. If he hadn't been so sympathetic to James and Gavin, none of them would be in this situation. Better yet, if he had listened to Craig—simply submitted to even *one* of his many requests to leave, they would presently be at the dining room table eating Mrs. Robertson's famous Saturday morning pancakes.

Yet here they were. He wondered if his mum knew they were missing by now, and what she was doing at this very moment.

James' mumbling cut through his thoughts. Fiona started crying. The cries echoed off the faded brick walls, amplifying as they travelled through the space.

Craig's body language shifted; the subtle flexing of his jaw muscle as he clenched his teeth; his forearm as he balled his hands into fists.

"Shut up!" shouted Craig. He jumped to his feet, towering over the other children. "Shut up! Shut up! Shut up!"

James fell silent. The blonde girl's wailing subsided.

"Listen here, Fiona." Craig stepped closer to her. "I don't want to hear ye cry. Because guess what? All four of us came down here of our own free will! Isn't that mental?" Craig pointed at Arun, still laser-focused on Fiona. "All because *he* felt bad for these loser orphans."

Fiona cowered in front of Craig with her knees to her chest. Her watery eyes overflowed once more—the shrill cries tore through the basement.

"And you!" shouted Craig, turning to James. "Al isn't going to let us go. He isn't going to bring you back to the Grounds. He's a killer who keeps kids like us in a floating freezer as his art! So stop lying to yourself before I make ye stop myself!"

"What?" Fiona looked at James. "Your da's a killer?"

James didn't give a nod of confirmation, nor a shake of his head in denial.

He just fell silent.

And the silence spoke volumes.

But it was different than all the bits of silence that had come before. All five of them accepted the truth. Craig's words were harsh but needed.

Hope founded on lies wasn't hope at all.

It was delusion.

Though the five of their minds were in various places, soaking in a stew of melancholy, one of the children's thoughts fixated on a single realisation.

Craig knew that the only hope they had of ever getting out of that basement was to stay rooted in reality. For now, that reality was exceptionally grim.

"Are we going to die?" asked Fiona.

No one answered.

Margaret parked her patrol car along the kerb on Mill Street. She stepped out and adjusted her belt, which had shifted uncomfortably on the drive over. There was an open field on one side of the street that was popular amongst the town's youth, and its southern edge backed up against the River Ayr.

She remembered Elaine's account of the lads going to play here after lunch.

Truthfully, there wasn't much for a twelve-year-old lad to do in this town. They could ride bikes, take a jump in the river, or play football. Much of Catrine's former liveliness had long since faded away. Private farms and rolling green hills spanned as far as the eye could see.

She surveyed the field, trying to discern any peculiarities that may be hiding within plain sight. There were none. She took a moment to notice the silence.

No cars. No laughter. No people.

She could only hear the faint gurgle of the river and the wind gently whipping through blades of grass. The field dropped off at one edge where it led to the riverbank. As she approached, she saw it:

A football bobbed around in an eddy, wedged between two rocks that kept it from floating downstream. She carefully shuffled down the embankment to retrieve it, shook off the water, and hoisted it under her arm.

Once back at her patrol car, it was just a short drive down the street to Aniqa's.

She lived in a modest semi-detached house at the far end of

Blackwood Avenue. The roof was splotched with grey, battle scars along its skin of roof tiles from the years subjected to the endless rain. Atop it sat an unassuming grey stone chimney. The original coat of beige paint on the house's face had been reduced to a faded champagne that had long since lost its fizzle.

With just a single rap on the front door, Aniqa appeared. She leaned into the open doorjamb and crossed her arms, giving a quick glance to the football tucked under Margaret's arm.

"Long time no see," she said.

Margaret fought the urge to chuckle, feeling it was inappropriate at a time like this, and instead produced a lukewarm smile.

"May I have a look?"

Margaret handed the football to Aniqa. She flipped the ball around a few times in her hands, studying it. Then she returned it to Margaret.

"I believe Arun's is inside. This one is likely Craig's."

"My thoughts exactly," said Margaret.

"Would you like to come in?"

"Aye. I'm going to take a quick look around the outside first."

During the walkaround, Margaret noticed a bike parked on the side of the house—so that eliminated the possibility of the lads getting too far on foot. Because when she had been at Craig's house earlier in the day, Craig's own bike was there as well.

When she returned to the front door, Aniqa raised a brow.

"Find anything?"

"Nae. Ye dropped Arun off before heading to Glasgow?"

"That's right," said Aniqa. Margaret saw a glazed look of reflection momentarily slide across her dark eyes.

Asking herself the dreaded *what if I hadn't left him*—

"Mind if I—?"

"Of course," said Aniqa shakily, quickly stepping out from the threshold. The interior of the Khan residence was standard fare.

Margaret assumed a single mother working the front desk at the Sorn Inn couldn't have been bringing in a lot of cash. Once in Arun's room, she found the bed unmade, dirty clothes—half on the floor, half in the hamper—and posters lining the walls. She saw a *Joe Brown and the Bruvvers* album sitting atop the armoire next to a dusty record player. Strung up on the wall above the bed was the blue and white striped flag of the Kilmarnock Football Club—the Killie—to locals.

Nothing out of the ordinary for a twelve-year-old boy's room.

"It still doesn't feel real," said Aniqa. "I keep thinking he's going to walk right through the door and ask me what's for lunch. Or plop down on his bed and blast whatever new record he found at the consignment shop until I yell at him to turn it down."

"By the state of his room it almost looks like he never left."

Margaret made sure the statement had a sombre air to it. The last thing she wanted was to upset the lad's mother. She stuck her thumbs in the loops of her belt, nodding to the door. "Onto the next," she said. Aniqa followed at her heels through the living room, the kitchen, and then into her bedroom.

The faint smell of sandalwood incense hung in the air, the carpet appeared to have been recently vacuumed, and the floral-pattern quilt atop Aniqa's bed was perfectly made, tucked in tightly with hospital corners.

"How often do you travel to Glasgow?" asked Margaret.

"Every weekend during the summers. I leave Friday afternoon and return Sunday night."

"How's your degree coming along?"

"Well, I suppose. My marks are above the class average. I've got another year left."

"If you don't mind me asking, what made you decide to enroll in school? By the time I married, I felt it was too late to go back."

Aniqa snorted. "I know the feeling. I'm always the oldest in my lectures. But my father got his degree in physics at the University of Dhaka before becoming a professor himself. I guess you could say I'm trying to follow in his footsteps."

A framed picture sitting on Aniqa's bedside table caught Margaret's eye. The black and white photo showed a handsome man with dark, slicked-back hair, and a strong, well-defined jaw. He wore a plain white Kaftan robe, with the curly black hairs covering his chest peeking through the V-neck slit. He sat on a set of stone steps attached to a large mosque behind him, and he was splayed out casually, resting his weight on one arm. There was a dreamy, content look on his face.

"Is that your father?"

"Yes. Not a day goes by where I don't miss him."

Margaret sucked her teeth. "I'm so sorry…"

"I'm sorry too. To think my father wasn't a soldier, but a scholar, and still got caught in the gunfire of Pakistani militants drives me mad. But then again, if he hadn't died, I would have never made it to London. Wouldn't have had Arun."

Margaret gazed at the photo a little longer before continuing her sweep of the room. What she hadn't bothered to ask her was why the photo had been torn in half. Its ragged, fringed edge signified to Margaret that it hadn't been cut neatly with a pair of scissors but ripped down the middle in the heat of the moment.

Aniqa had caught the glimmer of bewilderment in Margaret's eyes before she'd continued the search. She began fiddling with her crisscrossed fingers as she followed her around.

"I didn't have a good relationship with my mum, if that's what you were wondering."

"Wondering, yes," said Margaret nonchalantly. "But nothing more than that."

The answer didn't placate the awkwardness Aniqa felt.

"I got pregnant out of wedlock when I was twenty-three. She told me to marry the father or else she'd kick me out of the flat we were living at in London. Not long after, I packed what little I owned in a duffel and took a train north. Stumbled upon this quaint little village called Catrine after taking the wrong connection and decided to stay put."

Margaret turned to Aniqa. There was a darkness she hadn't seen before in those obsidian-black eyes of hers.

A wound that had clearly never fully healed.

"She was nothing like my father," she continued, "where he was calm and logical, she was impulsive and spiteful. She treated me more like a burden than her daughter. As if I were just an extra piece of luggage on the long flight to Britain that had cost her more than it was really worth taking." Aniqa steeled herself before speaking. "I'll never forgive her for what she did. Giving me an impossible ultimatum."

"They say the road to Hell is paved with good intentions," said Margaret, letting out a disheartened sigh.

A shrill ring came from the kitchen.

They both turned to each other.

"Expecting a call?" asked Margaret.

Aniqa shook her head. She led the way into the kitchen and picked up the receiver vibrating wildly at its base.

"Hello?"

A half-second passed before she extended the phone to Margaret.

"It's for you."

Margaret's brow furrowed as she put the receiver to her ear.

"Hello?"

"Margaret," Stu's tinny voice emerged. "Two orphans have gone missing. Get to Kissinger Grounds right away."

Margaret stepped out of her patrol car and headed down the pavement. As she cut onto the grass, she saw a dozen children playing football on the Grounds' recreation field. Kissinger Grounds took up a large area on the edge of the town's centre. Though she had been an attendee at the adjacent Catrine Kirk for the occasional holiday service, she'd never stepped foot on the portion of the Grounds that housed the orphanage. She had run into the deacons once or twice in passing but couldn't remember anything about them besides the fact they were mild-mannered.

"Excuse me," called a voice from across the field. A woman in a black pulpit robe closed in on her. She introduced herself as Gillian. Behind her, a tall man strode toward them through the field. Margaret recognised him as the owner but forgot his name.

"Albert Reid," he said as he approached, giving her a firm handshake. "But you can call me Al."

"Margaret Brown, pleasure. Although I wish we were meeting under better circumstances." She glanced between them nervously. "I was told someone phoned the station to report two missing kids."

Two more women walked down from a small building and flanked Al and Gillian.

"I believe it was Elder Louise who called." Al gave a gentle wave of his hand in the direction of the eldest woman of the three. She had a thin, pointed nose and half-grey, half-auburn hair whose ends danced about in the steady breeze blowing past.

"Aye," said Elder Louise. "That was me."

"So, get me up to speed. How did you discover the lads were missing?"

"When I checked the boys' dormitory this morning, their beds were empty. Sheets tossed back like they'd gone off somewhere and never came back."

"Mind if I have a look around?"

She had directed this question to Elder Louise; Margaret watched her defer to Al, waiting for him to respond.

"Of course, let's head up there," Al said.

As they ambled up from the entrance of Kissinger Grounds, grass was eventually replaced by brick walkway. They passed a burbling stone fountain that shot rivulets of water out its top in symmetrical arches, falling gracefully into the reservoir below. The whoops and hollers of the dozen children on the playground caught her attention as they passed, and she saw another small building where more children were talking inside.

"What are they doing in there?"

"Lunch just ended," began Al. "Some of the kids go straight back to the playground, others like to linger in the canteen and chat."

"I see."

"In the summers, they haven't the burden of school. So outside of doing arts and crafts that Louise, Angela, and Gillian head up, and the morning bible study on weekdays, they are free to do as they please."

Elder Louise scurried ahead and propped open the door to a long, rectangular building with a low-pitched roof. Two lines of twin beds, evenly spaced out, ran parallel the length of the dormitory. Elder Louise approached the two beds that clearly were unmade.

"My sergeant said the lads who went missing were James and Gavin…"

"—Hamill," added the woman Margaret believed to be Gillian. She was the one with the round face, just a bit younger than Elder Louise.

"Aye. Were they the type of lads to run off on their own?"

Elder Louise shot a furtive glance at Al.

There it is again, Margaret thought.

She could have sworn Al gave an imperceptible nod of his head.

Elder Louise finally said: "Given that they're brothers, when they do leave the Grounds, they're always together."

Angela piped in: "Attached at the hip since they were just wee bairns."

Margaret noticed she had a squirrelly disposition. A subtle restlessness to her beady brown eyes, and hands that were constantly fiddling with the fabric of her pulpit robe.

"Do ye have any idea where they might have run off to?"

The four of them all exchanged glances and shrugs, then turned back to Margaret.

"Your guess is as good as mine," said Al.

Now is the time, Margaret thought. *While they're all still together.*

"I'm not sure if you've all heard what happened," began Margaret. She shifted her weight, pausing to see if she caught an anticipatory glimmer in their eyes. "But two lads went missing yesterday. Arun Khan and Craig Robertson. I believe they're about the same age as James and Gavin."

A look of shock spread evenly across the three women, reaching Al last.

"You serious?" he asked.

"Aye. And I wouldn't joke about such things."

Elder Louise's face blanched, and she grasped Angela and Gillian's arms to steady herself.

"Four missing children in our little village…God help us," she mumbled.

Margaret aimed the next question at Al.

"Do you know if the lads got on well as friends?"

Angela cut in with a nervous snicker. "Not likely. There's a stigma the orphans from Kissinger carry. Others their age tend to bully or just ignore them altogether."

Margaret made a mental note of this, then walked past the four of them. She kept her gaze pointed and purposeful as she moved through the rest of the boys' dormitory, ensuring that any wandering eyes would find her sweep of the area believable. But truthfully, there was nothing out of the ordinary here she could find—she was simply giving herself time to think.

"Does one of you do checks to make sure the kids are accounted for?"

"At night, yes," answered Gillian. "We usually rotate."

"And who checked last night?"

"I did," Angela piped in.

"And James and Gavin were in bed?"

"Aye," she said with a nod, and continued kneading the fabric of her pulpit robe with those jittery hands of hers.

"And then in the morning, they were gone," said Margaret.

"That's right," said Elder Louise. "I was the one who found their beds empty."

"I see," said Margaret. She retraced her steps back to the group. Her eyes drifted past them to the grey light spilling in from outside.

"Well, I'll be honest with ye. My sergeant thinks the lads went off on some Huck Finn type adventure. And I hate to admit it, but if there's no sign of forced entry…" she said with a huff as she pulled upward to find the dormitory window locked. "Then it looks like my sergeant might be right. No open windows this morning?"

"Nae," said Elder Louise.

"Then my sergeant's theory may be likely."

Elder Louise tramped over to a chest of drawers and threw one open. "I don't see how they're going off on an adventure when they haven't even brought as much as a change of britches."

Margaret stared meditatively at the drawer filled to the brim with neatly folded clothes.

"Seems they might not be gone long, then," she said, resettling her gaze on the four of them. "May I see the lads' records?"

Elder Louise shot a half-second glance toward Al before speaking. "Of course, let me—"

"I'd actually prefer if Al could assist me; I'd like to have a word with him alone."

Elder Louise struggled to hold her wavering gaze, and Margaret could sense she had an internal itch that was begging for her to make eye contact with Al.

Al extended his arm towards the door, producing a warm smile. "After you."

Margaret strolled slowly while waiting for Al to take the lead. They continued up the stone path, passing the centre courtyard and gurgling fountain encircled by skirts of pink and white; hundreds of blooming heathers drifted lazily in the intermittent breeze. Their faint sweet scent tickled Margaret's nose.

"I'm curious as to what you think about all of this?"

Al's brow furrowed. "It's hard to say really…"

"You don't have any thoughts about lads going missing? Seems to me your life's work revolves around children, so I figured you might have some input."

Al chewed on this question a bit before speaking. "It's hard to believe. Especially in a place like Catrine. And now it's four boys instead of two, which before you arrived, seemed unthinkable on its own…"

"What do you think happened to them?" she asked, keeping a careful eye on Al's reaction.

He snorted and shot her a sidelong glance of disbelief. "I don't feel it's my place to conjecture about—"

"I insist," she said and then thought: *I'm pushing my luck.*

"If I were a betting man, I'd say your sergeant is correct. What Angela said about the orphans from Kissinger not being the most popular lot is true, but you never know. If they did hang out with the two you mentioned, James and Gavin never brought them to the Grounds. Plus, I remember what it was like being a lad that age and even on my best days I was up to no good. Doesn't seem too unlikely that they may have run off together."

Margaret and Al stopped as they reached a small stone cottage with creeping wisteria crawling up the sides of its stone faces; they looked like a crisscross of lavender-coloured veins pumping life back into the timeworn structure.

"Is that the only reason why you think my sergeant is right?"

Al cocked his head a bit, and a slight twinkle emerged in his icy blue eyes. "No," he said. "I think your sergeant is right because what kind of criminal is dumb enough to kidnap four lads from the same town and think he'd get away with it?"

Margaret smiled, and a tiny snort escaped her nose. "My thoughts exactly," she said as Al opened the door to the cottage. Inside, Margaret was met with worn tongue-and-groove wood floors and faded floral wallpaper that peeled back in certain spots along the skirting boards. At the centre of the room sat a sturdy-looking desk and plain wooden chair.

"Deacon's quarters," said Al as he began rifling through a drawer in the desk. "Louise, Gillian, and Angela all live here and run the Grounds' administration from this very desk. I told them long ago I'd help them secure residences nearby, but they chose to stay."

"I take it then that they like their boss."

Al chuckled. "Louise has been with me fifteen years; Angela and Gillian over ten. I'd like to think they're happy here."

A smile began to emerge on his face, revealing a set of straight white teeth. Margaret saw that same twinkle in his eye she'd seen earlier, and a warmth began spreading through her chest. She was unknowingly experiencing what the townspeople knew as Al's charm firsthand. When he spoke, there was an almost musical lilt to his voice, even though his tone was clear and confident.

He presented her two manila folders, and each tab was scrawled in ink that read:

Hamill, J.

Hamill, G.

"Thank ye," she said with a nod. As Margaret bid Al farewell and ambled back to her patrol car, she couldn't help but think that she understood exactly why Louise, Gillian, and Angela were happy. They worked for a kind, courteous man, one that cared for them. She felt a pang of jealousy, in a peculiar way. If only Sergeant Stu would show even an ounce of care about her happiness.

Al knelt at the foot of the crucifix and prayed. His first few years in the village, he'd spent all his free time here, at the Catrine High Kirk, long before he became the owner. He'd read hundreds of books throughout his life—thousands, maybe—but there was one he'd read more times than any other, cover to cover.

The Good Book.

And the more he read, the more he found contradictions. The harsh rules of Leviticus; the wrath of God ever-present in the Old Testament clashing with the one that was all-loving in the New Testament. But the longer he studied its text, he realised that these inconsistencies weren't contradictions at all. The first covenant was based on obeying a set of laws given to Moses. The second covenant was based on the realisation that humans couldn't keep the law perfectly. Their sacrifices became nothing more than empty ritual. So, the Lord sent his only son to be sacrificed for the whole of mankind. To give undeserved mercy to anyone who accepted Jesus Christ as their saviour.

To spare them condemnation by taking that condemnation unto himself.

Not only did Al find the story of Jesus inspiring, but rather fitting. For he, too, was full of contradiction—inconsistencies spawned by the internal tug-of-war between two sides of his soul.

The invisible battle those around him couldn't see.

Mercy was needed for a man like him.

He prayed now because he felt helpless. He wished with such fervour that the hands of time would turn back to the day prior, where he could have stopped the unthinkable from happening. But there was no undoing what was done. That truth ate away at him. He knew it would take a supreme cunning to restore balance to this situation.

The longer he knelt, the more he mused that if the Lord were listening, the last prayers he should answer were his own.

I've come this far unscathed. Who is watching over me?

Al nearly laughed at the thought. How could it be the Lord watching over him? If God had power to bring light into the world, He certainly had the power to snuff out the dark.

Then why hadn't his evils been extinguished? Why had he been allowed to roam free all these years? Maybe this wasn't the work of God. He, the benevolent Lord Almighty, surely wouldn't have permitted the type of endless darkness that existed throughout his childhood.

The blackness that stained everything Al touched throughout his life was more likely the work of the Devil. Perhaps to the Devil, this was all a sick game with no winner, where the pain and suffering of those dwelling on Earth was pleasure to Lucifer down below.

The church door groaned behind him and slammed shut. He came to, stood, and turned around to orient himself. Twilight slipped through the western windows; a fine dust floating in the air caught the light, diffusing it softly through the space.

A woman approached. Her dark skin and hair blended into the shadows. The silence was palpable, and Al felt exposed. Out of his element.

"Pardon me. Are you the minister here?"

Al cleared his throat. "No. I'm the owner."

"Oh," she said, her tone crestfallen.

"I'd better get going. It's getting late." Al sidestepped the woman. He was halfway through the pews before he heard her feet shuffle.

"Would you mind praying with me?" asked the woman.

He stopped, closed his eyes, and steadied his breath. She had beaten him to the punch.

"I normally wouldn't ask a stranger to pray…but I've just had the worst day of my entire life."

"Me too," muttered Al.

As much as it pained him, he submitted to the woman's plea. He turned and joined her. "Albert Reid." He extended a hand.

"Oh, I believe I know you. You own the orphanage and the restaurant too."

"That I do."

"I'm sorry to bother you. I wouldn't ask but I'm not very religious. And for the first time in a very long time, I'm afraid to be alone."

"You're not a member of the Kirk?"

"No. There's no mosque nearby. So, here I am."

The woman shifted her weight uncomfortably.

"I didn't catch your name, Miss."

"Aniqa."

"Well, Aniqa. Let us pray." He motioned to her in the dim light to come forward, and they knelt together in front of the crucifix. Aniqa offered an open hand to Al.

She rested her hand in his.

"What brings you to the church at such a late hour anyhow?"

Aniqa nearly choked on her reply. "My son went missing last night."

Al gently squeezed her hand, and froze. He only had a fragment of a moment left to craft his hand squeeze into something more benign. "That's horrible. I'm so sorry."

She nodded solemnly. It was in that moment that everything clicked for Al. The dark skin and eyes. *She is the mother of the precocious one.* The boy who demanded his friend to be brought into the basement first before he followed.

"Thank you for this," said Aniqa.

Al instantly snapped back to reality. "No need. Now, let us pray."

They awkwardly stared at each other, holding hands.

"You've never been to a Christian church…"

"No," she said.

"Do you know the Lord's prayer?"

"I believe so."

Al was brimming with an invisible fire that licked at his insides. "Our father who art in Heaven, hallowed be thy name."

They prayed in unison, with Aniqa taking Al's lead.

"Thy kingdom come, thy will be done, on earth as it is in Heaven."

"Give us this day our daily bread and forgive us our trespasses, as we forgive those who trespass against us."

A steady rain began thrumming on the old tin roof of the church.

"Lead us not into temptation but deliver us from evil."

Al and Aniqa finished their prayer and bid each other farewell.

Then, the rain turned into a downpour.

The Lord cried again for Catrine that night. For the fact Aniqa had just joined hands in prayer with her son's captor. His tears mirrored Arun's, who fell asleep fitfully on the cement floor of the damp, dark basement for the second night. He cried for Elaine, who through troubled, drunken eyes saw that the evening news made no mention of the boys' disappearance.

But wasn't that the nature of this cruel world?

When the Lord cries, the Devil laughs.

CHAPTER 6
THE LIE

Kensington
1934

Princess Edith traversed the last few blocks to her destination in Earl's Court. Being a part of the royal family meant she almost never got to enjoy a quick stroll. She was driven everywhere—even for the shortest of distances.

But today was an exception.

Queen Eleanor had returned to Buckingham Palace, and Princess Edith felt like she could finally breathe. Though she loved her mother, she noticed that every passing year a portion of that love was replaced by abhorrence.

There was one choice her mother had made that was unforgivable. A lie so powerful that it eliminated a world of potentials in an instant. A future of integrity, of living without fear. All that hope shattered by a single decision.

Princess Edith flushed with heat as her wandering mind reminded her of this upsetting reality. She pulled herself back to the present, drew in a breath of the musky summer air, focusing on the sounds of the cars sputtering as they went by, of the chirping birds in the trees. A woman pushing her newborn in a pram smiled at Princess Edith as she passed. She returned it, cherishing the small interaction.

There were seldom days when Princess Edith was happier than now. She walked the streets of London in commoner's clothes, able to blend in without issue. It was a simple pleasure, one that reminded her that this world, the real world, existed outside the palace walls.

Princess Edith arrived at 20 Courtfield Gardens. She combed her fingers through her windblown hair, climbed the four steps to the door, and knocked.

Sir Charles Stirling answered after a few moments. He was a wiry fellow with broad-set shoulders, brown curly hair, and eyes the colour of honey. Charles was a good man, and for this reason, he held a special place in Princess Edith's heart. He was equally enamoured with her. She had an attractive face with auburn hair and blue eyes.

"May I?" she asked but didn't wait, letting herself into the foyer. Sir Charles closed the door behind her. She took a seat on a chaise in the corner of the room. He offered her a cup of tea which she declined, and instead asked for some water. As she wet her parched mouth, she waited to speak until Charles sat and took a long sip of his tea.

"You can't send any more letters."

Charles took another sip, acting like he didn't hear her.

"I'm serious. You mustn't, or everything we did will go to waste."

"You sound just like her," he scoffed.

Princess Edith shifted in her seat uncomfortably—his comment stung.

"Did you even read the letter? I'm not spilling my guts to the boy. I just want to have a relationship with him. He has no idea who I am, but at least corresponding through letters is something. I've been barred from seeing him for thirteen years. At least you get to watch him grow."

Princess Edith's spirit sank, her countenance downcast.

"I understand your pain. But my predicament is both a blessing and a curse. Could you imagine seeing him every day, yet being limited to the conventional interactions between a brother and sister? Being in such proximity yet never able to hold, comfort, or love him? He is closer to Theodora than I."

They both fell silent. There was an unspoken pain shared between the two of them—it was their bond. Although Sir Charles' house was filled with the finest furnishings and artwork, and they sat mere feet apart, the room felt empty. Something irreplaceable was missing from the home, and for reasons beyond their control, it would always remain that way.

"You could take the boy and leave. We could live out our days in the countryside, but that would mean you have to leave the Crown."

She gave him an empty stare that conveyed far more than words could.

"*We* could leave," he added gently.

Princess Edith's blushing cheeks betrayed her. "You know how much I would love to, but I—"

"But you can't," he cut her off and stood. "There's no one holding a pistol to your head. You're a grown woman."

"I'm the Queen's daughter," she said, exasperated.

"And being the Queen's daughter robs you of your God-given free will?"

"More than you would ever know, Charles."

He watched Princess Edith deflate.

"Maybe one day," she said softly. She tried to meet his eyes for consolation but saw his sympathy sour into pity.

"One day?" he said, raising his voice. "The boy is going on fourteen. He'll be a grown man before you know it. And then what?"

In her heart, Princess Edith knew what she should do. But in her rational mind—the one that considered society, the Crown, her future— fell short in producing a substantive response.

"If not now, then when, Edith?"

She met his gaze with shameful eyes.

"Is that all you have for me?" he spat. "To tell me to stop writing our son?"

Princess Edith stared at the floor, unable to face him. An empty pit formed in her chest, and she felt like she couldn't breathe. Trapped by circumstance, by the fact that if she ever wanted to have her son to herself, she'd have to find the courage to face her mother. That thought terrified her. Because if she tried to take back what was rightfully hers it would unravel the lie.

"Edith," said Charles, cutting into her thoughts.

Her lower lip trembled as she realised that she didn't have the courage to break her mother's wishes. "That's all I have for you," she said just above a whisper.

Sir Charles looked at her with scorn. "I hope for the sake of our son that your decision to do nothing never comes back to haunt you."

He opened the door swiftly and outstretched his hand. She took the signal to leave. The moment she crossed the threshold, the door was slammed behind her. Tears welled in her eyes as she tried to compose herself before rejoining the busy streets of London.

As she walked down the pavement, the birds were singing, the sun glinted off the faces of the white stone buildings, and she caught the sweet aroma of blooming pink magnolias in the air. For a moment, it seemed as if everything were right in the world. But that moment proved fleeting.

Sir Charles' parting words hung in her mind like a fog that wouldn't lift.

In the instant after that thought, Princess Edith returned to baseline. The past thirteen years had been filled with guilt and regret, and every day she walked this earth joylessly—every colour seemed duller, every meal less flavourful.

Every moment that she spent alone; she was mourning the death of someone who was alive.

Mourning the death of a potential life that had yet to be lived.

Queen Eleanor sat in the parlour of her Buckingham Palace quarters. A nearly empty plate with a few shreds left of smoked haddock sat on the end table next to her. She was reading *Alice's Adventures in Wonderland,* reclining on her chaise. Today was the first day in over a week where she could focus on the words of the page because in every moment of solace, she'd have flashbacks to the dining table at Kensington Palace.

She still couldn't believe the audacity Leon had to blurt out that question in front of all his immediate family. She snorted and shook her head at the thought.

A knock came at the door.

"Come in," said the Queen.

Jean-Claude Marron, her trusted servant, entered the parlour. He grabbed her plate and stood still, facing her.

"I assume you came here for something other than just retrieving my plate," she said without glancing up from her book.

"Princess Edith is returning to Kensington Palace."

Queen Eleanor's interest was piqued. "Did she visit him?"

"Indeed, Your Majesty."

She smiled, pleased. "Very well then."

Jean-Claude began leaving the parlour.

"Jean-Claude," called the Queen.

He turned to her. "Yes?"

"Thank you."

Duke Leon dipped his paintbrush into green paint. He returned to the canvas and flicked the tip of his brush methodically, making little striations that filled in the ground with grass. He'd been sitting in front of the Brazilian walnut easel for half an hour. He had one of the servants play his favourite Gustav Holst record, the orchestral notes bouncing off the far-flung reaches of the gilded carvings on the ceiling.

What he loved most about art was the ability it had to calm his restless mind. Duke Leon was in a perpetual tug-of-war between his desire to quiet his mind and the need to fill the silence with something other than his thoughts in moments that were too quiet.

Now, he'd achieved the perfect balance—a quiet mind in a room full of music.

Footsteps slid between the sounds of the orchestra, but Duke Leon kept painting. He felt the familiar soft touch of Princess Theodora on his shoulder.

"Well, isn't this lovely," she said.

"Thank you."

Compliments from his aunt were the most cherished.

"I recognise that scenery," she said cheerfully. "Is that Balmoral?"

"Mhmm."

He craned his neck and a smile tugged at his lips. With his free hand, he wrapped an arm around her waist, embracing her.

She joined him on the cushioned bench and scooted in. "So, tell me about what's going on in this one."

"It's the family around the fire in the Balmoral Garden, just like in the summers," he explained, flipping around the paint brush to point with its end. "There's you and I." Princess Theodora smiled and nodded. "There's Eugenie and Lysander next to you." He pointed out Princess Maud, Prince Oliver, and Maud's four children.

Queen Eleanor stood alone.

Princess Theodora's brow furrowed. "Why is the Queen so much taller than everyone else?"

The question drew his attention to the peculiarity. He hadn't even noticed he had done that, and now he was struggling to produce a reason why she looked so much larger than the rest of the family, including all the men. "I don't know," he said. "Do you not feel that way sometimes?"

"What do you mean?"

Duke Leon attempted to find the right words. "Her presence takes up the most space in the room."

Princess Theodora smiled halfheartedly, shrugging. Her nonchalant body language didn't help Duke Leon intuit whether she confirmed his statement or not.

"She is a powerful woman." Princess Theodora bit her tongue, knowing that was the extent of her commentary. She wouldn't be caught speaking ill of her sister.

Duke Leon resumed painting. "So, what do you think? Do you like it?"

"I do." Princess Theodora gave the painting another look over. The green grass of the gardens was almost filled in, the skies were a twilight shade of blue, with a few spots of white left to serve as stars, and the castle had been painted impressively accurately to come from the memory of someone Leon's age.

"The fire could use some red," she added. "Or maybe for the Queen's dress."

Duke Leon forcefully dunked his paintbrush in the water cup to clean it, chose a new colour, and returned to the canvas. "I didn't pour any red paint," he said. "I hate that colour."

"Why?"

"I just do."

There was a finality to his tone that she'd never heard before.

A subtle push to *stop prodding*.

"Well, I'll leave you to it then, my dear." Princess Theodora began to leave the grand parlour. "I'll see you at dinner."

"See you then," he responded.

Around fifteen minutes passed, and Duke Leon had nearly finished the painting. He found himself thinking about Princess Theodora's comment, and each time it surfaced, his eyes flicked to the portrait of the Queen that loomed over the rest of the family around the fire.

Suddenly, the record player's needle scratched, and the music stopped.

He froze—paintbrush inches away from the canvas—and his stomach sank.

There it was again.

The silence.

He left the easel and hurriedly crossed the grand parlour. He checked the appearance of the record, the condition of the record player and its needle—all looked fine. He tried to reset the record, but the motor wouldn't spin it. His hands were beginning to tremble, pulse quickening. Heat flushed from his head to his toes, and panic rose within his gut.

He yelled for the servants.

After a few moments, one of them appeared.

"Fix this, please," he said.

The servant fiddled with the needle, then examined the motor. Unplugged and re-plugged some parts. Yet when he went to start the motor, the record wouldn't spin. The servant disconnected the power cord and hoisted the record player in his arms.

"My apologies, Your Grace. I'll bring this back straight away once it's fixed."

The servant left the grand parlour and Duke Leon stood there, rooted in front of the end table the record player had just been sitting on. His chest tightened as the crushing silence made him feel like he couldn't breathe. As much as he wanted to return to his painting, he knew the wave of panic surging through him wasn't going to dissipate. Sweat droplets formed along his forehead; he wiped them and tugged at the ever-tightening collar of his shirt, as if it were a boa constrictor slowly crushing his airway.

Little spots of light began to appear in his vision. He shook his head to clear them, but when they disappeared, they'd return a moment later. The only other time he'd seen spots of light in his vision was when…

Midnight, he thought. Flashes of the killing cut through his vision, and an electrical feeling danced along his skin.

The silence was like a petri dish; one thought would multiply exponentially into thousands of fragmented voices within his head.

Duke Leon fished in his pockets. *It's not there.*

He rounded the corner of the grand parlour and jogged back to his room. Thankfully, he passed no servants on the way. He pulled open the top drawer of his armoire and grabbed his knife. He raced back to the grand parlour as the flashes of light became rippling starbursts in his vision. To his dismay, the record player hadn't been returned.

Then the emptiness arrived.

The empty feeling slid into the centre of his chest, replacing the panic, removing the heat of his skin. An icy numbness that felt like death itself.

No sensations, no heartbeat, just emptiness.

Though it was only the second time it had arrived in his young life, he recognised that the emptiness scared him the most.

The inability to feel…anything.

He pulled out his knife and pressed its edge deep into the palm of his hand. The sharp pain allowed him to feel, and it chipped away at the emptiness.

Duke Leon walked back to the easel and stared at his painting. His gaze settled on the Queen. Her tall, looming figure stood centred in front of the fire, with family flanking both sides. He pressed his bloody palm onto the portrait of the Queen and dragged his hand into the fire beneath, smiling as he removed his hand from the canvas.

"Here you go, Mother," he whispered. "There's your beloved red."

CHAPTER 7
THE PATH

Arun's hands rested on the icy iron handles of the double doors. His first instinct was to pull away. He tried to jerk his body back, and his hands didn't budge.

It seemed as if a mystical force were holding him there.

No, I don't want to! he shouted voicelessly.

The inability to speak frightened him, and his hands became so cold they were starting to hurt. No matter how hard he tried, he couldn't break away from the handles. There was an unspoken rule between the door and Arun, one which they both knew, but Arun wouldn't admit its truth—because the moment he gave the rule validity, he would lose the battle. He groaned as the skin on his hands burned, like an invisible flame roared at full force beneath the handles.

No! he fought to pull away harder. *I won't do it.*

Come in, said the door's baritone voice, echoing like rolling thunder.

Arun looked down in horror as his hands were turning blueish grey. He wasn't met with numbness but instead the feeling of a thousand knives stabbing at his skin.

Please, make it stop! he begged, panic rising by the second.

Come in, said the door. *Come in and it stops.* Arun cried, screaming soundlessly in agony when the tears that slipped out of the corners of his eyes were ice crystals. Razor sharp, tiny and iridescent, they fell to the floor and shattered. Rivulets of blood slid down each of his cheeks.

He hiccupped, bawling an empty, mournful cry.

Make it stop…make it stop…

There was a moment of silence that felt like eternity. Arun was petrified that he'd lost connection to the voice of the door, and that he would soon be frozen from head to toe.

You know what to do.

Arun surrendered. The moment he made the decision to give in, the iciness faded out of his fingertips. The droplets of blood slid up his cheeks and disappeared back into his eyes.

The pain was gone.

Yet he kept his hands on the cold iron handles.

That was the unspoken rule, telepathically understood by them both.

The door wouldn't let Arun pull away. It would only let him pull the doors *open*.

A blast of frosty air hit him. He was back in the frozen room. He stood at the beginning of the dock that divided the room, and sitting cross-legged on the circular ice blocks—the frozen children. He shuffled forward along the wooden boards, stopping where one of the thick, frozen ropes attached to the dock. He unconsciously grabbed the rope and began pulling in one of the children's ice blocks toward him. Arun felt like someone was controlling his every move, and the only thing he could do was submit.

When the ice block reached the dock, he studied the girl. She was the same one he'd seen the first and only time he had ever stepped foot in this room a few days ago. Her matted hair was thick with ice crystals. Her cheeks a pale grey, lips a deep shade of blue. She looked so…peaceful. There was no chance this girl's last moments alive had been painful. She sat so still she seemed to be meditating. Arun slowly extended a cautious finger, getting closer to the skin of the girl's cheek. He wondered what her frozen skin would feel like—*would it be hard? Would it crack?* He was so close the tip of his index finger was only inches away…

A crunching sound ripped through the room as the frozen girl's right arm reached out and grabbed Arun by the wrist. He lurched back and nearly plunged into the water, slipping from her grip. Her arms and legs snapped and crunched unnaturally as she stood upright on the ice block. Arun shuffled towards the frozen room's doors, and she jumped onto the dock with a loud *thump*. Crushed ice spilled outward from her feet with every step. He scrambled onto his haunches but fell over again. She lunged and caught him by his ankle. The skin there started to freeze, spreading outward like a ravaging infection that couldn't be stopped. The muscles in his calf and thigh petrified into a blue-grey stone, and the paralysis crawled upwards through his pelvis and lower back. He thrashed with all his might to drag himself backwards, but she grabbed his other ankle, and the process repeated. The frozen blue raced up his other leg, merging with the other half. His abdomen began freezing over. He felt *so* cold, and his lungs were tightening up. Soon he felt his arms go numb, and he could no longer fight.

He felt the air leave his lungs as he took one last, frosty breath.

What terrified him the most was that he could still see.

The frozen girl leapt one final time and collapsed on top of him. Just moments ago, she had sat meditatively on the ice block, still and peaceful, but that girl was gone. She had been replaced by something far more sinister. Her lifeless eyes glowed with a fury Arun had never seen, their faces inches apart. The frozen girl raised an arm high above him, her frosty lips contorting into a wicked smile before she leaned in and whispered, "One day you'll be like me."

She struck him and he shattered into a million pieces.

Arun jolted awake, gasping for breath. The air that filled his lungs wasn't icy, and he glanced down at his arms to see the skin perfectly intact.

"Are you all right?" asked Fiona.

He nodded shakily, calming slowly as he realised he was safe.

"Just a nightmare."

Arun got the sense that Fiona was a sweet girl. Even at first glance she looked…angelic, pure. Porcelain skin with blonde hair and blue eyes. Today was day three inside the basement, and Gavin's panic had long since subsided.

All five of the children were finally on the same page regarding their abysmal predicament.

"You said when we got to the bottom of the stairs that you had seen this place before in a nightmare," said Craig. Arun turned to him, shellshocked—this was the first time Craig had addressed him since he'd regained consciousness from Al's blow to the head.

"I did."

Craig cast glances at the other children, then met eyes with Arun. "Can you tell us what you saw?"

Arun recounted the nightmare in its entirety. There was the squeaky, oscillating halide light that hung over the surgical table in the basement. The man with no skin, and how he begged to be killed. Then lastly, how Al put the man with no skin out of his misery by slipping a scalpel into his neck.

Fiona and James grimaced. Gavin listened with his standard stoic stare. But with Craig, an ember of resentment still burned within. It was like he could hear Craig's thoughts telepathically: *how could you let us come down here after a nightmare like that?*

Guilt panged in Arun's gut. As he held Craig's gaze, the resentment shifted ever so slightly to sympathy.

"The nightmare you just woke up from," said Craig. "What was that about?"

Arun struggled to form the right words. The adrenaline was fading fast, but the vivid details hadn't. He decided to save them from sharing his pain. "I became one of them."

"One of who?" asked Craig.

"The frozen children."

Fiona glanced around at them cluelessly. "Frozen children? You guys were serious?"

Arun mustered a solemn nod.

Fiona cradled her arms around her knees, tucking them in.

"We're going to die in here, aren't we?" blurted Gavin.

"Shame on you," said James, a scowl crawling across his pale face. "None of us are going to die. We're all going to leave this basement together. Alive."

Silence fell over the basement.

No one dared say a word.

"We will if we don't find a way out of here," said Craig. Everyone digested his statement, and Arun fought the urge to smile. The look on Craig's face when he spoke up was so reflective of his true character— courageous and bold. That's why Arun looked up to him. And why he felt so guilty for not listening to him when he tried to get them to leave.

"He's right," echoed Arun. Fiona, James, and Gavin turned to him. From the corner of his eye, Arun could have sworn he caught Craig cracking a small smile. "If we don't escape, we will probably die down here."

Fiona started to blubber. Craig wasn't one to be sentimental, but he stretched out his arm to gently pat her back. "Don't cry," he said. "It'll be okay."

"I don't think we'll have to escape," said James, nervously. "I think Al will let us go."

"Don't be an idiot," sneered Craig. "You saw what was in that room. Do you really think he'd ever let us go given what we've seen? He'd be hanged for what he's done. That's why our only option is to escape."

James shifted on the concrete uncomfortably.

"I think he's right," said Gavin, who stared vacantly at an empty corner of the room with wide eyes, looking like he'd seen the ghost of death itself. "No one is going to come for us."

Gavin had spoken a truth that weighed on all of them. In the silent hours that passed, those words were what Arun focused on. The likely outcome that no one was coming. He thought of ways to escape. In the three days they had been in the basement, Al had appeared a total of six times. Three to deliver breakfast, and three to deliver dinner. They weren't fed lunch. Al would put five servings of food in an emptied-out red toolbox. There would be napkins—but no cutlery, of course—Al was more intelligent than that. When they were finished, they'd toss it all back in the toolbox and when Al delivered the next meal, he'd remove the rubbish. Besides that, they had nothing. No tools. No weapons. In the corner of the room, there was a single toilet and a sink. There was no door separating it from the main room, not even a curtain. Each child that went would ask the others to turn away, and Fiona went a step further and demanded they plug their ears, too.

Despite the conditions, they were all alive and well, save for Craig, whose colourful bruises deepened on his face by the day.

Arun tried to remind himself of this every morning when he awoke: *I am alive.*

He promised himself that he would find a way out of here. Find a way back to his mother. But truthfully, there was a part of him that felt like he didn't deserve to leave at all. Every night when he fell asleep on the cold stone floor, he would fantasise about the one truth he knew to be real.

Finding a way up those stairs would be their salvation.

Margaret had just left the police station, and the conversation she had with Kenneth Creighton, a journalist from the *Cumnock Chronicle*, kept replaying in her head.

Kenneth had laughed when she told him the news—albeit nervously—because he didn't believe her at first.

"Kidnappings happen in the big cities, but surely not here," he had said.

How could someone take four children at the same time in broad daylight? Margaret thought. It was this specific question that had kept her up last night long after her husband fell asleep. Despite Stu being adamant that the lads were just off on some Huckleberry Finn type adventure, Margaret wasn't convinced. An inkling of intuition told her that the nature of the four lads' disappearance wasn't as innocuous as Stu imagined. More troubling was the fact that Catrine only had so much space. A handful of shops, a school, and enough homes for the three thousand residents dotted the verdant hills of East Ayrshire. There were only so many places for four teenage laddies to hide. Mauchline was nearly a three-mile walk away, and Cumnock close to ten. If they had travelled long distance on foot, someone would have seen them, and knowing the likes of folks in these parts, they would have offered to drive them back into town.

No. Margaret's gut told her that the lads went missing from Catrine, and they were likely still here. And that was why she parked her patrol car along the edge of Kissinger Grounds.

She had discovered something this morning, and she wanted to talk to the head honcho himself. She cut through the grass and heard the snickering laughter of the children as they gallivanted from the slide to the monkey bars, with another group hooting and hollering while they played a game of tag. A small smile tugged at the corners of her lips. Soon her feet met the brick walkway that wound past the courtyard and the burbling fountain surrounded by the fragrant blooming heathers.

Elder Louise, nor deacons Angela and Gillian, were anywhere to be found.

Good, she thought. *I don't want them interfering.*

Margaret arrived at the door to the deacons' quarters and gave it three raps of her knuckles.

Al opened the door, greeting her with a warm smile. "Back so soon?"

She chuckled. "You'll be seeing a lot of me until your lads are brought home."

"I figured as much." Al invited her in with a wave of his hand, gesturing to an open seat at the round pedestal table. "Do you take milk in your tea?" he asked as he tipped the kettle spout, filling up two teacups.

"Aye," she said. "Where are the deacons? Just a bit surprised we're in their quarters and got the place to ourselves."

"They're in the canteen prepping lunch," said Al as he approached a round table in an alcove off the kitchen. "Takes the three of them to get it all ready." He turned to her, expectant. "Please, sit."

She joined Al at the table and took a sip of her tea to be polite.

"Thank ye," she said. "For this and for your time."

"It's the least I can do." He took a sip of his tea, then crossed his hands, resting them on his lap before meeting her gaze. "To what do I owe the pleasure?"

Margaret slipped the manila folders from the inside of her coat and set them on the table. "There was something that piqued my interest in James and Gavin's files."

"And what might that be?"

"The notes about their parents. I read that in those first few years after the lads were given up, they came back to the Grounds three times. The first two visits, ye only permitted them to see James and Gavin from afar, as you said such an appearance would unsettle and confuse them. And the third time, the deacons barred them from entering the Grounds entirely."

"Those incidents were close to a decade ago. It hasn't crossed my mind in years. Do you really think it could be something?" Al began, scratching his chin pensively. "Perhaps…a lead?"

"I'm not necessarily saying it's a lead, but it does give me pause. Parents giving their bairns up for adoption, then coming back not once but three times to try and see them. To me that's a clear sign of regret. A longing for what they lost."

The occurrences in James and Gavin's files were certainly of interest, but Margaret found them rather benign. They were simply more stones that needed to be overturned. It was the only way she could sleep at night; cross all her *t*'s, dot all her *i*'s. What Al didn't know was that she had an ulterior motive for presenting these peculiarities.

To see his reaction.

Another opportunity to study the demeanour of the man in charge—alone—without the added burden of keeping track of the shared glances between Louise, Angela, and Gillian.

But Al didn't miss a beat. "The possibility that there might be more to what you said about their parents frightens me."

"Do you think they could have done it?" she countered.

"I remember them well," he began, a glimmer of reminiscence in his eyes. "They were good people. Just hardly had enough money for the two of them, let alone a child. They had James first, struggled to get by, and then the mum got pregnant with Gavin right after. They didn't want to give them both up, but they also hadn't the heart to separate the two brothers. So, they came to the Grounds." Al paused; a bit of melancholy tinged his voice. "I believe you are correct. They regretted what they did. That's why they came back those times. I remember thinking that back then, but now, with you pointing it out in these files…"

"If the parents were somehow involved, that would only explain James and Gavin's disappearance," she said.

"But what if the lads were altogether…" he mumbled.

"I thought you said the orphans weren't popular with lads their age."

"I did, but…anything's possible." Al pulled out a silver pocket watch. He flipped open its metal cover and looked at the time. "I'm afraid I must cut this visit short," he said, rising to his feet.

"Everything all right?"

"Yes, I'm just behind schedule. Ten minutes late to my daily trip to TLC."

"Your restaurant?"

"That's right," he said.

"Ye mind if I keep those?"

He gave the bottom of James' and Gavin's folders three sharp taps against the edge of the table, arranging the papers inside neatly, then handed them over.

"I'll walk you out."

He held the door open for her, and as they cut through the courtyard, Margaret studied him in her periphery. He looked calm and content.

Al ambled to his car, parked in a paved spot along the far side of the boy's dormitory. It was a handsome, older model black Vauxhall Velox, and as he reached it, he paused, turned to face her and shouted, "Call me if something comes up!"

"Aye," she yelled back.

As Margaret made her way back to her patrol car, she couldn't help but think that Al had passed the test. There was no hesitation in his answers; he was present, clear with his words, and didn't let his attention drift for even a second. She cranked her engine and sputtered onto the main road back to Cumnock, headed to the station to update the case paperwork and document her visit with Al.

Elder Louise let out a nervous sigh as she parked along the kerb of Holm Farm Road. A gentle pitter-patter of rain added to the gloom of the day, obscuring the sun behind the thick grey clouds. She strode up the gravel drive, stood in front of Al's door, and raised a fist to knock.

The door slowly swung open, and she was face to chest with Al. Him being a giant of a man, she always had to tilt her head upwards to get a good look at him. Her nerves melted away the moment he smiled.

"Louise," he said softly. "Please, come in."

Al ushered her inside. Elder Louise had never stepped foot in Al's house, and she was a bit taken aback. White crown mouldings lined the edges of the ceiling and the floors in the living room. The kitchen was filled with stone counters, polished wood floors, and stained wood cabinets. Even the carpet beneath her feet felt thick and buoyant. The more she looked around, the more she understood why Al spent so much time here; the space had a calming energy. All the colours in the house were earth tones—blues, greens, and browns.

"I'm afraid I know who took our lads," said Al, sitting down across from her on a plush grey loveseat.

Elder Louise crossed her legs under her pulpit robe to stop them from shaking. "Who?"

"You remember what happened in that first year after James and Gavin arrived?"

She nodded.

"Then surely you remember their mum's guilt. How she showed up those times wanting to see them…"

Though it was over a decade ago, she still remembered the poor hen's face when Al denied her plea to see her sons. "You can't possibly think…that after all this time…"

Al's eyes fell to the floor. She'd never seen this solemn countenance about him before.

"I just don't see any other plausible scenario. I've hardly slept since they went missing, and the one thing I can't seem to fathom is the idea that a stranger plucked these lads right out from under our noses. It had to be someone they were familiar with. Someone would have seen or heard something if the lads didn't go willingly."

"But if it *is* the parents, why now?" she asked.

"I haven't the slightest idea. That worries me the most. Why would two parents suddenly want their children back that they gave up so long ago?"

Elder Louise shrugged her shoulders without an adequate answer. "Should we call the police?"

"I already have. I talked to Margaret about it this morning."

She opened her mouth to speak but Al cut her off.

"Louise. I want you to go back to the Grounds and speak of this to no one—not even Gillian or Angela. Then tomorrow, you will go on a trip to retrieve the lads. If we have any issues, and the parents don't give them up quietly, the police there are already on standby to assist us."

"*Me*," she repeated, pointing a shaky finger at her chest.

"Of course. You are the only one I trust enough to bring them home."

A warmth spread throughout her chest. Al recognising the fact she cared about the lads was of the highest order of compliments.

They both chatted a little while longer about their plan for the day ahead, and then Al bid Louise farewell. She returned to her car with a newfound hope, feeling invigorated by the thought of taking the situation in her own two hands, with Al by her side—the man she admired like no other. An opportunity like this was rare in the life of an Elder of the Kirk.

When she returned to the Grounds, she knelt in front of the cross in her room and thanked God for calling her to walk this path.

As ten p.m. approached, the last remaining bit of twilight dimmed by the minute. A woman walked along the pathway that ran parallel to the river and encircled the town's edge. The slight evening chill in the breeze trickled into her light jacket. She buttoned it up with one hand, pushing her newborn baby in its pram with the other, crooning to it sweetly. The quiet of the path was accompanied only by the gurgling of the river, and the incoherent babblings of her baby. Just as she rounded a bend, something in the bushes caught her eye. She stopped and squinted. The mysterious object was encased in a hard, black material, with a glassy-looking piece that glinted in the fading daylight. She left the stroller for a moment and fished it out from the brambles.

A camera.

The lens was badly shattered; the exterior nicked and covered in scratches. She almost threw it back in the grass, but then mused that her husband might have some use for it if it could be fixed. He enjoyed photography with these new 35mms and at the very least, he could pawn it for parts if it was useless.

As she walked back to the pram, she studied the camera more closely.

Maybe it belonged to someone, she thought.

She turned the camera bottom side up and saw a one-by-one inch faded white sticker. She wiped the dirt off its face with her jacket sleeve to get a better look at it.

Scribbled in pen was the name *C. Clark*.

The woman laid the camera in the back of her pram and continued her walk.

CHAPTER 8
THE MEAL

Osborne House, Isle of Wight
1936

The wildflowers danced ever so slightly in the temperate, briny air; their fragrant scent wafted into the noses of those standing lengths away. Birds chirped happily throughout the array of trees on the grounds, and the honeybees meandered between the dahlias and canna lilies whose colours dazzled vibrantly in the peak of their bloom.

It was mid-July, and at Osborne House, summer was in full swing.

These two weeks served as one of the few times throughout the year when the Queen's family was together under the same roof. The adults surrounded a long table on the back terrace overlooking the garden, and the butlers were as busy as the bees—zipping around clearing plates and bringing fresh ones full of hors d'oeuvres, refilling wine glasses, and ensuring every need of the royal family was catered to.

Queen Eleanor was listening to Princess Theodora recount a story of her being mistaken in Baden-Baden as one of the Swedish royals. The two had grown up together in Kensington Palace, but when Theodora married Ernest, she moved to Germany. Queen Eleanor would only dare admit so in letters, but she always pressed her sister to stay in Britain as often as she liked.

Princess Theodora had also once admitted in her diary that the only time she could breathe was outside of the Palace gates. This truth stemmed more from the memories of their oppressive upbringing than it had anything to do with Eleanor. Once she took the throne as queen, Princess Theodora had noticed a shift in her behaviour. While she had always been a glutton with a voracious appetite, Princess Theodora watched her develop a taste for something that only being a reigning monarch could bring.

Power.

She feared that her sister was letting that taste cloud her better judgement, eclipsing the compassion she knew lay within.

Then again, how could a princess try to advise a queen?

Eleanor's laughter echoed into the far-flung reaches of the garden. Princess Theodora met eyes with Princess Maud, who seemed slightly annoyed she wasn't part of the conversation, but judging by the glassy look in her eyes, she also wished they would lower their boisterous voices, when the entire family sat in such close proximity.

Inside the galley, Princess Edith chatted with one of the longtime servants whom she found most endearing. She bit into a few succulent strawberries as they conversed. Princess Maud's husband, Prince Oliver, returned from the bathroom and made his way through the galley past the commotion of the chefs and the servants. He pinched Princess Edith's buttocks as he passed her, and she cast a subtle, cautionary glance in his direction while still mid-sentence with the servant. He was a married man and married to her sister, no less. She found it objectionable that he would dare to lay hands on her like that in front of the staff.

Down in the garden, Eugenie, Caroline, and Catherine, played with dolls in a hand-painted house that reached nearly the same height as them. Their wild imaginations fuelled all kinds of stories and events taking place between the dolls. On the other side of the garden, Duke Leon, Lysander, William, and Charlotte were playing croquet. Charlotte, being more tomboyish than her sisters, often spent time playing with her male cousins.

The game already well under way, Duke Leon and William were struggling to overtake one another. William had just hit the ball through the second-to-last wicket, still celebrating the hit while Duke Leon readied his mallet for his next move.

But then, William missed the last wicket before the turning stake. Duke Leon hit the ball and made it through the second-to-last wicket, following William's last move perfectly. William eyed him with a scowl. Duke Leon missed his bonus stroke as well.

Lysander and Charlotte took their turns, still a few wickets behind.

Now it was William's turn. If he made it through this last wicket and hit the turning stake, all he'd have to do was hit the final stake to win.

He missed again.

"Bollocks!" shouted William.

The girls turned from their dolls for a moment to see what the fuss was all about.

Duke Leon readied himself, took in a steadying breath, and hit the ball with his mallet.

It rolled smoothly through the wicket.

William crossed his arms, face flushing red. He kept his eyes glued on Duke Leon to see if he'd make his bonus stroke. But instead of going for the final wicket before the turning stake, he aimed for William's ball.

"What are you doing? Don't!" cried William.

Ignoring his protest, Duke Leon tapped the ball with his mallet just enough to run into William's ball. He now had two extra strokes. He planted his foot on his own ball and whacked it as hard as he could; the force transferred to William's ball and sent it hurtling towards the woods.

"No!" cried William.

On Duke Leon's second stroke, he made it through the second-to-last wicket and hit the turning stake. With a smug air of confidence, he hit the final stake and won the game.

Charlotte and Lysander congratulated him, but just as Duke Leon began relishing his moment to shine, William came tramping toward them and whacked his ball full force, sending it flying to the woods where William's ball had landed.

"Go get it!" shouted Duke Leon.

William shook his head. "No. You did the same to my ball."

"You lost," said Duke Leon. "Go get them."

William crossed his arms indignantly. "You cheated!"

"He won fair and square," said Charlotte with a roll of her eyes.

"You know he did, William…" Lysander echoed in a hushed tone.

"That freak cheated! I know it."

William brooded as he stared at Duke Leon, resentment building up within him.

"Will you two stop so we can finish the game?" asked Charlotte.

"Go get my ball," said Duke Leon.

"Okay. But you come with me."

Duke Leon compromised for the sake of Charlotte and Lysander, who wanted to finish playing. Both boys carried their mallets as they trudged towards the woods. Neither trusted the other enough to be alone together without some type of defence. Once they passed the edge of the garden and entered the woods, they were out of sight.

Duke Leon found his ball, and shot William a questioning glance, as he stood quietly alongside him.

"Are you going to get yours?"

William nodded. Duke Leon set his mallet down for a moment to climb through the twisted brush of the woods. He heard a quick flurry of shuffling steps behind him. William pushed him with all his might, and he fell face-first in the dirt. He scrambled to turn around, crawled backwards using his hands and elbows, and received sharp jabs of pain in his back from a thorny vine. Duke Leon was covered in dirt, muddied and moist from an overnight rain. "Why did you do that?" he cried.

"To put you in your place. You shouldn't even be here."

He tried to wipe the tears from his eyes, smearing dirt across his face.

"You're a bastard child." William chortled. "I overheard Mum saying that you aren't pure blood like us."

Duke Leon pounced at William's ankles, knocking the wind clean out of him as he fell on his back. He wriggled backward, mallet still in hand while Duke Leon pulled and clambered his way up William's calves. "Get off me!" he shouted.

Duke Leon punched at his thighs, progressively working his way up to get as close as possible to inflicting blows on his stomach. A sudden explosion of pain shot through his fist as William slammed his mallet down, and he cried out, recoiling away. His knuckles were puffy and already beginning to turn a faint purple, his hand pounding with a relentless throb. He quickly got to his feet, and William followed suit.

Although Duke Leon still coursed with anger, what he felt more than anything was sorrow.

"You're a bastard child." William's words took root in his mind, and Duke Leon fought the urge to cry.

William glanced down at himself; he was caked in mud. "Look what you've done!"

"You attacked me first!"

"They'll never believe you," scoffed William. "You're the black sheep of the family."

"They'll never believe you either. Charlotte and Lysander saw you're a sore loser."

William deflated, and Duke Leon watched giddily as his foe was forced to digest the bitter truth of the statement. But soon, an unknown darkness simmered in his eyes, accompanied by a warped grin that tugged at the corners of his mouth, sending chills down Duke Leon's spine. "What?" he asked shakily as he watched this maniacal smile bloom across William's face.

William swung the mallet upward, clubbing himself multiple times as hard as he could in the eye. He then dropped it, wincing, and cast another menacing glare at Duke Leon through his newly swelling eye.

"Try getting out of *this*." William turned toward the garden and began to wail. Duke Leon's stomach sank, and his legs trembled as he followed him out from behind the tree line.

William's howling cry caught the attention of the adults on the terrace. Princess Theodora jumped to her feet and descended the staircase, pulling her dress up while she ran. Queen Eleanor was intrigued but unfazed. She presumed it might be something as straightforward as a bee sting. Princess Maud's brow furrowed the longer she heard the distinctness of the cry, and then she too rose.

"My boy!" she cried out and began shuffling down the steps.

Down in the garden, the rest of the children surrounded the two boys. Princess Theodora knelt in front of William, horrified by the grotesqueness of his eye, that swelled more by the moment. She whipped around to face a muddied Duke Leon, whose wide eyes were pitiful and filled with tears. "Did you do this?"

Duke Leon shook his head.

Princess Maud barrelled into her son's side, kneeling next to Princess Theodora.

"My god! Who did this to you?" she asked frantically.

The bawling ceased for a half-moment, and with tears dripping off his face, William pointed a wavering finger at Duke Leon. Princess Maud clutched her son in revulsion, pulling him instinctively closer for protection.

Princess Theodora grabbed him by his shoulders. "Tell me the truth, dear. Did you do this?"

"He did it to himself," Duke Leon muttered.

"Liar!" shouted William, peppering in some more crocodile tears.

Queen Eleanor's arrival caused the chatter amongst the other children to hush. A few of the palace guards now stood on the terrace overlooking the scene to ensure it wouldn't escalate. Princess Theodora turned to

Leon. Her smooth features and kind gaze comforted his bruised spirit, and he could tell by the hint of reluctance in her gaze that there was a small part of her that believed his story.

"What happened here?" asked Queen Eleanor. She wove between them all, but not gracefully like the princesses—it was as if every step she took, the Earth felt.

"He clubbed me with the mallet!" cried William, pointing at Leon again.

Queen Eleanor craned her neck around to face him. "Is this true?"

Leon's throat turned to sandpaper as he struggled to maintain eye contact with his mother. "No," he said, with a shake of his head. "William clubbed himself."

Princess Maud cried out in disbelief. Princess Theodora stood helplessly between the Queen and Leon, weighing her choices of who to believe.

"He told me the same," blurted Theodora breathlessly.

"Preposterous!" shouted Maud, uncovering her hand to display William's bulbous eye. Some of the children echoed a chorus of "Ew!" at the sight.

Queen Eleanor's jaw dropped, and she whipped back around to Leon. "There's no way he did this to himself. Look at him!"

Leon obeyed his mother; he cast a quick glance to William and returned to staring at his feet. "I swear it," he said. "He framed me."

"Liar!" shouted William again.

"I beat him in croquet, and he accused me of cheating! Charlotte and Lysander will tell you."

The prolonged silence made Leon raise his head. He glanced between Charlotte and Lysander. He pleaded desperately with his eyes for them to do the right thing, to tell the truth...Their empty stares confirmed the worst—they had chosen to stand with William. When he looked around, the whole family stared at him as if he were nothing more than a garden pest.

"You're the black sheep of the family."

Forlorn and rooted where he stood, Leon's surroundings became muted. The shouts of Princess Maud calling for the servants to come and dress William's wounds, the whisperings of the children, and even the chirping of the birds and the sound of the breeze flitting through the trees—all silent. Princess Theodora gently rested a hand on his shoulder, but the comfort the gesture brought him was cut short the moment Queen Eleanor grabbed him by the wrist and dragged him away from the garden.

They stood on the side of the palace, and before she spoke, he flinched, preparing himself for the same blow he'd received three years earlier in her quarters. She caught him cowering. There was a part of Queen Eleanor that regretted having to go to that length to ensure the family secret *stayed* secret, but there was another part of her that relished in the fact he feared her.

"Leon, you must never hurt someone like that again. Do you understand?"

He nodded solemnly. When she gestured with her hands as she spoke, all he could imagine was that thunderous strike and how painful it was.

"You are a member of the royal family, and you must behave as such. There's no room for violence under this roof, or any other for that matter across the kingdom."

While the Queen spoke, all he could hear was William's voice, *"I overheard Mum saying that you aren't pure blood like us."*

His statement contradicted everything his mother was saying. As the chastising continued, all Leon heard were lies upon lies. Lies about royalty, about behaviour—how should he *really* behave when he wasn't even a true royal?

"Snap out of it!" cried the Queen, striking him in the face. "You will start behaving like the duke that you are this instant. Your behaviour is a reflection on me."

The blow was lighter than the one before, but it still stung. Leon was still too young to know it hurt him more mentally than it did physically.

What ate away at his being was that he hadn't even done anything wrong. He'd been framed. All of this made him realise that William was right.

He *was* the black sheep of the family.

When Duke Leon returned to his room in Osborne House, it didn't take long for the silence to start playing its tricks. Then arrived the deathly chill that accompanied the emptiness. His breath caught in his chest, and instead of letting panic get the better of him, he headed for a shower. Still covered in caked mud from head to toe, he decided to kill two birds with one stone—get clean and try to warm the numbness he felt in the centre of his chest.

Yet only the former worked; he returned to his room and put on some fresh clothes. Again, the emptiness reared its ugly head. It was like an unwanted houseguest—one who never notified anyone of their arrival and always overstayed their welcome.

He knew what he had to do.

He fished through his luggage until he found his handmade knapsack. One of the butlers had sewn it for him a little over two years ago. When he requested it to be made, he had told them it was for hunting with his friends outside the palace. While only half of that statement was true, having the knapsack definitely made things easier. It always astonished him how infrequently the Crown's staff contested his explanations. The dynamic by which they operated was one where they were yes-men. He had used this trait to his advantage time and time again.

Unbeknownst to the family and his loyal friend, John the Guardsman, Duke Leon had been killing animals off and on for the past two years. And now, at fifteen, every passing month he became more daring in his escapades.

He pulled out the blade that he had hidden in one of the soles of his dress shoes, grabbed a bag of old chocolates from his suitcase, and left the bedroom. He slipped out one of the side entrances and stealthily headed toward the tree line. Once in the woods and out of the view of any guards or adults that might be on the terrace, he retraced his footsteps back to where he'd left his croquet mallet. He picked it up and traipsed through the brushy floor, and then found an open clearing on the opposite side of the woods to settle in on the boundary between the denseness of the woods and the openness of the fields.

He plopped down, leaned against a tree trunk, and waited.

But before long, the gentle lilt of the breeze flitting through the leaves caused him to drift closer to the blackness of slumber.

A rustling sound roused Duke Leon. He rubbed his eyes groggily as the rustling sounds transformed into tearing and chomping. His eyes flickered open to see a small dog rummaging through his knapsack, pulling out the bag of chocolates. Its teeth tore through the bag, and its long pink tongue flailed wildly as it swallowed down as many chocolates as possible. The dog was unconcerned with Duke Leon as he slowly stood up, reaching for his mallet.

A rush of feeling returned to his body—a welcome relief to the emptiness.

Part of the excitement came from the fact he'd never killed a dog before. The other part stemmed from Duke Leon's psychology. There was something about the dog's disposition, how it could not care less about the boy sleeping beneath the tree and how it interpreted him to be harmless. Being seen as docile, but the dog not knowing his true nature, made him feel powerful.

Like a wolf in sheep's clothing.

He struck the dog on its head, and it yelped, trying to scramble away, but its legs buckled. With a few more blows to the head, the dog lay there, twitching for a few moments until it took its last breath.

A release of endorphins flooded through Duke Leon, and with that came the elimination of the emptiness. He could breathe again, and a newfound energy came over him. He stared down at the dog's corpse, then knelt to inspect it.

It had a collar, and he read its name tag: *Lady*.

It wasn't one of the royal dogs, so it had to be from a neighbouring residence. He unbuckled the collar and threw it aside. He returned to his feet, and the dog lay before him, still and peaceful. The wind gently whistled through the trees, and all was quiet along the edge of the woods of Osborne House.

Duke Leon's elation was short-lived.

Memories from the morning resurfaced in his mind: the disturbing images of William clubbing himself in the face, the other children refusing to defend him, and the conversation with the Queen.

"Your behaviour is a reflection on me."

He chuckled and thought: *If only Mother could see this behaviour.*

A new, perverse thought arose—one that had never crossed his mind before. He smiled wickedly and got to work skinning the dog. Grotesque popping and ripping filled his ears as he peeled the skin back. It took much longer than he expected, but after he finished, he could see that most of the parts of the dog he needed were exposed. Next, he began to carve out large pieces of the fatty meat and muscle with his knife, tossing them into his knapsack as he went. To most people, this process would be nauseating, but not to Duke Leon. To him it was akin to a science experiment or when a group of people stood around a table trying to piece together a puzzle.

Except in his case, he was pulling things apart.

Destruction, not creation.

After minutes stretched into hours, Duke Leon had harvested the viable pieces of the dog. He tied them tightly in his knapsack and disposed of the dog carcass beneath a pile of rotted wood, then hurriedly returned to the palace the same way he came, making sure to keep his grubby hands close to his pockets just in case he ran into someone. Once back in his room unscathed, he washed away the blood staining his hands.

The rush he felt from executing such a high-risk plan was more intense than the killing itself. But there was no time to relish the act. The next stop was the galley, where, knapsack still on his back, he announced to the handful of staff who were cutting various vegetables for tonight's dinner that Princess Maud had requested all of their presences immediately. He strategically chose Maud because her room was on the farthest side of the palace, but even so, he still wouldn't have much time. Once the chef and servants left, he moved to the sink, where he began rinsing the dog meat to remove any bits of hair or flecks of bone. He set the rinsed meat in a bowl and raced to the fridge. Inside, he looked at all the containers with thawing meat.

There was one labeled: Q.E.

He grinned because he knew its significance. His mother was known to be an adventurous eater, and often for large gatherings the chefs would prepare her something special. Mutton was her favourite, and it wouldn't have surprised him if that was the meat in this container. He pulled it out and brought it to one of the silver preparation tables. He threw the original meat from the container into his knapsack and swapped it with the rinsed dog meat, placing the strips of it one by one neatly in the container. After he finished, he quickly compared a piece of the original meat to the dog meat—they seemed similar enough.

Footsteps echoed in the distance, and he darted to put the meat container back in the fridge. Once finished, he left the galley and scurried back to his room.

He washed his hands and plopped onto his bed, breathless but happy.

Servants flowed endlessly in and out of the grand dining room of Osborne House as they began to serve the main course. The Royal Family sat around the long, oval dining room table adorned with the finest china and silverware. Leon especially hated this room—his mother's touch was pronounced in the decorations.

Red velvet curtains and red carpet to match.

Normally, Leon couldn't stand to be in such a red room for so long… but he was starving. He'd expended a lot of energy with the dog.

And now, he hoped he'd see his work come to life.

One element of family dinners he particularly enjoyed was the amount of noise they produced. Even if no one spoke, the clinging of silverware, the soft jabs and scraping sounds on the china, and the suppressed swigs of drinks and gobbling of food never gave his mind a moment to be left with his lone companion.

Leon stared at his plate; he wanted to avoid the judgmental looks if he could help it. The adults sat on one half of the table, and the children the other; the exception being William, wedged between his mother Maud and the Queen. He had confirmed with a passing glance when he first sat down that William's eye appeared much worse than it had in the morning. Leon nearly smiled, imagining William having to deal with that eye for the next week or two, and he deserved every bit of it.

The lunatic fell on his own sword.

As the final dishes were laid and the drinks poured, the Queen cleared her throat.

"Before we begin," she said. All the heads at the table swivelled to her. "I'd like to address the incident that happened this morning."

His gut twisted in a knot.

"Leon. I'd like you to apologise to your cousin so we can put this behind us."

Heat flushed over his body as the agonising scrutiny of all the eyes at the table bored into him. He was forced to look up from his plate and move his hands to his lap as they trembled wildly.

"Go on," said the Queen. All the princes, princesses, and his cousins waited. Their eyes flickered expectantly. They had that look—the one where all the jurors project nonchalance, but deep down they relish the chance to see the criminal admit their guilt and be punished.

"I'm sorry," he croaked. Leon caught a shimmer of sinful pleasure in William's eyes, and that look alone planted a seed of anger into the depths of his soul.

Queen Eleanor displayed a curt smile. "Very well then. Let us eat."

The dinner commenced, and while Leon cut into his braised mutton, he watched as his mother wolfed down her first bite. She chewed the second piece more carefully and displayed the tiniest sliver of ambivalence. He reeled with excitement as he studied her; it was as if her taste buds were hanging in balance like two sides of a seesaw. One side alerted her that something was off, and the other told her the meal was delectable.

As she swallowed, it was clear she had embraced the latter.

It nauseated him to watch his mother eat. If they were dining back in London and not at their summer house, she wouldn't be eating so unhurriedly. The dinner guests would be forced to consume everything within the narrow window of time before she finished, and then all the plates would be taken. Which was a nuisance to everyone except the Queen because she could polish off a five-course meal in under half an hour.

Although he had been framed, shamed, and forced to apologise in front of the family all in the same day, Leon felt pride. For not a single soul at the table knew the type of debauchery he was capable of. And that made him feel powerful. Untouchable.

A smile tugged at his lips that he fought to suppress.

He took another bite of his mutton, glancing over at his mother as she savoured another bite of Lady.

Dimly lit by candles that lined the walls in sconces, the hall to the east wing of Osborne House was gripped by silence. Duke Leon waited patiently in a nook a few doors down from William's room, having strategically placed himself in the corridor that leads to the kitchen. Though most of the rooms had an ensuite bathroom, he hoped that something, anything, would draw William out of his room. He'd also chosen a nook directly across from an empty room, and he'd already cracked the door open.

Now, all he had to do was wait.

Duke Leon imagined the scenario endlessly in his head.

William walks past, I tackle him, I pin him to the floor, and cover his mouth before he screams.

But then he waited. And he waited some more. He nearly dozed off in his nook until the sound of a door opening roused him. His heart galloped in his chest, and he readied himself to pounce, edging forward on the balls of his feet. The footfalls grew louder, and the swollen eye came into view just at the right moment for Duke Leon to ensure it was him.

He leapt out from the nook and tackled William, whose weight crashed into the door of the empty room as he fell, knocking it open. Duke Leon slammed the palm of his hand on a wide-eyed, panic-stricken William before he could scream. He tried to squirm away, and Duke Leon used that to his advantage, squirming with him deeper into the room. He kicked the door shut and straddled William's chest, pinning his elbows down with his knees. William hadn't a chance of overpowering Duke Leon—he'd had his growth spurt long before the other boys.

William screamed and blabbered, but all his efforts were extinguished by Duke Leon's forceful hand. A swirling rush of anger and power surged through him, and he reached to his pocket and pulled out his blade, flashing it in the dim moonlight that slipped through the windows. William screamed louder; Duke Leon could feel the shrill reverberations of his voice vibrating the skin of his palm. He pressed the edge of the blade against William's chest. "Stop screaming and listen," he said, pushing the edge just a hair tighter against his shirt.

The screams softened.

"Tomorrow morning at breakfast, you're going to tell everyone the truth about what happened to your eye."

William's brow furrowed in defiance; he squirmed and protested voicelessly under his grip. Duke Leon pushed the edge of the blade into his chest, drawing a line of blood that ran the length of the blade.

"If you don't, I'll bring you out to the woods and kill you with this very blade. And your sisters will go home without their beloved brother."

William winced in pain but still scowled at Duke Leon, not ready to surrender.

"Or maybe I'll kill your lying sister first and make you watch. And then I'll kill you and leave both your bodies for the birds to pick at."

Tears slipped out of William's closed eyes.

He couldn't face the monster that lay atop him.

"Look at me," said Duke Leon. "Do you understand?"

William opened his eyes and reluctantly nodded.

"Now get up, go to your room, and throw away that shirt. Let the wound dry and go to bed. I'll see you in the morning."

He eased the knife for just a moment, and William followed the motion by propping himself up shakily, but just as he took a deep breath, Duke Leon pressed the blade again in a new spot, threatening to make a fresh cut.

"If you tell a soul of this, I'll make sure to keep my promise."

William nodded. Duke Leon slowly rose to his feet, and when he did, he saw that the crotch of William's pyjamas was soaked in urine down to his knees. Just before he left the room, Duke Leon turned back to face him one last time.

"I'll be watching you."

A beautiful day met those sitting around the table on the terrace of Osborne House. The sun shone vibrantly, and the sugary tang of the freshly-squeezed orange juice Leon sipped on seemed to match its radiance. Even the warbling of the birds carried a falsetto intonation, but perhaps it was just his imagination.

The servants were busy pouring drinks and laying the plates, and as he noshed on the assorted berries, he cast a quick glance at William. His swollen eye was the worst he had seen—tinged with black and purple bruises. Though no one paid enough attention to notice, Leon took great pleasure in seeing William slightly tremble in his seat, and how he tried to project normality, yet his nerves were clearly wracked with fear and shame.

The breakfast was underway, and the longer time passed, the more Leon's enjoyment soured into uncertainty.

Will he ignore my threat? he wondered.

He shot a sidelong glance at William and made certain to display as menacing a glower as possible. William swallowed hard, shakily took a swig of water, and looked back one final time at Leon, fear filling his eyes.

"I have something to say," he blurted. The clinking of silverware stopped. Everyone at the table turned and stared at him, silent.

"I lied yesterday."

Gasps peppered the table.

"William! Why would you say such a thing?" asked Princess Maud.

William met eyes with Leon, and the beseeching look he sent was pitiful. It served as a final plea—that simply admitting he lied should suffice as fulfillment of Leon's demand.

He rebuked the request with a miniscule shake of his head, and Princess

Edith was the only one at the table that caught this slight interaction.

William sighed in defeat.

"I lost in croquet, and I clubbed myself to frame Leon."

Whispers scattered across the children's end of the table, and Princess Maud pressed her eldest son to stop spewing nonsense and to rescind what was an obvious fib. Princess Theodora met eyes with Leon, and he caught the relief in her countenance. It was as if he could hear her delicate voice: *you were telling the truth.* Leon slipped her a small smile.

"Is this true?" asked the Queen, voice crashing over the whispers like ocean waves eclipsing the shore.

William reluctantly met her stare and nodded. The chatter resurfaced.

"You will apologise to Leon this instant," she said through her teeth. Princess Maud huffed, and Queen Eleanor shot her a cautionary flick of her eyes.

The roles were entirely reversed from the night prior, and with his head hung low, William raised his gaze just enough to catch a glimpse of Leon.

"I'm sorry," he mumbled.

"If *I* could barely hear you, my dear, I highly doubt anyone else at the table did either," spat the Queen.

"I'm *sorry*," repeated William.

"Good," said the Queen as she forcefully stabbed her smoked haddock and eggs. "Carry on."

From that moment on, Leon ate and drank his fill, even going as far as smiling at some of his cousins and sisters when they met his gaze. He was experiencing a high unlike any that had come before it.

The euphoria stemmed from his successful retribution for William framing him, and that a raw display of power invoked a fear too frightening to disobey, allowing him to achieve the outcome he desired.

And that realisation proved far sweeter than the saccharine juice he drank.

CHAPTER 9
THE BULLSEYE

Margaret's body was caught in an all-too-familiar tug of war. Physically, she was half-awake from a sleepless night of tossing and turning, mind racing in circles as she thought about the lads' disappearance and her conversation with Albert Reid. In contrast, mentally, she felt wide awake, like there was an electric current feeding into her mind.

This juxtaposition of sensations would, she hoped, be levelled by a strong cup of black coffee.

"Margaret!" shouted Stu from down the hall. She nearly spilled her drink as she jumped in surprise. A moment later, Stu clung to the edge of the doorway.

"Please tell me why there are two reporters from Kilmarnock bangin' on my door."

Unfazed, she took a full swig of the coffee and escorted Stu back to his office. She grimaced, took another swig to wash down the first. The coffee had a burnt taste that she had gotten acquainted with over the years, but its bitterness still made itself known in the first sip. As they approached, one of the two reporters leapt forward—a scrawny fellow with tousled brown hair and shoulders that cowed forward.

"Sergeant, do you have any comments on the four missing lads?"

Stu rolled his eyes, glanced at Margaret, and threw out his hands as if saying, *"See what I mean?"*

"Well, Sergeant," she said, trying to sound polite while keeping her growing discontentment under wraps. *"Do* you?"

Stu motioned with his index finger. "In my office. Now."

She followed him in, and he sat down behind his desk.

"Sit," he said. Margaret took a nervous gulp of her coffee. Stu hadn't used this tone with her in years, maybe even a decade.

"Did ye call the newspapers about the lads?" he asked.

She always found it hard to focus on Stu's eyes because his caterpillar moustache would jump around his upper lip when he spoke.

"I did." The tone she gave sounded a bit too pleased. *Damn it,* she thought.

"May I ask, Margaret, why did you contact the press without speaking to me first?"

Margaret only now realised that she had broken the chain of command, but there was a bigger issue at hand that bothered her—one she knew she wouldn't be able to leave this office without getting off her chest.

"With all due respect, Sarge…why didn't you alert them yourself?"

Stu turned red as a tomato. "I just don't want to unnecessarily make parents think their kids are in danger."

"Four kids disappeared on the same day. I know we live in small towns where nothing bad ever happens, but *this* happened. Today is day four, and it's our duty to protect the people who live here. That's why they need to know."

Stu flipped a pen between his fingers meditatively. "I agree with you, Margaret. I do. Just please, don't make a bigger mess of this than it already is. All morning I've had calls from parents asking me if they should keep their children inside."

"It may be a pain, but the people deserve to know. Plus, it might bring out any potential witnesses. Speaking of witnesses…"

"What?"

"What do you know of him?"

Stu cocked his head. "Of who?"

"Albert Reid," she replied. "Or…*Al,* as you called him."

"Well," began Stu, smoothing out his moustache with his index finger and thumb. "I don't remember him growing up, but when I came back from living in Edinburgh, he had already been here for a long while. By that time, he had bought the Catrine High Kirk and had started building Kissinger Grounds."

"Is he married? Have any kids?"

"Not that I know of, and with an orphanage full of kids I see why he wouldn't want one." Stu chuckled at his little quip.

"Fair enough."

"Why are ye so curious about Albert Reid all of a sudden?"

"There's just something about him I can't put my finger on. For one, the tight schedule he keeps reminds me of the city folk. Doesn't seem like he'd fit in well in a small town like this."

Stu let out a throaty laugh. "He's a busy man, and he's done nothing but good for Catrine since the day he arrived."

"I see." Margaret stood and headed for the door. "Give them a quote, will ye?"

Stu gave a halfhearted nod.

Margaret returned to her desk where she was finalizing the report of yesterday's interaction with Al. She detailed the theory she presented him about James and Gavin's birth parents as a test to gauge his reaction, but nothing about it was off. He had passed the test.

At least for now.

"He's done nothing but good for Catrine since the day he arrived."

She put the report behind lock and key in her file cabinet. It was of the utmost importance to her to ensure all the reports were exactly where they needed to be.

Crossing her *t*'s and dotting her *i*'s.

Arun held the icy metal handles of the double doors, rooted where he stood. He waited for the baritone voice of the door to invite him in, but it never came. Instead, over the gurgle of the water, he heard soft cries. He pulled open the doors and a frosty blast of air sent goose pimples racing along his skin. At the far end of the dock, Craig sat cross-legged, facing away from him, crying. Arun's steps were measured; the wood of the dock groaned and wobbled as it undulated in the water.

He wondered why Craig hadn't turned around—his footsteps were noticeable.

"Craig," he said timidly. There was no answer. The closer Arun neared, the more he noticed the unnatural cadence to the cries. There was no variation to the sound, just the same cry, being repeated endlessly on a loop. He crept closer to him, now just a few feet away.

"Craig, it's me."

He reached out to tap him, slowly inching his index finger toward his back. When he gently tapped his shoulder, the crying stopped.

"Craig…"

Craig's shoulder blades rose and fell viscerally, poking against the stretched skin of his back, as if he were panting, yet Arun couldn't hear his breath.

Craig leapt backward and twisted mid-air, pouncing on Arun. The wind was knocked clean out of him, and he tried to wriggle away from his grip. Saliva slipped from the edges of Craig's mouth as he stared down at Arun like a rabid animal. Arun tried to kick and free himself, but Craig was bigger and stronger than most their age, and he didn't stand a chance of overpowering him.

When Arun was completely pinned, Craig slammed his hands against Arun's throat. He choked and spat as he tried to pull air through his constricted windpipe, but Craig wouldn't let up. Arun wrapped his hands around Craig's, tried to spit out the word "Stop", but it was eclipsed by Craig's snarling breaths. Arun's heart pounded, and his lungs strained, collapsing in on themselves as they fluttered, trying to use the last bit of air to saturate his starving blood with oxygen.

"You did this," growled Craig, as he choked the last bit of life out of him. Tears fell from the corners of Arun's eyes as his vision began to fade.

"You killed us!" he cried at the top of his lungs. The last thing Arun saw was that Craig's mask of rage was mixed with tears.

He was crying too.

"*You killed us…*"

"Arun!" shouted Craig.

Arun bolted awake, gasping for breath as he clutched at his throat. He choked and coughed, pulling in deep breaths to fill his hungry lungs. Craig stared at him confused; Arun had lurched back at the sight of him. Fiona, Gavin, and James all stared at him like they had witnessed something they would rather not have seen.

"You were choking in your sleep," said Craig.

Arun finally caught his breath. As he stared at Craig, his lower lip began to tremble, and guilt washed over him, forming a massive rock in his throat. He rested his head between his knees in an upright foetal position. He sobbed as if he were a newborn, except the world he had just been ripped from was a nightmare instead of a safe, warm womb. And the reality he awoke in was equally as wretched as the one he had just dreamt about.

His raw, guttural cries filled the basement.

Three nights sleeping on the cold, damp concrete and not a tear shed.

But now, he let it all out.

"I'm sorry," he blubbered. Although Fiona, Gavin, and James were all present, the only person those words were meant for—heard them.

"If I had listened to you, we wouldn't be stuck here. I'm sorry, I'm so sorry."

Arun groaned and blubbered until he was finally out of tears.

Craig didn't speak, but when Arun finally met his eyes, he could tell that the apology had hit a soft spot.

No words could replace what a single look conveyed between the two.

Margaret parked a quarter of a mile away from Al's house and walked the rest of the way. She hid behind the thick trunk of a sycamore tree with her head perched between a fork in the branches.

Al's property was situated on a larger lot than its neighbours. A long gravel drive snaked through the rolling lush greenery of the garden, and the house backed up against the River Ayr. While modest in size, Margaret took note of the well-kept exterior—the slate blue paint looked fresh, the black-stained shutters made from oakwood, and the many windows that adorned the house must have dappled its insides with a tremendous amount of light.

If they were open, she thought.

Hung from each window were thick grey curtains that had all been drawn shut.

She couldn't see in, but on the other hand, Al couldn't see out.

Margaret didn't know why she was here, exactly. She kept seeing Al whip out his silver pocket-watch in her mind's eye; the tinny *clack* of its lid being slammed shut still ringing in her ears. Al clearly valued punctuality, and Margaret hoped that she could leverage this trait to her benefit.

To gain a clearer picture of the man's busy schedule.

She had spoken to him twice at Kissinger Grounds, but now she wanted to see the place he called home.

The gentle whistle through the sycamore leaves became a hiss as the breeze swelled into a gust. She tilted her head back to gaze in awe at the thick, twisting woodwork. Its towering trunk groaned beneath the wind's force, emitting a series of hollow *pop-pop-pops*—each *pop* she felt as a percussive tremor through her chest as it pressed against the grooved bark.

She flinched and pushed away from the trunk.

The wind subsided, and the air held perfectly still as if it were holding its breath. But a moment later, a stronger gust rose until it became a roar, rattling the branches and causing the trunk to emit a cacophony of deafening groans and pops.

The sudden sensation that she was trespassing swept over Margaret— that the very ground she stood on wanted her elsewhere.

The hollow groans peppered with *pops* began to take on a malicious tenor.

A warning to *leave now*.

She then realised that the flurry of echoing sounds from the sycamore placed her dead centre atop a sonic bullseye.

If Al were to simply step outside—

Margaret flinched at the thought and tucked herself against the trunk once more. She peered through the fork in the branches carefully, only exposing the top of her head and a single eye.

The front door of the house opened, and Al bounded down the porch steps into the garden. Her instinct said to duck, but Al paid her no mind. He circled around the side of the house, weaving past his black Vauxhall Velox parked at the top of the gravel drive, and stopped in front of what looked to be an attached shed.

Al paused; he shot a sidelong glance in her direction. She quickly dipped her head beneath the fork in the branches, breath hitching, and slowly began to count to ten.

One…two…three…

Her imagination conjured up the sound of footsteps.

Four…five…six…

The looming figure of Al popping out from around the tree.

Seven…eight…nine…

"*Ten,*" she said in a hushed whisper.

When she rose back up to claim her original position, Al was gone.

Margaret wasn't certain if he'd gone inside the shed, but she would wait for his return, nonetheless. She rolled up her left sleeve and began flicking her eyes between the minute hand of her wristwatch and Al's shed.

Four minutes and forty-five seconds later, the door to the shed swung open. Her eyes immediately fixated on Al's right hand—he held a small black satchel. What piqued her curiosity was that what he'd emerged with wasn't a toolbox or a hammer or even a rake.

It just seemed...out of place.

Who disappears into a shed for almost five minutes only to return with just a satchel?

Perhaps it was her imagination, or the wind whistling through the leaves, but Margaret could have sworn that throughout the four minutes and forty-five seconds Al was inside the shed, he didn't make a sound.

Not a jiggle or jostle of tools. Not a bump or a bang.

Silence.

And that was enough to leave Margaret unsettled.

What could be in that shed?

She was determined to find out.

Five minutes earlier

The false wall of the basement room slid open, but instead of the normal toolbox containing their bags of food slipping through the opening, Al thundered in, slamming the door behind him. Fiona cowered at the sight of his presence. Gavin, Craig, and Arun stared at him coldly, as if trying to silently tell him he was unwelcome in their prison that he had made for them. James, on the other hand, seemed a bit relieved.

As if he were still clinging on to that shred of hope that he would be their saviour.

Al threw balled-up bundles of clothes at the boys. "Get undressed."

They all exchanged confused glances.

"Now!" he bellowed.

James and Gavin rose to their feet first, sheepishly looking at Fiona.

"Why?" asked Craig.

"Don't make me ask you again. Now get undressed."

Craig and Arun followed suit.

Arun studied Al's countenance. There were deep grooves along his forehead, jaw clenched. He wondered what was going on out there in the real world, up above, that could have made him this frazzled.

Al crept closer to them and pointed to the bundle of clothes on the ground.

"I don't care who is watching," he growled through his teeth. "Get undressed *now* and change into these clothes!"

The lads slipped off their filthy shirts and began reaching at their waistlines hesitantly.

"Please, don't look," said James.

Fiona respected their wishes and gave them a few moments until Gavin announced they had finished. Al gathered up the dirty clothes, shoved them inside a black satchel, and left the basement without a word.

An uncomfortable silence fell over the room.

"At least he gave us some new clothes," said James with lukewarm optimism.

Gavin turned to his brother but didn't say a word. No one did. He wasn't sure if this was his brother's way of looking for the silver lining in the situation, or if he simply couldn't see the truth of their reality.

The truth about Al.

The light drizzle Margaret encountered on her drive subsided as she pulled into the parking lot of the East Ayrshire Council building. It was a two-storey red brick building with long, rectangular windows and a faded grey roof. The architecture of the municipal buildings in Scotland always seemed to match the country's dreary weather. While she did pass a pop of colour from the flowers planted out front, the inside proved as drab as the exterior. As she climbed the stairs to the second floor, the distinct office smell hit her—subtle wafts of old carpet and large volumes of paper.

Once inside, a sharp floral scent penetrated her nose, masking the old carpet and paper smells entirely. The perfume of the elderly clerk that sat behind the counter was the likely culprit. She was a rather round-faced woman with thick arms and a short neck. Stringy grey hair that matched her crocheted shawl fell past her shoulders, and she sported a pair of thick-rimmed glasses with such strong prescription lenses that it gave her bulging bug eyes.

The woman hardly looked up from her desk at the sight of Margaret's arrival. She couldn't tell whether the woman was more stirred from the thought of having something finally to do or peeved by the fact her peace had been disturbed.

Margaret cracked a small smile at the thought, realising that she probably looked the exact same way at the station when the likes of Mrs. Young came in prattling on about a new grievance against the town's children.

"Can I help you?" asked the woman.

Margaret read her name tag as Agnes.

"Yes. I need to pull land records for someone."

Agnes' eyes slowly rolled up to meet Margaret's.

"Well, you came to the right place," she said flippantly.

"I'm investigating an active case and I need everything you have on Albert Reid." Margaret pulled out her badge and set it on the counter. "He's a resident of Catrine."

Agnes put down her paperwork, revealing a strained smile.

"Of course. I'll be right back." Her chair creaked as she slowly brought herself to her feet and waddled into the depths of the many rows of files. Minutes passed, and Margaret shifted uncomfortably as she waited. She craned her neck over the counter and peered to the right and left to see if there were any other signs of life in the office. After what seemed like an eternity, Agnes returned with a small manila file filled with papers.

"I'll need you to sign here for the copies." Agnes slapped a piece of paper on the counter and pushed her a pen. Margaret quickly signed her name, eager to get back to her patrol car so she could dig through the files.

"What were you able to find?"

"Just about everything. The deed, tax information, and blueprints for the orphanage and the residence at 42 Holm Farm Road."

"Cheers. Appreciate your help," she said.

Margaret bid her farewell and left the council building.

Agnes glanced at the clock that hung from the counter wall. The black plastic was in the shape of a cat, its squiggly tail shifting back and forth with the passing seconds. Red eyes made of jewels glimmered in the fluorescent lights running along the ceiling. She waited a full minute to make sure Margaret was gone and then picked up her phone to dial a number.

"Hello, yes. It's Agnes." She listened to the response and picked up the piece of paper Margaret had handed her. "I never thought I'd be making this phone call, but a woman by the name of Margaret Brown just came to collect your records."

There was a pause.

"Take care."

Agnes shakily put the phone back on the receiver. She took a gulp of her cold, bitter coffee and stared into the jewelled red eyes of the ticking cat clock.

Elder Louise grabbed her overnight bag and slipped out of the girl's dormitory. Early in the morning while Gillian and Angela were asleep, she had packed a bag, made the long walk to the girls' dormitory, and hidden it in one of the armoires. This way when her rounds were over, she could leave unseen without running into the deacons.

The drive to Al's was short, but it felt even shorter than usual as Elder Louise slipped into autopilot, just going through the motions without being consciously aware. Energy buzzed within her as she imagined the journey to get back the lads. Just stepping foot in Al's house was far closer than anyone else working for him had ever been to him. She relished the fact he thought highly enough of her to entrust her with this duty.

She struggled to round the corner onto Holm Farm Road, fighting to see through the sheets of rain pummelling her windshield, even with the wipers on. She fish-tailed up his gravel drive, and within a moment, Al came out of the front door with a black umbrella.

When he arrived at her window, she caught him fixating on something at the back of her car.

"The back window is open!" He struggled to make himself heard over the pouring rain. "Your duffel is getting soaked. Pop your boot, I'll put it in there."

She popped the boot and glanced back to confirm what was going on. Rain splattered all over her overnight bag and the back seat.

That's odd, she thought. *I don't remember leaving my window cracked.*

Al reached in, quickly grabbed the bag, shoved it in the boot, and slammed it closed. He proceeded to the passenger door and Louise unlocked it so he could slip in. He closed the umbrella and sat there next to her, half-soaked and breathing heavily.

"I slipped their adoption papers in your bag. Here is the address to the parents' house and their names. I called a hotel and made you a reservation for two nights."

She tried to speak, but Al kept going.

"Here is money for petrol, the hotel, and any food you might need for yourself and the lads. Take a night to rest with them when you get them back tomorrow. Who knows how they're feeling right now."

"I can only imagine."

"I think the Lord has sent for you to do this, Louise."

She sniffled, fighting to rein in her emotions.

"Now go," he said. "It's a long drive."

Al handed Louise the money, a map, and a piece of paper with the address to the hotel and the house of the lads' parents. He was about to grab his umbrella but instead, set it down on the passenger seat. "I'll leave this for you too." He smiled and ducked out of the car, ran back to his house, and disappeared inside.

A flurry of thoughts and emotions zipped through Louise's mind, but she didn't want to lose time. She placed the papers on the passenger seat, glancing at the address. She composed herself and turned the key in the ignition.

Louise made it onto the motorway within minutes, her ramshackle Mini sputtering along as she pressed the accelerator, cutting through the downpour.

She was headed to Aberdeen.

Aniqa sat behind the counter at the Sorn Inn, staring through the glass of the front door listlessly. She waited for something to break the stillness that had plagued her shift since she'd arrived. A weary traveler shuffling through the door, or even a ring from the telephone. Anything would be welcome relief. Instead, her only companion was the steady drip coming from a leak in the ceiling. It pitter-pattered into a bucket she had set below.

Today was the fourth full day Arun and Craig had been missing. Elaine wasn't holding up very well; on her last trip to check on her,

Aniqa had found her asleep, face pressed into the dining room table next to a half-empty bottle of wine.

It was only just after eleven in the morning.

Aniqa hadn't been holding up well either. Her nights were sleepless and filled with many tears. She'd called her professors in Glasgow and told them she couldn't make it for the weekend classes until her son was found. But she still had bills to pay, and coming to the Inn carried the additional benefit of getting her out of bed. What pushed her to maintain some form of normality was the hope she held onto fiercely—that her son was still alive. But each passing day, the worry grew stronger, syphoning power from the hope. It was the endless duel that waged inside her from the moment Arun went missing.

The clash between hope and fear.

The droplets hitting the bucket were beginning to drive her mad, and she wasn't sure if it was the slight must in the air, but her chest felt tight.

"Robert!" she called out. A few moments later, the Inn's owner appeared. Robert McCallum was an average-looking man with an average-looking body. He had brown hair that was balding and dark circles that made him appear tired, no matter how much rest he got at night.

"Yes?"

"Can I tap a fag off you?"

A little life came back into Robert's dead eyes.

"Ye don't smoke."

She tilted her head, pleading with a sharp flick of her gaze for him not to question. He fished one out of the pack, then turned back to his office.

"Lighter," she said. He pivoted, slipped it from his pocket, handed it to her. She hurried out the Inn door, and a bell jingled raucously against the glass. She positioned herself under the roof overhang, the pouring rain falling in a loud, cascading sheet in front of her. With a flick of her thumb, she lit the cigarette and took a puff. She savoured the tobacco flavour reminiscent of an equally troubled time in her life.

When she gave birth to Arun after she'd been kicked out of her mother's flat.

Although she pulled toxins into her lungs, she was still drawing breath, still alive. She whispered to Allah in her head, praying her son was doing the same.

Just as she enjoyed a few moments of solace, footfalls caught her attention.

Seeing his tall stature made her immediately recognise the man as Al. Aniqa was rather pleased to see a familiar face.

Al, on the other hand, tried to suppress his disappointment. If the evils he had committed throughout his life were made possible because of the amusement it brought the Devil, this happenstance surely was the work of his counterpart above.

The Lord has a peculiar sense of humour, he thought.

Al gave Aniqa a small smile as he moseyed past her, stopping in front of the Inn's door. She noticed his pause and pulled the cigarette forcefully, leaving a caterpillar of disintegrated ash wilting in its wake.

"I'll let you finish," said Al. He awkwardly shoved his hands in his pockets. This gesture of patience impressed her. To other male travellers, she was simply the lowly immigrant clerk there to give them a key and wait on their every need. This was why she pursued her university studies; the world was an unforgiving place for women, but for a Bangladeshi woman, it was twice as hard to earn her place.

A truth that seldom bothered her, for she had her father's spirit.

She flicked the butt onto the pavement, and it fizzled out in the rain. Al followed her inside, waiting until she walked around the reception desk.

"How can I help you?"

"I need a room."

"Single or a double?" she asked.

"Single is fine."

Aniqa collected his ID and payment. She flipped opened a lockbox and grabbed a key, pausing to caress the faded brass between her fingers as a thought crossed her mind; she re-hung that key and chose another—for a room closer to reception. Al would have to pass her again if he left his room unless he made the long trek to the back exit of the building. An unforeseen urge she placated on a whim, and when she faced Al again, she wondered why she'd done it.

"I know it's none of my business, but is everything all right?" She paused. "I know you live nearby…" Her voice trailed off.

Al smiled and let out a small chuckle.

"I needed a change of scenery." He paused, then added, "The orphanage can be hectic at times. My house is a bit too close to my work."

"I get it," she said, staring up at Al. For a moment she got lost in thought. When Aniqa finally snapped out of it, she broke away from his blue eyes and quickly handed him the key, grateful that he'd waited and not drawn attention to her pause. "Room 13. There's a breakfast from seven to ten as well."

There was something about Aniqa that held Al's attention for longer than normal, and that observation intrigued him. His mind flashed to the other night at the church when they'd been joined together in prayer. He remembered the softness of her hand clasped in his…warmth spread throughout his chest. A sensation he'd felt only a handful of times in his forty-three years.

"Is there anything else I can do for you, Mr. Reid?"

Aniqa's voice broke through his reminiscence. "No, thank you." He left the counter and headed down the hall. When he discovered his room was a mere ten feet away from reception, a mixture of feelings swept through his gut. The first a jolt of fear—did Aniqa purposely put him this close to her to keep a watchful eye on him? Out of suspicion?

No. It's not possible, argued his rational mind. The competing feeling was a fluttering sensation, like a swarm of uncoordinated butterflies trying to escape his gut. Something in the way that she looked at him made him realise the former assumption must be wrong. She couldn't be suspicious.

Perhaps she had just fallen into the net of charm he'd cast on the town for the past two decades.

Before he opened his door, he turned back to reception.

"Take care," he said before ducking into the room.

Though he didn't see it, Aniqa cracked a smile.

Margaret pulled into the empty drive in front of her house along Lorimer Crescent, in the Holmhead suburb of Cumnock. She often came home before her husband, Walter, although given the circumstances with the missing lads, she felt she shouldn't be home early, if at all.

There was still work to do.

Normally, her evening routine was the sole respite after a day of paper pushing and taking complaints from the locals. But not tonight. When she took off her uniform, she felt like a warrior removing their armour before the battle had been won. Every layer she peeled off, another coat of shame slid in its place. Even a shower proved futile in washing away the feeling that she was doing far too little for four children who were still out there somewhere.

Margaret headed to the kitchen and threw together leftover potatoes and veggies from the fridge into a casserole dish. Walter loved a good rumbledethumps, and she didn't want to waste a shred of mental energy on making her husband dinner from scratch. Her thoughts blared through her head, crowding out the sound of the knife hitting the cutting board in the background.

What about the lads made them a target? Why did the kidnapper choose them?

She mumbled the answers to herself out loud. "They were together. They are young…" She threw the cut veggies into a bowl and in a separate one began mashing the potatoes.

But why kidnap all four at the same time? Wouldn't they have run, fought, or cried for help?

"Maybe the kidnapper was someone they knew. Or at least someone they found harmless."

The front door swung open and caused Margaret to jump. Walter strode in, dressed in business wear, briefcase in hand, and disappeared into the bedroom. He reappeared in lounging clothes and came into the kitchen, drawing in a long breath as he entered.

"Smells good."

Margaret gave her husband a kiss and rubbed his back as he pulled her into an embrace. Mild-mannered Walter enjoyed a whisky neat, reading historical non-fiction, and the occasional trip to the Highlands in the summer. He, like Margaret, had grown up in East Ayrshire and never left. He'd taken a handful of business courses in Ayr before heading back to Cumnock, where he became a worker at the local branch of the Bank of Scotland. Some twenty years later, he was now the bank manager.

The two poured so much of their lives into work that the lust they'd once felt for each other had waned. Margaret felt that every passing year they became more like friends than lovers. Both having sedentary jobs, they had gained a bit of weight—not that either of them cared.

Margaret picked at her food. Compared to Walter, whose plate was nearly clear, she had hardly put a dent in the meal.

He finally noticed her listless gaze and returned a forkful of food to his plate. "What's wrong?"

She snapped out of it. "Nothing."

Walter ducked his head, giving her that look that said: *out with it.*

"It's the lads. I can't stop thinking about them."

"Do you have any leads?" he asked before shovelling another bite into his mouth.

"Nae."

She paused, watching him eat. It was against protocol to discuss an active investigation, but this was her husband.

"What do you know about Albert Reid?"

Walter nearly spat out his food.

"Albert Reid?" He covered his mouth, swallowing the bite down. "Is he a suspect?"

She pressed her lips together. "Not at all."

"Then why bring him up?"

"Now that I think about it, I probably shouldn't say."

"Way to tease me," he said, scooping up the final bite of rumbledethumps.

Silence fell over the table. Walter grabbed his plate and motioned for Margaret's.

"I'm finished," she said. He took hers and brought them to the sink. The detective in her spirit became curious.

"Do ye know anything of him?" asked Margaret, raising her voice over the running sink.

"His restaurant is phenomenal."

"Fair enough. But there's something off about him. Like he doesn't belong."

Walter shut off the tap and returned to the dining room. He rested a hand on Margaret's shoulder lovingly and put some thought into her statement. "Well besides the Grounds, the Kirk, and TLC, I don't know much."

"That's what gets me. Where did he come from?"

Walter paused. "It seems like he's always been here."

"But that's impossible. I don't remember him from school. Do you?"

"Nae. But there is one thing I do know."

"What's that?"

He flashed his wife a sympathetic smile. "That Catrine wouldn't be Catrine without Albert Reid."

For a moment, Margaret tried to stop being a cop and think about how she viewed Albert Reid through a different lens. A lens that existed before all of this happened. He was a man that everybody knew yet knew nothing about. And that was just fine, because the truth Walter spoke of was all that mattered to the townspeople.

Catrine wouldn't be Catrine without Albert Reid.

Walter's snores reverberated through the room, and Margaret lay on her back, staring at the nearly pitch-black ceiling. The twilight of the Scottish night barely slipped through the thick fabric curtains, illuminating their edges in a light-blue glow.

Her stomach ached, but not from the rumbledethumps. Because she couldn't move her thoughts away from her conversation with Walter.

"Catrine wouldn't be Catrine without Albert Reid…"

No matter which way she tossed or turned, the nagging pit in her stomach wouldn't lessen, nor would the intermittent lick of acid that accompanied it. The few times she did attempt to close her eyes, all she could see were the faces of the four missing lads.

The ticking of the wall clock served as a conscious reminder that every passing second was another second lost. That thought gave her a jolt of energy; she threw back the covers and changed into something other than pyjamas. But just as she headed for her bedroom door, she saw her—

The little girl. She sat with her knees tucked against her chest, arms wrapped around them, back pressed against the door.

She stared up at Margaret, unblinking. Her fearful eyes shimmered with misty tears, and she heard her say without words, *"Help me."*

An invisible fist punched Margaret in the gut, knocking the air clean out of her lungs. Seeing the girl before she fell asleep at night was haunting enough, but this was a first.

Blocking her exit.

"I'm sorry," Margaret said no louder than a whisper. "I can't make the same mistake twice."

She beelined for the door, walked through the girl, and left.

The patrol car brakes squealed as she came to a stop in front of the Cumnock station. Being just after ten, there wasn't a soul in the car park. The station was only open until nine, so she had to enter with her key.

Nothing changed at night except for the lack of people and sounds. The fluorescent lights still cast a harsh off-white glow on everything, illuminating the chipped paint and cracked skirting boards that showed the station's age.

Margaret carefully crept through the halls because she knew at any moment another officer might come in from their rounds. She felt a twinge of guilt as she approached her destination, popping open the door. Beneath it was a stronger force—a nagging curiosity that she desperately needed to alleviate.

Photos of Stu's family sat on his desk next to his nameplate. The faces seemed to baulk at her arrival—an intruder in their midst. A coffee cup held a few pens and a miniature Scottish flag. She rounded the desk and knelt in front of his private filing cabinet.

Margaret yanked the chrome handle—it caught on the lock with a loud clang. She tried the drawer beneath it and realised it too was locked. She felt underneath the desk, patting the nooks and the crannies, then checked beneath the photos and inside the coffee mug.

Nothing.

With a sigh, she accepted defeat. There was no master key to the cabinet, and there wasn't a chance in Hell she'd be able to break into it. Her mind played out all the possibilities if she were to get caught in the act…the most likely being her badge taken away without a question.

She went back in the direction she came, and when she reached the exit, her heart sank.

There was a car parked next to hers with its engine idling.

Her feet felt heavy as she descended the station steps. The headlights illuminated the evening mist, creating a blinding halo effect preventing her from getting a good look at the car. Instead of lollygagging, she headed straight for her patrol car. Only in her peripheral did she make out that it was another patrol car.

A car door popped open behind her.

"Margaret?"

That voice sounds familiar…

She turned around, awestruck at who she saw.

"Gordon?" she half-asked, half-exclaimed. She hadn't seen him in years. He stepped out from the idling car, grinning ear-to-ear. Margaret outstretched a hand; he swatted it away.

"None of that here," he said, pulling her into a hug.

It took her a moment to fully ease into his embrace, since it wasn't commonplace to greet another officer with a hug, especially a female. But she succumbed to his friendliness and gave him a few gentle pats on the back as a smile tugged at her lips.

Gordon Ross was a year older than Margaret, and he had black hair, hazel eyes, and olive skin that made him look like he'd just hopped off a sailboat from a Greek island rather than being born and raised in Scotland. A handsome man to say the least, and a good cop too. He quickly outgrew his hometown of Cumnock, transferred to Edinburgh, and had been working there since.

"Late night?" he asked.

"Nae, couldn't sleep. What about you? Why ye here?"

"If I were a betting man, I'd say the same reason you couldn't sleep."

"You mean…?"

"The missing lads," said Gordon.

"But this isn't your jurisdiction."

A smug smile blossomed across Gordon's face as he slipped out a shiny silver badge with an ornate crest imprinted on it.

"You're looking at Detective Chief Inspector Gordon Ross now."

"That's fantastic!" exclaimed Margaret. "Doesn't surprise me. I knew you were meant for bigger and better things."

"Thanks. It's what I've always been working toward, and now that I have it…" He paused, mulling his words. "Just a bit surreal is all."

"When did you get the promotion?"

"'Bout a year and a half ago."

"I'm proud of you, Gordon."

Margaret's mind refocused on something else Gordon had said.

"So, what exactly brought you here?"

Gordon stammered before letting out a defeated sigh. "Are ye headed home?"

"I was."

"Well if you're up for it, I'd like to show you something."

Margaret's brow furrowed.

"I—I've got a room at the Inn nearby. And I think you might be able to help me."

"Help you with what?"

Gordon smiled. "You'll see."

Elder Louise pulled up to the Gloucester Hotel. The rain had stopped, so that was a plus, but she was eager to get into bed. The level of excitement this journey had brought her was so uncommon that after the initial surge of energy, once it waned, her body was completely exhausted.

She checked in and paid in full. Once inside, she realized she had forgotten her duffel in the boot of the car. But her ageing legs told her to just take a shower and go straight to bed. Closing her eyes in the steamy hot shower caused her mind to flicker between scenes of what she imagined tomorrow would hold. Her only fear being that James and Gavin's parents wouldn't give them up without a struggle.

She reminded herself the Lord was on her side. That thought alone soothed her.

Without pyjamas from her duffel, she donned the hotel's cotton robe and began boiling water for her nightly cup of chamomile tea. While it steeped, she pulled out her bible. She laid it on the edge of the bed and knelt in front of it.

She thanked St. Christopher for providing her safe passage to Aberdeen, and then went about her usual prayers. Tonight, she ended on one she didn't repeat as often:

Psalm 23:1-6.

"The Lord is my shepherd; I shall not want. He makes me lie down in green pastures. He leads me beside still waters. He restores my soul. He leads me in paths of righteousness for his name's sake. Even though I walk through the valley of the shadow of death, I will fear no evil. For you are with me; your rod and your staff, they comfort me. You prepare a table before me in the presence of my enemies; you anoint my head with oil; my cup overflows. Surely goodness and mercy shall follow me all the days of my life, and I shall dwell in the house of the Lord forever. Amen."

Gordon opened the hotel room door and gestured with his hand. "After you."

Margaret's nose crinkled when she saw the mess of paperwork strewn across the king-sized bed, covered edge to edge. On the floor, cardboard boxes filled with manila folders encircled the room, along with a few red Magic Markers sitting on the bedside table.

"What is all of this?"

Gordon stood at the centre of all the paperwork. There was a twinkle of pride in his eyes, kind of like when an artist gazes at their creation. "It's my last shot at trying to prove a theory."

A fleck of curiosity arose in Margaret's gut. She felt the sudden urge to speak up…to say, for once, what she was thinking. But a long trail of memories throughout her time as an officer had conditioned her to do the exact opposite.

An unwanted memory flashed behind her eyes.

The dilapidated house on the outskirts of town. The young girl sitting in the corner of a filthy kitchen, looking up at her with those terrified eyes. The mum who incoherently babbled non-stop, painting the picture that everything was all right and everyone was fine. The phone call hours later that shattered her soul into a million pieces.

Margaret shook her head to rid herself of the memory.

Gordon isn't like them, she thought. *He won't shoot you down like the rest do.*

"I want to hear it," she said sternly. "Your theory."

Gordon revealed a broad smile and picked up some of the files.

"Let's get to work then."

Propped against the corner of the room was a large roll of paper that she helped him unfurl—on it was a massive map of Scotland.

"Gave my artist neighbour five quid to draw it," he explained with a nervous smile as Margaret helped him tack it to the far wall of the hotel room. Then, they both moved to the bed and began thumbing through the paperwork.

"It all began with the Queensferry case. An eleven-year-old girl from a rundown flat in the Muirhouse suburb. Kidnapped in broad daylight without a single witness. No suspects. The girl's mum was a heroin addict. Family, friends, and neighbours told police they suspected that she had died of neglect. Or maybe an accident she had covered up.

"Then, there was the six-year-old case. A laddie from the Hermiston suburb. According to the wife, in the days prior to the disappearance, her husband had been threatening to take the kids and swore she'd never see them again. He ended up getting charged with battery because the police assigned to the case found bruises on the wife. It's still unsolved, and the husband remained the only person of interest in the case.

"Both cases have long gone cold. Even after looking into them, my bosses brushed them off. That's when I remembered why they had gone cold in the first place."

"They're all children of addicts. Scroungers," said Margaret. "Parents who would have been better off not having kids in the first place."

"Exactly. But there's also one from two weeks ago that doesn't match that pattern. Fiona Campbell, twelve. Have a look at this…"

Gordon plotted the missing cases on the map, each with a distinct dab of red Magic Marker. The three near Edinburgh went up first. Then, two kidnappings in the Highlands. One in Fort William and another in Oban; each almost exactly a year apart. Lastly, he put up Fiona Campbell's case out of Cathkin. He recruited Margaret to help him pull the dates of the missing children from files. He put the date, gender, and a red dot on the map for each corresponding case.

"There are just over a dozen missing children's cases still unsolved. My superiors won't have a word of it. They're too far apart, too many have prime suspects who only needed a shred of real evidence to put them away. And that's what led me here," said Gordon, smiling as he tapped the map with his forefinger. Margaret had fallen into a trance, poring over the dates they went missing, and the towns.

"Margaret." He nudged her. "Look."

She glanced up at the map, and her breath hitched. A flutter in her chest contrasted with the sinking feeling in her stomach. All the red dots formed a perimeter—a misshapen circle of missing children around the edges of Scotland.

"This is why I came here unannounced," said Gordon. He bounded forward and popped open the cap of the Magic Marker. "None of these cases made sense," he began shakily. "But then four days ago, your lads went missing."

With forceful jabs, Gordon plotted four red dots atop the village of Catrine. "In the past ten years, your missing lads are the only cases to ever occur within this perimeter."

Electricity coursed through Margaret as she studied the map, both reigniting her investigative drive and stoking the coals of the fear that had burned since the day the lads went missing.

"It's not a perimeter," she said in a daze. "It's a bullseye."

CHAPTER 10
THE MISLED

The double doors didn't beckon him this time, but by now, Arun knew to open them. The frosty blast of air engulfed him as he slowly walked down the buoyant, swaying dock. This time, there was no one waiting at the end of it; just the frozen children on their ice blocks and the sound of the water lapping loudly against the underbelly of the dock.

Arun stayed quiet for what felt like an eternity.

"Hello." His voice seemed to dissipate instantly in the icy air.

He walked forward with measured steps, eyes nervously flicking between the frozen children. The longer he stood there, legs like jelly from keeping his balance on the dock, the more he felt time standing still.

"Why do I keep coming here?" he asked.

"Why are you here in the first place?" replied a deep voice from behind him. The hair on his neck stood and a crawling sensation slid down the length of his body.

He turned around slowly—

Al.

He stood at the beginning of the dock, the double doors framing his tall figure. "You know you shouldn't be in here," he said nonchalantly, yet there was a sharpness to his tone that served as a dire warning. Al put one foot out in front of the other and took a step forward.

"This isn't real," said Arun.

"Well, it sure feels real. Doesn't it?"

Arun swallowed dryly. Al outstretched his opposite foot and took another step.

"But it isn't," he spat back. "None of this is real."

"How can you be so certain?"

Arun's defiance tickled Al, and he cracked a smile.

"My art is real."

A cacophony of crunching ice filled the room. The frozen children's limbs bent grotesquely as they stood upright on their blocks, frost bursting at their icy joints with every ear-splitting movement.

"Don't you see?" laughed Al. "They're mine now." He took another step closer. "And here, they're safe. They're finally pure."

Arun crept backwards and bumped against the edge of the frozen wall. He had nowhere left to go.

A wicked grin slid across Al's face, and he pulled a knife out of his pocket.

"You're a good boy, Arun," he said mockingly. "But I think it's time *you* became like *them*."

Crunching sounds ripped through the air like exploding rubble as two frozen children jumped on the dock, one boy behind Al, and a girl in front.

Al stared at them in bewilderment. "Do you think this is some sort of game?" he taunted with his knife.

The two children began encroaching on his space.

"What do you think you're doing? Get back!" he shouted with a warning jab of the knife.

The frozen girl didn't flinch, just kept inching forward.

"I said get back!" In a last-ditch effort to keep them away, Al stabbed the frozen girl in the centre of her chest. The blade sank below her frosted skin, crunching as it went deeper. The frozen girl didn't even as much as register that she'd been stabbed. Her eyes slowly traced the length of Al's arm until they settled on the blade resting just below her breastbone. She stared at it for a few moments, and then slowly raised her head to meet Al's horrified gaze.

The blue skin of her lips cracked with frost as her mouth formed a broad, warped smile. Blade still in her chest, the girl lunged forward and shoved Al with otherworldly force, spittle flying as the air escaped his lungs. He fell backward into the arms of the frozen boy waiting behind him, whose forearms hooked around Al's shoulders, clamping down on them with a vice-like grip. Al flailed, bellowing expletives as the boy dragged him toward the double doors, with Al's attempts at landing uppercuts failing miserably. Every punch that landed sounded like a fist hitting solid metal. Al's flurry of blows caused blood from his knuckles to spread into the boy's frozen cheeks, like a wine-coloured paint seeping into a cold blue canvas.

The boy dragged Al out of the frozen room, and the girl paused just shy of the exit.

She twisted around and smiled at Arun.

He returned it; her arm crunched as she removed the knife from her chest. She then pointed to a random corner of the frozen room. As if an invisible set of nerves connected them, the rest of the frozen children mirrored her, raising their arms and pointing to the same spot with a staccato of crushing ice. She let her arm fall to her side and exited, double doors slamming behind her.

Al's muffled screams echoed from the hallway.

Arun grimaced.

Now that Al was gone, Arun's eyes darted between the remaining frozen children who stood petrified on their ice blocks, all with their arms outstretched, pointing to the left side of the room.

"What do you want?" he asked, to no one in particular.

The children didn't move a muscle.

Arun copied them by pointing at the same spot in the room. "What's over there?"

Crunching ice erupted from both sides, followed by two clipped thuds. The impact of the two frozen children caused Arun to struggle to maintain his balance with the amplified swaying of the dock beneath his feet. They approached slowly, and he twisted back and forth to try and keep both of them in his field of view. As they closed in, he had nowhere else to go. They calmly stopped and raised their arms to point.

"I don't understand," said Arun. The room exploded with a cascade of crunching ice; all the frozen children, one by one, jumped from their ice blocks onto the dock, and once fully upright, resumed their pointing.

"What is the point of all this? What do you want me to do?"

The two children closest lunged forward, grabbing him by his shoulders.

"Let me go!" he shouted, but his attempts to break free from their icy grasp were futile. They suddenly hoisted him off the dock, legs flailing, and threw him into the water. The wet cold crashed in around Arun, soaking through his clothes in an instant. Pins and needles danced along his skin, and in seconds he began violently shivering.

To his horror, the frozen children jumped in the water behind him in pairs, and they all swam toward him. He thrashed in the water to get away from them, but within a few feet he'd reached the edge of the room. He pounded at the frosty concrete wall, crying for help at the top of his lungs, inadvertently sucking in water, causing him to cough and choke. The children closed in, and he clamped his eyes shut to avoid witnessing what might happen next.

"Wake up!" he shouted, slapping himself in the head. "It's just a nightmare...it's just a nightmare," he muttered under his breath repeatedly until something clicked in his mind.

The children, he thought. *They haven't attacked me.*

He reluctantly turned around, opening his eyes.

All the frozen children were treading water in a semicircle. In this silent moment of respite, Arun was able to get a good look at them. Beneath the frosty veneer of blue skin was the inescapable visage of youth. A pit formed in his gut as he realised that they all appeared to be around the same age as him.

"...I think it's time you became like them..."

Al's words crept back into his mind, and along with them a lucid moment. He knew this was a nightmare; that soon enough he'd wake up on the cold concrete floor of Al's basement. Forced to go another disorienting day where time didn't exist. Another day without clean clothes, a warm bath, or his mother's embrace.

Arun had buried a thought deep within in those first hours after they got trapped. It resurfaced with a vengeance, rearing its ugly head to the point he couldn't avoid it. That every day spent in Al's basement was another day closer to death. Their fate was inching closer every hour, and if nothing changed, it would surely come true.

A rock formed in his throat and deep grooves etched his forehead as he began to blubber. "I don't want to die," he wailed, hiccupping violently. "I'm sorry he did this to you…I can't die down here…I don't want to die…"

And as he bobbed up and down in the water, he felt a cold pressure against his arm. The pressure spread to his other arm, shoulder, and back. He blinked deliberately to clear the tears and saw the frozen children embracing him. Their icy skin intensified his shivers, and even though they were all cold and dead, he could still feel the remnants of the warmth that had once existed.

All the children pulled back except for one. She grabbed his hand, and with it, manipulated his fingers to form a pointed index finger. She spun him around and, with her arm laying over his, pointed down into the inky black water.

"What's there?" he asked.

The girl took an exaggerated breath in and held it. Arun mimicked her inhalation, holding it too. She nodded, grabbed him by the wrist, and pulled him under. The frozen children dipped beneath the water's surface and followed, pushing against Arun's feet to propel him forward.

The girl pulled him deeper beneath the water. He could feel the pressure building in his ears, the light filtering in from the surface became incredibly dim, and he could barely see through the murky water in front of him.

She guided his hands toward something. He felt the circular metal edges of a drainpipe. She pointed into it, and without warning, swam inside. He followed her, trying to keep pace. It was just wide enough for him to kick the tips of his feet to propel himself forward.

There's an opening!

At the end of the drainpipe was a grated cover. The frozen girl interlaced her fingers with his, gently pushing his hand toward a certain spot where the bars were extremely corroded. They crumbled with just the bit of force of his hand. A small gap that had naturally eroded gave him a head start. The girl helped him; they hurriedly broke off the crumbling pieces until the hole was large enough for him to get through.

Arun pulled himself under, the corroded bars scraping along his back, but the frozen girl grabbed his legs and helped push him through. He darted towards the surface, kicking his feet with all his might. Because even though this was just a dream, he still had the sensation that his lungs were starved of oxygen. The faint grey light of day intensified as he approached the surface. When he broke through the waterline, he took in the most liberating breath of air.

Of fresh, outside air!

Arun gasped wildly, choking as he awoke in the real world. Fiona and Gavin stared at him as if they'd just watched something out of a horror movie. James sat next to Gavin along the wall, uninterested. Craig, on the other hand, knelt right in front of him, like he'd been waiting for him to wake.

There was a fire behind his green eyes, one Arun hadn't seen before.

Arun didn't know it, but Craig was simply mirroring the radiant hope he saw in Arun's eyes.

"What is it?" asked Craig.

"I found the way out."

Aniqa lit the cigarette dangling from her lips and took a long drag, holding it in before letting out a prolonged exhalation. Interspersed with the drags were sips of her tea; when the teacup reached her lips, her hand would shake ever so slightly.

Today was day five.

Nothing frightened her more than when her mind would play tricks and spiral out of control, negativity seeping into the cracks in her worn psyche, where all she could picture was the sixth day, the seventh day, the second week, the first month…where Arun wasn't found.

She took another nervous gulp of her tea.

It was eight in the morning, and she sat in the breakfast nook of the Sorn Inn donning her work uniform, even though her shift wasn't until later that afternoon. Aniqa couldn't reconcile the strangeness of her actions, or their origins for that matter, but something had drawn her here on an impulse. Perhaps it was the fact she was painfully alone. Visits to check in on Elaine had become so burdensome she felt ashamed she didn't want to return, for any time spent in the Robertson household was mostly George apologising for Elaine's condition. It seemed like every day she started drinking an hour earlier than the one prior.

Aniqa didn't blame her.

People find their own ways to survive.

Maybe that's what this was—a survival mechanism. She'd strategically chosen a table that gave her a clear view of reception. These decisions: to come to the Inn so early, to choose this specific seat, were both precipitated by a peculiar feeling uncharacteristic of her. Desperation. To spend time with another human being who could rescue her from the ever-constant thrumming in her head of Arun still being missing. To help her avoid the glaring truth that, of the only two people she interacted with, one was a drunk, and the other was her dead mother who Aniqa imagined took great joy in haunting her dreams.

Just as she'd become lost in her thoughts, a burly figure came into view at reception.

Al.

As he walked past, his gaze met hers; a sliver of surprise illuminated his face.

A smile tugged at Aniqa's lips, and she waved.

He had to have seen me, she thought.

Al hesitantly pulled up a chair and sat down at Aniqa's table, mirroring her growing smile.

Aniqa flagged down one of her colleagues working the breakfast area.

"Coffee, please. Black," Al said to the server.

She poured him a cup and whizzed on to other patrons.

"Back to work already?" he asked, sipping his coffee to try to hide his discomfort.

"Yeah, but not till later on."

"Why come here so early then?"

"Nothing better to do. And home hasn't felt quite the same since Arun went missing; I've avoided being there as much as possible."

"I can only imagine how terrible that must be," he said.

"I keep telling myself that all of this is just some nightmare. That I'll wake up to find Arun safe and sound in his room. But this is the nightmare." She gave a wave of her hands. "Reality."

"It's a cruel world we live in, isn't it?"

Aniqa digested his comment, pushing the pain as far down inside as possible. "What about you?" she asked, pivoting the conversation. "How was the room?"

"It was just what I needed."

"Sleep well?"

"The bed was a bit stiffer than I'm used to, but other than that, five stars." He smiled and chuckled; she joined him in the laughter. "Oh, and please tell your manager the concierge who checked me in was lovely."

Aniqa prayed her dark skin wouldn't betray her as her cheeks flushed.

"I'll be sure to pass that along."

Al gulped down the rest of his coffee and took a cursory glance at his pocket watch. "Well, I'd better get going."

"Off to work so soon?"

"The Lord's work is never done. Just as I finish one task, there's always another ready to replace it. But I'm blessed beyond measure. And so are you, even despite what's happened…"

Aniqa snorted. "After my mum died, truthfully I've felt more like I'm cursed."

Al reached out to rest his hand atop hers.

When she didn't pull it away, he looked surprised.

"Sometimes bad things happen to good people. That doesn't mean you're cursed."

His comment touched a soft spot within her. The reality of her situation resurfaced like bile licking her insides, and her eyes became glassy. "I'd take being cursed for the rest of my life as long as my son is spared. He's all I have left."

"I have a strong feeling that your son is going to be fine. He's a good boy, isn't he?"

"The best."

"The Lord will bring him back to you. I know it."

Al's words soothed Aniqa's worries, even if it was just for a moment. "Thank you."

"But I must head to the orphanage now or I'll be late. Pleasure running into you again."

"The pleasure's mine." Aniqa smiled. Al turned and headed out the Inn door. Full of breakfast and sufficiently caffeinated from her tea, Aniqa found the thought of sitting at work until her shift started ridiculous. And as she tidied up the table for her colleague, she wrestled with the uncomfortable truth that the only reason she'd come to the Inn in the first place was to run into Al. Staying home alone did make her uneasy, but it was his presence alone that calmed her—not just getting out of the house.

She left the Inn, heading down the pavement to her car. As she neared it, a muffled voice caught her attention. She turned. A block away, Al's tall frame was hunched over inside a telephone booth. Interest piqued, she slowly crept toward the booth.

"…Since, last Saturday. Yes, the address I already gave you is correct…I believe they are there."

Aniqa stood quietly out of view behind the booth.

"I haven't a clue why, but please call me when you know something."

Al hung up the phone and flinched when he turned around.

"You believe who are where?" asked Aniqa.

"Damn, you scared me." Al caught his breath and froze. He paused, then said, "Let me walk you back to your car."

Aniqa pursed her lips as she digested the tidbit of information she'd overheard. "You were saying you believed *who* are *where*?"

"Let's just say it's a problem that arose yesterday at the Grounds."

"And?"

"That's why I rented the room. I don't know who I can trust anymore, and I wanted to talk to those I do trust in a place where everything I say isn't within earshot."

"You said you just needed a change of scenery."

"I lied."

Aniqa glared at him disapprovingly. "Why?"

"Because I was worried, and I wanted to be ninety-nine percent certain that I was right."

"Right about what?"

Al smiled. "I believe I know who took your boy."

Elder Louise parked along the kerb in front of 11 Sandilands Drive and cut off the engine. She took a deep breath to try and calm her nerves, but the attempt proved futile as her heart pounded away like a drum.

Louise had never been fond of confrontation. That was why she worked with children; while they often didn't behave well, their youth made them far less intimidating than the average adult. She pulled out the paper Al had scribbled the address on to double-check she was at the right terrace.

11 Sandilands Drive would have been easy to miss if it weren't for the gilded numbers tacked next to the door that had long ago lost their shine. All the terraced houses on this street were identical—worn grey brick ran parallel along both sides, each three storeys high adorned with a red door. An empty pram had been left carelessly in the garden, and one of the neighbours side-eyed Louise as she walked past.

She formed a trembling fist and knocked.

Loud barking erupted behind the door, followed by the shrill cries of a baby. Muffled chatter grew closer, and Louise saw the speck of light in the peephole disappear.

A woman opened the door, the inconsolable baby cradled with only one arm—the other rested against her hip. The woman took a cursory glance at Louise's pulpit robe and said, "If it's a donation you're looking for, we don't have any money."

"Nae," replied Louise with a nervous laugh. A rock formed in her throat. *Stay strong, Louise. Stay strong.*

As the woman rhythmically bounced her baby, crooning to it so it would quiet, Louise feared she might have gotten the wrong house.

Why would they have another child if they abandoned their first two?

"Are you Mrs. Hamill?"

"Aye. What is it ye want?"

Louise stood a little taller and mustered the strength to croak out a response. "Where are they?"

"Where are who?"

"You *know* who I am talking about," said Louise through a clenched jaw.

Mrs. Hamill huffed. "I'm afraid you must be mistaken."

"Who is it?" called Mr. Hamill from inside.

"Just an old lass from the Kirk it looks like."

"What's she want?" he shouted.

"Yeah," echoed Mrs. Hamill, eyes locked on Louise with a steely gaze. "What is it you want?"

"Let me take the lads back to where they belong. Don't make a fuss about it or I'll call the police."

Mrs. Hamill's face blanched, and her rhythmic rocking of the baby stopped. "What did ye just say?"

"The lads," repeated Louise. "I know they're here."

"Is this some sort of sick prank?"

Mr. Hamill's brawny frame came to the threshold, and he glanced between Louise and his wife with a look of naivety that was wiped from his face the moment he saw his partner's expression.

"What's goin' on here?"

"I'm here to take the lads back."

Mr. and Mrs. Hamill exchanged a glance, and he leaned closer to her ear. "Is she not right in the head?"

Louise's anger spilled over. "James! Gavin!" she shouted, standing on her tiptoes to get a better view inside. "It's time to go home!"

The baby's wailing reached its peak, and Mrs. Hamill stared wide-eyed at Louise. "*How dare you*," she spat. "Comin' to my doorstep and saying those names." Tears pooled in the corners of her eyes.

"I'm not leaving until they are in my car and on the way back to Catrine."

Mr. Hamill stepped in front of his wife, staring down at Louise, but kept a calm demeanour. "Well, I hate to be the bearer of bad news, but they're not here."

"Fine. I'll see to it that the police come here and take them back for me."

"I'd let you come in and use our phone, but you've upset my wife and the bairn. So go along the way you came and see to it that ye don't come back."

"You should be ashamed of yourselves," sneered Louise. "First you abandon your boys, and then you have the nerve to snatch them up years later when they're finally settled in their new lives."

Mrs. Hamill slipped past her husband and jabbed a finger at Louise's chest. "Letting go of my children was the hardest thing I've ever had to do. But we were too young and too poor to give them a proper life." She wiped the tears off her face. "So, let's get something straight. If I weren't holding this baby, I'd have clocked you so hard you'd wake up halfway back to Catrine...but I get the sense that you care about my lads. Drove up all this way looking for 'em. Call the cops if you want. If you truly are a child of the Lord, you'll take my word that whatever you were told that brought you this way was a lie."

Mrs. Hamill began rocking the baby again, and her countenance soured. "Now get the hell off my property."

The door slammed in Louise's face. She raised her fist to bang on the door, but something stopped her. She wasn't sure if it was fear or intuition, but she could feel the pulse in her throat, so she decided to avoid another confrontation and trudged back to her car.

I'll call the police when I get to the hotel, she thought.

The closer she got to the hotel, the larger the knot in her stomach became. Doubt seeped into her mind like a poison, challenging her faith in a way she'd never experienced before.

"Whatever you were told that brought you this way was a lie."

Elder Louise chewed on the inside of her cheek as she ruminated over Mrs. Hamill's words. She parked in front of the hotel and hurried into the lobby. Her thoughts were frantic; she wondered if she'd call Al or the police first. In her peripheral vision as she darted past reception, she saw the concierge on the phone. When she caught sight of Louise, she lowered her voice and shifted away from the desk. While this puzzled her, it didn't slow her breakneck pace to the room.

Once inside, she dialled Al.

The tone rang endlessly, but he never answered.

In a last-ditch effort to contact him, she called Kissinger Grounds.

"Kissinger Grounds Orphanage, Deacon Gillian speaking."

"Gillian! Thank God you picked up. Is Al there?"

An unsettling silence filled the receiver. "Louise," she said, voice low. "What have ye done with them?"

"Come again?"

"The lads. Where did you take them?"

"I haven't taken them anywhere. I'm here in Aberdeen trying to get them back. Their parents took them—"

"You're sick!" interjected Gillian; she snorted sharply. "I hope you rot for what you've done! Everybody in the town is looking for…" Gillian's voice trailed off and became muted as a series of disjointed pieces in Louise's mind suddenly clicked. She slowly pulled the receiver from her ear, Gillian still spouting off accusations, and hung up. She opened the curtains listlessly and let the gloomy Scottish light spill in, staring at the street below with a scant number of passersby.

Two patrol cars approached from a distance and parked along the kerb, boxing in her Mini at both ends. Steps as loud as thunder filled the hallway moments later, and a loud banging shook the old wooden door.

"Open up!"

Each passing moment felt more dreamlike as she floated toward the door. Although her mind stewed in a mental fog so thick, she couldn't think straight, an unnatural calm permeated her. She let the officers cuff her without a fight, ignoring the scowls of the hotel staff and the prying eyes of patrons. They led her outside and asked for the car keys. She handed them over, and when one of the officers pushed her in the backseat of the patrol car, she watched the other open the boot of the Mini through the window. He grimaced, looking down at the asphalt shaking his head, then returned to the boot and delved into its contents.

Elder Louise barely caught a glimpse of him pulling out a heap of soiled children's clothes just as the patrol car zipped away. And though the air outside was still, she could hear the barrage of raindrops thrumming against the patrol car's exterior like liquid marbles. She could see the smile Al cast yesterday in a different light, hear his words with a different intonation.

"I think the Lord has sent for you to do this, Louise."

Now she knew the truth. That the lie he told simply existed to eclipse the *real* lie.

The lie whose devious purpose had come to fruition.

Margaret sped along the winding backroads to the Cumnock Station. Just after she'd returned from Gordon's hotel room, the phone rang. By the grave tone of Stu's voice, she knew it was urgent. Although she was running on hardly any sleep, she felt more energised than she had in weeks. She and Gordon were armed with their new theory, staying up into the wee hours of the morning cross-checking names and dates. Despite how compelling the findings appeared, she wasn't sure anyone would believe them.

It was half past eight, and the mist of the morning still hung in the air, trickling into the station car park. She hurried up the concrete steps, opened the door, and—

Her section of the office was a collection of empty desks and chairs. A few of the coffee mugs still had steam rising from them. *Freshly poured,* she thought.

To her right, the reception window in the lobby normally staffed by her colleague also sat vacant.

Where is everyone?

Murmurs ricocheted down the hall. She followed the voices that grew louder as she passed Stu's empty office, and finally located their source—the admin room.

Margaret froze like a deer in the headlights. All her fellow officers huddled around Stu, Aniqa, and Al. The whispers ground to an unsettling halt.

As she locked eyes with Aniqa, the coldness of her countenance caused a shiver to race down her spine.

"What's going on?" Margaret asked, eyes darting between the many faces.

Stu motioned with his index finger for her to enter. He rifled through some papers in front of him, hands trembling, breath shallow. All the while, she felt Aniqa's glowering side-eye.

"Do you care to explain to me why ye didn't report Mr. Reid's initial statements?"

Her eyes flicked between Al and Stu. "I don't understand."

Stu held up a piece of paper and said through gritted teeth, "He told you from the first day you went to the Grounds about his theory of Elder Louise having taken the lads."

"That's impossible," she said breathlessly. "And that's not what happened—"

"You could have at least returned my calls," said Al. Beneath his milky blue eyes and the look of sorrow he cast was the subtlest sliver of gratification.

"I never received any calls."

Stu outstretched his arm, shaking the paper in front of her. She recognised it immediately as the station call log. There were over three dozen calls from Al in the last four days, all containing the message of a request for a callback and an update on the report he had filed. Margaret shook her head, pulse pounding in her ears, a pit forming in her stomach.

"This is a load of shite."

"Margaret," warned Stu. She slapped the call log on the desk and glared at him.

"I did file a report, but his story is a lie. He didn't tell me anything. *I* was the one who presented him a theory about the birth parents potentially being suspect. But there was never any mention of Elder Louise."

"Margaret!" hollered Stu, cutting her off. She looked around at her colleagues, who filled in the back half of the room. These were people she respected and who respected her. The disdain in their expressions baffled her, and she snorted, chewing on the thought of how sixteen years of good policework could be tossed aside so easily.

"You never told me this theory," growled Stu.

"Because I didn't trust your reaction!" She turned to Al, fire burning in her eyes. "And if Elder Louise really was suspect from the beginning, why wouldn't I have brought her in for questioning straight away?"

Al's sombre gaze dropped. "You told me you were my direct contact. I trusted you to do the job and report my suspicions."

"You're lying through your teeth," she spat. "Don't use this poor woman to—"

"—*Failing* to report a potential suspect is enough to get you fired," interjected Stu. "But to have the nerve to stand here and outright deny your mistake in front of a mother whose son is also missing is sickening!"

Margaret couldn't believe her ears. Flashes of Al flicking open the metal lid of his pocket watch, the hurried departure—it all made sense now. She had mentioned James and Gavin's parents to test Al. But it had inadvertently sparked an ember she had never intended would become a flame.

An idea struck her. She slowly backed away from Stu and began barrelling toward her desk once she reached the hall.

"Margaret!" shouted Stu from behind her. "Where are ye going?"

She knelt beside her cubicle and fished out the keys from her pocket, struggling to quickly unlock her filing cabinet before anyone could stop her. A swarm of footsteps arose in the hallway, and her heart pounded uncomfortably in her chest. She pored through the manila folders until she found the private copy of her reports on Arun and Craig's case, then spilled the contents and spread them out in a semicircle on the floor.

Her eyes darted frantically as she speed-read the documents, and it only took a few seconds to fathom the unfathomable.

Her report was gone.

The rest were there.

But the one she needed for proof was gone.

The one which detailed her first conversation with Al.

What she knew as the truth was now a lie.

The lack of a report and the call log corroborated Al's accusations. She dropped the papers, put them back in the folder, and set them on her desk, turning to face the crowd behind her, fighting to maintain composure. The enormity of what Al had done hit Margaret like a freight train, but what frightened her the most was that she didn't know if he had done it alone.

Was it just Al, or was Stu in on it too?

She snorted, eyes settling on Al.

"How did you do it?"

"What are you talking about?"

"That's my private filing cabinet. No one has a key to it but me." Her breath shuddered as she struggled to counter. "Someone broke in and stole my report."

"Do ye need me to call Walter?" asked Stu in a patronising tone.

"You're sick!" she shouted, tears brimming. "You're sick if you believe him for a second." She glared at Stu with disgust, and then at some of the other faces in the room.

"All of you!"

Stu's pinched lips were hidden beneath his caterpillar moustache. He crossed his arms petulantly. "Are you done?" he asked.

She took a deep breath and turned to face Aniqa. "You can believe their lies if ye want. That won't change the fact that I'm going to keep the promise I made to you and find your son."

Margaret pushed past the crowd, cast an unforgiving look at Al, and headed towards the exit.

"You're off the case, Margaret!" yelled Stu from behind her. "Go home!"

Outside, a light rain fell that increased in intensity as she walked to her patrol car. Her lungs burned as she held her breath to stop from bursting into tears. By the time she started her car and drove away, the sky was falling.

And her tears fell too.

God cried with Margaret, for He knew they were fighting against a force of evil so formidable that His light wasn't strong enough to defeat it alone.

Elder Louise sat in a holding room in the Aberdeen police station. Its faded grey walls and dingy epoxy floors of the same colour created a drab, lifeless shell that seemed to syphon Louise's spirit as time slipped onward. The tightness in her stomach ratcheted down, her hands knotted together as she held them in her lap. The silence kept her marinating in Al's betrayal, and the uncertainty of her fate kept her soul trembling.

The door opened and two officers walked in; the first was the baby-faced one with straw-coloured hair who had driven her to the station. The second was a barrel-chested man with a square jaw outlined by a black beard. He sat by the young officer's side and gingerly placed a series of photos in front of Louise, staring at her with pursed lips and a dark, furrowed brow.

"Ms. Fleming. This is Officer Conway and I'm Detective Farland," said the burly man.

She mustered a polite nod.

Detective Farland slid the photos one-by-one into her line of sight. "Now, would ye like to tell me why four sets of soiled children's clothes were in the boot of your car?"

"I was framed."

Detective Farland and Officer Conway shared a chuckle.

"Here's what's going to happen," began Detective Farland, lowering his tone. "We're going to transport you back to Cumnock, where in a few days' time you'll stand before a judge for your preliminary hearing. I hate to rain on your parade, but the 'I was framed' story isn't going to hold up in court."

"Why would I have taken them? I'm their caretaker, for God's sake."

"Beats me. But even if we had a good answer to that, the soiled clothes were enough to get us an arrest warrant. So if I were in your shoes, I'd make this easier on yourself by admitting what you've done."

Louise stared back at Detective Farland with heavy eyes and an aching chest. This path she believed God had led her down wasn't God's path to begin with. The speculation of what could be in Al's testimony caused her reality to collapse, along with the crumbling foundation of faith which it was built upon.

How much of the past fifteen years was a lie? she wondered.

"I'm not admitting to a crime I didn't commit."

Detective Farland collected the pictures and stood up. "All right then. We'll be in later to transport you to Cumnock."

Officer Conway slipped out the door, and just before the detective followed him out, he turned back to Louise.

"You do get a phone call, if you'd like."

"I have no one to call," she said. "But I'd like you to bring me my bible."

He mulled over her request, and after a moment, nodded.

It took a half-hour for Detective Farland to bring her bible. She flipped through the fragile pages of the King James edition she'd kept since the beginning of her employment with Al. Alone in the holding cell, all she had was her pain and the belief that the Lord Almighty would save her from this mess.

She landed on a passage, and a solemnity crept through her veins until it engulfed her entirely.

"Even Satan disguises himself as an angel of light. So it is no surprise if his servants, also, disguise themselves as servants of righteousness. Their end will correspond to their deeds."

— 2 Corinthians 11:12–15

CHAPTER 11
THE CHASTENING

Kensington Palace
1938

The morning light spilled through the many east-facing windows, casting an amber glow throughout the palace. The quietness that commanded this hour was but an illusion, for the palace was like a living organism; there was always activity, even when it appeared to be dormant. If one listened closely enough, the muted pitter-patter of footsteps in far-flung halls could be heard, or the occasional clink of silverware followed by condescending whispers. The Queen may have been at rest, but her hive was very much alive.

Duke Leon had a pep in his step as he bounced along toward the eastern entrance of the palace. He'd spent the hour before dawn listening to records while replacing some bolts and twisting new metal wiring onto his main trap, now securely stowed away in the knapsack on his back.

Life had developed a new rhythm for Duke Leon, and for the first time in seventeen years, he was truly happy. He hummed the tunes from his record to fill the absence of sound. What he'd realised in the past two years was that when he tried to fight the emptiness, it consumed him. But when he killed, it kept that feeling at bay. So he no longer fought the urge—he would kill animals regularly at his whim, all without ever being caught.

He'd grown like a weed in the last few years, and now he opened the weighty palace doors with ease, passing his loyal friend, John the Guardsman.

"Good morning, Your Grace."

"Morning, John."

John's stomach twinged on the mornings he'd see Duke Leon with his knapsack. While its contents were unknown, the increase in frequency of these trips caused him to worry. Flashbacks of the night he saw the bloodied outline of Duke Leon's fist in his trousers always resurfaced. Yet he stayed quiet, reconciling the worry by assuming that if the boy was involved in mischief, surely he would slip up and be caught.

Once out of John's view, Duke Leon snaked through the gardens until he reached the far side of the palace gates. Exiting the grounds using the front entrance was off-limits—it was too exposed. He threw the knapsack over the edge of the gate and stuck his foot into the groove he'd fashioned in the red brick a year ago to make the climb easier.

While still property of the Crown, this side's foliage spanned acres, instead of the sparse and heavily manicured gardens within the palace gates. As he opened his knapsack, he was shrouded by shadow, the thick treetops blotting out the morning sun. This wooded area was Duke Leon's favourite.

He set the trap, placing a bit of food he'd grabbed from the galley strategically on one side. He'd mastered the art of not killing the animal with the trap itself. The goal was to snag a leg so it would still be alive for him to put it out of its misery.

Now came the hardest part—waiting.

Back in the palace, the chefs made him breakfast to take to his room. His steps were light and carefree; he cherished these morning hours when the palace slumbered, because he was the only royal roaming its halls, the dominant force in spaces where he so often had to fight to be acknowledged.

He turned a corner and nearly crashed into Princess Theodora. She clutched her chest and caught her breath from the scare. "Leon. There you are. You weren't in your room, so I checked Prince Alfred's salon, but you weren't there either."

"Did you need me?"

"I just wanted to ask what time you wanted to take your piano lesson."

"After lunch. Is one all right?"

"See you then." She brushed his shoulder gently and carried on down the hall. He began scarfing down his breakfast before he reached his room, filling his stomach, and because of the rest of the morning's plans, also his heart.

A full belly, the trap set, and piano lessons with his favourite person. *Today is going to be a great day.*

"Have you told her you intend to accompany her back to Germany?" asked Jean-Claude.

"No," said Queen Eleanor, powdering her neck in front of the bedroom mirror. "She's my sister. I know she loves our time together here, but she loathes these halls even more than I do. Reminds her of our childhood."

Jean Claude filled the eighth piece of luggage with more of the Queen's belongings.

"You should take advantage of any chance you get to leave the palaces. You seem happier."

The air between them went still, and Queen Eleanor slowly turned around to face Jean Claude.

He caught this pause and peered upwards bashfully to meet her eyes. "Have I spoken out of turn?"

Her pinched lips turned into a slight smile. The tiniest snort escaped her nose, and she shook her head. "No. You're right."

It was as if admitting this truth, even to her trusted servant, pained her.

It was half past noon, and Duke Leon had retired to Prince Alfred's salon. He cosied up with a book, and though the crackling fire delighted him, he couldn't keep his focus fixed on the story. Flashes of an animal in the trap jarred his thoughts—imagining the life leaving its eyes when it lost enough blood, the look of peace that would follow, and the sweet release of endorphins coursing through his body.

He closed the book and left the salon, retrieved his knife from his room, and headed toward the eastern entrance. Impatience intermingled with curiosity, both reaching their zenith as he passed John the Guardsman.

The sight of Duke Leon twice during the same shift caused John's brow to furrow.

Duke Leon retraced his path to the woods, and still some distance away, he heard the whimpering of an animal that had been maimed by the trap. Excitement riddled him as he knelt in the lush grasses to find it was a black dog. No collar. It must have been a stray. The dog trembled and whimpered and held Duke Leon's gaze longingly.

A plea for help.

He smiled down at the dog, knowing that in a few moments he'd relieve it of its earthly suffering.

The last of Queen Eleanor's luggage was packed, and Jean Claude instructed two other servants on where it should be stored until departure. The Queen devoured the last few bites of her smoked haddock and eggs on toast. She'd slept in late and requested the chefs to bring her breakfast in her quarters rather than lunch at this hour.

A knock sounded at the door.

"Yes?" called Queen Eleanor, setting down her fork.

"It's me."

She recognised Princess Theodora's voice. "Come in."

Princess Theodora opened the double doors and entered the sitting room. Queen Eleanor turned in her chair and gave her a welcoming smile. A racket in the corridor proceeded the arrival of Jean Claude and two servants trailing him with a cart stacked with the Queen's luggage that towered above their heads. Princess Theodora tilted her head slightly as she witnessed this monstrosity enter the space, then turned back to her sister. "Another state trip so soon?"

"No," she said curtly. "I wouldn't allow it even if they demanded my presence."

Jean Claude shifted his weight uncomfortably, anticipating the interaction he knew would come. Even the Queen displayed a hint of reticence before speaking.

"I thought I'd accompany you when you return home to Villa Hohenlohe."

Princess Theodora's face pinched into a slight, strained smile, and although subtle, Queen Eleanor caught this reserve. "Forget it if it's too much trouble. I don't want to be a burden on you."

"No, not at all. You know I love your company," Theodora cajoled.

"Don't patronise me dear sister." Queen Eleanor rose from her chaise. "I saw the hesitancy in your face. You are my elder, but I will not accept an invitation laden with pity. So spare me the cordiality and be frank."

Princess Theodora forced an expression of calm upon her face. "I'd be happy to have you."

Queen Eleanor nodded. "Very well then." She almost admitted her gratitude to Princess Theodora, but worried it would make her appear weak. A prolonged silence filled the room, and Queen Eleanor realised that Theodora hadn't departed; she looked as if a frog was stuck in her throat.

"What is it?"

"I can't find Leon."

Queen Eleanor chuckled. "Well, he's bound to be around here somewhere."

"It's not like him to miss our piano lesson. I've checked all his normal spots, and I exhausted all my efforts first before coming here, as to not bother you…but I do have to admit I'm a bit worried."

The Queen registered her sister's discomfort and bridged the gap between them.

"Do you think he's left the grounds?" asked Princess Theodora.

"On occasion. But he's always asked permission beforehand."

"Where should we look?"

"Pardon my interruption," said Jean Claude, stepping forward. "But I have an idea of who will know his whereabouts."

John the Guardsman's stomach sank as Queen Eleanor approached, Princess Theodora trailing at her heels. He bowed to the Queen as she arrived.

"Have you seen Leon?"

"Yes, Your Majesty."

She snorted slightly. "And where might he have run off to?"

The Queen had pushed John into a quandary he never imagined having to face. One morning, after his shift change, he had walked the palace gates and seen where someone had carved out a foothold. The distance from the foothold to the top of the gate was around the height of Duke Leon. He'd brushed this knowledge aside to give his young friend the benefit of the doubt, but now he was face to face with his mother, the Queen, and he tried to hide the fact his knees were buckling.

"Let me show you," he said.

Duke Leon soared over the euphoric apex of the kill. The dog gutted, ribs split open, and blood covering his hands. Over the years, he'd developed a method of sneaking back into the palace without bringing back evidence of his slayings—he kept a rag in the knapsack that would rid him of most of the blood, and then he'd rinse his hands in one of the many palace fountains back in the gardens. Most important was the spade; he'd dig a makeshift grave for the animals, for he was shrewd enough to know that if carcasses started popping up outside the palace gates, the Crown would see it as some sort of threat, then the guards would be on high alert and patrol the area, and his killings would come to a halt.

He heard a rustling in the grass, and looked up to scan the horizon for activity. Nothing. He began wiping his hands with the rag and heard the rustling again, only this time, louder. With the spade, he hurriedly dug a grave for the dog because he realised the sounds couldn't have been an animal. The rustling seemed to emanate from multiple sources.

Come on, come on, he thought, pulse pounding in his neck, hacking away at the dirt.

The rustling became identifiable as footsteps, and a moment later Queen Eleanor rounded the corner, flanked by Princess Theodora, John, and two other guardsmen. His heart nearly stopped; he dropped the spade, grabbed the knapsack, and began to run.

"Guards!" shouted the Queen. "Stop him!"

Leon ran but had no idea where to go. Even if he hid on the streets of London, it wouldn't be long before some of the common folk recognised him. He wasn't one of them, and he loathed that he couldn't be, no matter how hard he tried. He sprinted to one of the footholds he'd fashioned on the palace gate to get back in and began pulling himself up the brick. Just as he reached the top edge, one of the guardsmen clasped his ankle and yanked him down. The wind was knocked from his lungs as he landed on his back, the two burly guardsmen dragging him by his shoulders back to the gruesome scene he was responsible for creating. He fought to evade their grip, but his attempts were futile.

The Queen's face scrunched up with rage as she stood over the dog's corpse. Princess Theodora clutched her open mouth, the miniscule bit of colour she naturally had fled her face in an instant. Tears pooled in Leon's eyes, for it was her reaction that truly pained him; the unmistakable sadness as she stared at the lifeless dog. Their eyes met for a split-second, and with one look it was as if she was speaking to him. *How could you do this to a helpless animal?*

Leon fought the tears back as he began to cry. For the first time since his killings began, he felt truly ashamed of his actions. This mortifying moment had swallowed up the years of bliss that preceded it.

The guards dropped him to his knees in front of the splayed dog corpse.

"So this is what you do when you disappear," spat Queen Eleanor.

He didn't say a word. He just cried.

Behind Queen Eleanor's eyes, the gears were turning.

"Guards. Draw your weapons and keep them held on Leon."

"Eleanor—" said Theodora.

"Don't you *dare* challenge my commands, sister."

The guards hoisted their rifles up, bemused. John's hands trembled as he aimed his weapon at his young friend, filled with a turbulent dichotomy of anger and sadness. After all these years, he wondered how many animals had been slain because of his negligence.

"This…" began Queen Eleanor, gesturing with an open hand to the corpse, "is far from the noble sport of hunting. What you've done here is clearly something else."

Leon blubbered, feeling the eyes of the guards and Princess Theodora digging into him.

"How vile. To kill an animal and to let it rot and go to waste…"

A hardness slid across Queen Eleanor's face. "Leon. Fetch your knife from the bag."

He craned his head up at his mother with confusion.

"*Now!*" she said, voice like thunder.

He slipped the knife into his hand and held it steady. A thought crossed his mind: *I could stab her right now as close as I am.*

But he knew the outcome—bullets filling his body. He probably wouldn't even be able to put a scratch on the Queen before all three guards turned him into Swiss cheese.

"Cut a piece of flesh from it," instructed Queen Eleanor.

Leon reluctantly chose a sinewy piece of thigh to begin hacking at it with his blade.

Princess Theodora glanced between the guards and Queen Eleanor, horrified. "What on Earth are you doing?" she rasped.

Queen Eleanor held a hand up to signal submission in her sister. She watched Leon carve the piece of meat with the tiniest beginnings of a smile tugging at the corners of her mouth. When he was finished, he stared up at her, half in shame, half in naivety of the meaning behind her instructions.

"Eat it."

The words seemed to sap the air of oxygen when uttered, for all those surrounding Leon froze, and along with them, the sounds of the world ground to an unsettling halt.

"You're serious," muttered Leon.

She never once let her gaze fall from his. She knew it would make her look weak. "Guards. If Leon tries to run, you have my permission to fire."

His soul deflated, gut trembling. He'd backed himself into a corner he couldn't escape from. All from being careless. From breaking his routine. As he let his head drop, he was face to face with the slain dog, whose mangled leg caught in the trap served as a blatant reminder that he too was trapped.

Predator turned prey.

"Now eat."

Leon brought the piece of raw flesh to his lips, the gamey scent of the freshly killed dog filling his nostrils before he could even take a bite. Princess Theodora turned away from the scene. She covered her mouth with a gloved hand and began to cry.

Leon closed his eyes as he chomped down on the piece of dog meat. The few coarse hairs that had stuck to the moist, bloodstained flesh exacerbated the chewy texture. The acrid flavour was enough to make him gag, bile rising at his throat.

"Swallow it."

The metallic taste of blood accompanying every bite made the Queen's demand seem impossible, but he chomped down quickly and repeatedly in attempt to get the meat soft enough to swallow.

He gulped it down.

The horrific moment was over. He fought the urge to retch by steadying his breath, soothing the bubbling nausea from the thought of what he'd just eaten.

"Stand down and return to your posts."

The guards dropped their weapons; as John passed and Leon met his eyes, he saw a mixture of disgust and sadness etched into the grooves of John's weathered skin. Theodora still faced away from the gruesome scene, hushing her cries with the sleeve of her dress. Leon dropped his head, staring at the carnage his hands had created. An incomprehensible humiliation seeped through him. Beneath it, a spark—an infinitesimally small ember of rage forming in the depths of his soul. And though remorse smothered this ember, one day it would reignite and turn into a blaze.

Only then would he process the truth of who held the flints.

After Queen Eleanor, Princess Theodora, and the guards had left, he finished digging a shallow grave for the dog before returning to the palace. He stared at his feet the entire way back, intentionally avoiding the eastern entrance, unable to face the reproach in John the Guardsman's gaze another time.

Despite his head being tucked down as he navigated the palace solely by memory, his hearing was on high alert. The moment he heard a pair of footsteps rustle or an airy whisper nearby, he'd dart down an adjacent hall. He feared the possibility that word of his heinous act had quickly travelled through the palace.

Once he made it back to his bedroom unnoticed, his stomach broke the quiet with a gurgling groan; he'd been so preoccupied with the anticipatory high of a potential kill that he'd forgotten to eat.

Another growl ripped through his gut.

While he was petrified of facing those in the palace who might have become privy to his demons, his hunger strongarmed the fear. He ditched his room and zipped through the halls, internally pleading his favourite chef, who'd given him vegetables for the rabbits over the years, was working. In the final stretch to the galley, something made him stop in his tracks.

Voices. The first of which sounded irate, and the other more hushed. Duke Leon shelved his hunger for the time being to placate his curiosity and followed the voices growing louder, trembling as he realised their source.

The Queen's chamber.

He inched towards the chamber doors, gingerly placing one foot in front of the other to avoid making a sound. He glanced around to ensure he was alone before placing an ear against the wood.

"…and what might you suggest we do instead?"

Mother, he thought.

"Eleanor. He's still a child," said Theodora.

"You're going to stand there and tell me you believe what you saw today was the work of a child?"

Duke Leon gulped hard at the silence that followed.

"That's what I thought," said Eleanor.

"Regardless of what I believe, what you've suggested as a solution is cruel."

"He needs help, Theodora."

"And throwing him in a looney bin suffices as help?"

"If he's capable of doing that to helpless animals, imagine what he could do once he bores of them. He may decide to direct that violence onto a person if they cross him."

"Don't speak of such things," gasped Theodora.

"You should know by now, dear sister, that I do not proclaim such things on a whim. In my conversations with the staff today it seems Leon has been outwitting them for years. He's a sharp one. And if you had witnessed that level of cunning in your lifetime it would frighten you as it does me."

Is she really scared of me? Duke Leon wondered.

"He needs love."

"What he needs is discipline," spat Queen Eleanor, voice rising. "If it weren't for my daughter's mistake, we wouldn't be in this predicament in the first place. He doesn't deserve this life because he's not truly a royal. And now it's obvious as he's becoming a man that his father's sins have stained him."

"You're sick!"

He heard a few muted footsteps within the long pause.

"If it were *anyone* else but you, Theodora, who spoke to me so freely I'd have them exiled. Not even Alfred dared so before his passing. I'm going to have the boy sent to a psychiatric hospital. If you feel so strongly on the matter, you can take him into your care."

The hull of the boat groaned as it rose and fell over the billowy ocean waves; with every lurch forward, the bow slapped against the peaks of the whitecaps, causing a salty spray to splatter the windows. Thick clouds hung low in a bruised sky, dappled with blotches of black and blue. The chill of autumn was more pronounced out at sea, and Duke Leon wasn't sure what to make of the ominous backdrop for their crossing from Dover to Calais. Was it symbolic of leaving the darkness of his past behind on the shores of Britain, or a glimpse of a stormier future to come?

The croaking gulls pulled him from the thought, and the sight of them playfully swooping around the vessel brought him joy. He tried to keep his focus outside the cabin windows, for if his gaze drifted inward, he'd be face-to-face with Eugenie and Lysander who sat across from him, casting perpetual scorn.

It pained Duke Leon that they saw him as an invader, clueless to the reason behind his return with them to Baden-Baden. But that didn't matter.

Today was a new start.

A second chance at a normal life.

And that thought made him the happiest he'd been in years.

Theodora sat at his side. Her presence seemed to keep the suffocating emptiness that plagued him at bay; he wasn't sure if it would return, but he prayed it wouldn't, for that feeling was the harbinger of the bloodshed he brought into the world.

Theodora and Duke Leon hadn't spoken much since she delivered the news that he'd be staying with her in Baden-Baden. He feared she'd let him come purely out of obligation to Queen Eleanor. This possibility frightened him the most, because if she now viewed him the way Mother and the others did, he wasn't sure he could cope with that level of bereavement.

He took a deep breath of the briny ocean air and tried to imagine the waves washing away his ill thoughts.

Everything will be okay in the end, he mused.

Just then, Theodora gently placed her hand on top of his.

The smallest beginnings of a smile tugged at his lips.

CHAPTER 12
THE WAY OUT

No one knew whether today would end in success or failure, but Arun hoped the extensive preparation that had gone into this plan would help when it came time to execute it. Four days had passed since Arun awoke from the dream. Its lucidity told his soul that the crumbling section of the drainpipe really did exist, and if he could just hold his breath long enough to swim through, he'd get to feel that ecstatic sensation again: breaking the surface of the river and inhaling the fresh, outside air. But this time, it would be in the waking world.

It would be *real*.

Gavin and Fiona had said it was dangerous to base an escape plan off a dream. Even Craig cast some doubts. James warned against trying to escape at all. Part of Arun worried that he was reading too much into it, but then he remembered the man with no skin.

He admitted he'd never had premonitions before that nightmare, but he also imagined that something bigger was at play here. Something beyond the physical realm.

He just didn't know what.

To improve their chances of escape, they formulated two escape plans to carry out simultaneously. The first was the drainpipe to the frozen room. Arun, holding steadfast in his belief in the dream, offered to attempt the swim alone. The second plan was to use the stairwell that led to the shed.

The barrier separating the children from escape was the stairwell gate lock. Tiny and metallic, Arun reeled at the thought that something so small had the power to keep them imprisoned. As a group, they had pushed open the false wall of their room many times—it took the strength of four of them to do so. They found three other holding rooms identical to theirs. At one end of the hall was the frozen room, and the other, the stairwell.

The only chance they had to escape, using the stairwell, was if they found a way to study the locking mechanism of the gate. Gavin volunteered, being the smallest of the four lads. A dangerous task, considering they had to wait until Al came down into the basement to feed them for Gavin to study the mechanism, while it was unlocked and opened, quickly enough without getting caught.

Gavin had waited patiently in the holding room parallel to theirs for Al's arrival, nervous in the knowledge that he was only allotted fifteen to thirty seconds at most to study the stairwell gate lock. He heard the heavy footsteps, pulse pounding in his throat. He watched as Al approached the false basement wall, pushed it open, and slid inside.

Go, he thought. He scurried to the lock and studied the mechanism. One half was a simple metal latch, and the other a concave opening for the latch to attach to. He imagined if you were to push the two sides of the lock together, they would catch. *Fifteen seconds*, he counted. As he stared at the open lock, a part of him thought he should just make a run for it. Sprint to freedom and find help. But would he be able to get out in time? Would anyone hear his screams? He shrugged the thought aside and stuck to the plan; the day of the escape would be more successful for all of them if they did this right. He hurried back to the adjacent room and waited for Al to return the way he came. Once he reentered the stairwell, he heard the gate lock close with a *click*.

The click, he thought. *How will we rig the lock if Al is used to hearing the click?*

When Gavin had brought this information back to the others, Craig suggested they use thread from the blanket to tie a loop around the latch itself. That way they could pull it open once it was closed.

It would be like picking a lock without the pick.

That was the plan of action they had decided on as a group yesterday. Today, they would execute it. Last night Arun had prayed for what felt like hours that their plan would succeed, until he finally met the blackness of slumber.

And now he wondered if perhaps he hadn't prayed hard enough. For this morning's attempt had failed. Gavin had been in position, thread in hand, but when Al came down, Craig's attempt at getting his attention didn't work. He simply threw their breakfast in the room and ignored Craig. After Al took the stairwell back to the surface, Gavin returned to the room, head hung low.

None of them exchanged a word.

All they could do was what they had done for days. Wait.

And now more than ever, the moments that met the five children in Al's basement slipped by with an excruciating slowness as they waited for the next escape attempt.

Dinner.

Stu taking Margaret off the case poured fuel on the fire still burning in her soul to find the lads. Holding the forged station call log that corroborated Al's version of events gave her newfound clarity. Al's tendrils of influence ran deeper than she ever could have imagined, and every night since that discovery she had lain sleepless, wondering how she could ever discover the truth about Al.

Despite the entire department turning their back on her, Gordon hadn't. They were set to meet at half past six, and she still had an hour to kill. Margaret passed the time the same way she had been since being thrown off the case.

Trailing Al.

Unable to use her patrol car, she borrowed Walter's car instead, with the caveat of having to take him to and from work. An easy compromise for her given the situation. But the past three days spying on Al from afar hadn't borne anything of value.

In the idle time Margaret had, she wondered if her suspicions of Al's guilt were getting the better of her. Even the most miniscule details struck her mind with great importance. Like when Al walked down the drive to fetch his car for his morning and evening trips, he would enter that shed, always spending three to five minutes. Sometimes he entered and left with a red toolbox in hand; other times, he carried the same black satchel she had seen the other day.

What on earth is he doing in that shed?

It was observations like these that Margaret fixated on. And she hoped that in time, one of them would lead her to finding the lads.

The baritone voice of Dr. Ian MacQueen droning from Margaret's car radio was welcome relief from the dreadful thoughts plaguing her day in and day out. She wondered if she felt that way simply because the sentiments weren't her own. Truth be told, the doctor's twice daily updates on the typhoid outbreak in Aberdeen were far from peachy. What had begun with just a few infections had now grown into nearly four hundred cases since the end of May. The typhoid hadn't left the borders of Aberdeen, yet Margaret worried they were dealing with an infection of their own. And like a pathogen, it too was invisible, and she wondered how long those who were sick could hide it.

Out of the corner of her eye, Aniqa came into view. She strolled down the street wearing a long-sleeved dress and slowed as she approached Al's house. She checked her surroundings with a sweeping glance—her eyes settled on Walter's truck.

"Shit!" Margaret slid down in the seat. She waited a few moments before peeking out the windshield. Aniqa strode toward the truck with a furrowed brow. Margaret quickly hopped out of the truck to face her. The last thing she wanted was for Al to come outside and realise what vehicle she'd been using this whole time.

"Are you following me?"

"Nae. I've been watching him." Margaret nodded in the direction of Al's house.

Aniqa huffed. "You can't just let it go, can you?"

"Not when I believe your son's life is on the line."

Those words caused an emptiness to slide across Aniqa's dark eyes. She snorted, shaking her head.

"I'm sorry…that was a crass way to word it. But what if I'm right? Everything I said back at the station was true. I swear it. I know you probably think I'm messed in the head for sticking to my guns but I'm not going to stop until I find him and Craig—"

"Just stop," said Aniqa. She wiped her misty eyes with her sleeve. "Stu told me about what happened. Why you are the way you are."

Margaret froze, petrified where she stood.

"How you didn't listen to your gut on that domestic call and go back. And then that little girl got beaten to death."

Flashes of that night lit up behind Margaret's eyes. Her lower lip trembled as the emotions she had fought to keep at bay over the past sixteen years flooded her mind.

Aniqa leaned in toward Margaret and held her finger in front of her chest. "So forgive me if I'm appalled at your inability to admit that your judgement might be clouded by the fact my son's missing case is your only chance to try and right your wrongs."

Aniqa's words broke Margaret's soul into a million pieces. She desperately tried to hold herself together in front of her.

"And how will you feel if you're wrong?" continued Aniqa. "What if

Arun and Craig's kidnapper is still out there, and you're so fixated on believing that we've all been duped by Al that you ignore everything else? Think how much regret you'll feel then."

Margaret kept her eyes glued to the ground.

"No," she muttered. "The girl died because I didn't listen to my instinct. I'm—I'm listening this time…"

"Are we having an extra guest tonight?" called Al from his garden.

His booming voice snapped Margaret from her depressive daze, and her eyes flicked back to Aniqa. "You can't go in there," she whispered.

Aniqa stared at her with pity. "You've truly gone mad."

"Aniqa, please—"

She turned and headed toward Al's gate.

Al gave Margaret a smile as he let Aniqa in. "I'd invite you in for dinner, but I have a feeling you'd ruin it with your conspiracies."

Margaret held her steely gaze on Al until he disappeared inside with Aniqa. She waited a few minutes before returning to the truck.

She glanced at her wristwatch—6:15. As uncomfortable as it made her thinking about Aniqa's dinner inside Al's house, she had to be logical. If Al really was who she believed him to be, he would be an idiot to harm the missing lad's own mother.

Margaret shifted the truck into gear and headed to Gordon's hotel.

It was time. Half an hour had passed since Al brought down their dinner, and Craig had successfully kept him in the room long enough for Gavin to thread the loop around the lock clasp.

Fiona stood shivering next to Arun on the dock and chewed her nails. She nestled her arm against him for the body heat. "Are you ready?" she asked.

He nodded. "If something happens and Al comes after me, save yourself."

"Don't say that. You're going to make it out."

He rested a hand on her forearm and smiled. Over the past week he'd enjoyed her company more each passing day. Her kind blue eyes always seemed to sparkle, matted yellow hair sprung out in every direction from nearly a week without a wash, but beneath the dirt and grime, Arun knew she was beautiful.

Craig propped open the doors to the frozen room. "We're about to head up. Ye remember the signal?"

Arun held up the stone Craig had given him. "I bang this against the drainpipe to let you know I made it through."

Craig turned to Fiona. "When I swam to the bottom last night, I counted how many seconds it takes to get to the grate. Arun should get through and signal us in thirty seconds at most."

"Got it," said Fiona.

Gavin stood behind Craig, listening intently. Arun saw him crack a smile. He shifted his gaze to James, who stood a few feet behind Gavin, staring listlessly at the wall. He looked like all the life had been sucked from his eyes, and all that remained was his hollow stare.

"Are you all right?" asked Arun.

James snapped out of his daze, shifting glances between them. "I'm fine."

"We need you to be focused," said Craig.

"I know."

Craig continued explaining things to the group, and Arun noticed that after a few moments, James fell back into his trance.

"Would you like some wine?" asked Al from the kitchen.

"No thanks. Do you mind if I light up?"

"Not at all. I'll join you in a minute."

Aniqa lit a cigarette and took a long drag. The sizzling sounds and fragrant smells of Al's cooking carried over from the kitchen. She caught herself marvelling at the detail-work of his home—ornate fixtures and antique decorations. Each room was painted with earth tones, and it made her feel calm, just as Al's presence did. The longer she studied the space, the more she wondered how a man as handsome and kind as Al didn't have a partner to share it with.

Al whipped around the corner with two steaming plates of food. "Dinner is served," he said, setting the plates down and joining her.

Aniqa's mouth watered as she stared down at what looked like a creamy vegetable curry. "How did you know I'm not fond of meat?"

"I didn't," Al said with a smile. "I just don't eat it myself."

Aniqa gave him a queer look. "I've never met a Scotsman who doesn't eat meat."

"Well, I guess I'm not much of a good Scotsman then, am I?" He swallowed a bite of the curry. "I can tell by your accent you're not from Scotland either."

"Good ear. I went to an international school in Bangladesh and lived in London the first five years I was in England."

She chewed another bite and processed his statement. "You said *either*. If you're not from Scotland, then where are you from?"

"I guess you'll just have to find out," Al said with a smug wink.

Their plates were almost empty. Al poured himself another heavy-handed glass of wine and scooted closer to Aniqa. He poured a little in the empty glass that sat in front of Aniqa, and before she could open her mouth to protest—

"Just for a cheers."

She obliged, holding up the glass. "Cheers to?" she asked with a playful grin blossoming.

"To new friends."

"To new friends," repeated Aniqa.

They clinked the glasses and Aniqa took a sip. She fished another cigarette out of the pack and looked around for the lighter. It had fallen off the table; Al picked it up before she could and flicked the lighter, holding the flame up to light Aniqa's cigarette for her. The two held each other's gazes the whole time, even while she took the first drag.

Al scooted his chair over again to the point where he was practically side-by-side with Aniqa. Stomach in knots, he hoped she didn't notice his nervousness. He gulped down another acidy swig of the wine before gingerly brushing the hair away from her face, tucking it behind her ear.

She stared back into his eyes with a warmness, an intensity he'd never seen from her before.

"You have the same eyes," he whispered.

It took a few seconds for the alarm bells in Aniqa's head to sound. "*Who* has the same eyes?"

"My—my mother," he sputtered. "She had that same…fire in her eyes you do."

Al placed his hand on hers and she pulled away.

She hurriedly shoved her cigarettes in her purse and stood up. "I more than appreciate the delicious meal, Al, but I'd better be on my way."

"Why the hurry? At least stay for dessert."

Aniqa shook her head, emotion welling up within her. "No thank you." Guilty thoughts bombarded her as she put on her coat. *Your son is missing and you're here on a date. You are an awful mother! You should be ashamed!* What bothered Aniqa the most was that her conscience was voiced by her mother. She couldn't escape her scolding tongue even after half a decade of her being dead.

"Did I say something wrong?" asked Al, following Aniqa through the living room.

"No, I just shouldn't be here. It's not right."

"Please, just—"

"Goodbye, Al," said Aniqa, closing the front door behind her and disappearing down the street.

Arun hugged Fiona tightly. "I'll get help. I promise."

"I know you will," she said softly.

He released her and balanced on the floating dock of the frozen room. The loud *clack* of the stairwell gate latch echoed through the basement. Craig, James, and Gavin waited in front of the now open gate.

"It'll take us thirty seconds to get to the exit. Go then."

"Aye," shouted Arun.

They disappeared up the stairwell to the shed.

"*Īśbara āpanāra sāthē thākabēna,*" muttered Arun. He closed his eyes and began counting. "…fifteen, sixteen, seventeen…" He visualised the crumbling gap in the drainpipe from his dream, and breathed deeply to prepare for the lack of oxygen he would feel below.

"…twenty-eight, twenty-nine, thirty."

Arun dove into the water, letting the weight of the rock pull him toward the bottom faster. He kicked his feet ferociously, uncertain of when he'd reach the pipe. His ears popped and the water became even colder the deeper he went. After a few moments, his hands met the metal rim of the drainpipe, and he attempted to calm his mind as he began to swim through, hoping he'd find the crumbling grate he had seen only in slumber.

Craig and Gavin sprang up the same stairwell that had brought them to Al's basement a week earlier. They nearly slammed into the exit door that led to the alleyway, and they both began shouting at the top of their lungs.

"Help!" cried Craig and Gavin repeatedly, pounding on the door.

After a few seconds, Craig's face blanched. "The door," he said, breathless. "He covered the slats of the shed door."

Gavin shook his head, chest rising and falling with every breath. "No," he mumbled. "No, no, no, no."

The original slatted, wooden door which Gavin had slipped his hand through to unlock had been boarded up. No light poured in from outside. Their screams for help were useless, for not a soul on Holm Farm Road could hear them.

"He's going to have to kill us," croaked Gavin. Pale-faced and choking on emotion, he stared up at Craig, searching for answers.

But Craig didn't respond. Eyes empty, the ember of hope that had filled them in the days prior during the plotting of their escape was being squelched by the second.

Scurrying footsteps made Craig and Gavin snap their heads around. James bounded down the stairwell and locked the gate shut when he reached the bottom. Craig sprinted after him. A frenzied look of desperation was all Craig saw on James' face as he disappeared down the hall.

Craig cursed him and began fiddling with the string to re-open the latch.

"Thirty-nine, forty, forty-one…" Every second past thirty caused the knot in Fiona's gut to ratchet tighter. She stared into the inky water and listened carefully for any sign of the rock clanging against the drainpipe.

Beneath the surface, Arun's knee was stuck halfway through the crumbling grate. As he kicked and pulled and shimmied with his free limbs, precious oxygen was being expended rapidly. Rock still in hand, he dug it into the ground as a means to pull himself forward. But each time, the rock slipped loose. His lungs flexed inwards as the starvation for air became worse by the second. Terror clutched his floundering heart with its unforgiving grip as he realised that he couldn't bang the rock against the bars for help…

Because Fiona would think he'd made it through.

They were so confident the plan would work they'd never thought of a danger signal.

"Fiona!" shouted Craig.

"Craig," called Fiona, still staring into the water. She heard footsteps from the hallway and glanced over her shoulder. James was yanking a string that hung along the wall, panting wildly, and staring up at the ceiling.

"They're trying to escape! They're trying to escape, Da!"

"Craig!" Fiona hollered. "Something's wrong!"

The bell in the dining room reverberated through the house with a shrill *ding* that didn't stop ringing once it began. A chill raced down Al's spine as he tried to imagine what was going on down there. He ran to his kitchen closet and threw back the antique rug that covered the trap door to the basement. He needed to use it to reach the kids faster, having avoided it until now because he didn't want them to know it existed.

Once the *click* sound signalled the latch had unhooked, Craig barrelled down the hall.

"Stop! You bastard!"

He pounced on James, shimmying his way on top of him until he straddled his chest; Craig pummelled him repeatedly in the face. Gavin watched his brother being beaten—eyes vacant. James cackled in between punches, and as Craig bloodied his swelling face with each subsequent punch, the laughter only made him angrier.

"Craig, stop!" cried Fiona. "Arun hasn't made it!"

Craig's arms went limp. It was almost like Fiona could see him mentally calculating the time that had passed, and she watched fear replace the blood draining from his blanched face.

"Two minutes," she whimpered. Craig sprung from James and ran across the dock, diving into the water. He swam down to the drainpipe and felt the lower half of Arun's body sticking through the grate.

He's limp, Craig thought.

He had to make a split-second decision. Pull Arun back into the frozen room or push him through and hope he made it to the surface. Craig found where Arun's knee had caught and pulled the corroding grate bars back, freeing him. With a big shove, he pushed him through. He tried to swim through after him but realised quickly that his shoulders were too broad to fit, so he floated back to the surface of the frozen room.

"I stopped them, Da," said James.

Craig threw his arms on the edge of the dock, sucking in air, and watched as Al's eyes glanced between the four of them.

His gaze fell to meet Craig's. "Where's Arun?"

A smug smile tugged at the corners of Craig's lips.

Al's eyes bulged and he dashed out of the frozen room.

Craig pulled himself onto the dock and chased after Al, following him into their holding room. Al dangled from the rungs of a trap door ladder; Craig jumped and caught the bottom rung and began to climb. Once Al made it through, he purposely waited until Craig reached the top rung, then smashed his fingers with a forceful stomp of his boot.

Craig yelped, pulling back his hand, now hanging only by one. Al stepped on it without a second thought. Craig slipped off the rung, falling back onto the cold basement floor.

Al quickly hoisted up the metal rungs, locked the trap door, and covered it with the rug.

Adrenaline surged through his veins as he imagined Arun banging on the door of a neighbour's house and screaming for help. Al spun the lock dial of his black metal safe until it clicked; from it he retrieved a syringe and a vial of Droperidol. He carefully syphoned the liquid into the syringe and covered its tip with a piece of felt before putting it into his lapel. He then grabbed the black wig and ran out the back entrance of his home, headed to his cargo van.

Temperate June air tickled Arun's back and neck. Cold water lapped at his skin. The muted gurgles of the running river filled his ears.

Sensations—*I am alive.*

He jolted upright and sucked in a deep breath of air, violently coughing up water at the same time.

"I made it," he gasped. *"I made it!"*

Arun looked around; he was floating in an eddy right beneath Al's house. He thrashed his arms and legs, swam out of the eddy, and the swirling current took him farther downstream along the River Ayr, away from Al's house. As he fought to get to the other side of the riverbank, he swallowed down gulps of water in between choking breaths.

He hoisted himself onto the muddy riverbank and began to climb it, slipping a few times on the wet grass. He dug his fingers into the viscous mud to hurry to the top, and once he rose to his feet and saw what faced him, his soul deflated.

Arun stood at the beginning of what made up the outskirts of Catrine.

He'd been so preoccupied with getting away from Al's house that he'd climbed up the rural side of the riverbank, where houses were few and far between. The side that ran adjacent to Holm Farm Road. He scanned the horizon and saw chimney smoke just over the hillside.

Run! screamed his subconscious, prodding his waking mind with a red-hot fire iron of adrenaline. His trembling legs flurried into action as he ran down the footpath.

"Help! Can anyone hear me?"

His cries were met with silence. Within that silence came the steady growl of a vehicle's engine. Arun's heart leapt out of his chest as he tried to pinpoint the direction the sound was coming from.

He paused for a moment to listen.

It grew louder until a black van crested the horizon. He waved his arms wildly and approached the road to get the driver's attention.

"Stop! Help me, please!"

The van accelerated as it neared, and every bit of the elation he'd felt moments earlier flatlined. Long black hair flowed over the shoulders of the person driving the van. Arun gasped and turned to run for his life. The emptiness of the rolling green hills around him filled him with a dread unlike he'd ever felt before.

It was as if he were trapped in a nightmare, and the only two people in it were him and Al.

"Help! Help me, please!" he shrieked at the top of his lungs as he ran towards the chimney smoke. He heard the car door slam behind him, followed by another pair of footsteps in the grass. He didn't know whether to cry, fight, or to give up. An irreconcilable mixture of emotions ran rampant within Arun, but with each breath, the sharp reminder that he was breathing *outside* air reinvigorated his survival instinct, pushing his burning muscles to go on.

He glanced over his shoulder to see Al gaining on him, and then suddenly felt his foot hitting a piece of uneven ground followed by a grotesque *pop* of his ankle. He yelped in pain and tried to keep hobbling with the injury, but Al tackled him to the ground, slamming a cupped hand over his mouth. Tears streamed down his face as he stared up at Al through blurry vision. The black hair of Al's wig formed a misshapen perimeter that eclipsed his view of the grey light of day. He sobbed at the realisation that no one had heard his muffled cries, and then a pinch in his neck caused him to wince, and it was followed by black.

Nothingness.

A harsh chemical smell jolted Arun awake as Al took a piece of fabric away from his nose.

"*There he is,*" said Al in a singsong trill, a disturbing contrast to the crazed look etched into his face. "Welcome back."

Arun tried to move; his wrists and ankles smacked against chain links strapping him to a chrome table. A quick look around made him realise he was in *that* room again.

Where he met the man with no skin.

"Are ye going to kill me?"

Al paused, mulling over his answer. "Death is no punishment. It's too easy." His maniacal grin soured into a scowl. "I have something better." He disappeared from the room. Hardly a moment passed before the shrill cries of Fiona and the helpless pleas of Gavin echoed from down the hall.

"No, no! Let me go!" Craig's blood-curdling screams formed a pit of nausea in Arun's stomach. "Burn in Hell!"

Arun closed his eyes, trying to ignore Al's grunts intermingled with the sound of Craig being dragged down the cement floor of the hall. The scraping grew louder, and Al and Craig rounded the corner. Craig tried to squirm free, but Al pinned him down and started duct taping his wrists together, all while Craig shouted expletives, spat at him, and did everything he could to break free. Al shifted and knelt on his shins, taping his ankles together. He hoisted Craig onto the surgical table next to Arun.

It was in that exact moment that reality hit Arun—they were both going to die in here.

Tears slipped from his eyes as he thought of never seeing his mum again, of the pain she'd face having to bury him, and of wondering what death would feel like.

He turned to face Craig.

"I'm sorry," he said. "It's my fault."

Craig caught his breath, and Arun could see in his emerald eyes that he too had accepted the same fate he'd just realised a moment ago.

"No," he said, panting. "James ruined it. He pulled the tripwire."

Arun furrowed his brow, shaking his head. "Why would he—"

"Because he's a bloody kiss ass. I tried to tell ye."

Craig's personality shining through couldn't help but make him smile. The sound of metal clanging together came from the other side of the room. Al was elbow deep in a large black bag. "…if it weren't for that goddamn nosy cop, I'd have this over with by now…" mumbled Al. His mutterings were that of a mad man.

Al returned to their sides with a meat cleaver. The lads writhed at the sight of the gleaming blade.

Craig's eyes bulged and his breathing intensified. "I'm sorry, Arun," he said, quivering. "I should have been a better friend."

Arun blubbered at these words. "You're my only friend."

Al cocked his hand back, holding the blade high above his head, staring straight at Arun. "You're going to pay for what you've done."

Arun closed his eyes and heard the whoosh of the blade slicing through the air. A wet thud and a cracking split came after; Craig cried out the most guttural scream he'd ever heard. Arun opened his eyes to see Al pull the cleaver out from Craig's shinbone. Thick maroon blood seeped from the gaping wound and spilled off the metal table onto the floor, his calf almost split in two. The mixture of Craig's shrieks of pain and Arun's hoarse pleas for Al to stop was an indecipherable agony that only the two boys could understand. Al raised the cleaver again and sank it into Craig's stomach and chest over, and over, and over.

"No!" Arun bawled, his throat raw. More blood trickled over the table's edge, and Craig's gaze drifted over to him. His skin was now a pasty grey, the shimmer from his green eyes fading. Arun held the gaze of his only friend, his dearest friend, and hoped the look of love he gave was enough to comfort him, even if it be just for a moment.

Craig, choking on blood, mouthed the words, *"You will get out."*

Arun nodded, sobbing silently, and watched the life leave Craig's eyes.

The room fell silent, and Arun couldn't perceive anything other than the pain he felt carving a hole in the centre of his chest. For what felt like eternity, everything around him went black. Al wasn't there. Nor could he smell the sickly metallic scent of blood all over the floor.

"Look what you've done." Al's voice brought him back to reality. He held the knife, pointing at Craig's lifeless body, and he almost looked sad. Al walked behind him and grabbed the back of his head, forcing it towards Craig.

"Look what you've done!" he bellowed, spittle flying from his lips. Al slid between the tables and used the cleaver to slice a chunk out of Craig's thigh. The red flesh oozed between Al's forefinger and thumb, and he stared at Arun with disdain. "Eat it," he uttered.

"No."

"Eat it or you'll never leave this room."

"What's wrong with you?" spat Arun.

A fire lit behind Al's eyes. "What's wrong with me? Look what you did!" He waved the cleaver wildly over Craig's body. "You killed this innocent boy and now you must learn your lesson. Eat it!"

Arun protested but Al dropped the cleaver and lurched toward him, piece of flesh in hand, and Arun thrashed against his restraints, attempting to knock over the table. Al pried open Arun's mouth with his free hand; he tried biting, but it was pointless against the thick, blood-soaked gardeners' gloves. "Eat it!" Al shrieked endlessly, trembling with anger, and forced the bloody piece of human meat into Arun's mouth.

When Fiona, Gavin, and James saw Arun slip back into the room, they didn't utter a word. His clothes were peppered with blood spatter, his black eyes empty.

James was in one corner of the room, Gavin in another, with Fiona sitting next to him. Arun acted as if none of the other children were there. He simply lay in the middle of the floor and curled up into a foetal position.

Fiona cast a glance at Gavin. He nodded solemnly. She pressed her lips together and held back the tears. She stood up, grabbed the only blanket in the room, and covered Arun. Then, she lay behind him and slipped under the blanket, curling her arm around his waist.

Arun wondered if he'd ever feel anything again besides the iciness that permeated from his core. But after a while, a new sensation lulled his bruised body and broken spirit to sleep.

Fiona's warmth.

CHAPTER 13
THE SPIDER'S WEB

Kensington Palace
1938

A faint shout in the distance pulled Queen Eleanor from her slumber. Her eyes flicked across the ceiling, and she went from groggy to alert in a second, for an unknown voice was scratching at her subconscious—*something is wrong.*

She whipped back the covers and followed the noise until it grew louder, heart pounding as the same shout that awoke her became clearer, and she feared she'd identified who it came from. Her pace quickened as she pushed open the doors to the palace terrace, the dewy mist of morning clinging to the white silk pyjamas the Spitalfields weavers had gifted her.

John the Guardsman held back Sir Charles, struggling to pull him away from the palace gardens. A feverish expression slid across Sir Charles' face the moment he laid eyes on Queen Eleanor.

"I want to see my son!"

She chewed on the inside of her lip as her eyes flicked from Sir Charles to the passersby far off in the distance on the streets of Kensington.

"You don't have a son," said Queen Eleanor. "And even if you did, he wouldn't be living here."

"Let me see him!" His cries crackled with desperation. His eyes were reddened and moist with a sadness cloaked behind anger.

Queen Eleanor didn't respond, just glowered at him like an insect who had invaded her garden.

"I hope you hang in chains!"

Sir Charles spat at the ground, trembling beneath the hefty grip of John, just as the southern entrance guardsman barrelled into him and aided John in pulling him away. He sputtered and slandered the Queen until the commotion faded away as the guards dragged him off the palace grounds.

Queen Eleanor returned through the terrace door and came face to face with a stony Princess Edith. Her hands were clenched in front of her dress with a white-knuckled grip, as if she were teetering between holding herself back or clawing her mother's eyes out.

"You could have at least had the heart to tell him."

"So he can take the next ferry across the Channel to shout outside Theodora's gates?"

Princess Edith stared back at her, unblinking. "Regardless of whether it's valid in your mind, he *is* his father. You can't keep him away forever."

"I have no intention to do so. I told you the night the letter arrived that you were to ensure it didn't happen again."

"A task I did reluctantly."

It was then Queen Eleanor noticed the dark bags under Princess Edith's eyes were more pronounced than she remembered, and her skin was an ashen grey.

"And what about the hundreds of letters that have——"

"I have *tried!*"

Queen Eleanor's brow furrowed, and she clicked her tongue.

"Well it seems your attempts have failed."

Princess Edith sighed, failing to produce a quick response.

"As I thought," said Queen Eleanor, walking past Princess Edith.

Queen Eleanor donned street clothes: a black wig, a pair of sunglasses, and a headscarf as she walked down Courtfield Gardens. She fought back a smile as she navigated the crowded street; it amused her being the most beloved figurehead of a nation, yet invisible to all who passed. With a brown leather briefcase in hand, she climbed the steps to 20 Courtfield Gardens and knocked.

An eye replaced the light slipping through the peephole.

Sir Charles opened the door. He glared at her, then craned his head out, scanning the street to both sides of her, and spotted one of the guardsmen dressed in common clothes. "I see you've brought company."

"He's here just in case you try to kill me," she said with a smile. "But I'll give you the benefit of the doubt and make him stand outside the door."

The Queen's cheery demeanour caused his brow to furrow. Just this morning she'd glared at him as if she wanted him dead.

"Are you going to let me in, or shall we stay out here?"

He stepped out of the way and let Queen Eleanor pass. She whipped around the foyer, taking a few cursory glances at the decorations and sighed, then plopped into an armchair. "I see the Crown's money isn't a precursor to good taste."

Sir Charles ignored her insult. "I know why you're here."

"Do you?"

"To tell me the same thing you've told me since Edith birthed our son."

Queen Eleanor pressed her lips together, shifting in her seat, and the playfulness in her expression began to sour. "You are correct." She kicked the leather briefcase that she'd sat next to her, and it slid half the distance between them.

"What's in there?"

"Fifty thousand pounds. But you can only have it on one condition."

"That I may never see my son."

"*And,*" said Queen Eleanor, leaning in his direction, "you have to leave London." She paused. "Permanently."

"You think you can just throw money at me and I'll disappear?"

"Believe it or not…Yes, in fact I do."

The Queen's response was laden with a whimsical tone that made Sir Charles sick to his stomach. "That's what's wrong with you. With the Crown. You think you can simply throw money at your problems to make them go away."

He stood up and kicked the suitcase; it went sliding until it hit the Queen's shins.

"I would never trade my own blood for money. Now get out of my house."

Sir Charles stared down at the Queen, jaw clenched. The indifference in her expression made him wonder if she'd heard him at all. It was almost as if, to her ears, his vehement denial was nothing more than the wind quietly whistling through a cracked window frame.

Her eyes flicked from the floor to meet his gaze. "I must warn you," she said. "This offer will only be given to you once."

He snorted. "Good. Then I shan't have to deny it a second time."

Queen Eleanor rose to her feet without breaking their shared gaze, eyes like daggers, and snatched the briefcase.

Sir Charles opened the door and gestured for her to exit. "Eleanor," he said.

She turned back to him halfway down the steps, raising her brows.

"I hope to see the day your money becomes the source of your misery."

Queen Eleanor exhaled the tiniest of laughs and disappeared into the streets of Kensington.

Sir Charles hurled his belongings into the duffel on his bed—clothes, toiletries, and the valuables in his safe, just in case he needed to sell them for sustenance along the way. The moment Queen Eleanor left, he'd gone to the bank, withdrawn everything, and closed the account. Now he was mere minutes away from leaving not only London but Britain altogether.

For he knew Queen Eleanor's offer was one she'd never intended to let him refuse.

Wearing the plainest coat and trousers he owned, he grabbed the duffel and hurried out the door. "Taxi!" A black cab zipped out from traffic and stopped in front of his door. Before Sir Charles ducked into it, he saw that a few houses down, a man hailed a cab a moment after he had. "King's Cross Station," he said to the driver. The entire ride, his eyes were glued to the rearview mirror as he watched the same cab the man hailed snake through the streets of London, following the exact route his was taking.

"Hurry," he told the driver.

He jumped out of the cab when he arrived at King's Cross, because if he was being followed as he suspected, now was his only chance to lose him. He turned around and caught a good glimpse of the man who'd emerged from the trailing cab. He was tall with dark features and a square jaw, wearing a standard business suit.

Sir Charles didn't want to draw attention to himself by sprinting through the station, but he powerwalked through the crowd, heading to his true destination of St. Pancras International across the way. Every offshoot hallway he saw, he ducked down, and every large crowd of people, he squeezed through. He pleaded internally that his efforts to evade the view of this man would pay off, and he sighed with relief when he saw he'd timed his arrival just as perfectly as he had planned it. The conductor was shouting the final call to board the southeastern. He slipped into the closest carriage and sat in the first corner spot he found away from windows. He tapped his foot, counting the seconds since he'd sat down, praying the train would start moving.

"…sixteen…seventeen…eighteen…"

The train lurched forward with a metallic groan as it began to crawl out of the station. Sir Charles leaned forward in his seat and glanced through the glass doors to the neighbouring carriages—he didn't see the man. Only then did the tension in his muscles begin to relax, and the fear subsided long enough for him to rest his eyes.

Princess Edith meandered through the palace garden, with the chill of a winter night sweeping in to replace the fading light of dusk. She wore a shawl to keep warm, but it proved futile, just as it always had. For even when the spring frost melted away and the summer warmth bore fields of colourful flowers, a perennial winter existed within her.

This was why she walked the garden, even now. Because she could still find beauty in it, even as the liveliness of seasons past were dying on the vine. She moved slowly on the manicured paths, just as the pensive thoughts seeped through her mind. Guilt, regret, pain. All emotions she purposely held onto, to feel them as intensely as possible.

It was the only way she could get some sleep at night.

To punish herself.

Although it was an endless battle with no winner, she knew it was what she deserved. There were other thoughts, too. Ones in which she imagined herself in a future where she had the courage to buck the Crown, to defy her mother in the hopes that she may one day hold her son in her arms and have him know the truth. But then, her greatest fear crept back into the centre of her chest, just as the blackness of night slid over the world every evening.

That the future she dreamed of would never arrive.

Tears pooled in the corners of her eyes as she wept silently. The last thing she wanted was the guardsman to see her in this condition and run to her side. With Leon's sudden departure to Baden-Baden, the inability to see him on a regular basis had damaged her spirit past a point of no return. Every time she closed her eyes, she pictured a beaming Theodora side-by-side with her son, fingers bouncing along the ivory keys of the grand piano as they played in harmony.

Princess Edith swallowed against the lump in her throat. She had never felt such an all-consuming envy, and there was a part of her that wished to walk right out the palace gates, take the train to Dover, and catch the last ferry across the Channel. Alas, her depression was like a leech, but instead of blood it drained her of energy, so she circled back toward the eastern entrance to retire for the night.

As she neared the glow of the palace lights, a shimmer of silver in the air caught her eye. She froze just in time to avoid walking into a spider's web. Its size was impressive, spanning the distance between a palm and a shrub. As she looked in awe at this spectacle, a clumsy moth flew into the centre of the web. It thrashed its wings and threw its body back and forth in an attempt to free itself, but hardly a second passed before the flickering legs of a spider raced down the strands to wrap its prey in fresh silk.

Princess Edith watched the slaying, mesmerised yet mournful. She imagined that the moth just moments ago was on its own version of an evening stroll, unaware of its fate that had been woven by the spider.

"End of the line, Dover Priory station," called the conductor over the speaker.

Sir Charles flinched awake and quickly scanned his surroundings. He peered into the neighbouring carriages, and just like before—no man. The train slowly ground to a halt, and he and the handful of remaining passengers exited onto the platform. The balmy air of Dover was pleasant, but it was no respite for his frayed nerves that had his senses on high alert. He slipped out of the station briskly and looked over his shoulder every few seconds.

During one glance he swore he caught sight of the man who had trailed him in the station. He did a double take, but he wasn't there now. The potential that his eyes hadn't lied caused him to pick up his pace and not stray too far away from the streetlights.

The ferry blew its horn in the harbour; Sir Charles hurried as he saw only a handful of passengers left to board. Sweat beaded along his forehead, breath trailing from his mouth as he broke into a jog. The yellow lights lining the docks of the port twinkled, their glow diffusing through the mist that came off the ocean.

To him, they were like little beacons of hope in an otherwise black night.

"Ticket please," said the crewman as he approached the boarding ramp.

Breathless, he gave the crewman a polite nod as he tore his ticket. He trudged up the walkway onto the ferry and took a full minute to scan the dock below and the passengers around him, and there wasn't a sign of *him* anywhere.

An hour passed, and Sir Charles saw through the main cabin's windows that the mist had cleared. He went up on deck and discovered he had the entire space to himself. A chill crept through to his skin; he zipped his jacket and shoved his hands in his pockets as he wandered the deck, head tilted back while marvelling at the stars he could never see so clearly in London. The briny ocean air mixed with the cold stung his nose as he took a deep breath in. He rested his arms along the railings and wondered where he would go once he reached the mainland. The thought reminded him of the newest letter he'd written. He pulled it out of his breast pocket and smiled as he began to read.

Dear Leon,

I know you have no idea who I am to you, but just know this is one of hundreds of letters I've sent over the years that never made it. Sadly, this one more than likely won't make it either. I wish more than anything for one of these letters to arrive in your hands. For then you would know that your father is very much alive, and his name isn't Alfred. And that your mother is a princess whom you've known your whole life, which is a luxury I envy. But I promise, if I must burn down the palace gates to get to you, I will. I love you, my son, and I hope one day we meet again.

Your loving father,

Sir Charles Stir—

A gloved hand covered his mouth, and a blade sunk slowly into his back. He groaned into the man's hand as he was stabbed repeatedly, felt the warmth of blood seeping from his gut and through his clothes. A dizziness swept over him as his view of the starry sky began to blur.

"Should have taken the money," said the man under his breath.

He pushed Sir Charles over the railing and watched as he disappeared in the wake of the ferry. He shook his head, wiped the few drops of blood off the railing and the deck with a rag. As he knelt, he saw the bloodstained letter in front of him.

The man rose to his feet and read the letter, shaking his head with a snort.

He ripped the letter into pieces and let it be whisked away by the wind, where it would come to rest in the indigo waters of the Channel alongside the man who wrote it.

CHAPTER 14
THE BAD MAN

Baden-Baden
1938

Nearly a month had passed since Duke Leon had arrived at Villa Friesenberg, and throughout that time, the emptiness never once returned. But as he sat on the piano bench waiting for his aunt, he was reminded of what had replaced it.

The sound of Princess Theodora and Prince Ernest fighting.

A dish shattered, and Duke Leon flinched, closing his eyes, taking a deep breath. Theodora strained her vocal cords until they were raw, her raspy shouts leaving an imprint in his mind long after they subsided. In his peripheral, Theodora's only servant walked along the hall parallel to the great room.

"Klaus," he called out.

"Yes, Your Grace?"

Klaus pivoted and approached him; his stride so graceful that it always appeared like he was gliding rather than taking individual steps.

"Tea with lemon and honey for Theodora. Bring it here, please."

"Right away, Your Grace." Klaus bowed and disappeared down the hall. Perhaps it was from all the screaming, but Duke Leon noticed in the weeks after his arrival that it was Theodora's drink of choice.

Ernest's bellows echoed farther down the halls than Theodora's, and Duke Leon struggled to maintain his stoic gaze. Theodora was already thirty minutes late for their playing time, and he prayed the argument would end soon.

But he had his doubts.

Instead of waiting for the tea, he left the great room and headed to the west wing of the house. Even a month later, he still marvelled at the architecture of the villa Theodora called home. Years earlier, he'd heard her describe it as a Swiss chalet. Three storeys tall and adorned with countless windows, it felt almost like the inside and outside were merged as one. To Duke Leon, the most noticeable difference between Kensington Palace and Villa Friesenberg was that in the villa it was easier for him to breathe; an added benefit being there wasn't any red in sight. Only earth tones; green shutters that matched the ivy crawling up the clay-coloured brick, wooden beams that disappeared high into the ceilings, and an airy essence that pervaded the space.

Duke Leon stopped at the threshold of the west wing sitting room. Eugenie was lazily flipping through a book and Lysander was engrossed in painting a model airplane.

"Does it ever stop?"

"Only when he's off to war," said Lysander, not looking up from his work.

Eugenie turned the book over on her lap and let out an apathetic sigh. "I told you the truth your first night here. You'll get used to it."

"I don't even hear it anymore," added Lysander. "Learnt to tune it out."

Duke Leon left them to their leisure. As he traversed the halls leading back to the great room, he thought his ears had fooled him because the yelling had suddenly stopped. When he turned the corner, he saw Theodora settling in on the piano bench, smoothing out her dress. He joined her, and the first thing that caught his attention was her bloodshot eyes.

"Are you ready?" asked Theodora.

"I am. Are you?"

She sniffled and produced a strained smile. "Of course. Sorry I'm late."

Klaus appeared at Theodora's side, placing a teacup in front of her with two slices of lemon at the bottom. He poured the steaming tea and left the carafe on an end table nearby.

"Klaus, how did you know?"

"It wasn't my doing. Duke Leon requested it on your behalf."

A bit of Theodora's sadness faded from her expression, and she turned to him. "How thoughtful of you."

She took a long sip of the tea and set it aside. Her hands trembled as they rested above the ivory keys; she shook them out and made a second attempt at playing, but just as she developed a rhythm, she would hit an off note and ruin the tune.

"I'm sorry…" She dropped her gaze, rubbing her hands together in her lap.

"Why do you let him treat you that way?"

His question was met with silence.

Theodora fidgeted and refused to meet Duke Leon's stare. "Have you ever been in love?"

"No."

"Then you wouldn't understand."

Duke Leon rested his hand on her forearm. "Can you help me understand?"

She relented with a sigh and turned to face him. There was a gentleness in her honey-brown eyes as she held his gaze. "When you love someone, you fight for the things that matter. But…" She paused, wiping tears with her sleeve. "You also realise that fighting won't change everything. So you must accept them for who they are."

Duke Leon decided not to press her further.

"Let's get back to playing, shall we?" said Theodora. Then, it was as if she had suddenly turned off a light switch; the emotions previously revealed to Duke Leon were wiped away in an instant, the melancholy replaced by the lively striking of the piano keys.

A slammed door drew Duke Leon from his slumber. He glanced at the clock on his bedroom wall—1:33 in the morning. Once he came to, the faint shouts of Prince Ernest reached his ears, intercut by Theodora's rasped responses. He rolled over and tried to fall back asleep, but as the intensity of the argument increased, he found it more difficult to ignore.

He sat on the edge of his bed and rubbed his eyes. He wondered if Eugenie and Lysander were woken by these fights or if they'd learnt to sleep through them entirely. A flurry of thuds echoed; it sounded like books were being thrown against the wall. Still in his pyjamas, Duke Leon traversed the halls of Villa Friesenberg until he reached the spiral staircase that led to the master suite on the third floor. His bare feet helped him quietly creep up the stairs without making a sound, and as he ascended, he began to hear the content of their argument. Theodora was going on about Ernest's drinking problem, and he was griping about the war and the state of their finances. Just as he reached the top of the stairs, he saw Prince Ernest hurl his tumbler full of whisky against the wall; it exploded with a spray of glass. Theodora cursed him and stepped away from the mess, a newfound rage sliding over her pale skin. She bridged the space between them and jabbed her finger against his chest, spewing a warning that one day the children might catch him like this.

Prince Ernest struck Theodora across the face; his tree trunk of an arm producing a thunderous clap that echoed throughout the master suite.

"Stop!" called Duke Leon.

The two whipped around. Theodora's eyes bulged as she cradled her swollen cheek. Prince Ernest stared at Duke Leon like a bull seeing red. His steps were measured as he approached, and Theodora attempted to follow.

"Don't you lay a finger on him."

Prince Ernest cocked his head back. "I'm simply escorting Leon back to his room." He pointed silently toward the stairwell with his index finger. The calm tone he had just used seemed inconsistent with his previous display of anger toward Theodora.

Duke Leon descended the stairs, and with his back to Prince Ernest, he prepared himself for an imminent blow.

Just as he was about to reach his bedroom door, Prince Ernest grabbed him by the collar of his pyjamas and flipped him around, slamming his back against the wall. He snarled, and Duke Leon caught the pungent smell of whisky on his breath. All the air was knocked from his lungs, as Prince Ernest tightened the grip around his throat.

"Don't you *ever* interfere with my marriage again. Or I will throw you to the streets where you belong."

Prince Ernest dropped him, and he coughed violently to catch his breath, rubbing his sore neck as he watched him return up the staircase. Once he disappeared, Duke Leon retired to his bed, and it wasn't long before a realisation arrived.

Princess Theodora's love had kept the emptiness at bay, and her husband's rage had brought it back. Except now, it was sharper than before—more potent. As if the time spent away from the feeling had made its newfound presence even stronger.

And after what he'd just witnessed upstairs, he wasn't afraid of the return of the emptiness.

He was happy.

CHAPTER 15
THE ARCHITECT

Margaret pulled into her drive, and the light from her headlamps revealed Aniqa sitting on the pavement. She hurriedly switched off the ignition.

"Aniqa. What are ye doing here?"

"I've been waiting for you to get home," she said, staring off in the distance listlessly.

"What happened?"

Margaret watched as Aniqa's eyes went glassy, and they flicked back and forth as if she were replaying a memory. "He had a few glasses of wine, and just for a moment, the way he looked at me changed…and he said *you have the same eyes*."

"Same eyes as who?"

"That's what I asked. It's like he realised he'd slipped up, and so he claimed I had the same eyes as his mother."

Margaret sat on the hood of her patrol car, crossed her arms. "So that's what brought you here?"

"He lied to me. And all my instincts as a mother tell me that Al has not only met my son, but knows exactly where he is."

"You really think that?"

Aniqa sat a little straighter, holding her composure. "I do. Don't you?"

Margaret revealed the beginnings of a smile and let out the tiniest of laughs. "Aye. I'm just thankful. Last thing I want is to have the mum of the lad I'm looking for against me."

Aniqa chewed on her lower lip and fidgeted with her car keys.

Margaret got off the hood of the car, kneeling in front of her. "Hey," she said. "Look at me."

Aniqa reluctantly met Margaret's gaze. There were tears pooling in the corners of her eyes.

"Don't blame yourself for a second."

"I fell for it," said Aniqa.

"Yeah, but so has everyone else in Catrine. The whole police department. Even Stu." She paused, letting out a sigh. "He's good. I'll give him that."

"What if he's so good that we don't find Arun?"

"I made you a promise," began Margaret. "And despite what ye may think of me, I intend to keep that promise. We'll get your lad back. And Elaine's. And the orphans."

Aniqa rose to her feet, nervously playing with the edges of her sleeve. "I'm sorry for what I said earlier."

"Nae. No harm," said Margaret. "You were right, anyway. I refuse to let someone innocent get hurt on my watch ever again."

The fog that rolled into Cumnock at this late an hour formed a blanket of grey across the land. It was as if, just for a moment, Margaret and Aniqa were insulated from the horrors transpiring around them.

"So what now? You're the only one who suspects him."

"I'm not the *only* one," Margaret said. "Detective Ross has his suspicions. But unlike me, he has inside access to the case and hasn't been written off as a loon by the whole department." Margaret grinned. "I also just came from his hotel room."

"And?"

"No leads."

Aniqa looked crestfallen.

"*But*," continued Margaret, "Elder Louise's arraignment is tomorrow. She's requested to talk to me, but since I'm off the case, Gordon is the next best thing."

"Who?"

"Sorry," Margaret said, shifted her weight and in the dim light, seemed to blush. "Detective Ross."

"You like him."

Margaret snorted. "I'm married!"

Aniqa pressed her lips together, cocking her head.

"Fine, he's a handsome lad. But I love Walter."

"I get it," Aniqa said.

Margaret quickly switched back to her normal professional disposition. "So, tomorrow Detective Ross will go to the arraignment, and I have loads of his files I need to comb over. It would be nice to have a second pair of eyes on them."

A triumphant smile slid across Aniqa's face. "I never thought you'd let me help you look for my son."

"Oh, piss off," Margaret said with a cackle. "That was before I got the boot."

"I'm teasing."

A flicker of determination lit up behind Margaret's eyes. "I'm through playing by their rules. We're gonna get this bastard."

Gavin lifted his head, yawning and rubbing his eyes as he awoke. He shook out the ants from his right arm—it went numb every morning from it being used in place of a pillow. The basement felt the coldest it ever had, and he wasn't sure why. A quick look around confirmed his worst fear; the screams he had heard last night were real. He gulped against the lump in his throat and fought back the urge to cry.

Part of him didn't understand why he was tearing up, because he wasn't particularly fond of Craig. He hadn't been kind to him, nor the other Kissinger kids in school. Despite this, images from yesterday's events flashed behind his eyes. Craig diving into the freezing water to help Arun, and how he'd fought so hard to climb up Al's ladder before getting his fingers crushed. In a way, he was their leader. He delegated roles and led them to a nearly successful escape. And their plan would have worked too if it weren't for…

Gavin wiped the tears from his eyes and swivelled his head to face his brother. James sat in the corner of the room with his knees to his chest, bug-eyed and flicking his gaze between him, Fiona, and Arun.

A gnawing pit formed in his stomach as he stared at James. He was so disgusted at what he'd done he wasn't even sure he could speak to him.

Craig was dead. And *that* realisation brought the tears back to his eyes.

"Why are ye crying?" asked James.

He cast a look of disbelief at his brother. "Are you blind? Craig isn't here."

"Da must have let him go."

"You've gone mad," he said with a snort. "He's dead."

James heard those two words and his eyes bulged wider. He shook his head side to side, muttering denials under his breath.

Gavin couldn't find the right words to respond to his brother's delusion. He rose to his feet and walked to the opposite side of the room, where Fiona and Arun lay together, joining them.

Elder Louise sat in her windowless cell, stroking the worn cover of her bible. She shifted positions on her bed every so often because the cinder block walls made her back ache. Without windows or a clock, she tracked time by when she received meals. That was how she knew it had been four days since she'd been brought here from Aberdeen. The guard told her this morning that her arraignment was tomorrow, and after those words were uttered, a black cloud of fear hung over her head.

While she still sought comfort in the Lord and His word, there was a part of her that felt betrayed. For it was her faith that had enabled her to believe Al's lies.

You're being too hard on yourself, she thought. Al used his authority to pervert her faith, to do his bidding. When the pangs of guilt grew too strong, she opened her bible to Psalms 37:32-33.

> *The wicked lie in wait for the righteous,*
> *intent on putting them to death;*
> *but the Lord will not leave them in the power of the wicked*
> *or let them be condemned when brought to trial.*

She smiled as she reread the passage and clutched the cross at her neck. Though she'd been misled, she knew staying connected to the Lord would see her through this mess. But beneath the bedrock of her faith, a tiny ember of fear still existed; that perhaps the picture Al had painted by framing her would solidify in the mind of the court. The memory of the officer rifling through the children's clothes in the boot of her car flashed behind her eyes, and she flinched.

The door to her cell swung open.

"You have a visitor," said the guardsman. Elder Louise slid her wrists through the opening in her cell door without hesitation—muscle memory. The guardsman led her to the same interrogation room she'd been in a few days earlier, when they transferred her here from Aberdeen, and to her surprise when she entered, it wasn't the Cumnock officers she was familiar with. Instead, on the opposite side of the table was a handsome man with hazel eyes and sun-kissed skin he must have been born with, for the sun hadn't poked through the clouds around these parts in months.

Arms crossed, she studied the man's countenance, trying to get a read of him and what his intentions were, because there hadn't been a soul yet that took her version of events seriously.

He responded to her cagey body language with a smile and extended his hand. "Detective Gordon Ross," he said.

She let his arm hang there while eyeing him, but after a few long, awkward moments, she quickly shook his hand and sat across from him. "I've already spoken with the Cumnock detectives. So I'm curious, where exactly are you from, Detective Ross?"

"Edinburgh. I'm Detective Chief Inspector for the Major Crimes Unit."

"And why have ye come to see me?"

"You asked for Officer Brown."

"Aye, I did," she said. "Yet here you are instead of her."

The warmth in Detective Ross' expression faded, a grave look taking its place. "I'm here despite the fact I've held the children's clothes with my own hands, heard the full story from every high-ranking officer in this department, and read your intake interviews a dozen times over."

Elder Louise's gaze fell to her lap, acid licking at her insides at the thought of having to sit across from another cop staring into her eyes like she was the source of this evil act.

"I'm here because I believe you."

"You believe me?"

Detective Ross nodded. "Aye." He pulled out a little black notebook and a ballpoint pen from his coat pocket. "Now, Louise. I want ye to tell me everything that happened from the morning the lads went missing until you were arrested at that hotel."

The scratching of Detective Ross' pen stopped. Elder Louise felt as if a weight had been lifted off her shoulders.

"I'm going to be honest with you, Louise. The evidence against you is strong, and the charges will likely stick. You might have to stay in prison until we have enough proof to convince the judge otherwise."

"I'm not worried," she said.

"Makes one of us. I haven't slept a wink all week."

"Do you keep a bible by your bed, Detective?"

A laugh slipped out from Detective Ross' mouth, and when Louise remained stoic, a look of chagrin slid across his face. "Uh…I regretfully admit I don't. I'm not very religious."

"Not *very* religious is different from *not* religious," she said with a raised brow. Elder Louise watched as he shifted in his seat, rolling a pen between his fingers.

"My dear, I am a woman of God, but I haven't His power to be the judge of men."

"Not religious," he admitted sheepishly.

The beginnings of a smile tugged at her lips. "He sent you here, you know."

"Who?"

"God," she said.

"I wish I could believe that was true. If only you knew the dark places I've had to go over the past year trying to prove my theory."

Elder Louise chuckled again. She reached up to brush her cross between her finger and thumb. "It's true, Detective. Whether you believe it or not. God works through all His children, and He's with you in the darkness." She continued rubbing her cross, and as she stared at Detective Ross, she felt herself slip into a trance.

The Holy Spirit is with us, she thought.

"God is working through ye and Margaret. I believed that the path Al led me down was a righteous one, but I was mistaken. His work is the work of the Devil himself."

Detective Ross shifted uncomfortably in his seat.

"I've been reading the Bible all my life, but in the past few days I can't help but return to Psalm 37." Her eyes roamed around the room as she mulled over her thoughts. "There's a verse in that chapter that reminds me so much of Al. Of the life he leads, and the lies he fed me in the name of God. It reminds me of the fate he will meet once the Lord finishes his work."

> *I have seen a wicked and ruthless man*
> *flourishing like a luxuriant native tree,*
> *but he soon passed away and was no more;*
> *though I looked for him, he could not be found*

"Ow!" winced Aniqa. A drop of blood slid off her finger and landed on one of the many papers strewn on the living room floor. "Papercut," she said, sticking her finger in her mouth.

"I'll grab you a plaster." Margaret dashed into the bathroom and rifled through the medicine cabinet. She found the box of plasters and returned to the living room.

"You mind?" Aniqa asked, holding her finger out.

Margaret shook her head and began peeling open a plaster; as she did this, a tiny red rivulet trickled towards the edge of Aniqa's finger. Margaret hesitated with the plaster open—she took a deep breath and sighed.

"Are you all right?" asked Aniqa.

"I'm just not the best with blood," she said with a nervous laugh. Aniqa sucked her finger again and cleaned the cut of the blood. "There."

Margaret quickly wrapped the plaster around the wound and sat down on the couch, returning to the task at hand—poring over all of Gordon's paperwork on the lads' case. He had dropped them off before Elder Louise's arraignment, and along with it, all the copies of Margaret's case files.

"I'm sorry," said Margaret. "Ever since that night I haven't been able to stomach blood."

Aniqa sat next to Margaret, resting a hand on her forearm. "The girl?"

A solemnness settled into Margaret's expression.

"You can't blame yourself forever."

"But it's my fault," blurted Margaret. "No matter how you dice it, it's her blood on my hands."

"How long has it been?"

"Sixteen years."

"You have to forgive yourself. You don't deserve to put yourself through that day after day."

"How can ye say that?" Margaret asked, raising her voice. "That child would be here if it weren't for me. I saw her crying in the hall, knees to her chest, staring up at me but refusing to say a word. But deep down I knew. And because of the fact the mum assured me and the other officer that things were fine, we left. I ignored my gut and that girl died trying to protect her mum, putting herself square in the path of her bastard father's drunken swing of a baseball bat…"

Aniqa winced. "You made a mistake. But you can't let it define you."

"She's the reason why Walter and I never tried." Margaret sniffled, blinking deliberately to clear the tears in her eyes. "If I let that happen to someone else's child, imagine what I might do to my own."

"That's shite if I've ever heard it," said Aniqa, giving Margaret a gentle shake. "After everything you've done for my son. You'd be a great mum."

Margaret pulled her arm out from beneath Aniqa's hand and straightened her posture. "I appreciate what you're trying to do, but you wouldn't understand."

Aniqa huffed.

Margaret watched as her eyes began wandering the room with a thousand-yard stare.

"I let my mother die alone. And I didn't even go to the funeral."

Margaret stayed silent, giving her room to think.

"And now ever since Arun went missing, she's haunting my dreams."

"Do you think they mean anything?"

Aniqa chewed on her lower lip and let out a sigh. "I think they are my mum's way of telling me that no matter how much I hated her, and how hard I try to forget about her, she's still my mother. And it's funny because I remember how she had this saying—'a mother's love never dies'. She would say it *over* and *over* and *over*, any time I was cross, but especially once she got sick. I swear sometimes even now I still hear it ringing through my head. *A mother's love never dies! A mother's love never dies!* Deep down I think she said it simply out of spite. To remind me that, yes, she would soon die but a piece of her will always live with me." Aniqa laughed, a flicker of anger behind her dark eyes. "And she was right. Her love is still very much alive. Because it was given to me in such a misguided and cruel manner that I still resent her to this day."

Hours passed, and Aniqa and Margaret were three-quarters of the way through the case files. Margaret looked up at the wall clock—4:30. Walter was due to be home within an hour.

"We've got to clean this up soon," said Margaret. "I don't want Walter to find us here like Sherlock and Watson."

"Do you think he'd be mad?"

"I'm not sure, but I'm not willing to make that gamble either." Margaret leaned over and wrapped her arms around a large pile of paperwork, shovelling it into the centre of the floor between them. "This is the last bit," she said. They split the pile and continued working.

Aniqa's brow furrowed as she came across a manila envelope jutting out from the rest of the case files. She unfastened the metal clamp and slipped out a paper that was so thin and delicate she was afraid it might rip. Her mind lit up as she realised what it was. "Whose house is this?" she asked, handing the blueprint to Margaret.

She glanced at it and handed it right back to Aniqa. "It's Al's house," she said, returning to her files.

"Is that not a big deal to you?"

"It was when I had the idea," she said. "But once I got it from the council building, I realised there was nothing there. It's just a normal house."

"There's nothing *normal* about that house. You can tell that much from the outside, but I noticed it even more when I went in. There isn't another like it in town."

"I agree with you, but there's nothing there. I took it to a local builder just to make sure."

Aniqa's momentary rush of excitement flatlined. The thought that she might have a lead worth following had given her the first bit of hope she'd felt since Arun went missing. She pondered Margaret's words and continued inspecting the blueprint, looking for anything out of the ordinary. The longer she looked, the more she feared Margaret was right.

Suddenly, an idea struck her.

Aniqa stood up and held the blueprint up to the light.

"What are you doing?" asked Margaret.

But she didn't answer, just smiled. "Stand up and look at this."

Margaret shuffled onto her feet and stood next to Aniqa, who without hesitation smacked her finger to the bottom right corner of the blueprint.

"It's a watermark," said Aniqa.

"I can't make out what it says." Margaret squinted, pushing the blueprint closer to the light.

"I think it's a name."

Margaret's eyes widened as the two turned to each other, speechless.

"The name of whoever designed this house."

"Do you think the builder you took it to before is open?" asked Aniqa.

"It's worth a shot. Can you drive?"

Aniqa grabbed her keys and slipped on her coat.

Margaret began shuffling together the papers strewn across the floor, Aniqa kneeling to give her a hand. As they were cleaning, the front door swung open and in came Walter.

"Whose car is in the drive?" he asked absentmindedly, not looking into the living room.

Margaret and Aniqa froze.

Aniqa mustered a shrug of her shoulders, deferring to Margaret on what to do.

Walter hung up his business coat in the foyer and then stopped in his tracks when he reached the threshold of the living room. He quickly cut his eyes between the papers, Aniqa, and Margaret.

"What's going on here?"

"Aniqa is helping me look over my case files."

Walter produced a thin smile and shifted his gaze to Aniqa. "Do ye mind if my wife and I have a moment alone?"

Aniqa looked at Margaret for confirmation it was okay to oblige, and Margaret confirmed with a small nod. "I'll go start the car," she told Walter.

Aniqa shuffled awkwardly past him and left through the front door; once it was closed, the smile he'd feigned in front of Aniqa soured instantly.

"Are ye out of your damn mind?"

"Far from it."

"Then surely you can imagine how this looks. If people see you two together, they're going to assume the worst."

"What will they assume, Walter?" she asked while gathering the rest of the case files. "Enlighten me."

"Don't patronise me," he growled. "You were taken off the case. And now you're playing detective with the lad's mum!"

Margaret rose to her feet and met Walter eye to eye. "If I just sit back and take my leave those lads won't be found."

"And when they throw the sicko in jail who took them, you'll be in the cell next door."

The possibility Walter spoke of was a likely one. Nevertheless, she couldn't hide the truth that was in her heart. Not even from her husband.

"I'd rather rot away in jail and still be able to sleep at night because I did what was right, not what was easy."

She turned to the door and opened it; a flurry of footsteps came behind her and Walter slammed it shut before she could walk out. His nostrils flared, jaw clenched. Margaret yanked at the door, but he used his forearm to keep it closed.

"If I see that lass set foot in this house again, I'll go to Stu myself."

She stared back at him with disbelief. "Do that and see whether *I* set foot in this house again." She pushed his arm away and slid out the door.

"I'm trying to protect ye, Margaret!" he shouted from the threshold.

She kept her eyes glued on Aniqa as she walked away from Walter, the lump in her throat expanding with every step. Sadness bubbled up within her gut as she processed her husband's threat, but she decided she wouldn't let it overcome her to the point of tears. Not now. Not in front of Aniqa. Because submerged in the river of sadness flowing through her was the determination she'd held tightly to since day one. Its flame like a beacon, guiding her through the darkness. And she knew without a doubt that despite Walter's threats, Stu's actions, and the mockery being made of her character—she would fan the flame until her job was done.

"What was that about?" asked Aniqa as she sat in the passenger seat.

"Nothing," she said, holding her composure. "But I might need to stay with you until we find the lads."

Aniqa turned to her, conveying with only a look that she understood.

Margaret watched in the rearview mirror as her house shrunk in size until it disappeared over the horizon.

She wasn't sure when she'd see it again.

The office of Sutherland Builders smelt like a mixture of freshly cut wood and musty carpet. Duncan Sutherland, the owner, carried the same scent, but with an added tinge of cigar smoke that rolled off his breath. The sparse hair he had remaining was all but grey, although what he lacked on his head existed threefold on his bushy eyebrows and thick caterpillar moustache that entirely eclipsed his mouth.

He held the blueprint to Al's house up to his desk lamp, and the watermark appeared.

"That's it," blurted Aniqa.

Duncan croaked out a raspy chuckle. "Aye. I see it all right."

Aniqa leaned over the counter to try to get a better look at what he was doing. "How interesting," he said under his breath, squinting as he held a magnifying glass over the watermark.

"What is it?" asked Margaret. Duncan grabbed a piece of paper and twisted the desk lamp to where he could hold the paper above the glowing bulb. Then, he slipped a pencil out of his pocket and began tracing the watermark.

"Well, I'll be damned," said Duncan. He returned to the counter and smacked the traced paper in front of Margaret, pointing to the watermark with a wrinkled, stubby finger.

"Malcolm Wright."

Margaret tilted her head, waiting for an explanation.

A toothy grin emerged on Duncan's face. "The architect."

"Do you have his number, by any chance?" Aniqa asked.

"Nae. Ye won't find him in a phone book around here either. He's out of Edinburgh."

Aniqa sucked her teeth. Margaret watched as she shifted her weight from foot to foot and nervously stroked the cuff of her jacket sleeve with her forefinger and thumb. She could tell Aniqa thought this might become another dead end, and she wondered how many times she'd been faced with that same terrifying thought over the past week.

"Do you happen to know who the builder was?" asked Margaret.

Duncan chortled, shaking his head before he spoke. "Whoever they were, they built that house faster than any I've seen before. Not from around here either."

"Thanks for all your help," she said, signalling to Aniqa with a nod for them to leave.

"So what now?" asked Aniqa.

"I need to head to Edinburgh and find the architect."

"*I?*"

Margaret sighed. "Look, if I find anything out that requires the police to get involved, you can't be there with me."

"Am I supposed to just sit at home?"

"If you don't mind, I'd like you to do what I've been doing since I've been off the case. Trailing Al."

"And who do I call if I see something important?"

"Just call the station. I'll find ye once I get back."

Aniqa's lower lip began to quiver, and she opened her arms, embracing Margaret. It took Margaret a second to accept the gesture, but she wrapped her arms around her as well.

"Thank you for everything," whispered Aniqa.

In that fleeting moment, and for the first time in months, Margaret felt happy.

Margaret was gasping for air as she cleared the top of the News Steps and approached the bright red telephone booth at the corner of St. Giles' Street. A local had told her it was the closest one from where she parked her rental car on Market Street, not realising the hundred-step climb she had to embark on to reach it. She had all the years pencil pushing back at the station and many evenings at home spent channel-surfing to thank for being so out of shape. Once she caught her breath, she dialled Malcolm Wright's number. She'd stopped at a nearby pub, whose owner allowed her to copy it down from the phone book.

"Hello," sprung a hoarse voice from the receiver.

Even though he'd just said a single word, both syllables sounded as if they had pushed past a frog in his throat to escape. Certainly not the intonation of a young lad.

"Hi, am I speaking with Malcolm Wright?"

"Aye, you are. And who might I have the pleasure to be speaking with?"

Nerves got the better of Margaret; she paused, hand trembling on the receiver. "My name is Margaret Brown, I'm an officer from Cumnock." The line went silent, and for a moment, she feared he'd hung up. "Are ye there?"

"I'm still here."

"Are you an architect, Mr. Wright?"

"Former," he croaked. "What's the nature of this call, Ms. Brown?"

"My apologies for not getting right to the point. Did you happen to design a house for a man by the name of Albert Reid?"

The bustling city behind her went quiet as she met another bout of silence. She plugged her finger in her open ear, waiting for him to speak again. "Mr. Wright?"

"Yes, many years ago." There was a twinge of breathlessness to his statement that Margaret took note of. Almost as if he'd been holding in that exact breath of air for decades and finally had the opportunity to let it out.

"If you don't mind, I'd like to meet with you and ask some specifics about the blueprint—"

"I'll do ye one better. You can come by my home office, in say, an hour?"

Thinking on her feet, Margaret replied, "Make it an hour and a half."

With that, Malcolm Wright gave Margaret his home address. Before she left the booth, she phoned Gordon and told him all about the new lead and her morning with Aniqa. He said he would leave Cumnock right away.

Margaret knew that whatever they discovered in the meeting with Malcolm, if it were something that warranted an arrest, Gordon had to be the one to do it. Pursuing this lead alone was a surefire way for her to get arrested. Despite her fear, an electrical excitement danced along the nape of her neck and tickled her temples. For this was the closest she'd been to answers since the lads went missing.

"All rise," said the judge with a booming voice. Elder Louise entered the courtroom with her head held high, hearing the swell of hushed whispers from onlookers as she approached the stand. She wondered if this room had ever been so full; especially considering the paltry crimes that came through these doors, day after day. A few journalists snapped their cameras, the loud clicks threatening to breach her inner calm.

The judge pounded the gavel and ordered the court room to sit.

"Louise Anne Fleming, the court has found you guilty of four counts of abduction." Gasps peppered the crowd like flurries of fireworks. Elder Louise closed her eyes and took a steadying breath. "You will be sentenced to ten years for each count, amounting to forty years in prison, without the possibility of parole. If by chance the children's bodies are found, you will face a separate trial for murder."

Applause erupted at the judge pounding the gavel, and as Elder Louise rose to her feet, a few of the townspeople spat expletives at her. "Order!" commanded the judge. The officer guiding her to the exit tugged roughly at her shackles, and Louise could see the disgust on the man's face just from his profile. It was then she quickly scanned the hundreds of faces in the room, and she saw how they too looked at her as if she was the Devil herself. Her stomach ratcheted tighter, and she decided to close her eyes for the remainder of the walk. She took a deep breath and reminded herself that man could never judge her—only the Lord Almighty.

Margaret left the car the moment she saw Gordon parallel park on the opposite side of the street. The day had gone from cloudy and calm to blustery, with the wind biting straight through her clothes. She struggled to stand still as Gordon approached, and there was something about this sudden change in weather that rubbed her the wrong way. The violent wind whipping in different directions, stirring up the air in Edinburgh. Perhaps it would surface whatever secrets had lain here for far too long.

"Two blocks north, isn't it?"

She nodded, and they zigzagged down the footpath against the wind, arriving at the address Malcolm had given.

23 ½ Leamington Terrace was a corner terraced house built of grey and brown stone at the very end of a long row. Two storeys high, with multiple bay windows jutting out from its stony visage. A black Jaguar sat in the tiny slip of a drive just below the entranceway.

A gust of wind threw Margaret off-balance, pushing her forward a few steps. She glanced over at Gordon; he seemed to mirror her discomfort. The ease with which she'd been able to arrange a meeting with Malcolm prickled her sixth sense. He was either perfectly innocent and had nothing to hide, or he was so plagued with guilt that he was ready to let the truth out.

Margaret led the way up the handful of steps to the door. She rapped three times with her knuckles and waited.

Nearly thirty seconds passed—no response. She and Gordon exchanged pensive glances, and Gordon gave her a signal to try again. She knocked harder, and it was then the door popped open slightly.

"Hello?" she called out.

No response.

Gordon peeped his head through the opening. "Mr. Wright?"

Even with the fierce wind, there was an unnatural stillness to Malcolm Wright's house.

"Hello, Mr. Wright? It's Margaret Brown."

Yet Margaret's words fell on dead air.

"Let's go in," said Gordon.

They tiptoed into the foyer and closed the door behind them.

"Wow," said Margaret, marvelling at the craftmanship present in every nook and cranny. The floors were crafted of real wood, bannisters lining the stairwell made of the finest mahogany, ornate crown mouldings, and wallpapers that had likely cost a small fortune.

"Mr. Wright!" shouted Gordon.

A sudden pitter patter emanated from upstairs, followed by the tiniest of mewls.

"Is that a cat?" asked Margaret.

"Sounds like it." They carefully crept up the stairs, the old bones of the house creaking beneath their feet. As they reached the second floor, Margaret scrunched her nose at the metallic scent. "Do you smell that?" she asked, turning to Gordon. He nodded, and they began down a small hall. They passed an empty room, but at the end of the hall, they faced a closed door. "It's getting stronger," she said, and groaned into her cuff, trying to avoid the sickly smell. Before they opened the door, they gave it one final set of knocks.

"Mr. Wright! Officer Brown here." She didn't know why, but her heart began to pound in her chest. Margaret had to turn the glass knob with a bit of force; its bearings were worn out, made in an era before their time. When the door popped open, she gagged at the smell. The scene which her eyes fell upon caused every muscle in her body to tense up.

"Oh God," she gasped, nearly keeling forward. Malcolm Wright was leaning back in a stationary chair in the centre of the room, with a pistol lying at his side. A gaping gunshot wound marred his left temple, and on the other side, his neck, arm, and side were stained with blood. Beneath him, a thick maroon puddle formed a perimeter around the chair.

"Jesus Christ," said Gordon, holding his composure with a closed fist to his mouth. He coughed from the inescapable iron smell stinging his nose.

"The bastard killed himself," muttered Margaret as she approached. Her limbs felt numb, and each step closer put her more in a dreamlike daze.

"Did he sound off when ye called him?"

"A little. But nothing like this."

"What do you mean, a little?"

"It was more his tone. Almost like he was expecting a call. Like he'd been waiting for it."

"What exactly did he say?"

"He just said we could meet and talk about the blueprint. Not much more."

Margaret pulled the blueprint from her pocket, unfurling it. She sighed as she scanned along the finely drawn outlines of Al's house. *What now?* she thought.

Gordon picked up the pistol and let the barrel rest in his palm. "It's still warm," he said.

"I wonder if the neighbours heard anything."

"If they did, they're probably already on their way," replied Gordon, setting the pistol back on the floor. "I just don't get it." He crossed his arms. "Why would he invite you over just to blow his brains out right before you arrived?"

She snorted and stared down at the corpse of the architect.

"Because he knew he was guilty." Margaret stepped over the puddle of blood and knelt beside Malcolm. She fingered through his pockets and dumped their contents onto the floor. "I know this blueprint is shite. And by the looks of it," she said, nodding at the body, "*he* knew that too."

"Margaret, if the cops show up with you rifling through his belongings—"

"We don't have time for ethics, Gordon. Help me. Check his desk."

They spent the next few minutes poring through his desk and file cabinet. "Look for the matching design year," she instructed. "1944." But they found nothing. Nearly all of Malcolm's work was done around Edinburgh and Glasgow, along with sparing summer houses in the Highlands. Gordon discovered a safe in the closet; Margaret tried all the keys on Malcolm's key ring, but none were able to open it.

"I hear sirens," said Gordon.

Margaret tilted her head and heard the faint oscillating whine in the distance. She relocked the safe and returned to the centre of the room.

"You have to get out of here," he pressed.

She knew he was right, but the tiniest fleck of rebellion kept her rooted where she stood.

"Margaret!" yelled Gordon, trying to break her out of her daze.

She shook her head, thinking. "He knew the cops would come. But what he wanted to tell *me* wasn't meant for *them*…"

"You're not making sense—"

"Someone who went to the lengths to kill himself just to avoid facing the consequences of his involvement is a guilty soul. He was following the case…and he knew I was taken off it, too."

Just then, Gordon picked up a few charred newspapers from the fireplace. "You're right…"

Margaret saw the miniature faces of the four lads on the front page of the *Scotsman*. Her mind darted in a million directions as the sirens approached. "It wouldn't be somewhere the cops could find easily. He knew I'd be here first."

She scanned the room, panic rising in her gut, and it was after she'd exhausted every nook and cranny that her eyes fell back to Malcolm's dead body. Eyelids stuck half-open, eyes rolled back, and every limb in his body hung lifelessly.

But then, she noticed his mouth.

Her brow furrowed, as it took her a second to process what she was seeing. His lips were closed, but the positioning of his jaw was as if he were about to speak.

Like there was something—

She stepped as close as she could without her boots getting in the puddle of blood, and she stretched out her arms, grabbing Malcolm by the jaw. When she opened his mouth, she couldn't see anything but his pink tongue and the darkness of the back of his throat.

"Margaret! What the hell are you doing?"

She fetched her torch and flicked it on, and just past his tonsils was the tip of something metallic that glinted in the light. She delicately fished her forefinger and thumb into Malcolm's mouth and fought to pull it out. She shook her hand of saliva and held up a slobbery silver key.

"Christ Almighty," gasped Gordon.

Margaret bounded back to the closet and slid the key into the safe's lock.

Her heart leapt out of her chest as she heard a *click*, and the black iron door swung open. Inside lay a tightly rolled white paper. She grabbed it, quickly unfurling it on a nearby desk and then placed the city's blueprint of Al's house side-by-side with this copy. Gordon rushed to her side.

Margaret's jaw dropped.

Malcolm's blueprint, the *real* blueprint, showed a third level existing in Al's home, containing a sprawling basement bisected by a long hall. There were four identical rooms off-shooting it, two on each side, and then a fifth room at the end of the hall that was bigger than the rest. It seemed as if there was a large pipe and a water source feeding into it.

Knocks sounded at Malcolm's front door. "Police!"

Gordon and Margaret snapped back to reality, and she rolled the blueprint up, slipping it in her breast pocket.

"Go out the back!" he shouted. "Wait for me at the hotel. Don't ye let a soul see it."

Margaret's pulse pounded at her neck as she scurried down the stairs and escaped out the back door. An overjoyed grin blossomed on her face as she snuck around the back garden into the alleyway, peering over a brick wall to wait for the Edinburgh officers to enter Malcolm's home. She practically bounced to her car and cranked the ignition, and as she drove off, she quickly patted her breast pocket to ensure she wasn't dreaming, to make sure the blueprint was still there.

She laughed and couldn't hold back her exhilaration, with the sweet taste of victory fresh on her palate.

CHAPTER 16
THE WALLFLOWER

Annie Stewart speculated she was born unlucky. Until age eight she couldn't pronounce her R's, and the other kids at primary school teased her for it. In her first year of secondary school, her formal date left her on the dancefloor without a word and disappeared to an afterparty, never caring enough to invite her. She had to call her parents from the headmaster's phone to pick her up early because she was too embarrassed to finish out the rest of the night. As she developed into a woman, the mirror was a constant reminder that she hadn't blossomed like some of her peers had, although her mother was the first to tell her she was the most beautiful girl in the world. She had a bit of an overbite, gums that showed unreasonably when she would grin, and two front teeth that were at odds with each other and formed crookedly.

She just felt…plain.

A woman whose physical appearance never warranted a second glance.

Despite these shortcomings, she met a man at university who fell for her. They married just a few months later and, after graduating, decided to settle down in her hometown of Cumnock. But much like the rest of Annie's life, within a year and a half their marriage began to fall apart. Her husband's parents died, a month apart, sending him into a depressive spiral. He began drinking excessively. Missing work. Verbally abusing her. Weeks turned into months. Bills started piling up. The first time he struck her, she dragged him against his will to the local church and got the marriage annulled. But then she was alone with no job and a pile of her ex-husband's debt. Her parents weren't happy she was hardly twenty-five and yet she'd already been married, had the marriage annulled, and gotten divorced to settle the legalities. The icing on the cake was discovering that she was pregnant. All it took was a few mornings of retching and a missed period to inform her something was off. She hadn't a clue what to do, nor a soul to guide her outside of her disappointed parents. She figured if she were to bring a baby into this world, she needed to find a way to provide for herself and the bairn. That was when she stumbled across an advert for an office clerk job at the police station. She applied and got the job. It wasn't much, but it allowed her to fend for herself and her newborn baby without the help of the father.

In the nearly twenty years of her employment at the Cumnock station, the officers and staff had never paid her much attention. They'd walk past her, seldom giving her even as much as a nod, like she was more a ghost than a living, breathing human being. Some were even so aloof in her presence that, despite her bringing the same lunch every day for twenty years—a chicken salad sandwich with extra mayonnaise—they'd sometimes take it as their own.

But that was life for Annie Stewart.

She felt invisible, and she had accepted that as her fate.

All her yearly reviews at the station were uneventful. She was always timely and rarely phoned in sick. She'd get her meagre raises and there were never any complaints about her performance. It was almost comfortable in a way, being a wallflower. Albeit a mundane, unappealing variety of a dull shade no one cared to take notice of.

Yet that was the defining trait of what made Annie unique. In the silence that was her everyday life, she had time to watch. To listen. A reticent observer who, in her endless watching, had amassed a mental stockpile of all the station's characters and their intricacies. She unknowingly knew some of them better than they knew themselves.

It was this specific quality that led Annie to notice a change in

Sergeant Stu's behaviour. In all the years she'd worked under him, he'd never arrived before 8:30 in the morning. She was typically the first to arrive out of the office staff at around 8, so she'd been very surprised when, two weeks earlier, she'd seen him in his office when she got to work. She chalked it up as a one-off, but the next day, there he was again. After a few days of this pattern, she decided to come in at 7 instead of 8. There wasn't a chance in Hell the sergeant would come in that early. Yet again, there he was when she arrived. She would quietly walk past his office and enter her own, shutting the door soundlessly behind her. She kept the admin office's blinds cracked so she could see into his office directly across the hall. After a few more mornings of studying him, something about his countenance caused an inkling of suspicion to hijack her mind. She caught an unbridled stress within Stu. It surfaced in the grooves of his forehead and the pallid hue of his cheeks and lips. Even his caterpillar moustache seemed to droop. But outside of that, he wasn't doing anything out of the ordinary. Just poring over paperwork.

Why come in so early? she thought. Paperwork went hand in hand with being an officer in a town with little to no real crime, but that didn't explain the tension about Stu's body language. The number of papers he had strewn across his desk served as a reminder for her to check her own files. In the Cumnock station, Annie was the gatekeeper. She had two administrative assistants working for her, but she was still the head of it all. Every police or arrest report, every warrant, financial records—all barred behind locked rows of filing cabinets.

And only she held the key.

An itch arose within her mind that told her to check her records. So, she spent a large part of the morning going row by row to check the integrity of the files, and nothing appeared off. When she reached the rows that housed the financial records, she noticed that, while everything was where it was supposed to be, the keyhole of that cabinet had nicks and scratches surrounding the metal opening.

That's odd, she thought. *I don't remember those being there.*

This damage gave her pause. When she returned to her desk, she felt the sudden sensation that she was being watched. A quick glance across the hall confirmed Stu was watching her, and the moment their eyes met, he shifted his gaze back onto his paperwork.

Now she wondered if he had been watching her just as much as she'd been watching him. She had to shift her strategy. Be more discreet. When she left that night, she went home, cooked a tasteless TV dinner, and then lay awake into the wee hours of the morning. She couldn't sleep, wondering if Stu had rummaged around her office after she departed.

The next morning, she decided to wake up and head into the station even earlier. The blue and grey building lay dormant with most of its lights off. When she entered, she wandered down the long hall to the admin office, flicking on the lights as she went.

To her surprise, she found Stu's office empty.

Annie glanced down each length of the hall. A split-second decision set her in motion, quickly striding toward the front of the station. She knew she only had minutes before the thick metal door would swing open and another employee arrived.

A coded lockbox was all that separated her from the master key to the station. It opened every door, including Stu's. Only he and a few longtime officers knew the code. But one of the many observations in her long tenure was the lock's four numbers that never seemed to change—7878. The address of the station was 78 Ayr Road. Not the least bit secure. She grabbed the master key and hurried back to Stu's office. The door creaked loudly as it opened, almost as if it were trying to alert the rest of the slumbering station that an intruder was in its midst. She stepped gently into the room and a quick glance at the paperwork left on Stu's desk revealed that it was all benign.

Police reports, officer performance reviews, witness statements.

She pulled at the handle to his filing cabinet—it clanked loudly against the metal lock. She knelt and fished the Kirby grip from her bun, inserting it slowly into the lock. This was a trick her mum had taught her as a young girl. Her father always kept his study door locked, and her mum was far too curious about what he might have been hiding in there. She couldn't help herself.

The lock clicked, and she slid the drawer open. The files she fingered through yielded nothing of any interest. She huffed, and for a moment, she wondered if her paranoia was even warranted. There was a good possibility she would leave Stu's office without alleviating that little tickle of suspicion in the back of her mind. When she reached the last file, its weight fell backwards against the other files, like a toppling of dominos. The shift revealed a black notebook obscured beneath the many manila folders.

She slipped out the notebook and flipped through the most recent entries. Stu's scribblings bristled the hairs on the back of her neck. They were dates. One date written for each month, going back at least a year… A fleck of familiarity made Annie wonder why it was *these* dates that were written. She also noticed that Stu had scribbled out some of the dates, re-writing them a day or two differently, as if he weren't sure of himself.

Guessing.

A light switched on in her mind, and suddenly, it all made sense.

The dates. The scratches at her filing cabinet's keyhole. The stress on Stu's face.

She took a final look over the journal, holding as many of the dates in her mind's eye as possible, and hurriedly re-locked it. She strode across the hall, and once in the admin office, locked the door so no one could barge in on her. Annie's heart pounded in her chest as she unlocked a specific filing cabinet that housed the station's financial records. The same one which had the keyhole damage. The file she was after was the one which recorded outside charitable donations. It was commonplace for a handful of patriotic locals to donate to their local station, but that wasn't why her blood ran hot through her veins.

It was the *who*—and the *why*.

She fingered through the first two months and froze when she saw two dates that matched.

Albert Reid had donated five hundred pounds this month and the last. She continued going back in time, realising that not only had he donated this amount every month before it, but he was also the station's largest donor by a hefty margin. Although she didn't yet understand the *why*, she knew her colleagues would be in any minute now. She retrieved all the donation records that housed Al's contributions as far back as she could, and realised that he'd been donating that amount for close to ten years. She carefully carried over the originals to the station's new copier machine and began duplicating the records.

If it was these donations Stu was trying so hard to get, it was her job to see the originals were protected.

Later that morning, when the humdrum of office life was in full swing, Stu gave the admin office a quick rap of his knuckles and walked in. The face that stared back at Annie was ghastly—a slight hue of purple in the bags beneath his eyes, and a dewy peppering of sweat lined his forehead.

He approached her desk sheepishly, hands shoved in his pockets.

"Mornin', Annie."

"Mornin', Stu."

An awkward pause blossomed between the two.

"What can I do for ye?" she asked.

"I—I'm doing some reports for the National Police in Edinburgh. Can I borrow our donation files for a bit?"

"Aye," she said with a quick nod. "Be right back."

When she turned away from Stu, she fought the urge to smile. *He is up to something*, she thought. Mirroring the exact route she had taken earlier,

Annie stuck her key into the damaged lock and opened it. She retrieved all the donation files and then returned to her desk, holding out the large bundle of manila folders to Stu.

"Here ye go."

He produced a thin smile and said, "Cheers," before slinking back to his office. Annie watched as he settled in, and as he was about to open one of the files, he must have felt her prying gaze, because his eyes flicked up to meet her own. She nervously broke the stare, fixing her attention on some trivial paper lying about her desk in the hopes of allaying Stu's suspicions.

Just then, he walked over to his office windows and slanted the shades shut.

Hours later, Stu emerged from his office with a visage so white it appeared as if all the blood had drained from his head. He left the station in a hurry, and after peeking out from her office, she saw a handful of officers shuffling out the door behind Stu.

She casually walked over to reception and stood in front of the dispatcher, Norman—a young lad in his early twenties with a face much younger.

"What was that about?"

Norman over-blinked, the corners of his mouth somewhere in between tugging into a fervent grin or curling up in disgust. He looked like he might jump out from his seat.

"The magistrate just approved a search warrant for Albert Reid's home."

She gulped in absence of a response and had to lean into her years of being the office wallflower to feign nonchalance.

"Hmm," she said. "How odd."

"I'll say," replied Norman, fidgeting with a pen between his fingers.

His body was buzzing from the excitement of a search warrant. Likely his first.

He opened his mouth to continue but she cut him off with, "I'll be back in a bit."

She returned to her office, and in the privacy of her own company, found herself replaying the events of the last few days and unable to escape the feeling that the amount of serendipity required for these happenings to be purely coincidence was…nearly impossible.

Stu's stressed demeanour for the past week.

The damage to the financial records filing cabinet.

Albert Reid's prolific donations over the past decade.

Stu's blundering request for the donation records.

And the icing on the cake—a search warrant being granted for Albert Reid's home.

She spent the next few minutes securing the copied donation records in the filing drawer attached to her desk, not only behind the drawer's key lock, but with the additional protection of a padlock as well.

Oh Stu, she thought, emitting a disenchanted sigh. *I hope you're not caught up in all this mess…*

But if he was involved in something sinister, she was prepared. The paper trail, whatever its significance, was hers alone to protect.

And for the first time in as long as she could remember, Annie Stewart felt lucky.

CHAPTER 17
THE LIGHT

Baden-Baden
1939

"You're tense," Freidrich Weber scolded, grabbing Duke Leon's wrists. "Let your arms rest naturally at your side." He mumbled something to his coworker in German and stretched out the measuring tape along Duke Leon's inseam. Freidrich was a petite man whose fingers were equally as nimble as his mind. The latter had to remain sharp to deal with the plethora of idiosyncrasies each royal—or former royal for those seeking refuge—brought with them when they crossed the threshold into his shop.

For twenty years, he had tailored for both the average person and the celebrity. When spring became summer, and the town's population of ten thousand quadrupled, business boomed. He made more in those three months than the other nine combined, and the surplus money pleased Freidrich to such a high degree that he could easily shoulder the stress, snipping it from his mind like the useless ends of fabric on a pair of trousers or the sleeves of a dress.

Today he was taking care of Princess Theodora and company. She was one of the few royals he found agreeable, and despite the dislike he held for her husband's temperament, he caught himself smiling often in her presence. He found Theodora's children to be rather dull, their eyes wandering aimlessly along the walls of clothing that encircled the store. But the new addition to her household, her nephew Duke Leon, was quite the opposite. His icy blue eyes sat beneath a furrowed brow, precipitated by the hassle of his suit fitting. His gaze didn't wander like his cousins, it darted pointedly between himself, Princess Theodora, and Prince Ernest.

Behind the mechanical clacking of the sewing machine in the back room, Freidrich overheard Princess Theodora and Prince Ernest bickering. When he focused his attention, he discerned its triviality—the guest list for tonight's gala.

As he finished the fitting, Freidrich caught Duke Leon's eyes fixating on something over his shoulder. A quick glance confirmed who the look was directed at—Prince Ernest. He swivelled his head to face Duke Leon again; he was so transfixed that he hadn't noticed the jostling of the fitting had stopped.

Freidrich had seen that look before, but not on a child. Sure, Duke Leon was built like a man, but his real age of seventeen was still readily apparent by the lack of lines on his smooth face.

But those eyes. They radiated anger, like pools of lava spilling over a volcano's edge.

"Has he wronged you?" asked Freidrich in a hushed whisper.

Duke Leon broke from his trance and stared down at Freidrich, slightly offput by the fact his countenance had been unknowingly studied.

Freidrich watched as the fire in the boy's eyes reduced to embers. As if the realisation that a lowly tailor had borne witness to his true feelings spurred a calculated extinguishing.

"No," said Duke Leon, adjusting his collar and settling into the fitted suit.

Freidrich rolled up his measuring tape and fought the urge to scoff.

For anyone with ears would have known that the boy lied.

Princess Theodora rested on the chaise in the master sitting room, cherishing the last full breaths she'd be able to take. Soon, her servant would assist in cinching her corset. It was such a dreaded garment, that represented everything wrong with how the world expected women to be. Society was more concerned with the size of their waists than the knowledge in their heads.

A shame, thought Theodora.

Her moment of respite wasn't as restful as she'd intended, for it was being polluted by her thoughts. She swallowed the bit of acid that rose at the back of her throat, instigated by the dread that in a week's time she was to leave the airy, beloved haven of Villa Friesenberg and return to Schloss Langenburg. She had convinced Ernest several times to leave without her; each of her trips to London prolonged the time away from her troubled husband. But with no plans to see Eleanor on the horizon due to Leon's incident, she feared Ernest would use the permanence of her homecoming to Germany to his advantage, and she and the children would be carted off to stay with him in Langenburg indefinitely.

Theodora often felt more like a piece of property than a living, breathing person.

These thoughts were a large part of the reason why she decided on hosting a gala. A party served both as a lively distraction and a bittersweet goodbye to Baden-Baden. Because once she arrived at Schloss Langenburg, she knew the trips Ernest permitted would be seldom at best. She could practically hear the groans of him contesting her pleas, shooting them down like birds attempting to fly through the path of a sportsman's shotgun.

"I don't want him in my home."

Ernest's words shook her from her daze.

"Pardon?"

He turned to her, adjusting the cufflinks of his suit. It was then she noticed the touches Freidrich had added—both the buttons and the suit's inside lining were royal blue, and the pocket square was yellow—colours of the Langenburg family coat of arms.

Ernest was a handsome man, but his good looks were obscured entirely by the abuse he subjected her to. It was frighteningly more frequent than the affection he doled out. The love she'd once held for her husband had soured like a bottle of red wine left uncapped, its richness and body replaced by an acrid vinegar that made her nose turn every time she encountered it.

"I don't want Leon coming to my house."

"Is it not *our* house, my dear?" Theodora straightened up in the chaise, curling back her shoulders.

"That may be true of *this* house. But not Schloss Langenburg."

She snorted. "And where might you suggest he go?"

"Anywhere but with us. It disgusts me the Queen thinks she can dump her property on you like we're her inferior." He threw back the rest of his whisky glass, grunting as it burned on the way down his gullet and proceeded to straighten his tie.

"He's my blood, Ernest."

A guffaw burst from his mouth, and he whipped around in front of the mirror.

"That lie may work across the Channel, but it doesn't here. I know he's the bastard son of that commoner tutor—"

"You shut your mouth."

"—Pardon me?" Ernest cocked his head to the side and approached her with measured steps. She didn't cower beneath his looming presence because she'd learned that the more vulnerable she appeared, the worse his abuse. It was as if the very sight of weakness stoked his fire. "That child *will not* step foot in the royal residence."

"Then I presume I must stay here."

"You will do nothing of the sort."

"Try to stop me."

Ernest struck Theodora across the face, his arm thick as a piece of timber; the sound it produced reverberated like an echoing thunder throughout their chambers.

She cupped her cheek, nursing the stinging, enflamed skin, and got to her feet. "You'll be lucky if I have enough powder to cover this up."

He ignored her and returned to the top of his armoire, which he'd fashioned into a makeshift bar. The soft squeaking of glass on glass filled the room as Ernest unscrewed the plug of the decanter, sloppily pouring up another drink.

"*Try to stop me,*" he mocked with a snort. "It's almost as if you wanted me to hit you."

Theodora chewed on the inside of her lower lip as she applied the porcelain powder, tapping the brush in circles to conceal her reddening cheek. She met her own gaze, studying her reflection, and it was then she realised she didn't recognise the woman staring back at her. How could she have allowed this to go on for so long? Their shoddy attempts at obscuring the abuse were no match for the children's acute hearing. While she knew they'd never have the courage to admit it, she wondered if they perceived her the same way she did in this mirror.

Weak. Subservient. Perhaps even complicit in the abuse itself.

Ernest slammed his empty glass on the armoire and caused her skin to jump. The metal nail file on the vanity glinted in the light, catching her eye. She fixated on it for longer than normal, and a little voice in her head said to pick it up. She caressed its weighted handle and ran her fingertip along its serrated underbelly until she reached the pointed tip, tapping it lightly. It didn't break the skin, but with a bit of force, she was certain it would.

Holding the nail file parallel against her breastbone, she spun around—deliberately not producing a sound. Ernest's back was turned towards her, and she gingerly inched closer.

A perverse thought suddenly swept into her mind: *you can put an end to this right now.*

Fear accompanied by a rush of adrenaline coursed through her veins, because she wasn't certain the voice which had produced that thought was entirely hers. Its tenor stronger, more commanding. Perhaps it was just a future version of herself, living in a reality where Ernest no longer posed a threat.

Ernest got the particular tickle on his neck he hadn't felt since he was off at war, one that signified danger. He whipped around. In her daze, Theodora wasn't quick enough to hide the nail file before Ernest caught sight of it. He glanced between the tiny blade and her shellshocked expression, chuckling. "You really think that would do the job?"

She shook her head, falling back a few steps as he began to encroach on her space. "I…I don't know what I was think—"

Ernest lunged forward and grabbed her forearm, shaking it forcefully until the nail file fell to the floor. With his free hand, he struck her again in the face and once in the stomach. A guttural groan escaped as she keeled over on the chaise, sucking in air.

"You never learn," he said.

Droplets of blood pitter-pattered onto the bedspread, and she gently touched her busted lip. She rose to her feet, dashed for the bathroom, and grabbed a washcloth to soak up the blood. Her hands trembled wildly as she fished for the faucet, but she managed to get the water on and warm enough to rinse the wound. A quick glance in the mirror confirmed her worst fear—it would take a lot more than powder to camouflage her lip.

"I'll call Klaus to come mend it," said Ernest unflinchingly. He patted down his suit and slipped in through the open door. "And you'll tell him you fell. He's already familiar with your proclivity for clumsiness."

He proceeded to the end table by their bed and phoned Klaus. With the washcloth pinched against her lip, Theodora left the bathroom and slowly approached the nail file resting within the thick fibres of the lush carpeting. As she retraced her steps back to the vanity from which the nail file came, she sheepishly tried to avoid her reflection in the oblong mirror. When she accidentally caught a glance, her disfigured lip and what remained of the evanescent face powder on her swollen cheek were like blemishes belonging to a woman she no longer knew.

The Theodora she used to be was long gone. A ghost in a shell. Then, the paralysing weakness she felt daily crept back into her bones, like a late spring frost whose unexpected appearance extinguishes the budding plants' chance of life in an instant.

She settled back into the chaise, glancing at the grandfather clock along the far wall. There were three hours left until the gala. Klaus entered the sitting room and knelt at her side, and as he began dabbing a numbing crème on her lip, she continued staring at the clock's brass pendulum, watching its endless and unchanging, rhythmic swinging.

Tick tock. Tick tock.

The sounds of the room fell to the wayside. All she could hear was the clock.

Perhaps the years she had left on this earth were like that of the pendulum, swinging in perpetuity, trapped in a glass cage, propelled solely by the hundreds of powerful mechanisms that, together, kept it exactly where it was and where it would always be.

Klaus mended Theodora's lip with a careful hand, Prince Ernest polished off another tumbler full of whisky, and Theodora gazed listlessly at the grandfather clock.

None of the three noticed that Duke Leon had slipped away from behind the chamber doors.

Theodora delicately touched her scabbed lip in front of the vanity. It took a keen eye to match the right shade of red to blend with the dried blood from the scab, but she was impressed with how the wound disappeared almost entirely. She felt a bit like a chameleon, but instead of camouflaging to avoid prey, she was disguising the fact she had already been preyed upon.

For now, she was safe. Ernest's snores could be heard from down the hall, amidst a whisky-induced nap on the daybed in his study. She wished she could let him sleep all night, but she'd instructed Klaus to wake him just before the gala began. In an hour's time the first guests would arrive.

Her chamber door swung open.

Duke Leon entered, his hands interlaced, resting at his waist. His styled hair glistened with a sheen from hair wax, and his tailored suit fit snugly, making him appear more like a man than a boy on the cusp of adulthood. A sense of pride swelled within Theodora, and she couldn't help but grin. "Leon, you look so handsome."

Although the warble in her voice conveyed to him that Theodora meant what she said, Duke Leon struggled to produce a smile in reaction to the compliment.

"Thank you," he said.

A long pause filled the space between them. Theodora noticed the reserve in his demeanour. She approached him in the hopes of breaking the quiet. "Is something wrong?"

He neither affirmed her question with a nod nor denied it with a shake of his head. He just stared up at her with a hint of pensiveness swirling around his blue eyes.

"I wanted to ask your advice."

"Why of course," she said, bridging the gap and gesturing for him to join her on the chaise. "What is it?"

Theodora wondered what could be bothering a boy who hadn't yet faced the quandaries which the world doled out to nearly everyone who walked its surface.

"There's something I want to do."

"And what's that?"

"I'd rather not say."

Theodora let out a suppressed chuckle. Almost as if to ease the awkwardness she felt. "Well, then I can't be of much help to you."

Duke Leon's shoulders hunched over toward his lap.

"Okay, let me ask you this, then," she said, thinking on her feet. "Is what you want to do good or bad?"

"I think it would be good. Not only for me but for you and the whole family."

"Well, that sounds wonderful!" chirped Theodora. "Then what is it that's stopping you?"

"I'm scared."

She clicked her tongue and scooted closer to him, rubbing his back soothingly. "Sometimes in life the things that scare us the most deeply are exactly the ones we're meant to do."

Theodora watched as Duke Leon met her advice with a thin smile, eyes still vacant. She took a deep breath laden with disappointment, rooted in the thought that her words hadn't helped the boy in the slightest. She shifted positions next to him, and looked a bit more inward. "Leon, may I ask you a question?"

He nodded.

"Do you have a little voice inside that tells you what you should do?"

She tapped two fingers delicately at the centre of his chest.

He nodded again.

Flashes from this morning jarred her psyche—the weighty blows to the face, the air being knocked clean from her lungs—the pain endured a mere fragment of the full damage the abuse had caused over the years. "It's hard to admit this, but every single time I've ignored the exact voice that's telling you to do what you want to do, I've regretted it." Her mouth trembled as her true feelings began to surface, and she pressed her lips together to fight back against the nervous twitch.

A fleck of hope shimmered in his widening eyes. "Really?"

"Honest to God. I'd likely be better off if I'd listened to that voice years sooner."

A genuine smile emerged on Duke Leon's face, and she opened her arms and took him into an embrace.

"I love you," he mumbled with his chin against her shoulder.

"I love you too, Leon. You have a good heart."

Leon left her chamber, and she gave her appearance a final look over in front of the vanity. She applied a bit more blush to her right cheek to better mirror the natural redness from Ernest's blow. A warming sense of pride swelled within her as she reflected on her conversation with Leon. Her sister's parenting left a lot to be desired, even for her own children. Never mind the fact that since Leon was a living, breathing reminder of the man who had infected her bloodline, she refused to form a loving connection with him.

Theodora felt no shame in playing the role of a mother to a child who wasn't hers.

Someone had to, for a boy who grows into a man without love is destined to bring nothing but hate into the world.

That thought struck a chord of fear within her.

Perhaps I'm too late.

Theodora's kindness made her susceptible to naivete. For she didn't realise that while the voices of instinct guiding both her and Leon were the same, the hearts they spoke to were profoundly different.

Night had fallen on Baden-Baden, but for the townspeople who lived in the vicinity of the bustling chalet that sat atop the hill, the light pouring out of Villa Friesenberg shone so brilliantly it illuminated the sky as if the sun had never sunk below the horizon. Cars chugging along the winding back roads slowed as they passed to get a glimpse of the action going on inside;

boisterous laughter coalesced with the string quartet's lively plucking of their instruments, women's bosoms adorned with rare jewellery glinting in the light as they moved about, and those living in the hills across the French border saw the house as but a twinkling star in the distance.

All it took to fuel the sun was hydrogen and helium, but for Villa Friesenberg to shine the way it did required far more moving parts and dozens of chain reactions to keep it burning bright. Libations were the first and most important ingredient—there was enough alcohol in the Villa to keep the whole of Baden-Baden plastered until the first frost of winter arrived. The sprightly music was the next piece of the equation, both lifting the spirits of those inside and channelling the gala's liveliness through the windows, down the hillside, to eddy around the homes of the commonfolk, forcing them to marinate in envy. Last, but certainly not least, were the guests themselves. Royals from all corners of Europe donned their finest garb, each of them adding personal touches in homage to their houses' colours. Their reasons for attending the gala varied, but broadly speaking could be lumped into two categories—those who desired to be in Theodora's company and those who feared what damage their reputation might take if they were to ignore an invitation from Queen Eleanor's only sister.

Duke Leon stood at the core of it all, but neither the bright lights, the hot, sticky air from the hundreds of bodies filling the chalet, nor the vibration from the music bouncing off the walls were enough to melt him away.

The gala achieved the exact opposite effect; it held him together.

For the chattering chaos served as a hefty dose of his favourite medicine—the antidote to silence.

Tonight, he hadn't a shred of desire to eliminate the emptiness. He welcomed it with open arms. Its icy chill kept him focused on the evening's chief task at hand.

A burst of merriment spilled into the main foyer where Duke Leon stood against the wall. He poked his head around the corner to see Princess Theodora belly-laughing with a glass of wine in hand, side-by-side with her dear friend Elisa. She had kind eyes, like his aunt, and she had introduced herself as Elisa de Montijo, reminding him that they had met before when he was a young boy at Osborne House. Apparently, she had recently become godmother to one of Princess Maud's daughters.

Catching a glimpse of the sprawling joy across Theodora's face stirred up the same feelings within him; a welcome change from what he'd witnessed her go through hours earlier. Flashes of the forceful blows Prince Ernest delivered to her face and stomach caused a tremor to rise in his gut. He swallowed hard, forcing down the anger, bottling it up so as to not let a speck of it escape.

There were only a handful of other royal children in attendance, and a few of them had tried to interact with Duke Leon earlier in the evening. He gracefully traversed through the mind-numbing small talk, doing his best attempt at feigning mutual engagement, but those he spoke to soon found his curt temperament belittling and wandered off.

It wasn't his fault, for his mind was elsewhere. And if anyone in attendance were to watch his eyes carefully, they would discover the object of his attention happened to be the most important man in the room.

Duke Leon had eaten his fill of hors d'oeuvres, drunk enough of the sickly-sweet grenadine drinks the servants whipped up for the children, and had made multiple trips to the bathroom—all to keep Prince Ernest within view.

Wherever he went, Duke Leon sneakily followed.

He'd been keeping count of how many glasses of whisky he'd knocked back.

Eight. And they were only two hours into the gala.

In the many months since his arrival at Villa Friesenberg, he'd studied Prince Ernest fastidiously. Sometimes the surveillance was accomplished with ease, like when guests came over and he could position himself between the railings of the bannisters along the walkway encircling the third floor. Others were more difficult, like when he wedged himself behind the master chamber's door where his vantage point was merely a narrow crack.

What he'd learnt was that somewhere between drink twelve and fifteen was when Prince Ernest retired for the night, and he could always be found in one of two places. Either the master chamber or his study.

Prince Ernest tossed the rest of his eighth drink down his gullet, laughing heartily as he told stories too vulgar for his wife's ears to an engrossed circle of fellow aristocrats, enjoying the camaraderie only the company of other men could bring.

Perhaps it was the Louis XIII cognac whose bite was too strong or the company too lively, but Prince Ernest missed the distinct tickle on his neck that signified danger.

Two hours had passed. Prince Ernest was on his fifteenth drink and more cognisant than the remaining men around him who'd drunk half as much. Most of the guests had left, and the ones still lingering at the Villa were either close friends or merely acquaintances, struggling to see out whatever ulterior motives had brought them there in the first place. Eugenie, Lysander, and two other children had invited him to play a game of croquet in the garden, but he declined.

For the *little voice* Theodora had mentioned earlier informed him that his patience would soon be rewarded. The finish line he'd waited months to finally cross was coming into view.

He positioned himself behind the spiral staircase, eclipsed from Theodora's eyeline as she bid farewell to the never-ending flow of departing guests.

Here, he'd be ready the moment Prince Ernest polished off his final drink.

The gravelly voice of his uncle suddenly grew louder. Alarm bells sounded in Duke Leon's mind. He scurried up the staircase and slipped into the master chamber, trying to quiet his heavy breathing. Without hesitation, he bounded to the vanity and slipped the nail file into the lapel of his suit. Prince Ernest's drunken groans became clearer as he lumbered up the stairs. Duke Leon was out of time. His eyes darted frantically around the bedroom and, with seconds to spare, he ducked behind the bathroom door.

Prince Ernest entered the master chamber and stopped in front of his armoire, pouring himself another glass of whisky from the decanter. He loosened his tie, grumbling under his breath about something one of the other men had said; he was recounting a pissing match between Ernest and the friend who asserted he was the superior marksman during their military training. Duke Leon often wondered if all adult men possessed egos as fragile as Prince Ernest's, but he had no one to compare him to, since he had been raised solely by women.

Prince Ernest guzzled down the rest of his drink, setting down the empty glass heavy-handedly on the armoire with a loud clink. He stumbled over to the bed and collapsed on his back, legs partly hanging off its foot.

Time seemed to freeze in the quiet moments that followed. Duke Leon listened intently and noticed Prince Ernest's breathing change.

Do it, commanded his gut. *The time is now.*

He slid out from behind the bathroom door and tiptoed toward his target, ensuring with perfect certainty that he wouldn't produce shuffling sounds on the luscious carpet. His blood pulsed in his neck as he became close enough to Prince Ernest to smell the whisky seeping from his pores.

This is it, the voice said again. *Now.*

Duke Leon slipped the nail file from his suit pocket and let it slide into his hand. He clenched his fist tightly around it to keep from trembling. He stood just inches away from Prince Ernest's legs, and the man he'd harboured a visceral hatred for since he'd stepped foot in Villa Friesenberg was fast asleep, right in his grasp like a sitting duck.

His stomach rolled as he raised the nail file over his head, clutching it with two hands. He paused for a moment, taking note of how he felt almost completely numb. The emptiness had consumed him entirely. A tiny thought arose that contrasted the deeper, more powerful voice of his gut, reminding him that what he was about to do was irrevocable. It proved no match against the rage, dissolving instantly in the presence of the black hole in Duke Leon's heart.

Now! bellowed the voice.

He sank the blade into Prince Ernest's stomach, watching as he jolted awake with eyes as wide as saucers.

It took only a second for him to process what had happened—a quick glance between Duke Leon's devious glare and the blade confirmed he was not dreaming.

Duke Leon withdrew the blade and repeated the stabbing motion, watching in what felt like slow motion as Prince Ernest's nostrils flared and he knocked the nail file out of Duke Leon's hand, snapping to his feet as if he hadn't a single drink throughout the night.

A rush of adrenaline surged through Prince Ernest, and he watched in delight as fear flooded across Duke Leon's expression. He pushed the boy with both hands, catapulting him off his feet and causing him to nearly crash his head against the base of the armoire.

Pain radiated through Duke Leon's back. He was so shaken by Prince Ernest's defences that he hadn't formulated another plan of attack.

Prince Ernest guffawed, shaking his head while lumbering toward him. "The bastard child thinks he can put an end to me."

Duke Leon scrambled halfway to his feet and scurried toward the nail file, but Prince Ernest reached him the moment he grabbed it again and stomped on his hand with all his weight. Duke Leon groaned and fought not to scream. The only thing he feared more than being killed by Prince Ernest was Theodora coming through the chamber doors and putting an end to their brawl before he could fulfill the rest of the plan. Prince Ernest kicked him in the stomach, and Duke Leon gasped for air, unable to catch a full breath. Prince Ernest let out a primal hoot and holler, spittle flying from his mouth.

I can't go out like this, thought Duke Leon.

Then don't, the commanding voice said.

He curled up in a ball, exaggerating his pain by clutching his stomach and scooting away. Through squinted eyes, he watched Prince Ernest take a few steps, each stride longer than the one before it, with the final step outstretched as if he were going to kick a football a league away. Duke Leon whipped his legs around and kicked Prince Ernest's back leg out from under him, dropping him to the ground with a loud thud. He growled and pounced on Duke Leon, throwing heavy swings at him until one stuck and knocked his jaw sideways, emitting a grotesque popping sound. He flailed as he crawled backwards, desperately trying to escape Prince Ernest's log-like arms. His back bumped against the corner of the bedroom wall and the armoire; he leveraged the pressure to push himself upright, sliding up the wall until he was standing. Without a second thought, he grabbed the decanter and slammed it on Prince Ernest's head—it erupted deafeningly into a spray of shimmering pieces that spread across the carpet.

The prince went limp.

"I did it," muttered Duke Leon, the beginnings of a smile tugging at his lips.

Prince Ernest began to stir, pushing his hands into the carpet laced with shards of glass, gritting his teeth, groaning through the seething pain. Duke Leon scanned his immediate surroundings for another object, but there was nothing, and the nail file sat in a far-flung corner of the room. Prince Ernest rose totteringly to his feet and threw a punch at Duke Leon, which landed. But it didn't cause him to falter.

It was then Prince Ernest realised that the boy was only seventeen and just an inch or two shorter than he.

Duke Leon caught his uncle sizing him up, and quickly jabbed at the man, catching his nose and lip. And just as Duke Leon had reacted to his punch moments earlier, he hardly flinched.

Prince Ernest lunged at him, and they became entangled in a grapple of sorts, each with a vice-like grasp on the other's shoulders. Prince Ernest removed one of his hands from his grip on Duke Leon, taking the risk of being overpowered, and swiftly delivered an uppercut to the boy's jaw. Duke Leon mirrored his motions precisely and countered with an uppercut of his own.

The next minute became a perilous dance.

They struggled against each other's grip, bobbing and weaving in circles around the master chamber, trading off punches one after another. Neither of the two realised how much damage they were taking in the heat of the moment, but Duke Leon did recognise the distinct metallic taste of blood in his mouth, and also noticed that after every punch from Prince Ernest, a ripple of bright white stars cascaded through his vision.

More importantly, he took note of how unbalanced Prince Ernest was becoming—more so after every punch he inflicted on him. A growling crescendo arose from Prince Ernest's throat, and he used his grip on Duke Leon to force him into a spin. Duke Leon tried to fight back but was no match for the stubbornness and grit that only many more years of suffering on this earth could fashion.

Prince Ernest hurled Duke Leon and sent him crashing into Theodora's vanity. The impact shattered the elliptical mirror, sending a spray of reflective shards over him, the tiniest of which seemed to lodge in his scalp, throbbing separately like a dozen bee stings. Prince Ernest was sucking wind like he'd just run a marathon, but just as the welcome relief of a momentary break began to wash over him, he saw Duke Leon pulling himself up to his feet. He eyed the nail file in the corner of the room and ran to retrieve it.

Duke Leon watched in horror as Prince Ernest picked up the nail file he'd been stabbed with just minutes ago; he chortled, shaking his head as he stared at the bloodstained, four-inch blade. An arrogant smirk slid across his face. He slowly waved the blade in front of him, taunting him.

He thinks he's won, thought Duke Leon. He glanced down at his sides—a few of the mirror shards were sufficiently sized to do some damage—but holding them in his bare hand would be excruciating. He didn't trust himself against Prince Ernest's brute force. While his drunkenness could be seen as a hindrance, it also meant that he could thwart more of the pain.

And that was a task proving difficult to accomplish for Duke Leon. Every passing second the aches and throbs lapping at his wounds intensified, his body like a riverbank about to crumble away as the agony continued crashing over him in waves. Every fibre of his physical being pleaded for him to surrender, yet his mind couldn't cope with the thought of failing, nor the repercussions that accompanied it.

"Throwing in the towel, are you?" mocked Prince Ernest. He inched toward him, smacking the thin blade against his palm. "You know, it's not your fault you're weak. Your real father was the same way."

Real father. Those two words stirred up a vortex of emotions within Duke Leon, but he knew better. Prince Ernest was simply trying to roil him up, to get him to attack.

"And like the saying goes, the apple doesn't fall far from the tree," said Prince Ernest. "That's why you are the way you are."

The hatred Duke Leon felt for Prince Ernest festered in his soul, bubbling up to the point where he had to let it out.

"Does that mean your father beat women too? Or are you an apple that fell from his own bastard tree?"

Prince Ernest snarled and lunged at him with the nail file, but Duke Leon hopped out of the way at the last second and ran out the chamber door.

"You snivelling little shit," spat Prince Ernest, panting, spittle flying from his lips. "Ungrateful for all you've been given, that shouldn't have been yours to begin with."

That's when Duke Leon saw it.

The bloodshot eyes, the death grip on the hilt of the nail file, his lurching posture, standing on the balls of his feet—Prince Ernest was seeing red.

And just like a bull glowering at the matador's cloth, he was unaware of the fate that would meet him if he would charge.

But I don't have a knife, Duke Leon thought.

"You think you're going to run?" asked Prince Ernest, voice rising as he inched forward. "I'll have you hung before the sun rises tomorrow if you try."

Duke Leon didn't realise he had been shuffling backwards from the chamber doors, and his lower back bumped against the bannister. He flinched and a jolt of fear coursed through his veins from the momentary sensation of almost falling—

He fought the urge to smile, trying his best to suppress the cunning thought that surfaced. He hocked the slimiest wad of bloody spit he could stomach onto the floor.

"Let's see you try, wifebeater."

Prince Ernest charged at him blade-first, a guttural snarl escaping his throat as he built up speed. Duke Leon leaned forward with his fists outstretched. His heart pounded in his chest and his vision became tunnelled. Adrenaline caused time to dilate, everything went silent. He could practically hear his subconscious counting as Prince Ernest bridged the last few feet between them.

Three... Two... One—

Duke Leon ducked just as Prince Ernest lunged at him, the nail file completely missing its target, and Duke Leon clenched his teeth through the blow of being kneed in the face, but he only had a second to execute the motion with Prince Ernest's own momentum. He clutched Prince Ernest's legs and used all his strength to heave him upward, sending him hurtling over the bannister.

He cried out in shock, and Duke Leon wished he could have seen the look in his eyes as he faced the three-storey fall to the foyer floor; he took a deep breath and awaited the sweet relief Prince Ernest's body thudding against the ground would bring.

The hairs on his neck bristled as his senses registered the impossible… because he didn't hear anything.

A crunching of glass and a choking gurgle broke the silence. Duke Leon pulled himself up by the bannister and couldn't believe what he saw.

Prince Ernest hung from the grand chandelier, impaled on one of its metal arms. The momentum of his fall must have crushed the light fixture fastened to the end of the arm and the weight of his body did the rest of the work. He thrashed, sputtering blood from his mouth, each attempt to move revealing more of the gilded metal arm protruding from his back. A grotesque pitter-patter of blood began accumulating on the foyer floor, dripping from the worsening wound. The sound of Prince Ernest's last gurgling breaths was music to his ears. A jubilant smile tugged at Duke Leon's lips, for it was still before sunrise, yet it was *Prince Ernest* who was hanging.

Elisa de Montijo entered the foyer, saw the pooling blood, and swivelled her head skywards to find the source. She let out a bloodcurdling scream and fainted.

The Polizei had left. They'd made Duke Leon recount his story many times over. Each time, the two senior officers scribbled something new in their notepads. This worried him, because in each retelling, he kept the details the same; he and Prince Ernest got into a fist fight, and then Prince Ernest picked up the nail file, charged at him, and when Duke Leon ducked to avoid being stabbed, Prince Ernest went flying over the bannister. The only element of truth he omitted was that he had stabbed his uncle first, and the only falsity he added in were the tears he shed.

Duke Leon wasn't sure the Polizei believed his story, but he overheard the word "accident" more than once as they talked amongst each other and to Theodora. Duke Leon had been sneaking sidelong glances at her since the moment she walked in on the scene a few steps behind Elisa de Montijo. She exhibited the same horrific reaction as her friend, save the fainting, but once the immediate shock of the gruesome imagery wore off, she fell silent.

She didn't even shed a tear.

While the last few lingering guests had rushed to her and Elisa's side, her eyes remained transfixed on Prince Ernest's hanging body.

Duke Leon wasn't sure if he was imprinting, but he felt it was almost as if he could read her thoughts from her expression alone: *is he really gone?*

There seemed to be equal parts fear and awe in her honey-brown eyes, and he wondered which of the two emotions would prevail. The paramedics that arrived shortly after the Polizei had to locate a ladder tall enough to remove the body from the chandelier, and it wasn't until they laid Prince Ernest's lifeless body on the gurney that Duke Leon saw the bit of fear in Theodora's countenance dissolve away.

Perhaps she was afraid he might wake up, he thought.

The paramedics had informed her there was nothing a doctor could do; her husband lacked a pulse and most of his blood lay in a viscous puddle at the centre of the foyer. She nodded listlessly as they explained the next steps. They were to bring his body to the local morgue and a medical examiner would be in contact in the next few weeks to discuss his findings. But as they had continued speaking, Duke Leon noticed she couldn't look them in the eye. All she could do was stare at the gaping hole in the centre of her late husband's chest.

Now the commotion was long gone, and Villa Friesenberg was empty. The only sounds that could be heard were Klaus scrubbing the floors and the muted cries of Eugenie and Lysander in the west wing. Klaus and the remaining guests had shielded them from witnessing the gruesome aftermath of their father's death, and because they didn't see, they couldn't understand the suddenness of his passing. The only thing they *could* see was Duke Leon's disfigured face. Both eyes were swollen, one almost entirely shut, and his bottom lip had split open in multiple spots, causing it to resemble a swollen, blood-crusted caterpillar on the verge of popping.

The master chamber was far enough away to mask the scrubbing sounds and the cries. It was only the percussive thumping of Princess Theodora's own heart she could hear. After snapping a few photos of the nail file in the bloody puddle for evidence, the Polizei handed it back to her. It took less than a minute to rinse and return it to the vanity, but in that time, a thousand different scenarios of the little blade's journey played out in her mind—from the last time she held it before the gala to its final resting place beneath her husband's hanging corpse. Leon's account was one possibility given the injuries he'd accumulated, but she knew there were likely others…

If being a royal in the world's most powerful empire had taught her one thing, it was that nothing is ever as it seems on the surface.

She grabbed the nail file with a trembling hand and shoved it in one of the vanity's drawers. She couldn't handle seeing it any longer, especially having earlier clutched its handle with an idea so perverse that it had only previously arisen in her dreams.

She then reflected on Leon's visit and the vague string of questions he'd presented her. And the longer she replayed their conversation in her mind's eye, the more she wondered its true meaning.

I think it would be good. Not only for me but for you and the whole family.

Two thoughts caused guilt to eddy in her gut.

The first was that at the heart of Leon's guarded solicitation for advice was the desire to kill Prince Ernest.

The second was the notion that she'd encouraged him to do exactly that.

After an exhausting and unforgettable day, Princess Theodora retired to her chaise. Despite the troubling contemplations that weighed on her soul and the corset she had forgotten to untie, she could breathe deeply for the first time in years.

She fell asleep quickly. It was a blank and solid slumber.

CHAPTER 18
THE ANTIDOTE

Baden-Baden
1939

August.

Theodora stared at her reflection in the vanity. She picked up a brush, twirled it gently in a porcelain-coloured powder, and tapped it along the edge to discard the excess. Although she hadn't a single item on today's schedule, she still began the morning the same way she had for years now—with a bit of makeup. Klaus cleared his throat behind her; she didn't turn around, just found him waiting at the threshold in the reflection of the mirror.

"Come in."

He zipped across the carpet, holding a cup of tea with such nimble balance that not a single ripple emerged along the liquid's surface. He set it on the vanity, slipped a spoon from his breast pocket, and stirred to blend the milk and tea together.

"Anything else you might need?" he asked.

Theodora shook her head and smiled warmly at him. "You're too good to me, Klaus. I don't know what I'd do without you."

Klaus reddened from her compliment and let out a stifled chuckle, attempting to keep rein of his professionalism.

"I feel similarly," he said, giving a quick bow before leaving her chambers.

An immense gratitude swelled in her chest, for someone as devoted as

Klaus was a diamond in the rough. Every servant she'd encountered across the kingdom performed their duties adequately and appeared dedicated, but their paltry wages were hardly sufficient, and she imagined they likely wished ill upon the royals they served hand and foot who often treated them as substandard. Whatever loyalty they displayed was feigned—but not Klaus. Against Ernest's advice, she paid him handsomely compared to his counterparts in London. Not only did he deserve the compensation for always going above and beyond what was expected of him, but she knew his loyalty was authentic. For even a worthy wage wouldn't be enough to retain the average servant after witnessing the horrors from the night of the gala. He scrubbed away the bloodstains long into the morning with a nonchalance akin to cleaning a simple spill of wine.

And yet he stayed. If it weren't for Klaus, she'd be alone with the children. A tiny snort slipped from her nose; such a habit it was to imagine them still as *children*. Leon had just turned eighteen in June, with Lysander only a year behind him, and Eugenie a month away from turning sixteen. They were practically grown.

She took a sip of the milky tea, and when she closed her eyes to savour the taste, the warm liquid caused the memory of Ernest's funeral to resurface. The day had been the hottest of the year, and the muggy air permeated the mourners' attire, making it cumbersome and sticky, adhering like a second skin that would have to be peeled off when they returned home. Bloated cumulonimbus clouds loomed over the horizon like black-and-blue pillars shouldering the weight of the heavens, and minutes into the service, the sky fell. The droplets were warm like bath water, and as the priest spoke, deafening claps of thunder rocked the eulogy. Theodora remembered how hard her heart pounded as the cracks of lightning and thunder intensified around them. Leon grasped her hand to comfort her, and the moment he did, a bolt of lightning struck a tree on the opposite side of the cemetery, whiting out their vision for a moment. A few of the mourners gasped out in fear, children leaning into their sides for protection. The pallbearers rushed to assist the groundskeepers in covering the casket more hastily considering the worsening weather. The cries of Eugenie and Lysander snuck through the curtains of rain smacking against the ground as they watched the dirt being shovelled begin to fill their father's grave.

The funeral was pure chaos, and she knew Ernest wouldn't have had it any other way.

Leon had been crying too, but Theodora wondered if the tears shed were analogous to how the rain fell, quenching the parched earth.

Out of necessity.

The steam wafting from the teacup tickled her nose and drew her from the memory.

She set it down and applied a bit of blush along her cheekbones. The reflection staring back at her in the mirror seemed to harbour contempt.

Why are you still doing this?

She dropped the brush and grimaced, for she didn't have a sufficient answer to her conscience's question. The bruises had long faded away— there was nothing left to conceal. Perhaps the rhythmic brush strokes of applying the makeup were more of a compulsion, and the parts of her she was attempting to conceal weren't visible on the surface.

A stained soul.

The years of abuse had affected her psychologically in a way that even she hadn't yet fully grasped. And the damage inflicted was exacerbated by something new, a pernicious force that seemed to chip away at what little remained of her spirit day by day.

The thought of Ernest's death.

Although he no longer posed a threat, the way in which she had been alleviated of her problem felt suspiciously easy. There was an unnaturalness to how abruptly it ended, all without ever having to lift a finger. It was as if God himself had reached His celestial arm down from the heavens and plucked Ernest away. She knew better. His untimely death was far too macabre for God to have been involved. She wondered if people like Ernest even made it to heaven at all, because the hatred he held in his heart surely had been a product of the Devil's work.

She sighed nervously, fidgeting with the fabric of her dress. The final police report deemed it a horrific accident, and that was the reality she had accepted; for she remembered how early that morning, when the blood had finally been scrubbed clean, and the cries of her children had been replaced with a fitful slumber, she visited Leon in his room. He sat on the edge of his bed, sulking with his head hung low. She joined him and calmly requested he look her in the eyes.

Then, she asked the unthinkable.

"Did you kill him?"

There wasn't the tiniest fragment of change in his expression. His icy blue eyes conveyed a cold, calculated confidence that signified one of two things. Either he was innocent, or he had committed the act without the slightest bit of remorse.

"No. I didn't," he said.

The look of indifference on Leon's face still haunted her. While she was thankful she no longer had to face the wicked acts of her husband, she ruminated over the authenticity of the account Leon gave that night.

For she wondered if Ernest had been deliberately removed from this world by *another* act of wickedness.

Theodora shook herself from her trance, letting go of the dress fabric that had become damp in her clammy grip. She met her vacant stare in the mirror once again. Whether she realised it at the time or not, doubt had infected her mind like a parasite, ruthlessly burrowing itself deeper by the hour.

These fretful thoughts were what had contributed to a new piece of her morning routine. She listlessly picked up a little white pill that sat adjacent to the teacup and placed it on her tongue.

She washed it down with a gulp of tea.

September.

The Mercedes engine chugged noisily as Klaus pulled around to the front entrance of Villa Friesenberg. The late summer sun was at its apex in the sky, eradicating both the morning's crispness and the long shadows of dawn with tremendous ease. The lingering humidity of the season made Duke Leon pull at his collared shirt; the saturated fabric seemed to lick at his neck; coupled with the unbearable heat, he was growing more uncomfortable by the minute. Eugenie and Lysander stood next to him.

Eugenie fiddled with the strings of her bonnet, which rubbed annoyingly against her chin. While the brim protected her fair skin from burning under the midday sun, she wasn't fond of the garment and saw it as a nuisance. It never failed to ruin her hair, but after everything she'd seen her mother go through since the death of her father, she hadn't the heart to protest the ensembles she chose.

Lysander shifted his weight from foot to foot, growing impatient. He'd recently hit a growth spurt but still stood two inches shy of six feet tall, and there was a piece of him that was bothered by the fact the top of his head barely cleared Leon's chin. He'd been digesting his father's death for a few months, and there was a large part of him that was relieved he was gone. Sometimes he wondered if he was still a good person in God's eyes if he hadn't mourned the loss of his father the same way Eugenie had. Pondering the circumstances of *how* he died always left him conflicted, for he didn't know the exact details of what had happened. He couldn't even pry the information out of Klaus, who normally always cracked when harbouring a secret. There was one thing he knew for certain, though, and that was the distaste he had for Leon being there. While their family life had been chaotic long before he arrived, at least it was *their* chaos. It was as if when Leon came, he superimposed his own brand of madness. One in which Lysander suspected he might be responsible, in some way, shape or form—for his father's death.

Klaus rolled down the car window and stuck his head out. "How long have you been waiting?"

"Fifteen minutes at least," said Eugenie, wiping away the sweat hanging beneath her bonnet brim.

Klaus scratched the scruff of his chin. "Mind seeing what's taking her so long?"

Eugenie agreed with a nod and headed into the house.

The three men waited silently, and it was in that silence that Klaus' question prodded Duke Leon's conscience. *Why hasn't Princess Theodora yet joined us?* Less than an hour ago she had told them to get ready for a lunch out in town.

A set of rapidly clacking footsteps grew louder. Eugenie barrelled out of the entrance, bonnet nearly flying off, breath staggered. "Come quick!" she gasped. "Mum won't wake up."

In the span of one second, Duke Leon's mind wildly imagined the worst. The shock of Eugenie's words paralysed him where he stood, but Lysander yanked his arm and shook him from his daze, pulling him inside. Klaus left the car running and bounded ahead of the group, fear glowing in his eyes. The news had flipped an internal switch within the family's docile servant, and there was a grave determination etched into the wrinkles of his face. None of the children had ever witnessed him with such a countenance.

As they reached the master chamber, Klaus made it in first with Lysander close behind him. They both arrived at Princess Theodora's side; she lay on the chaise, apparently at rest, yet there was a troubled expression plastered on her porcelain skin.

Lysander shook her. "Mum!"

Her limbs jiggled limply under his grip. Klaus held up a hand to stop him. Duke Leon stood at the foot of the chaise with Eugenie by his side. She clutched her mouth to dampen her sniffing cries. Those were the same cries he'd heard echoing from her room the night of Prince

Ernest's death. He imagined the horror she must have felt at the idea of losing another parent.

Klaus pressed two fingers along her wrist, then raised them in front of her nose. "She has a pulse and is breathing."

Eugenie let out a trembling sigh. "Thank God."

"Wake up!" Lysander raised his voice, giving her another shake.

She didn't respond to his touch. Klaus darted off to the bathroom and a moment later returned with a wet washcloth. He gently pressed it along her forehead, a few droplets of water trickling down her cheek.

A lethargic groan escaped Princess Theodora's mouth and she began to stir. She blinked deliberately a few times, and when she opened her eyes, Klaus and Lysander flanking her provided a jolt of surprise that roused her from her slumber. She pushed herself up on the chaise, straightened her posture. She cast glances at Eugenie and Duke Leon. He noticed her gaze lingered on him a bit longer than the others.

"Here, let me help you," said Klaus, offering a hand.

She rose slowly, and a small glass bottle fell to the floor, its contents clinking together rhythmically as it rolled to a stop on the carpet.

It was filled with little white pills. They all stared at it for a split-second before Princess Theodora quickly knelt, picked it up, and brought it over to the vanity.

Klaus shifted uncomfortably and stood between Princess Theodora and the vanity, blocking the children's view of her. "Come along now. Let's wait down by the car."

"I'll be right behind you," added Princess Theodora.

Eugenie began to move towards the door, but Lysander refused to leave.

"Mum. What are those pills?"

"It's nothing," she answered dryly, shoving the bottle in the vanity drawer.

"It's not *nothing* when whatever they are, they put you in a sleep so deep I couldn't even shake you conscious."

Eugenie and Duke Leon paused by the master chamber door, curious for an answer to Lysander's question. Klaus chewed on the inside of his lip, positioned awkwardly between the children and Princess Theodora.

She let out a stifled sigh and mustered up the energy to look her son in the eye. "It's medicine."

"Medicine for what?"

"Are you ill?" asked Eugenie, chiming in with her brother.

Princess Theodora's eyes flicked between them both. "No, I'm not sick—"

"Then what's it for?" pressed Lysander.

She let out a tiny snort. Her gaze fell to the floor for a few moments before she reluctantly returned to meet her son's gaze.

"My pain."

The lunch went by quicker than usual because it was devoid of conversation. Everyone ate their food, only exchanging sidelong glances. Princess Theodora set the tone by not uttering a word, not even to the waiter; she chose her meal by pointing a delicate finger at the menu. Lysander consumed his food with tremendous speed, and judging by the grooves etched in his forehead, it wasn't due to ravenous hunger, but rather the fact he couldn't bear to face his mother.

When Klaus announced he was fetching the car, Eugenie and Lysander were quick to follow him out of the restaurant, unable to handle the tense silence any longer.

Duke Leon stayed behind. He pushed around lukewarm roasted potatoes that were beginning to soften into a mush from the constant prodding of his fork.

Princess Theodora glanced between Duke Leon and his half-eaten plate a few times, waiting to see if he noticed her examining him. "Did you not like the food?" she asked.

The mindless fiddling ceased. He glanced up at her just to confirm he hadn't imagined her speaking. She tilted her head expectantly.

"It was fine. I just don't have much of an appetite."

"That's not like you."

He stared back at her blankly, a slight squint to his eyes, for this comment was unlike her, and he couldn't discern its meaning.

Is she trying to press me?

"Is something bothering you?"

"Not particularly," he mumbled.

Princess Theodora saw through his ambiguous answer. His countenance spoke louder than his words. "Was it what transpired this morning?"

He nodded without meeting her eyes. "You shouldn't have to take those."

"Is that right?" she asked. The rise in her pitch, her canny tone, and the thin smile she produced told Duke Leon the question was purely rhetorical.

He nodded.

She let out a dispirited sigh.

The nonchalance she displayed perturbed him—as if this morning's events were not an issue worth discussing. It was then that Duke Leon came to the realisation that the normal warmth his beloved aunt exuded had been squelched by an unknown force. For now, when he looked into her eyes, he couldn't read a single emotion. It was as if he were looking at a two-way mirror.

Theodora could see out, but he was unable to see in.

"So, I have upset you it seems—"

"Not just me," he blurted. "Eugenie and Lysander too. Did you not see the scowl on his face or the veins bulging along his temples as he ate?"

Duke Leon leaned forward against the table and clenched his hands together with a white-knuckled grip. They held a shared gaze, neither yielding to the other, even when Duke Leon thought he saw a momentary crack in Theodora's veneer of apathy—the distinct rosy hue of embarrassment flushed her cheeks.

"I apologise."

The two words eased Duke Leon's steely gaze, but only marginally.

"I took one too many pills and fell asleep. But look at me," she said, showcasing herself with a wave of her hands. "I'm fine."

The waiter appeared and interrupted their exchange. He registered the palpable awkwardness between them, quickly removed the remaining plates from the table, and left the bill for Theodora to settle. She turned back to face Duke Leon and could see that her apology hadn't placated the tension that permeated through him. "What is it?" she asked.

He chewed the inside of his cheek, mulling over his words. "I'm more upset by the fact you aren't happy he's gone."

The indifference that had guarded Princess Theodora's emotions slid off her face in an instant. Duke Leon's words prodded her spirit; unbeknownst to him, she had slowly and deliberately peeled back the layers of his sentiments during this conversation and had finally reached the core.

"Happy is not the appropriate word. Relieved? That might be more fitting."

"If you are relieved then why are you taking medicine?"

She snorted. "Because despite the fact I am relieved, a death is a death. You are far too young to know the insidious nature of grief, let alone understand the intricacies of the bond of marriage which Prince Ernest and I shared. Don't play fool with me, Leon. You were aware I was being beaten."

A croak rose from Duke Leon's throat as he tried to form a response.

"*Happy*," huffed Theodora. "Seeing the man who I bore children with hanging from a chandelier like a bloody Christmas ornament left me anything but."

Duke Leon took the last remaining swig of water in his glass, wetting his parched mouth. He didn't respond to Princess Theodora for he had nothing to say. Nor would he meet her gaze.

"I'll see you in the car," he said as he stood up and left the table.

It was nearly a year ago, she thought. The early autumn day which became the first domino to topple in the chain of events that led them to this reality. Memories flooded her mind. The grotesque image of the slain dog, its chest cavity splayed open like a lab experiment gone wrong. It was *that* day that she had witnessed what she believed to be genuine remorse. Shame.

But what if his display was feigned?

A display strategically meant to pull at the heart strings of the aunt who had shown him nothing but love since he was a young boy.

Perhaps her sister's plans for him weren't cruel, but well-intentioned given the circumstance. They had always known Duke Leon as the black sheep of the family, for a reason beyond his control. But as he had grown into a man, his actions were pointing to a different conclusion—that he was a wolf in sheep's clothing.

And by taking pity on him, Theodora feared she'd done the unthinkable.

Let the wolf into her home.

October.

Princess Theodora rubbed the envelope's fragile edges between her forefinger and thumb. It was marked for the Attention of: Princess Theodora of Langenburg, and the return address was the coroner's office. When Klaus delivered the news of the letter's arrival, she took it and immediately went to the second-floor balcony. She figured the crisp autumn air might alleviate the heat flushing her skin. The sun had begun its late afternoon descent, painting the rolling green hills of Baden-Baden with an amber shimmer, and her view of the garden over the parapet was marvelously serene. The warbling of a lone blackbird atop a linden tree with brilliant burnt-orange leaves represented her only company.

She tore the envelope's seal, pulling out the paper. Her eyes zipped through the lines, sounding the sentences aloud, hurriedly looking for—

Her breath hitched.

3. A second puncture wound approximately 4.5 centimetres deep was found in the lower-right abdomen, 1 centimetre from the subject's appendix.

CAUSE OF DEATH: Internal haemorrhage due to impalement of the thoracic cavity and subsequent rupture of the descending aorta.

MANNER OF DEATH: Accidental.

Princess Theodora folded the report and slipped it back into the envelope. Although the sun shone upon her skin, she could no longer feel its warmth, nor could she hear the song of the lone blackbird, and she wasn't certain whether the silence was real or imagined. Each listless step led her back inside; she stared straight ahead, eyes vacant, unconsciously gravitating toward Klaus' chambers. When she reached his door, she rapped her knuckles twice against it.

"Come in!" he called out.

She found Klaus mending an old curtain. He popped his head up from behind the sewing machine, its mechanical needle clacking raucously. The moment he saw Theodora's faraway gaze and austere expression he cut the machine off and jumped to his feet.

"My dear, are you all right?"

She produced a miniscule nod, its meaning imperceptible.

"Klaus, might you be able to find a measuring tape and bring it to my chambers?"

"Right away." He darted out of the room. Princess Theodora retraced her steps to the staircase and unhurriedly ascended the three floors to her chambers. She made her way to the chaise and sat, smoothing out the fabric of her dress with her hands.

Then, she waited.

Not a minute went by before Klaus strode through the door, extending his arm before he fully crossed the threshold, measuring tape in hand. "Here you are."

A constrained smile tugged at her lips but faded away just as quickly as it came. She was thankful for Klaus, but the deathly chill she felt in the centre of her chest smothered any verve that remained. She took the measuring tape and dismissed him, watching as he disappeared down the stairs. Now alone, she took a deep breath and walked to her final destination.

The vanity.

She eyed the drawer where she knew it rested, nearly laughing at the absurd notion that such a tiny space could have ever kept the memory of Ernest's death hidden forever. It was like a tiny coffin behind a layer of faded, eggshell white paint. She gingerly pulled the drawer open, heart pounding as the nail file glinted in the soft light slipping through the windows. A part of her wished for nothing more than to slam the drawer shut and turn around. But she couldn't. Her hand was drawn to the blade, pulled along by a force so strong it felt like a magnet. But this time, when she picked it up, holding it in the palm of her hand, there was no diabolical thought of how it might be used. No immediate threat to her safety. She had reunited with it for a different reason.

Princess Theodora laid the nail file on the vanity and unfurled the measuring tape, starting from the top of the hilt and stopping at the end of the blade.

Its length was exactly 4.5 centimetres.

November.

The torrential downpour obscured the loud jingle that signalled Princess Theodora's entrance into Fredrich's garment shop. Its warmth enveloped her as she stepped inside, and she took a deep breath in—the scent of worn leathers and cotton, intermingled with the distinct piney cologne Freidrich habitually wore, all of which were welcome reminders that she was finally somewhere other than home.

She collapsed her umbrella, tucking it under her arm just before Freidrich appeared and took it from her, along with the two dresses she had draped over her other arm. He set them aside and turned back to her with open arms. She met his embrace, holding it for longer than normal. Typically, Freidrich wouldn't dare touch a royal, only bow to the women and the occasional handshake from the men. But this was Theodora, and in his eyes, she was a diamond among a kingdom of gold.

"My dear Theodora," he said softly as he pulled back from her, scanning her eyes. "I pray you've been well."

A tiny sigh escaped her lips. "Your prayers must have fallen on agreeable ears, because despite this weather I'm feeling well today."

"Splendid news indeed." A moment of silence passed before Freidrich shook himself from his prolonged gaze at Theodora; he feared if his true feelings rose too close to the surface, she would register the fondness he held for her. "Come, come," he said, gesturing for her to follow.

Once he'd turned around, her cheeks flushed slightly. She wondered if Freidrich had always eyed her in such a way, or perhaps this was a new phenomenon now that Ernest was gone. As he led her through the many racks of formal clothes, she felt a minor pang of guilt for telling the only person she considered a friend in Baden-Baden a half-truth.

"While I feel well today, Freidrich, I cannot lie to you. There have been many days…months, really, where I've felt quite unwell."

"Nothing a strong cup of tea can't fix." He pulled out an extra seat and placed it adjacent to his. "I'll be right back. Make yourself comfortable."

Princess Theodora soon found her eyes wandering the different spaces of Freidrich's mending room. The wall she faced had been fashioned into a bulletin board, filled edge-to-edge with cuts of fabric pinned by thumbtacks, papers sketched with designs, measurements, and delivery dates. The table beneath it housed a solid black sewing machine, and littered across its surface were metal thimbles and pin cushions filled with needles. Truthfully, she wasn't interested in the minutia of Freidrich's shop; observing was merely a way to ignore her thoughts, and just as she ran out of things to look at, the shrill whistle of a kettle preceded Freidrich's return.

He placed the cups of tea on the table, sat down across from her, and wasted no time in taking a slurping sip of the milky liquid.

"Now," he said with a warm smile. "Tell me what's been bothering you."

Nearly half an hour passed. She'd recounted the night of Ernest's death and the details of the autopsy report. But what she had failed to divulge was the true catalyst to her unrest. It was like there was an invisible rope strung between them and the conversation had become a verbal tug-of-war. When Freidrich pulled for details, Princess Theodora tugged back conservatively and remained tight-lipped.

"What I'm hearing is that Prince Ernest's death was an accident. A misfortunate one at that, but nonetheless an accident. That's what the police say. That's what the boy says. If the autopsy shows a stab wound, perhaps the boy was defending himself." Freidrich took a long breath, tilted his head down to line up with Princess Theodora's low, listless gaze. He continued at just above a whisper. "But I have the faintest inkling that if you sincerely believed it all to be an accident, you wouldn't have come into my shop in the first place. I've known you for ten years, and you never would have gone through the trouble of bringing me these two dresses with tears so minor Klaus could have mended them at home."

Princess Theodora snapped from her daze, and she stared wide-eyed at Freidrich.

"Have I spoken out of turn?" he asked.

She shook her head. Almost indiscernibly.

"Very well," he said, taking a sip of tea. "Let's try this again. What is really bothering you?"

"Leon."

When the name slipped out, a weight lifted off her chest; simply hearing the truth out loud instead of in her mind for the first time was freeing. Before Friedrich could open his mouth to question her, every thought she'd pent up since the night of the gala came pouring out. She took him word for word through the cryptic conversation she and Leon shared, the funeral, their exchange at lunch, and most importantly—how his original story conflicted with the autopsy report.

Princess Theodora divulged all of it while hardly taking a breath. A hint of astonishment pinched Freidrich's face; his bushy brows were raised, mouth slightly agape, but for the most part, he held his composure.

"You know..." he pushed the words out against a hesitant breath. "No, never mind. It might cause you unnecessary grief."

"No, you must say it!" she exclaimed, scooting her chair closer.

Freidrich saw the slight trembling of her hands, which she quickly concealed in her lap. Her eyes were wide as saucers, and they flicked back and forth frantically, searching his own. It was then he realised that whatever conviction she held about her nephew, it had consumed her entirely. The gentle spirit inside her had been snuffed out by obsession.

"Please," she said, eyes glistening.

Freidrich acquiesced with a sigh. "The day of the gala, when I was finishing Leon's fitting, I caught him staring at Ernest..."

"And?" asked Princess Theodora, unblinking.

"He stared at him like he was looking at the Devil himself. I remember thinking of how I'd never seen a boy his age staring at someone with such abhorrence."

Princess Theodora took a sharp breath through her nose and revealed a broad smile as she let go of the fistful of dress fabric she had been clenching. "Thank you," she said.

She stood, fetching the two dresses she had brought and draping them over her arm.

"Theodora, please don't let what I've said upset you."

"Nonsense," she said with a chipper tone. "I appreciate your honesty, my dear friend, but I must go now."

Friedrich followed Princess Theodora at her heels, who was making a hasty exit. "Will you at least stay and let me mend your garments?"

"Klaus will take care of it. Thank you, Freidrich, really." She pushed out the words breathlessly as she carved her way through the racks of clothes. When she reached the shop's entrance, she swung the door open, its bell jingling more violently than when she had entered.

"Theodora!" shouted Freidrich as he reached the threshold, watching helplessly as she walked out into the pouring rain. "You forgot your umbrella…" His voice trailed off, replaced by the deafening downpour.

But she didn't turn around. Despite his clothes beginning to soak through, his gaze remained fixed on Princess Theodora trudging along the empty brick street. A light mist rose from the ground, and in the amber rays of dusk slipping through an open crack in the clouds, her silhouette looked ethereal. When she finally crested the hill, and her figure had disappeared, Freidrich felt frozen there, being pelted by the barrage of frigid droplets, and in the stillness of the moment he was met with a paralysing feeling of dread.

For he realised that his dear friend hadn't come into his shop to pick his brain; her sole intention had been to confirm precisely what she already knew.

When Princess Theodora returned to Villa Friesenberg, she was met with the smell of garlic, roasted potatoes, and the savoury scent of a pot roast—Klaus preparing dinner. Him being occupied allowed her to leave the dresses to mend in his chambers whilst quickly ascending the stairwell to her own. She couldn't imagine how Klaus would react if he saw her clothes soaked through and a dripping mess. Once in the privacy of her room, she stripped down, left the sopping wet dress on the floor of the bathroom, and slipped into a bath robe.

Although dry, she still felt the phantom raindrops peppering her skin, and despite her chamber's quietness, her mind was anything but. Thoughts zipped around like an angry hive of bees trying to escape a crumbling nest, and she knew only one way to rid herself of the calamity.

She walked over to the vanity and fished out the little glass bottle from a drawer, unscrewing its lid and placing one of the white pills atop her tongue. She let it dissolve a bit before filling a drinking glass with water from the bathroom sink to wash away the bitter sting of the medicine. As she returned to the vanity, with an unconscious survival instinct tickling at her amygdala, she caught herself eyeing the pill bottle once more. The calmness she craved so desperately hadn't washed over yet, and it wouldn't for at least another twenty minutes. She shakily tapped out two more pills into her palm and threw them back; this time crushing them with her back molars until they were nothing more than an acrid, chalky paste she had to gulp down.

The slightest bit of the medicine absorbed sublingually and the storm in Princess Theodora's mind began to clear. She took a deep, steadying breath and straightened her posture. Then, she reached into another drawer and pulled out her stationery and fountain pen.

She had never imagined this day would come, yet here she was. This wasn't something she wanted to do, but fate had forced her hand. She clicked the pen and started writing.

The letter began with two words:

Dear Sister.

Christmas.

The faint sound of "Jingle Bells" crept into Duke Leon's room, stirring him from his slumber. He groggily lifted his head and rubbed his eyes until he came to, then noticed that outside the window, daylight hadn't yet arrived. Beyond the snowflakes piling up on the windowsill, the darkness of night was amidst its waning from black to a deep shade of blue. The woods encircling the eastern side of the Villa were varnished white from the layer of snow weighing down their thick, knotted branches.

He let out an elated sigh; the calm that blanketed the world on a snowy morning was something he cherished greatly, and coupled with the distant music coming from the record player, the two proved a perfect pair. The murmurs of Eugenie and Lysander drew him from his blissful daze, and he threw back the covers, heading out the door and down the hall. Once he passed the grand foyer, his footfalls were silenced by the thick carpet that led to the west wing living room, and each step he took seemed just as hushed as the winter wonderland swirling just outside the frosted windows.

Turning the corner into the west wing, he saw Lysander thrust the fire-iron into the blazing logs; a crackling burst of reinvigorated flames licked the soot-covered stone of the hearth. Eugenie sat in an armchair near the Christmas tree, watching her brother stoke the fire. Duke Leon joined Eugenie by the tree, a ring of wrapped presents at their feet. He took a deep breath, the scent of balsam fir intermingling pleasantly with the wood in the fire. Contentment welled within his spirit, for this was the first Christmas where all felt right.

No Mother. No Prince Ernest, he thought.

But as he settled into the room, he noticed Princess Theodora hadn't yet joined them.

And while the room was warmed by fire, the space felt incomplete without her presence.

"Where's Theodora?" he asked.

"Still in bed I bet," said Lysander, hanging the fire-iron back on its holder. "She's been sleeping through the morning most days because of that bloody medicine."

He only half-pondered his statement before Klaus rounded the corner with a silver serving tray carrying two steaming mugs. "Your Christmas favourite!" he chirped. "Hot chocolate." He handed one each to Lysander and Eugenie, then quickly caught Duke Leon's presence in his peripheral. "Master Leon, would you care for one?"

He nodded, but his mind was elsewhere. Klaus returned to the galley, leaving him with the sounds of the crackling fire and Eugenie's crude slurping. He couldn't help but wonder why his aunt would sleep in on *Christmas* of all mornings.

He couldn't help himself.

"Should we wake her?"

They both turned to him; Eugenie shrugged her shoulders.

"I tried to one morning this week. She was cross with me," said Lysander. "If she's not awake soon we can send Klaus to get her."

His statement almost placated Duke Leon.

Almost.

But then the minutes passed, and no Theodora. Klaus brought him the hot chocolate. He sipped it listlessly. The hot liquid wasn't sufficient in settling the uneasy feeling crawling around his gut. Then he felt a sharp jolt of pain, as if an invisible whip cracked against his back, and it jolted him to his feet. He set down his drink and walked deliberately away from the west wing.

"Where are you going?" asked Eugenie.

"To wake your mum."

Klaus exited the galley door and stopped in his tracks when he saw Duke Leon.

"Are you all right?" he asked as he tilted his head, following Leon up the spiral staircase with his eyes.

"Just waking up Theodora," he said.

Duke Leon didn't witness Klaus' reaction, but the jovial air to his demeanour flatlined. He'd gotten so caught up in preparing the morning's splendour that he hadn't realised she'd yet to come down. He glanced at the clock that hung in the grand foyer—8:25. Whatever alarm Duke Leon sensed transferred to Klaus. He began the ascent to Princess Theodora's chambers.

Duke Leon gave the thick wooden door three raps with his knuckles.

"Theodora," he said.

No answer. This time, he beat it with his fist, shaking the wood to the edge of the frame.

"Theodora!"

Still, no answer.

He entered her chambers, gingerly stepping in, unconsciously mirroring the silence that met him inside. He swivelled his head to survey the room—no Theodora.

"Theodora!" he called out.

His imagination almost conjured up the sounds of rustling footsteps and Theodora appearing from the bathroom, greeting him with a "Merry Christmas."

But none of that was real. Duke Leon slowly directed himself towards the bathroom, and he stopped just short of the threshold. "Theodora!" he called again, giving the door a few knocks. In the moment after, that's when he heard it.

Every few seconds—*drip, drip, drip.*

He opened the door.

At first glance, everything looked normal. Shower on the right, mirror and sink in front of him, and tub on the far left of the room.

Another *drip.* He cocked his head in the direction of the tub and eyed a tiny droplet fall from its edge onto the tile floor, and as he inched forward, he saw a small puddle had formed. A tightness spread through his chest, every breath shallower than the one previous. Fear pumped through his veins, like a poisonous liquid spreading head to toe, pooling at his feet which he had to drag forward, as they seemed to be petrifying to the floor.

Then, his heart skipped a beat.

Princess Theodora lay naked in the tub with water up to her neck. Her eyes were closed, and she looked oddly peaceful.

"Theodora," he said, voice trembling.

She did not stir.

Why isn't she waking? he thought. The tiniest ember of panic rose in his gut, and he instinctively knelt along the edge of the tub, eyes flicking across her exposed body, alabaster and smooth.

"Theodora," he said a little louder, shaking her shoulder.

Her skin was cold, and her head rolled grotesquely to rest against the opposite shoulder. Duke Leon winced and jumped to his feet. He shook Theodora more forcefully; her body bobbed limply in the water, creating splashes that spilled over the tub's edges.

"Theodora!" he shouted, tears welling in his eyes.

A tremor unlike any other he'd experienced ripped through his soul, tearing him apart from the inside out. He began shaking her violently, screaming her name at the top of his lungs. *"Theodora! Wake up!"*

"Master Leon!" shouted Klaus from the bathroom threshold. "What are you do—?"

He froze in his tracks behind Duke Leon, processing the gravity of the situation. "Oh my God," he muttered as he spotted the bottle of Theodora's pills on the windowsill above the tub.

"Wake up!" Duke Leon blubbered, shaking Princess Theodora's cold, *lifeless* body. He flinched beneath Klaus' gentle grip on his shoulder.

Klaus reached over and placed the back of his palm on Theodora's face, instantly recoiling, then turned to Duke Leon and harnessed every modicum of composure he possessed to look the boy in the eyes. "Leon," he said. "She's gone."

Duke Leon listlessly released his grip, letting her body rest. A dizzying spiral of misery was set into motion, and with it came a powerful wave of nausea. When Klaus went to the bedroom to phone the Polizei, Duke Leon stayed at Theodora's side, emitting drawn out, guttural cries. His tears rolled off his cheeks into the water, and he pulled her shoulders toward him, cradling her cold head against his chest.

The peace of the morning had been obliterated by the finality of death, and for the first time in Duke Leon's life, he cried. And he would continue to cry until night fell on snow-covered Baden-Baden, as well as when the sun rose the following morning. And he would cry in the days and weeks to come, for he had lost the only person whom he had ever truly loved.

His dearest Theodora.

A bit of nostalgia washed over Queen Eleanor as she watched her grandchildren opening presents. The air was filled with hints of mistletoe and peppermint; the sounds of wrapping paper being torn coupled with joyous yelps of excitement were music to her ears. Although the grandchildren were still the little ones in *her* mind, they weren't so little anymore. Princess Maud's children, William, Caroline, Charlotte, and Catherine ranged from their mid-to-late teens, but their excitement hadn't dulled over the years and nonetheless still pleased her.

Christmas was the fondest of holidays to Queen Eleanor, for when she was still *Eleanor* and not yet *Queen*, it was the one day where the crushing isolation of her strict upbringing was eased. The whole family would come together, and the palace was lively and gay.

Princess Maud met eyes with the Queen, and they shared a warm smile. Footsteps came from behind the Queen, and she turned to see Jean-Claude Marron at her side.

"A letter has arrived," he said.

She raised a brow in disbelief. "Can it wait until tomorrow?"

Jean-Claude avoided eye contact with any of the other family members and leaned in next to her ear. "It's from Theodora."

"Oh, how wonderful!" she chirped. "Give it here."

Jean-Claude slid a paper knife through its seal and handed Queen Eleanor the envelope.

Her broad smile diminished the moment she began reading.

Dear Sister,

It pains me greatly to even hold this pen, but I must relieve myself of the weight that has been burdening my soul since the passing of Ernest. I write this letter in confidence that you will ensure it is read by your eyes and your eyes only, for what I am about to tell you is something I can neither fully prove nor disprove by facts alone. I admit this shortcoming candidly, but I also implore you to understand that I have not by any means come to these conclusions solely on intuition. I believe the circumstances that led to the labelling of my late husband's death as accidental was the only true accident that transpired. Firstly, the day of the gala, I had a conversation with Leon. I will not go into the details of that conversation, but in short, I only understood the true nature of his words after Ernest's death. Secondly, the coroner's report revealed an anomaly about a stab wound that begot many sleepless nights. Lastly, a conversation with a trusted friend confirmed my suspicions with enough certainty that I am able to produce this letter. In whole, this knowledge has suffocated your dear sister's spirit for months, and it is truly with an unimaginable guilt that I say to you I believe I let a monster in with open arms and subsequently allowed him to bid his will in my home. I have now learned the grave lesson that it is impossible to love an illness into extinction. I see the truth, that Leon is afflicted with a forever sickness. The same sickness that led to him being responsible for Prince Ernest's death. This is my conclusion. That you were correct, Eleanor, in your original assessment. For the horror we witnessed that day outside the garden walls was just a preview of what he is capable of. Yet all is not hopeless. I have faith that with enough fortitude this situation can be remedied, but unfortunately, I see no other way for him to be healed within the walls of our kingdom. Nevertheless, I believe this is a problem we can solve together.

Please do visit soon. I regretfully admit I am not well enough to make the trip across the Channel. For by some stroke of misfortune, it seems harbouring this knowledge has caused me to develop a sickness of my own. But don't fret, dear sister. A good doctor has prescribed a medicine that will make me all the better. I pray the information in this letter does not burden you with the same severity as it has me. You have always been the stronger of the two of us. I trust you will know what to do when the time comes.

All my love,

Theodora

Queen Eleanor did not realise the tearing of wrapping paper and lively conversation had all but disappeared. Princess Maud and the grandchildren were staring at her, silent.

"Pardon me for a moment," she said through a thin smile. Jean-Claude followed at her side as she manoeuvred her way from the grand parlour, down the walkway, and into the galley to use the phone. She quickly dialled the number for Villa Hohenlohe and impatiently waited as it rang.

Klaus was crying when he answered.

New Year's Day.

"Master Leon," whispered Klaus, gently nudging his arm. "Wake up."

Duke Leon stirred beneath the covers, emitting a reluctant groan before his eyes flickered open. The face that stared back at him was unrecognisable compared to the one he'd grown accustomed to over the past year; beneath Klaus' eyes were saggy skin and dark circles a faint hue of violet.

It was then he noticed that outside it still appeared to be night. "What time is it?"

"Half five."

Duke Leon raised a brow. "Then why are you waking me?"

Klaus' lower lip twitched. Much like Duke Leon, Princess Theodora's death tore at his heart night after sleepless night, and ever since, his lone companion during the days was exhaustion.

"I'm afraid I don't know the reason, but you must. Get dressed now, and when you're done, meet me downstairs."

The vague answer didn't placate Duke Leon's curiosity. Klaus left the room, and he quickly got dressed. When he traipsed down the slumbering halls of Villa Friesenberg and arrived in the grand foyer, he was alone. A few seconds passed before he heard the distinct chugging of the Mercedes engine outside. He followed the sound and found it had already been pulled up in the drive. Klaus was in the driver's seat and the back door was popped open, awaiting his entry.

He crouched in, closed the door, and before he could settle in his seat Klaus accelerated away from the drive. The Mercedes jostled him around over every bump and pothole on the rural roads outside of Baden-Baden, and the twinkling of the houses dotting the dark hills made him feel peaceful—but only for a fleeting moment—for he realised that they were passing the city centre altogether.

"Where are we going?" he asked, a hint of alarm tickling his vocal cords.

Klaus met his eyes in the rearview mirror.

"Not to worry. We're almost there."

He dodged my question, he thought. Duke Leon leaned back into his seat, and the normally soft leather seemed to poke and prod him so that he couldn't find a suitable position to relax.

The car rolled to a stop in an empty parking lot in front of a square, plain white building. Klaus hopped out and opened the door for him. Duke Leon stood there with his arms crossed, and the discomfort he felt in the car had followed him outside as he studied his surroundings. There was one other vehicle parked in a shadowy corner behind the building's alleyway.

"Come along," said Klaus, gesturing with an open hand.

Duke Leon looked away from the unknown car and followed him toward the building's entrance. Just above the doorframe were brass letters that read:

AMTSGERICHT BADEN-BADEN.

Gericht… he thought, attempting to recall the bits of German he had learned in class, but he couldn't put his finger on the meaning. Once inside, Duke Leon was hit with a slight musty smell, intermixed with old wood and paper. It was too dark to discern the building's purpose, but Klaus led him to a set of heavy-looking wooden doors. He stopped in his tracks and stood off to the side.

"What?" asked Duke Leon, glancing between the door and Klaus.

Klaus held out his hand, and with faint remnants of the streetlights slipping in, Duke Leon could have sworn he saw his Adam's apple bob up and down before he spoke.

"You must go in alone."

He wanted to contest Klaus' instructions, but a little voice told him it was no use. He managed to muster up the strength to ask a single question.

"Is it safe?"

"Of course, Master Leon."

He pushed open the double doors, the old hinges groaning beneath the weight of the wood. The room was encircled by rows of what looked to be pews, and at the centre of the large space was a podium. His steps were measured as he approached, all while his senses were on high alert for any movement outside his own. Just as he reached the podium, the wooden double doors groaned raucously as they swung shut, followed by the forceful clank of a metal lock. Fear crawled up his spine and made the hairs on the nape of his neck bristle, for he instantly realised two things; the first was that Klaus had lied, and the second was that he was *not* alone.

The sound of a match sliding against sandpaper came from the far side of the room. He frantically searched for the flame and found it amidst lighting a candle. When the candle wick caught, it revealed the glowing white visage of Queen Eleanor. The clacks of her footfalls echoed throughout the cavernous ceilings as she approached the centre of the room.

"Hello, Leon," she said, without a trace of surprise in her voice. She exhibited the confidence of someone who had not only expected his arrival but had been patiently awaiting it. From the opposite side of the room, a second pair of footsteps arose.

Leon whipped around to find a man approaching. He donned a full robe and a long, white wig whose tight, ringlet curls fell past the shoulders. When he reached the podium, he climbed up behind it.

"What is this?" asked Leon, eyes flicking between the man and Queen Eleanor.

Neither the man nor the Queen answered. His question simply fell past the periphery of the candlelight and disappeared into the shadows. Suddenly, his mind flashed back to the brass letters spelling AMSTGERICHT above the doorway of the building, and as he stared at the man's outfit and headdress, he realised its meaning.

Gericht—court.

He opened his mouth to speak but Queen Eleanor held up a finger.

"Not a word."

The judge drew an envelope from his court dress and slid his finger through its edge. In the dim light, Leon could make out the red wax seal of the Queen. He watched as the judge unfolded a letter and cleared his throat.

"I, Queen Eleanor of Lancaster, with all royal powers vested in me, on this first day of the first month of the year 1940, decree the immediate and permanent removal of Duke Leon of Albemarle's ducal title—"

"Have you gone mad?" he blurted, voice jumping to a higher-than-normal pitch.

Queen Eleanor chewed on the inside of her cheek and glowered at him. She took a steadying breath and held it, unnaturally puffing up her chest.

"If you speak again—even a word—you will not only have to suffer the punishment outlined within this decree, but you will be exiled to a far-flung island in the middle of the Atlantic never to be seen again."

Leon gulped, his throat dry. He had never heard such finality accompanying his mother's caustic tone.

"Continue," she said to the judge, holding her eyes on Leon.

"From this day forward, you shall be banished from your residence at Villa Hohenlohe and barred from entering all the royal residences. You will also be prohibited from bearing any name or title similar to your ducal title of Albemarle or the Lancaster name. Any association to the Royal Family will be seen as a violation of this decree."

Leon felt a tremor rise through his gut; his eyes flicked between the judge and the Queen imperceptibly in the pale blue light of dawn slipping through the lone skylight. He tried terribly hard to keep his face from contorting, but in the sickly silence that hung in the air after the judge spoke, it was as if the emotional weight of Theodora's death had doubled in a fraction of a second. Physically, too. Every shallow breath he drew in was met with a barrage of invisible knives lodging between the spaces of his ribs, and the pressure on his sternum was comparable to being crushed by an elephant.

"Leon, you must say you agree for the record."

He stared blankly at his mother, speechless.

"*Out loud,*" she said, voice lowering an octave.

For a moment, he wondered if the alternative Queen Eleanor had mentioned was the better option. If he were abandoned on some remote island in the mid-Atlantic, at least he'd still be *Duke* Leon. He'd still have his name. His dignity.

But that thought dissolved away just as quickly as it had materialised, and reality cradled him back into its thorny arms.

"I agree." He forced out the words. The statement reverberated longer than normal, and even though that peculiarity fell only on Queen Eleanor and the judge's ears, it almost seemed like the shadows occupying the rows of encircling benches had absorbed the raw misery of the two uttered words. For the wooden benches, carvings of the walls, and the high ceilings had borne witness to so much raw emotion over the years the very materials themselves were imbued with it.

The judge dragged his fountain pen along the bottom of the decree and rolled it up.

That's it, Leon thought. *Something as simple as a signature stole my name.*

"May I have a moment alone with my son?" asked Queen Eleanor without diverting her gaze from Leon.

The judge obliged with a nod and stepped down from the podium. He casually walked toward the exit, giving the double doors a quick rap of his knuckles. The bolt unlatched and Klaus swung it open. He quickly relocked it.

Fear suddenly coursed through Leon's veins. He was *alone* with his mother. And much like Pavlov's dogs who would salivate at the sound of a whistle, Leon's past had trained his natural instincts inversely.

That when he was alone in a room with his mother, nothing good was in store for him.

"This will be the last time you see me," she said unflinchingly.

Little did she know, Leon would have preferred precisely that outcome the first time she struck him after dinner so many years ago. The air between them seemed to thicken.

"I know what you did," Queen Eleanor said in the lowest of whispers.

A petrifying force slid down his spine, straightening his posture unnaturally as he fought not to tremble under his mother's gaze. "What are you talking ab—"

"Do not play fool with me, Leon. I cannot prove it in a court of law, nor could Theodora, but it was you." Her chest heaved and fell as she spoke, and the rage she held back caused her to shake. "My sister was kinder than I, and that is why she took you into her home. Because she loved you like you were her own. And yet you were so selfish that you decided to abuse that kindness. To play God. To rob her of her husband and Eugenie and Lysander of their father!"

"He *beat* her," he croaked as tears welled in his eyes. "Violently. It wasn't once in a blue moon; it was every goddamn week! Shattering plates, broken furniture, bruises and bloody lips. He would have killed her himself if I wouldn't have put an end to it!" Leon's lip curled up in irrevocable disgust.

"You thought you could save her." She exhaled out a tiny, pity-laden titter through her nose. "That's the irony of it all, isn't it? You tried to protect her and yet you're the one responsible for her death."

"I am *not!*" he bellowed, clamping his eyes shut.

Queen Eleanor bridged the space between them and prodded his chest with an index finger. "Bruises heal, Leon. Grief can kill." She grabbed Leon's cheeks, cradling his face. "Look at me."

He couldn't. Not when she was this close.

"*Look at me!*"

He broke, meeting his mother's icy blue eyes that mirrored his own.

"It was grief that killed Theodora, and for as long as you live, I hope you remember that it was *you* who brought grief to her doorstep. You and no one else." She dropped his face from her grip as if his skin was dirty and turned away from him. She began up the gentle incline toward the courtroom exit and stopped halfway, turning back.

"If you try and test the boundaries of this decree, I can promise you the consequences will not be pleasant. Your father tried to test me once, and it didn't end well for him."

"Alfred?"

Queen Eleanor snorted. "No, Leon. Your *real* father."

She left and let the double doors slam behind her. Moments later, Leon heard the cranking of the Mercedes' ignition followed by tyres spinning across the gravel drive. A numbness began spreading through his chest, and as he lumbered out of the courtroom, his legs felt like lead. When he exited the building, it seemed as if the liveliness of morning had come to a screeching halt. The songbirds stopped their warbling. The trees held still despite the breeze. And even the distant sounds of the city seemed to disappear altogether. He followed the sidewalks aimlessly, uncertain of where he would sleep tonight. For the first time in his life, he worried about what the future held. The comforts of his royal upbringing had been eradicated in the blink of an eye.

The sun that rose over the horizon in Baden-Baden that morning was soft; it cast a warm, dewy glow across the landscape, and as it slipped through the cracks of the trees it touched his face, like a warm hand cupping his cheek, a welcome replacement to the cold, loveless hands that had touched him minutes earlier. As the sun rose higher, the trees stretched out their branches, soaking up the light, and the birds returned to their song, and a few cars sputtered past him along the street. Leon paused to notice the reawakening of morning life, and it made him realise that even though his life as *Duke* Leon was over, life itself would still go on.

He drew in a sharp breath of the cold winter air and continued walking.

Kensington
Two days later

Princess Edith closed the door to 20 Courtfield Gardens and began sobbing into her palm; she prayed her muted cries wouldn't carry through the cracked bay window and reach Queen Eleanor's ears as she walked away. The news she'd brought invoked such sudden, strong nausea that she thought she might retch all over the foyer.

Theodora was dead.

And her only son had been banished from the kingdom for reasons Queen Eleanor would not explain. She fetched a handkerchief from the dishevelled living room, having to step around an overabundance of boxed-up belongings, useless furniture, and miscellaneous memorabilia strewn about to reach the master bedroom. It had been nearly a year since she moved from apartment 1A in Kensington Palace to the townhouse Sir Charles lived in before he went missing, yet she had never fully unpacked. It was as if she wasn't satisfied with the idea of settling here, of all places. It was too close to home. Too close to her mother. She often daydreamed of chartering a sailboat and heading to Bermuda. Or perhaps disappearing and taking up sculpture in Morocco.

Anything to get far away from this Godforsaken island.

The real reason Princess Edith craved escape was that she simply wanted to run as far away from her mistake as possible. Run away from herself, from the woman whose cowardice had only pushed Leon further from any chance of receiving her love. First, he left the palace, and she could barely stomach him being across the Channel. Now, there was a large possibility she might never see his face again. The thought caused a painful groove to form in her forehead as she blubbered, and she felt like she couldn't take a good breath. She moved to her bed and haphazardly threw her pillow across the room, revealing the only photo she had of herself and Leon. It was taken on Easter Sunday at Osborne House, away from the Queen's eyes.

She collapsed to her knees, clutched the picture to her chest, and continued crying for the rest of the afternoon. Her lone companion was the sickening knowledge that her son was gone, and there was not a thing she could do to bring him back.

CHAPTER 19
THE CAT'S CRADLE

Irene Murray had been a waitress at TLC for ten years—since it opened, in fact—and she didn't have plans to leave any time soon. Al had paid her fairly from day one, and within a short amount of time he made her the head waitress. She helped with hiring, firing, making the schedule, and even a bit of inventory. If she ever had a friend from university that she ran into on the street poke fun at the fact she still waited tables, she'd laugh it off, for she knew with the many raises she received she likely made a better living than whatever job the poor lass' degree gleaned her.

And throughout all that time, she'd never had any complaints. But there were two days every year that stood out to her at TLC. Each occurrence tickled a part of her brain that caused her perception to be heightened. She wasn't sure if it was fear, curiosity, or a mix of the two, but the peculiarity of the scene and Al's behaviour always left a strong imprint on her memory. After some time, the memory would begin to fade, but like clockwork, six months to the day, the rendezvous would happen again and reinvigorate her palate with strangeness.

Today was one of those days.

Al would notify only she and the head chef the evening before the guest's arrival. By now, Irene had all but memorised her set of instructions to prepare. She was to have the wait staff cover the restaurant except for the one table set aside for the guest, in a narrow alcove near the restrooms. Irene found this preference intriguing. If the guest were Al's family or a good friend, why did he give them the worst seat in the house, so far removed that they were not only out of the view of the customers but also most of the wait staff? The head chef would prepare a special meal for the guest, and Al would serve. He would spend the entirety of the guest's meal at their side, talking. Sometimes he even pulled up a chair.

She always wondered what they talked about. The guest was an elderly woman, with pale skin and even paler blue eyes. Even at a distance, Irene could see the powdery makeup lying heavily in the creases of the crow's feet around her eyes and the sagging skin of her jowls. None of that was unusual for a woman her age, but the predominant trait that puzzled Irene was the choice of wardrobe. A gaudy brooch rested on her bosom, yet the rest of her outfit was deliberately bland. But then those earrings. My God! Those gleaming, ruby earrings must have cost a fortune. It was almost as if the woman was wealthy but doing everything in her power to appear the contrary. Irene was no fool, though. She could see right through the façade because for most of her life, all she knew was poverty. And the one thing she had learned about the rich was that there were very few of their kind who could withstand the temptation of flaunting their wealth. Irene snorted at the thought. It was as if at a certain point, the excess didn't even exist if there was no one around to witness it.

"Irene. Jack's on hold for the flour order," called a waitress from around the corner of the galley. She sighed, dropping her gaze from Al and the old woman. She walked back toward the phone and suppressed a giggle; it amused her how carried away she got with wondering about the mysterious woman's origins.

Even so, she knew once she confirmed the flour order with Jack, she'd drift right back to the corner where she could discreetly watch the interactions between the two.

Oh, what I'd do just to hear their conversation, she thought before picking up the phone.

Al watched Queen Eleanor cut three slices of meat, dipping each in the gravy reduction before popping them in her mouth. She closed her eyes and emitted a tiny groan of pleasure as she chewed, fully engrossed in devouring what was left on her plate.

"I take it you like the food."

She broke her focus from the plate, cheeks flushing as she quickly swallowed. "I swear it gets better every time. I don't know how you do it."

"Trade secret," he said with a smile.

Queen Eleanor tilted her head, sucking her teeth with playful reprove. "Shame. One of these days I hope you'll tell me."

She settled back in her seat and smoothed out her dress. Al always found it interesting to sit across from his mother in full disguise. He still to this day wondered what spurred the visits, and after all these years he could only guess. One thing he noticed was how the way she looked at him had evolved. Perhaps it was the power of time, but every subsequent visit revealed more cracks in the callous woman he'd always known. A twinkle of admiration glimmered in her eyes every so often, but he didn't understand its impetus.

"You know," she began, pausing to mull over her words. "You've done very well for yourself."

"You told me so the last few times."

Queen Eleanor glanced down at her wrinkled hands, fiddling with the edge of the tablecloth. She drew in a few small breaths and opened her mouth as if she were going to speak, but then her chest collapsed with a sigh.

"What's the matter?" he asked.

She clicked her tongue, almost like she was chiding herself for her hesitance. She sat up a little straighter, then looked him directly in the eyes.

"I'm proud of you," she said. "Proud of the man you've become."

A powerful conflux of emotions eddied in Al's gut. His windpipe constricted, making it hard to breathe. One second, he felt gratitude. The next, fear. Beneath all of that were the embers of anger he'd stoked for as long as he could remember. Flashbacks to the courtroom twenty-four years ago surfaced in his mind's eye.

His last day as *family*.

"Thank you," he pushed out.

In his peripheral, he saw Irene waving from around the corner, eyes wide as saucers. He wondered what it could be because she was well aware she should never, under any circumstances, interrupt *this* meal.

"Pardon me a moment," he said and rose to his feet. When he approached Irene, she pulled him around the corner away from the Queen's earshot.

"What is it?"

"The police sergeant is out front. He says they have a warrant to search your home."

A black hole formed at the centre of Al's chest; it slipped slowly downward with the weight of its own gravity into the furthest reaches of his gut, swallowing everything in its path. In a matter of seconds his whole world seemed to cave in around him. Everything he'd built to hedge the pain—the beauty he'd brought to the town, the charm, the good deeds—all of which were propped up by his elaborate charade, toppled down off its feeble foundation. And all that was left was the darkness within Al.

The black soul he fought so hard to hide.

To keep out of the light.

Fiona groaned, legs squirming slightly on the cool concrete floor.

"It hurts," she whimpered.

"Is yours a kind of gnawing feeling?" asked Gavin quietly. He sat upright, arms wrapped around his shins, chin resting atop his knees.

"Worse. I'm not sure I can take it much longer." She cast a glance at Arun when she said this.

He met her gaze briefly before breaking away. He couldn't handle the pain in her pleading eyes; it stimulated an endless nausea that only ceased when he slept, because he was powerless to help his soft-spoken, angel-faced new friend. Powerless to turn back time.

To when the group of four was still five.

He grimaced at the thought of what had happened that night. He swore he could still taste the metallic blood on his tongue, and he feared the smell would cling to his nostrils until he was a wrinkly old man. It had been over half a week since Craig was killed, and today was the fourth full day without any food.

They were slowly starving. On the first day after Craig's death, all of them pressed their shoulders against the false wall of the room in an attempt to drink the water within the frozen room. But it took four of them to push it open. With Craig gone, that left them dependent on James, who refused to help. They had no other choice but to drink straight from their toilet. Even though they avoided the bowl for the sake of a bit of hygiene and instead drank from the cistern, Fiona still gagged as she held the water cupped in her hands. James drank from it as well, but never at the same times as they did. Every day that passed, the distance between him and the rest of the group grew larger. The two brothers hadn't uttered a word to each other. Gavin couldn't bear to look in James' direction.

Arun conjured that he might have gone delirious. Despite his ramblings about Al coming to save them, he wasn't blind. James *must* know Al murdered Craig. Perhaps this was all a big defence mechanism. A way for him to ignore the truth.

Arun's stomach gurgled violently, pulling him from his thoughts. The sudden shaking of his innards made him silently beg to God that the emptiness he felt inside could be swapped with the teeming thoughts threatening to make his brain explode. Then, all would be right. Just for a moment.

A full stomach and an empty mind.

Just then, shuffling sounds came from the ceiling above. Arun craned his head upward, staring.

"What was that?" asked Fiona.

"I don't know," he answered, glancing quickly at Fiona and Gavin to see them staring at the same spot of the ceiling he was studying. Suddenly, the sound came again. But different this time. There were multiple sounds coming from different spots. Though a layer of concrete was above their heads, Arun heard the faintest creaking of Al's wood floors.

"Footsteps," said Gavin flatly.

The deathly chill that had taken root in the centre of Arun's chest since Craig's death, the ravenous hunger, and his noisy mind instantly fell to the wayside. There wasn't just one person above them. There were *people*.

He jumped to his feet and began shouting, "Help! Help us!"

Fiona and Gavin joined him in the pleas for help. They all stood side-by-side, bellowing the most fervent SOS they could produce. But not James. He pushed his head deeper between his knees and cupped his hands over his ears.

Three were fighting to be saved.

The fourth refused and was waiting for his saviour.

"This is what our tax dollars are paying for," scoffed Al.

"Protect and serve," said Margaret as she slid a bookshelf away from the wall. "I'd wager that saving four lads who've been missing for almost two weeks suffices for 'protect' and throwing you in jail for the rest of your life will fit the bill for 'serve'."

"Is she supposed to be here?" Al glanced at Stu, who stood awkwardly in the centre of the living room, checking the area with lacklustre enthusiasm. "We saw she's capable of lying," he added sourly.

"She was brought back on the moment she found your architect's blueprint."

"Malcolm? He was sick in the head! Always rambling about delusional fantasies, designs he wished he could create." Al tapped his foot, arms crossed, eyes darting between the many officers desecrating his beloved home. "You found a fake copy of a blueprint. Was a bloody madman, I tell you! Should have taken a gander at his journals. They'll be far more enlightening than what you'll find here."

Margaret attempted to silence Al's agitated murmurs and focus on the blueprint which she held to the light. She noticed in the area she assumed to be the kitchen, in what looked to be a closet, there was a square on the floor of that room.

"Move to the pantry, empty it!" she called out to the officers.

Al gave them all a roll of his eyes. "I assure you; this is all a waste of time. You won't find anything."

In the pantry, a small throw rug sat in the centre of the floor. One of the officers yanked it up to find nothing. Just a smooth, epoxy finish. Margaret revisited the blueprint, frustrated. "Let me through," she instructed. The two officers in front of her stood back against the walls and watched as she knelt to the ground. "Be quiet." She began knocking around forcefully on the floor, keeping the intensity of the knocks equally distributed. When she knocked at the edges of the pantry, the sound was deeper. Duller. But when she knocked in the area that the rug had covered, it was slightly lighter—echoey.

"This space here in the middle is not as solid as the rest," she said.

Some of the officers behind Stu and Al mumbled soundlessly to each other. Al snorted, shifted his weight, arms still crossed. "And that, I assume, means you've hit the jackpot?" he mocked.

She ignored him, glancing up at Stu. "We need to cut through this floor."

"Oh, this is ridiculous, you can't possibly—"

"Get him out of here!" yelled Margaret. "I can't think, for Christ's sake."

Two officers escorted Al from the kitchen, and now she was alone with her sergeant for the first time in weeks. Stu's lips trembled beneath his moustache, and there was a peculiar reticence behind his eyes.

"We can tear apart his house, but we can't physically tear through walls and floors. You know that."

"There's a square on this blueprint, right here in the pantry. This spot is hollower than the rest. And you're telling me that if the four lads are beneath our feet we can't break through and save them?"

She held his gaze, pleading with her own.

He shook his head. "We can't."

"Unbelievable," she huffed.

If she couldn't legally break through the floor, she'd find another way. There had to be something they were missing. She returned to the blueprint once more.

Aniqa's eyes grew wide as she saw the many officers surrounding Al's house. They buzzed around the garden and the gravel drive like bees who had just found a stockpile of honey. She'd just finished her shift at the Inn and was returning to do what Margaret had asked of her the last time they spoke—to keep an eye on Al. She parked along the kerb and began the short walk to his home. As she approached, a nervous fluttering arose in her stomach. It made her stop in her tracks, and she took a deep, steadying breath.

Her imagination was the culprit; she visualised rounding the corner to Al's garden and seeing Arun standing next to Margaret, his big black eyes flicking toward her the moment she called out his name, hearing his mother's voice. She could see him in a full-on sprint, running into her arms, holding her with the softness of his boyish embrace.

Aniqa blinked deliberately to rid herself of the vision along with the tears welling in her eyes. Her beloved son was not safe.

Not yet at least.

When she reached the edge of Al's garden, she noticed Stu and Margaret weren't among the officers outside. Through the slits of the blinds, she caught sight of Al talking to an officer in the foyer. She dipped around the corner to obscure herself from his potential view.

"Shite," blurted a voice from behind her. "What's goin' on here?"

She whipped around to see the postman, Brian, standing on the tips of his toes to get a better look over Al's hedges.

"No idea. Guess they're looking for something," she said.

"Never thought I'd see police at Al's of all places. He's a kind fellow."

Aniqa mustered a lukewarm nod.

"Well, say, I'm headed to yours in a wee bit. Mind if I give ye your mail?"

"Sure."

Brian fished through his mailbag and handed her a few envelopes with a warm smile.

"Take care, Miss Khan."

He departed with a nod, but just a few steps out, stopped at Al's mailbox. He shoved a bundle of mail inside and continued walking, soon disappearing down an adjacent street.

An idea dawned on her. She casually walked over to the mailbox, casting sidelong glances at the pavement and double-checking to ensure none of the officers nor Al were looking in her direction. She hastily opened the black iron box and pulled out the mail, quickly cycling through the bundle. All mundane in nature. Bill after bill—electric, telephone, water.

The sudden weightiness of one of the envelopes piqued her interest. She held it above the bundle, gently setting the rest of the mail back inside the box. It had no sender name or return address, but it was made out to Albert Reid.

The shiny red wax seal intrigued her the most. She rubbed her thumb across its slippery texture, wondering what the ornate crest impressed on it signified. Without hesitation, she put the envelope into her bag and returned the rest of the mail into the box. Aniqa wasn't sure what triggered that reflex, but the part of her brain that had ruminated over the peculiarities of Al: the Scottish accent so subtle it felt contrived, the fact no one in town seemed to know where he came from—seemed a sufficient catalyst to take what was not hers.

She glanced up at the house and felt fear race down her spine; Al was staring at her. And even through the membrane of the cracked blinds and the gleaming glass, it was glaringly evident that Al saw what she had taken. She flinched into motion and began back down the pavement. When she cranked the ignition, the logical part of her wondered if she had made a mistake. *Why did I steal that?* she thought. But the other part of her felt—*sbajñā*—intuition—rising to the surface of her soul, making her believe that this anonymous letter was important. A compulsive glance in her bag confirmed that it was still there.

Aniqa drove home in silence, brooding over the fact her son had been missing for close to two weeks.

"When was this repair made, again?" asked Margaret, fighting the urge to clench her teeth.

"A few weeks ago," Al said, glancing between Stu and her. He had his hands in his pockets and his countenance had taken on a casual air. Like he knew he was almost in the clear. There was nothing left for him to fear.

"We have good reason to believe there is an entryway on this side of the house. A stairwell or a passageway inside the shed."

"Does this look like an entryway?"

Margaret chewed on the inside of her lip. She loathed Al's arrogance, but what she detested more was the fact that she was staring at a brick wall. Tools hung haphazardly on jagged hooks. The only visible sign that there was anything suspicious being that some of the bricks were brighter, less worn.

Indicating that a section of this wall was new.

"Excuse us for a minute," she said, pulling Stu toward the back of the drive, out of Al's earshot. Stu's pallor hadn't improved. She wondered why he looked so ill.

"Is there no way we can tear down that shed? Pay for the damages if he's innocent. Arrest him if he's not. There must be a—"

"There isn't. We can empty this place if we want, but the warrant doesn't allow for what you're asking."

"But the blueprint *shows*—"

"Enough, Margaret. We simply can't."

Stu left her and returned to the main search. She let out a sigh; once her subconscious reminded her she was alone in the drive with Al, she looked up.

"I'm sorry you didn't find what you were looking for," he said flatly.

Margaret didn't respond to the comment, just walked past him and returned to the main search. Al may have won the battle, but Margaret intended to win the war.

By any means necessary.

The footsteps above them had long since subsided, and a deathly quiet hung in the basement air. The absence of sound unnaturally amplified the noise of their breathing. Despite the annoyance of this heightened perception, it was the sole reminder to each of the children that they were still alive.

"I miss my mum," said Fiona.

Arun and Gavin looked over at her to see her chest rising and falling as she fixated on a random spot of concrete floor, mouth contorting wildly, and her scrunched up brow fighting the skin on her forehead.

An exasperated cry escaped her. "I'm never going to see her again. I can just feel it."

"Don't say that," chided Arun. He bridged the few steps to her side, wrapping an arm around her as she began to blubber.

"We can't lose hope." Arun projected his voice more than necessary, almost like he was trying to bolster his own belief in what he'd said.

"He's going to kill us before they can get down here," said Gavin distantly. "Throw our bodies somewhere they'll never find them."

"Stop!" shouted James, cupping his hands tightly over his ears, clenching his eyes shut.

Gavin ignored him.

"I just keep thinking about that room. What are there, ten kids? Floating like ice sculptures for God knows how long. If he's good enough to have never been caught before, he's not going to get caught now. He won't let us be the reason he gets caught."

"Shut up! Shut up! Shut up!" cried James.

"Gavin," said Arun, nodding in the direction of Fiona, who was crying into his shirt sleeve. "If you think like that we'll never—"

"No, I'm tired. We're all tired!" Gavin shouted, chest heaving as he spoke. "He's left us down here in the hope that we'll die of hunger before he has to do the job himself. He's bigger, stronger, and smarter than us. And we think we're somehow going to get out of this? I'm *sick* of empty hope, *sick* that my brother's gone loony, and *sick* that I'm going to die before I even get the chance to have a real family! Don't give me false hope just to make Fiona feel a little better before she gets the axe too. Look what happened to Craig."

That name caused a blow of pain to Arun's gut. Though he hadn't moved, the wind was knocked clean from his lungs. He opened his mouth to contest what Gavin had said, to salvage the spirit in the room, but empty air came out. Arun didn't want to admit it, but he was right. If nothing changed, death would be their fate.

Although he had kept the horrific moment locked away in the furthest reaches of his mind, the memory of Craig mouthing his silent last words suddenly resurfaced.

You will get out.

He winced from the visualisation of his gaping wounds, and the blood oozing from his mouth before the life left his eyes. The words reverberated in his mind again, and this time, they were voiced confidently by Craig himself.

You will get out!

"*We* will get out," he said absentmindedly.

Gavin looked over at him, and Fiona's cries softened.

"What?" asked Gavin.

"We are going to get out of here. Alive."

"How?" whimpered Fiona.

"The next time Al comes down here, we are going to attack him."

Elder Louise knelt at the edge of her bed, praying. The guards had taken her rosary when she was booked, so she ripped two strips off the bedsheet and used them to fashion a makeshift cross that she laid on her mattress. She spent many hours around her cell praying, because the bed itself was so stiff she could hardly endure sitting on it, let alone sleep on the dreaded thing.

She prayed for Catrine. For the lads to be found. For the righteousness of the Lord's will to prevail over the evil that had infected the town. She didn't pray for herself, because she had faith her circumstance was but a byproduct of the bigger plan—His plan.

All would be well once the light won out over the darkness.

Suddenly, light spilled onto her bed, illuminating the cross and the mattress in a celestial white glow. She held up her hand and moved her fingers delicately in the light, watching the shadows dance along the wall. She turned and saw that, through the little square window at the top of her cell wall, the full moon shone brilliantly through a broken space in the clouds.

"Oh my," she said breathlessly, a wave of emotion washing over her. Not a single ray of light had touched the ground of East Ayrshire in as long as she could remember. Weeks, months even. The thick grey clouds had never once yielded.

Something powerful is happening, she thought. She hurriedly retrieved her bible and turned to Ephesians 5:11-13.

Take no part in the unfruitful works of darkness, but instead expose them. For it is shameful even to speak of the things that they do in secret. But when anything is exposed by the light, it becomes visible.

The downpour started sometime before midnight. It thrummed ferociously against the land, the roofs, and anyone who was unlucky enough to be caught outside. It was almost as if God were attempting to wash away the sin that had leached into every nook and cranny of the town.

A crack of lightning caused the lights in Aniqa's house to flicker. The delayed boom of thunder seemed to reverberate through the foundation, making every piece of furniture and décor tremble slightly. Scotland received a handful of storms a year, but none this severe. Despite the calamity that ensued beyond her windows, Aniqa much preferred it to the silence and the emptiness that had occupied her home since the day Arun went missing.

She gingerly lit the last candle and walked over to the armchair, moving an extra coat of Margaret's out of the way. She'd been staying with her since the fight with Walter, and truthfully, Aniqa didn't mind the company. Once the chair was clear, she clicked on the television. Loud static filled the room, and Aniqa raised a brow at the lack of signal. She returned to the TV set and changed the channel. Nothing.

She switched to the next—nothing.

A crack of lightning struck so close that the thunder rocked the house simultaneously, and the bright white light illuminated the entire street. The sudden flash allowed her to catch the outline of a dark silhouette walking through her garden. A chill made her skin crawl, goose pimples racing from the nape of her neck down her arms, and a sixth sense prodded her mind with one word.

Danger.

Three forceful knocks came at her door. She took measured steps to the peephole, carefully ensuring she'd make no noise to reveal her location. Her efforts to remain stealthy were futile because the living room was aglow with a ring of candles and her car was parked out front. Just as she neared the peephole with her eye, the knocks came again; this time so violent they shook the door along its frame. She held steady until they ceased, then repositioned her eye against the glass circle.

Al.

Fear spread like a fire in her chest, and she jolted away from the door, hightailing it to the kitchen. She dialled the number for the police station and prayed whoever worked the overnight shift wasn't out back having a fag.

The line rang, rang, and continued ringing.

Panic rose in her throat as Al pounded the door endlessly with all his might. She closed her eyes, imagining the door flying off its hinges and Al doing his worst.

Suddenly, the knocking ceased.

All that remained were the howling wind and curtains of rain slapping against the roof, intermingled with the rolling echo of thunder.

She left the phone off its receiver, the station line still ringing, and slowly inched toward the door. The deafening storm hindered her ability to focus on what might be transpiring beyond the door.

Was Al still there?

In the dim candlelight, aided by the intermittent flashes of lightning, she watched in horror as the doorknob jiggled slightly. Clicking sounds came from inside the lock mechanism, and not a moment later, the door slowly swung open.

A crash of lightning caused Al to momentarily appear as a black shadow standing in her doorway. The thunder that followed caused her to quiver beneath his looming presence. He took two steps forward, and in the warm glow of the candlelight, all she could see were his icy blue eyes and the grave look on his face.

Aniqa casually crept backwards, keeping her eyes on Al, carefully placing each foot down slowly to avoid tripping. She was intentionally leading them toward the kitchen. With each step, Al mirrored her motions, following her deeper into the house.

"Al," she began, steadying her voice. "I'm not sure what this is, but you need to leave my house. Right now."

"Now?" He sucked his teeth a few times as he shook his head. "Why do you think I would leave so fast? You have something that's mine, and

I'm afraid I need it back."

Aniqa's throat was like sandpaper as she swallowed, snaking her way backwards into the kitchen. "I'm afraid you're mistaken," she said, her voice cracking beneath faltering courage.

"I watched you take it with my own eyes."

Her back slid along the countertops, and she knew she was only a few feet from the knife set.

"Give me the letter and I'll be gone."

She felt around the counters blindly with her right hand obscured behind her back. She bumped into the knife block and ran her hand up it, quickly retrieving the largest chef's knife of the set and outstretching it in front of her.

"Back up!" she shouted, jabbing the knife toward him.

Al just laughed. "You think you know how to use that?"

"Take another step and you'll find out."

He shrugged his shoulders, holding up his hands as if he were surrendering to her warning, yet still inched forward.

"That would be a terrific headline, you know. *Mother of Missing Boy Murders Local Philanthropist.* I can see the evening news now: 'It was the evening of their second date that the desk clerk by day, distraught with her son's disappearance, stabbed Albert Reid repeatedly to death. The vicious attack left the area's largest orphanage without its founder, a church without its leader, and a popular restaurant without its owner. The killer's son, Arun Khan, has been taken into custody of the state—'"

"*Quiet!* Not another word or I'll do it."

But Al didn't listen. As their tête-à-tête led them deeper into the kitchen, the blaring sound of the dial tone crept through the noise of the storm. Al walked over to the phone and held it to his ear.

"Called someone for help," he muttered, shaking his head. He placed the phone back on its receiver. "I'm still confused as to why you're scared. I just want the letter."

"Fine," she said. "I'll get it."

She had outright lied but prayed this would buy her more time. Knife in hand, she circled around to the living room and began digging through her purse. Before Al could get near her, she swivelled around to ensure her back wasn't facing him. She didn't want to let her eyes off him for even a second.

"I could have sworn I put it here…"

Al huffed. "Stop playing around. Get the damn letter, now!"

"I had it in my purse," she said, feigning distress. "I swear."

Aniqa held the knife out shakily, glancing around as she navigated backwards through the living room, attempting to increase the space between her and Al.

Squealing brakes were followed by headlamps that illuminated the front of her house. A car door slammed, and Al walked over to the window to peek out the blinds. "Damnit," he said with a shake of his head. "You're playing a dangerous game, Aniqa. If your suspicions about me are true, don't you want him to come home safely?"

Him.

The word jabbed her in the gut like a red-hot fire iron, electrifying her motherly instinct. He had threatened her with the only thing that mattered to her in this world.

Arun.

"Aniqa, get behind me," said Margaret as she appeared in the doorway, pointing a pistol at Al.

"I don't ever remember you carrying a handgun," said Al whimsically. "Might get in trouble for taking something that's not yours." He side-eyed Aniqa as he said that.

"I had a feeling I might need it," she said, her jaw clenched.

"He broke in, picked my lock," muttered Aniqa, breathless. "Threatened me."

"Albert Reid, you are under arrest for trespassing." Margaret continued her reading of Al's rights and approached him cautiously.

He lackadaisically lifted his hands in surrender, then slipped them around to his lower back. She put the handcuffs on without a fight and began leading him to her patrol car. Once he was in the back seat, Margaret returned to the door. "You all right?"

Aniqa produced an unconvincing nod.

"He didn't hurt you?"

"No."

"What did he want?"

"No idea."

She wasn't sure why she lied to Margaret and chose to keep the existence of the letter a secret. But a little voice inside told her to.

"I'll be back later tonight. Stay put."

Margaret walked down the drive and carted Al off in her patrol car, disappearing moments later.

The tumultuous storm had passed Catrine, and now Aniqa was acutely aware of how she was alone again. In the quiet of the house, the faraway rolling thunder echoed softly, and beyond her windows, the flashes of heat lightning silently danced through the clouds, the rain but a pitter-patter along the roof.

"If your suspicions about me are true, don't you want him to come home safely?"

Al's ominous words caused her imagination to run wild. The thought of her beloved boy trapped somewhere cold, dank, and dark—missing his mother—desperately wanting to come home made the knot in her stomach twist tighter.

These ruminations spurred an idea. She went to her bedroom, began packing a duffel bag with clothes and toiletries. She circled back, blowing out the ring of candles, then returned the knife back to its block. Lastly, she ensured the mysterious letter was packed safely away.

Aniqa left her house and drove away, unsure of her destination. All she could focus on was the fact that Al needed that letter. He was so desperate to get it back that he'd broken into her home and threatened her.

There was something special about this rogue piece of mail…

And she was determined to figure out why.

Margaret pulled along the kerb and slung a backpack over her shoulder as she exited her patrol car. It was just after one in the morning, and a misty steam rose from the streets. The rain had subsided, and Catrine slumbered peacefully. She was around a half kilometre from her destination. She walked along the footpath, keeping an eye on her surroundings. The last thing she wanted was for someone to bear witness to what she was about to do.

The incessant drone of the crickets' summer song was much akin to the thoughts circulating through Margaret's mind. Flashes to the day's failed search of Al's house plagued her, and the notion that the boys may have been just beneath their feet ate away at her spirit. The failure wasn't any fault of the department, but more so a result of Al's cunning. It was as if before their arrival he had filled every crack to make it impenetrable, every path severed and replaced with a dead end.

When she reached Al's drive, she took a steadying breath.

No going back now, she thought. She crept around his vehicle and stood face-to-face with the attached shed. It took her a minute to pick the lock, but once in, she was presented with an ordinary tool shed. She waved her torch around and began circling the perimeter. On the back wall, there was a section of the brick that appeared newer, like puzzle pieces that had been replaced. Too new, not fitting the rest of the design. From her backpack, she retrieved a mallet she'd taken from Walter's tool set when he was at work. She raised it over her shoulder, readying herself for a swing. She let it fall forward, and it came down against the brick with a deep thud. It barely budged. She swung against the wall a few more times and noticed one brick in the centre whose caulking was loosening, sliding back.

There we go. She kept hitting, and the brick fully separated from the others, almost at a point where it would fall backward, creating an opening she could peer into.

"A little late for an evening stroll, isn't it, Officer?"

The hair on the nape of her neck bristled, and a shiver of fear shot down her spine, petrifying her with the mallet raised above her shoulder. Her throat parched so quickly she couldn't swallow. She didn't even have to turn to identify him.

That voice told her exactly who had caught her.

"How—I just—"

"I paid my bail. Seems the charge of trespassing is quite affordable," he said, casually leaning on his car. "Should have charged me with assault or something that would have kept me locked up longer." He crept closer. "Are you damaging my house?" He clicked his tongue patronisingly. "Oh, Margaret. This won't look good at all. Especially since you were off the case for failing to log my initial statement, and now, you're flying by night and breaking the law."

I have nowhere to run, she thought. *He has me cornered.*

Just when she thought he'd creep closer, he turned away without saying a word. A moment later, the glow of his kitchen lights flicked on. She listlessly walked out of the drive, mallet in hand, and through the deliberately opened window saw Al on the phone. He glanced out and they met eyes. He didn't smile, but even in the dim kitchen light she could see the distinct look Al always shot her out of the view of others. The look that said clearly and confidently:

I have won.

It was Stu who carted her off in handcuffs. His salt and pepper strands were tousled, eyes red, and his silver badge hung crookedly from his shirt pocket.

"Couldn't let me get a good night's sleep, could ye?" he grumbled from the driver's seat.

Margaret sat silently behind him.

"What on earth's gotten into ye, Margaret? They're gonna throw the book at you hard for this one. Never thought my best would do something like…"

She tuned out his disgruntled ramblings and stared out the window. The clouds had thickened to such a degree that the existence of the moon and stars were but a far-flung memory to those in East Ayrshire.

The night was black.

Empty.

Margaret was thankful there was only one person besides Stu to witness her arrest—the night guard at the station. Despite the circumstance, he still gave a respectful nod as she passed. She reciprocated the greeting, and Stu led her to one of the holding cells in the basement. They were in good condition, seeing that they never got much use outside of the occasional flagrant drunk needing to sleep off their buzz. All the real criminals got transferred to Ayr.

Stu opened the barred, iron cell door and locked it once she was inside. "I'm sorry about this."

She produced a small, sympathetic smile. "It's okay. Didn't give ye much of a choice."

"I'm sure this'll be the talk of the town by morning. I'll do my best to keep the reporters out."

"Cheers, Stu. Get some sleep."

He nodded and left. It was then the day's failure reared its ugly head yet again, accompanied by an irrevocable fear. Fear that she wouldn't be able to keep her promise to Aniqa. Fear that the boys would never be found, or worse, that they might already be dead.

Margaret didn't know what morning would bring. But in the isolation of her dank cell, with fear as her lone companion, she decided to pray.

She mustered up the courage to ask the Lord for a single request.

A miracle.

A deafening crash filled the basement as Arun slammed the cistern's cover against the ground; it shattered into pieces. He picked up a large shard of the ceramic and ran his finger along its jagged edge, bouncing his finger atop the pointed tip.

"It's sharp," he said to no one in particular. "Come pick one."

Gavin and Fiona joined Arun.

Fiona knelt and chose a narrower shard that fit well in her hand. Gavin chose the second biggest after Arun's. James, on the other hand, stared at them like they were lepers. No one minded him at this point, just left him be. Nothing they could say or do would help him snap out of it.

The trio stood together, staring at each other and the makeshift knives they held.

"So, this is it," said Gavin solemnly.

Arun nodded, looked at them both soberly.

"When we attack Al, we don't stop until he's dead. If no one is coming to save us, we have to save ourselves."

Neither Fiona nor Gavin responded, but the looks shared between the three children all confirmed they understood the commitment they had made to each other.

A full twenty-four hours had passed, and Margaret's cell had begun to wear on her. The isolation caused her imagination to run wild. She wondered what Stu and the rest of the department were doing to further the case, but also, thoughts of how Al might be spending his days as a free man terrified her. The more time passed, the more he could buttress the barriers he'd built to shield whatever it was he was trying so desperately to hide.

She had attempted to make bail but was unsuccessful.

Walter was the only one with access to their account, and he wouldn't answer the phone.

Aniqa, oddly enough, didn't seem to be home either.

Margaret was stuck. Surrounded by the dreary concrete brick that perfectly paired with the flavourless food she was served morning, noon, and night.

A jostle of the basement door caught her attention. She stood and went to the cell door, tilting her head to better source the sound. A jingle of keys was followed by the mechanical clicking of the lock being opened.

"Gordon," she said, surprise taking her breath.

He smiled warmly at her as he opened her cell door. "Think I was just going to let you rot away in here?"

"I was beginning to wonder."

"Hurry. Guard's on a piss break."

"Anyone else up there?"

"Nae."

They climbed the stairs together and left the basement. Gordon headed for the door, but Margaret stopped suddenly, then began down the hall. The lack of a second pair of footsteps caused him to whip around.

"What are ye doing?"

"Something I should have had the courage to do a long time ago."

"Margaret!" Gordon hissed.

She headed towards the maintenance closet. The room was filled top to bottom with tools, cleaning supplies, and electrical wiring. Her eyes quickly scanned the room until she found a crowbar. She hoisted it into her grip and returned to the bathroom door. She slipped the crowbar into the door handle of the men's bathroom and left it without a second thought.

"Are you out of your mind?"

"I need time," she said, then rushed to Stu's office door. "Keys," she demanded with an open hand. Gordon handed her the weighty key ring, and she sifted through them all. When she reached the master key, she quickly slipped it into the keyhole, and it unlocked with a click.

Margaret fell to her knees behind Stu's desk and slid out every drawer that would open. She frantically pulled out all his files, unsure of what she was looking for, but she knew more than anything that after what happened yesterday, precious time was slipping away.

She pleaded God would give her the miracle she had prayed for.

Something real. Something that would allow the department to surpass the normal constraints of the search warrant.

But as she pored through the paperwork, its banality flatlined her hope of finding a clue. The missing piece to the puzzle that was Al.

"Why are you going through his things?" asked Gordon.

"Did you not see how Stu was acting during the search? That queasy expression. Like he was waiting for us to round a corner and find a dead body. He knows something we don't about Al. Or at the very least, suspects it."

Margaret's bulbous brown eyes flicked quickly across each set of files, discarding them just as fast if they yielded nothing out of the ordinary. She then came across a manila folder that wasn't labelled, and it gave her pause.

Gordon noticed her stop. "What?"

"It's unmarked."

She opened it and her chest began to tighten. She saw the serial number logged on the first page, and the date. The first was six months ago. Next to the serial number was the word scribbled in Stu's chicken scratch handwriting—complaint.

The name that accompanied it sent her memory spiralling.

Colin Clark.

Her eyes blazed through the many complaint forms.

```
Clark, Colin. 21-03-64
Rambled on for half an hour about how Al is
hiding something. Asks for patrols to watch his
movements. I decline.
```

The subsequent files revealed more of the same. But then she reached the most recent complaint.

```
Clark, Colin. 13-06-64
Says Al turned off the lights in his house on two
different days, once in May and once in March. Says
the night when Al's lights were off corresponds
to missing children's cases around Scotland. I
dismissed him.
```

Her heart leapt in her chest as she recalled the homeless lad being dragged out of the station. Shouting absurdities, as Stu had called them.

"Messed in the head from drugs, can't believe a word he says."

Stu had shrugged aside the boy and his beliefs. A sickly feeling began slinking through her gut. She glanced at the date and realised the last complaint was the day before the four lads went missing.

"What is it?"

Margaret turned to him, face blanched.

"Read this." She handed the file to Gordon.

"Why would Stu not pass this kind of tip to the national police?"

"Exactly," she said.

"And this Colin Clark lad?"

"Local drunk. Parents kicked him out onto the street a few years back."

"Stu passed him off as mad," mumbled Gordon.

"That's how I remember it. The morning before the lads went missing, he got dragged out of the station, screaming about how we'd regret not listening to him. And for my conscience's sake, I hope he's wrong."

Margaret returned Stu's files back in their respective cabinets, and stood, facing Gordon with a faraway expression in her eyes.

"Who would have believed him? Not a soul. If Colin had come to me a month ago, I would have sent him off just the same. It's Al, for Christ's sake. But the lad *knew*…"

"And?"

She locked eyes with Gordon.

"Now we go find him."

Ships that pass in the night, and speak each other in passing, only a signal shown, and a distant voice in the darkness; So on the ocean of life, we pass and speak one another, only a look and a voice, then darkness again and a silence.

—Henry Wadsworth Longsfellow

CHAPTER 20
THE LOST BOY

January 3rd, 1940—past

The ferry's hull careened down the trough of the wave, sending salty spray over the bow and misting the faces of passengers along the deck. Leon drew in a full breath of the briny air, and the chilly sea spritzes were a welcome relief to his pale skin as it began to burn beneath the midday sun.

Today was a rarity for the British Isles—a bright, cloudless day in the dead of winter.

Despite having experienced the agonising loss of Theodora and being banished from the Royal Family all in the span of a little over a week, the sounds and smells of the ferry voyage across the Channel were enough to make Leon smile. Even the croaks of the swooping gulls seemed unusually jovial, almost as if they were laughing with each other. But then suddenly, the lively croaks of the gulls transformed, and he imagined they were mocking him, scoffing at the fact he'd had the courage to get on this boat to begin with.

A large part of Leon was petrified to step foot back on the shores of Britain. His mother's last words had been etched in the forefront of his mind, not with a chisel, but with her sharp tongue. He wondered if he'd ever have a single moment where the fear her warning caused would ease. For he knew that once he arrived, every waking moment would be tainted with the worry that he would cross an invisible line—say something, do something—to reveal he'd breached the decree which held his fate.

A gasp came from behind. "No!"

Leon whipped around to see the boy who had cried out trip and skid across the ship deck. A black and silver camera hurtled through the air, headed directly at his face; he jumped up and cradled his arms to catch it against his chest.

"Oi, nice save!"

Leon emitted a sheepish laugh as several passengers had turned to find the source of the commotion. The many pairs of eyes made him uncomfortable. He held out the camera as the boy strode over to him with a broad, childlike grin.

"You know what this is?" he asked, giving the camera a shake in front of him.

"A camera?"

"Not just any camera," chided the boy with a creased brow. "It's the Kodak 35."

Leon stared at him silently, unsure of how to respond. The seriousness in the boy's expression slowly eroded and a playful smile slid across his face. He roughhoused Leon with a few pats of his back and stepped in close, looking him in the eyes.

"Mate, you just saved me loads of money with that brilliant catch. Took me a whole year to save up for this beauty."

He couldn't help but smile in the presence of this amiable stranger.

"Right time and place, I guess."

The boy began tinkering with the camera, glancing between it and Leon, then wound the film wheel with its distinct clicking sound. "You mind?" he asked as he brought the camera up to his eye.

"I, um…I'm not sure——"

"Come on, I want to remember the bloke who saved my camera."

Just as he opened his mouth, the boy yelled, "Smile!"

Leon stared down the camera lens and produced as genuine a smile he could muster given his discomfort.

The shutter clicked and the boy bounded over to him and proceeded to throw his arm around Leon's shoulder. "Let me buy you a Coke," he said.

"You don't have to, I've got to…" he stammered as he failed to come up with a lie quickly enough.

"What, you got family waiting on you or something?"

That word stung. The boy noticed the subtle change in Leon's expression.

"You seem gutted, mate. You alone then?"

He nodded, eyeline hardly lifting from the ship deck.

The boy took a sharp breath in through his nose, then stared out at the sea with a faraway gaze. He wasn't sure if it was just the steady wind blowing or if the boy had choked up from hearing that Leon was alone, but his eyes were becoming misty. "I am too." The boy wiped his sleeve across his eyes before turning back. "It's a bit of a happy-sad, isn't it? New beginnings."

"More sad than happy," said Leon. "Especially if it's the end that keeps you up at night."

He snorted. "What's your story then? Bastard father? Loony mum?"

"No bastard father; he died when I was young. Bastard *uncle*, though. I was living with him and my aunt in Germany. He died last summer. Aunt passed away on Christmas, and my mum decided to kick me out three days ago."

"Bollocks year if I've ever heard it."

"What about you?" asked Leon.

"No idea who my real mum and dad are. The woman who ran the orphanage told me that one morning she checked the letterbox and found me in a pram on the doorstep. Spent my whole life there, in Ipswich. Four years ago, a Belgian couple adopted me into their foster family, but not once did I feel an ounce of real love in that house. The head of the orphanage was more of a mother to me than the woman who *chose* to make me her son." The boy steeled himself with his hands on the railing. "I turned eighteen two days ago. Packed my bag, and now I'm here, having a conversation with you."

"Happy birthday."

He let out a small snort and smiled at Leon. "Life's one hell of a ride, innit?"

Leon studied the bittersweet expression on a face that was otherwise smooth and youthful. There was a bit of nostalgia behind his hazel eyes. He wondered whether the boy was reminiscing about the good times or ruminating over the bad. Maybe it was a bit of both—a faint appreciation for the fact that the joyous highs and harrowing lows had led to this present moment.

Leon leaned against the railing, looking toward the west. He swore he could see the tiny, jagged line of white cliffs appear on the horizon. The boy joined him and handed him the Coke. Leon took a few sips of it and the chilled bottle numbed his lips.

"I never caught your name, mate."

"Le—"

He faked a choke and began coughing. *I'm a bloody idiot,* he thought.

"Lee?"

"Lee."

The boy's brow furrowed at his pause.

"Lee…what?"

Leon combed through his memories for a name, all while the echo of his mother's decree haunted him. *Lancaster, Gothe, Saxon…*

"Marron," he blurted.

The boy cocked his head. "Is that French?"

"Father was a Frenchman. Bloody shame."

They exchanged a laugh, and Leon tried to hide the discomfort of blurting out a French name despite being born and bred a Briton. But in the moment, the only surname he could recall that would ensure anonymity was that of his mother's longtime servant, Jean-Claude.

"And yours?"

"Albert," said the boy with a slight grimace, like there was acid on his tongue. "Albert Reid. But that's my old man. You can call me Al."

"Al," said Leon. "Good to meet you."

The ferry blew its horn as it approached the congested port of Dover. The two boys looked out in awe at the staggering white cliffs of the coastline, whilst unknowingly standing atop a precipice of their own—turning away from the children they were and taking the leap into manhood.

"What will you do once you get there?" asked Al.

Leon didn't yet know the answer to the question. But he wasn't about to deny his new friend the conversation.

"Start a new life. Take it a day at a time." He struggled to swallow down the emotions that were trying to surface. Every night when he finally fell asleep, he relived the horror of Christmas Day in his dreams. He'd walk into the bathroom and tiptoe toward the tub, the incessant drip of water slipping over its edge. He fought so hard to turn away, yet the motion of his feet seemed outside of his control. They always led him to the tub, and he stared down at the lifeless body of Theodora, skin as white as stone, face angelic and peaceful.

Take it a day at a time.

Those words were what he'd been telling himself since the day she died. It felt more like naïve optimism rather than a mantra to lead his new life by.

The ferry's horn drew him from his trance, and he tried to compose himself. He turned to face Al, revealing his glistening eyes. He displayed his sorrow earnestly.

"There's a little voice inside my head that says the life awaiting me on those shores will be just as awful as the one I left. Or worse."

"Lee—"

"My past is dark. I'm afraid it's only a matter of time before it'll find me again."

Leon felt Al's hand on his back.

"Mate, you said it yourself. Your mum kicked you out. She made her decision, and that's on her. Just because everything behind you is dark, that doesn't mean for a second that you don't deserve a bright future."

Al shook Leon's shoulder, "Look at me."

Leon shifted to face him, and now they were eye-to-eye.

"See all these people?" Al nodded over his shoulder in the direction of the passengers. "They don't have a clue the kind of shit we've been through. I can see it in your eyes, and I know you see it in me."

Leon bristled. The innocent boy he'd met an hour ago had dissolved away, and before him stood an equal.

"In a few minutes, you and I are about to get off this boat and go our separate ways. Unless fate has other plans, we likely won't see each other again. So, I want you to listen to what I'm about to say."

Leon nodded humbly.

"If you give up; whether its tomorrow, or the next day, or even years from now—the darkness wins." Al took a deep breath as he steadied his emotions. He placed a firm hand at the centre of Leon's chest.

"Even though this life has broken us, we are still capable of good. The darkness only defines us if we let it."

June 28th, 1964—present

The old wooden door's hinges groaned as Aniqa entered Martha's Antique Shoppe. Its ambience was a welcome change to the hustle and bustle of downtown Ayr outside. Two lonely looking lights were tucked in each corner of the room, casting a dingy yellow glow across the space. All the walls were lined with bookshelves from floor to ceiling, and along them sat worn, dusty hardcovers. She wondered if the unusual quietness was due to the many books that absorbed the street noise or just the lack of customers. On the floors were several antiques—furniture, collectibles, and artwork. The front counter sat barren, and as she approached, she saw a few candles burning. She caught a whiff of amber, and it intermingled with the strong musk of old books. She leaned against the front counter and waited.

"Hello?" She craned her head over, peering into the back room eclipsed in shadow.

No response.

She realised there was a silver service bell near her hand, and she struck it.

A chair creaked from within the back room, and the sound was followed by slow, lumbering footsteps. Out of the darkness emerged a fragile-looking elderly woman, who moved at the pace of someone who has lived long enough that they disregard time altogether. She saw Aniqa and seemed to be both slightly annoyed and intrigued at the fact she had a customer.

"What can I do for ye?" she asked unflinchingly in a thick Scottish accent.

"Are you Ms. Mitchell? My boss, Robert McCallum, recommended you," began Aniqa, flipping open her purse.

"*Miss* Mitchell is my mum, and she's pushing up daises," said the woman dryly. "I'm Martha."

Aniqa emitted a small chuckle. Being called *miss* still irritated her even at a ripe old age.

"McCallum?" repeated Martha with a creased brow. "Not sure I remember the lad."

"He remembers you, said you were the best history professor he had at uni."

Martha produced a halfhearted smile. "Very kind of him to say," she said. "So, what is it I can do for ye?"

"I was wondering if you could help me identify where this letter came from." She slipped it out of her purse and rubbed its edges in her hands. "It has no return address."

Martha scoffed. "The post office is down the street. Might be better off there." She turned away from Aniqa.

"No, please—" Aniqa's voice rasped. "I know you're not a mail clerk. There's no address, but there's a seal. I was hoping that it might tell you who the letter came from."

Martha ceased her retreat, turning to face Aniqa. "Give it here."

Aniqa traced the seal gently with her thumb one last time before handing it over.

Martha's brow furrowed immediately as she held the letter. She pushed her spectacles up to the bridge of her nose, squinted, and then glanced at Aniqa with a look of bewilderment. "Where did you get this?"

"Does it matter?"

The bewildered look took on a tinge of suspicion. Martha reached out with her free hand and swivelled the desk lamp shade to illuminate the letter as she held it more closely to the light.

"Well?" asked Aniqa, pitch rising.

A smug smile tugged at the corners of Martha's lips. "You did well in bringing this to me. I'm afraid a historian wouldn't be able to tell you where this came from," she said, tilting the letter at different angles beneath the light, staring at its red wax seal with a wistful gaze. "But just before postgrad, I interned at the Royal Archives."

"The Royal Archives, as in—"

Martha peered over the brim of her specs. "*The* Royal Archives. Windsor Castle."

"And?"

"This seal," she began, turning the letter under the light to face Aniqa, "is impressed with the Lancaster family crest. Which is why I'm still curious as to how this letter came to be in your possession."

"I'm not following."

"I saw this crest while I was at the Archives. And it's not something you can find at your local library reading about the Royal Family."

Aniqa's parched throat felt like sandpaper as she swallowed. "You mean to tell me that letter is from a royal?"

Martha smiled warmly, took off her glasses, folding the arms and placing them gently on the counter.

"Not just any royal," she said. "The Queen."

Her grip on the edge of Martha's desk tightened. "Queen Eleanor?"

She nodded and handed the letter back to Aniqa. "The Queen was born a Lancaster, and *that* is her family crest."

Aniqa's mind drifted away from Martha. She didn't realise it, but her hand trembled slightly as she held the letter.

"Now that I think about it…" Martha's voice drew Aniqa from her daze. "You asked me if I knew where the letter came *from*. That must mean you already know who the letter was sent *to*."

She met Martha's scrutinising gaze, and a single question came to her mind.

Why did Queen Eleanor send Albert Reid a letter?

January 11ᵗʰ, 1940—past

When he and Al had separated after disembarking the ferry, Leon quickly fell into what he had always imagined a life of poverty would be. He was a street kid. All it took to make him realise he needed money was a single night in a cold, damp alleyway with a stomach grumbling so raucously it wouldn't let him sleep. But when he sat on the side of the walkways with his cap overturned, asking businessmen and passerby for spare cash, he felt pathetic. Most people wouldn't even meet his gaze.

He was invisible, and he wondered if anyone who passed would have believed that the dishevelled young man begging on the streets of London was a former royal. One who had lived a life of excess and opulence that none of them had likely experienced, not even for a day.

The thought made him chuckle. A bit of morose irony.

By the end of the first week, sleeping in the alley had caused a thin layer of grime to accumulate over his face and neck. His matted hair sprung out in a hundred different directions. A few times a day he'd dart into the many storefronts, trying to discreetly pop into their washrooms without being kicked out by the clerks. He'd use the toilet and leave, but always took a second to glance at his reflection before departing.

He could hardly remember the Leon he used to be.

The one who was a duke. The one whose skin was squeaky clean, hair fixed, clothes fine, and hands soft and smooth from never having to do a day of physical labour.

But in this new life, every inch of his body was caked in dirt and dust, his clothes were tattered, and his back ached terribly from sleeping in that godforsaken alley. He wasn't going to give up and go crawling to the palace gates, though.

A part of him thought about pickpocketing, but when the sinister thought crossed into the plane of his conscience, Al's parting words echoed loudly in his mind.

"The darkness only defines us if we let it."

And he was unrelenting in his desire to not let the darkness define him any longer.

So, he'd continue to resort to begging. Reliant on the kindness of strangers.

Then, on a dreary Monday morning, a plump woman with a kind, round face stopped in front of his overturned cap and stared down at him inquisitively.

"What?" he asked curtly.

She let out a pitied sigh, and her eyes drifted away from him. "Nothing, love," she said, rifling through her handbag.

She pulled out a bank note, and Leon's eyes widened when he saw the distinct purple hue of a twenty-pound note. The woman rolled up the note, slipped it between her index and middle fingers, and knelt, extending her hand downward into his cap, but at the last second, she whipped her arm back, holding the money close to her chest.

"What if I told you I could do you better than this twenty?"

The question gave Leon pause, but the primitive pull of his insatiable hunger coupled with unrelenting lethargy got the better of his manners.

"I'm not greedy. Give it here."

He opened his palm. The woman didn't yield.

"If you're going to yank my chain, piss off."

She chuckled and dropped the twenty into the cap but didn't walk away. Her eyes deliberately flicked across his filthy face, then down to his tattered, grubby clothes. There wasn't a trace of revulsion on the woman's expression, but instead, an air of gentleness in the way she studied him. It wasn't long before he found himself doing the same to her. Subtle signs of the woman's true age appeared in the crow's feet around her eyes, and the smile lines around her mouth, but to him, the softness of her spirit seemed to carry over onto her face. Leon mused that there might be a truth to the thought—those souls who were pure and kind aged more gracefully than those who were bitter.

"How old are you?" she asked.

"Eighteen."

She clicked her tongue. "When I said I could do better than the twenty," she began, nodding down toward the note that rested in the cap, "I meant I know a place where you could get a good night's sleep. A hot shower, although you have to make it short. And a home-cooked meal, but I'll admit it's nothing to write home about. How does that sound?"

Leon wasn't sure what to make of the woman's offer. But the warmth she exuded was alluring, and the compassion he felt as he stared into her amber eyes reminded him of Theo—

He couldn't muster the strength to even think of *her* name.

"So what is this place?"

"It's a place for youth who…" She paused, searching for the right words "…are in a similar situation as yourself. You won't have to beg. We'll get you some clean clothes and you can get started on finding some work."

"*…are in a similar situation as yourself…*"

The words struck a nerve that existed only in *Duke* Leon's former life. For a moment, her proposition seemed abhorrent, and he couldn't imagine shelving the pride that came along with his title and luxuriant upbringing.

"An orphanage?" He spat the words out as if they were poison. "Is that where you're offering to bring me?"

"I'm not *bringing* you anywhere," she chided. "You're a grown man, and if you decide to come it's of your own accord."

He fell silent, and the woman let out a sigh. "Orphanage. Halfway house. Call it what you please," she began, ducking her head to better meet his eyeline. "But I know from experience, my dear, that the stiffest twin bed is a better night's sleep than that alleyway."

She pointed a crooked finger behind him and stared into his blue eyes knowingly.

The humbling realisation that this woman *knew*…hit a soft spot in the fresh wound that had formed during the week prior of having no proper place to lay his head.

He gave her a nod and began transferring the cash he'd collected in the cap to his trouser pockets. "I'll go, but I won't stay at your orphanage long. Just want to get a train ticket north."

"Fine by me." She smiled, extending a wrinkled hand. "Greta," she said softly.

He took her hand and stood, and they traversed the busy streets of London as the rising sun broke through the thick layer of clouds. The rays of light met the skin on his face, gently cupping his chin, tilting his head slightly upward, almost as if the morning light was forcing him to look ahead at the brighter days to come.

June 29th, 1964—present

Aniqa pinched the teabag strings between her forefinger and thumb, bouncing the steeped bags a few times in the hot water before tossing them into the trash. After a night of fitful sleep, she'd desperately needed a boost.

Her trusted black tea with a splash of milk should do the trick.

After leaving Martha's shop yesterday she had made the nearly eight-hour drive to London. The exhilaration she'd felt from such a split-second decision lingered long after she arrived at a run-down budget hotel just off the motorway. She tossed and turned beneath the worn, outdated comforter, and even with the curtains drawn and the room eclipsed in total darkness, she couldn't drift into proper slumber. And despite her conscious mind trying to convince her otherwise, she knew the root cause of her unrest.

The letter.

It rested on the coffee table. And though *it* did not stir, Aniqa could not ignore its presence. It called to her, begging to be opened.

The faint jingle of a bell atop the reception office door sounded, and it threw her right back into Martha's shop. Just as she had opened the door to depart, Martha called out from behind her.

"My dear," she had said.

Aniqa turned back. The door did not groan; even the shop's bell seemed to hold still in anticipation.

Martha stared at her through those old, wise eyes. "I'm not telling you to break the law, but if you do open it, I bet you'd learn more about the person you're looking for."

The muted thud of another guest slamming a car boot closed drew her from the memory. It was followed by the ignition cranking and the car driving off toward the motorway.

Watching the hotel carpark slowly empty reminded her that time was of the essence. She was eight hours from home, and her son was still missing.

"Why are you even here?" asked her mother's scathing voice. *"You are a bad mother."*

"Shut up!" she shouted. Her heart pounded, anger tickling her skin with its hot touch. She looked around at the empty, quiet room, and shook her head worryingly at the fact her mother's voice was becoming more frequent.

She took a long sip of her tea. Its strong, caffeinated bite revitalised her senses as the hot liquid settled in her gut. She guzzled down the rest of it and grabbed her overnight bag before walking out to the car park.

The day that met her was gloomy and grey. She hadn't the slightest clue what it might bring.

A twinge of worry poked her insides. The *why* behind this letter was what was driving her, but it was the *how* that scared her most. If Martha had identified it accurately, what on earth was she supposed to do? Jump the palace gates and ring the doorbell?

She scoffed at the thought.

But for the moment, she shelved her fear, threw her bag in the boot, and began the drive to her destination.

Buckingham Palace.

March 17th, 1940—past

A sudden rocking of the carriage awoke Leon. He slowly came to and saw the elderly couple still beside him. The man perused a newspaper whilst his wife had her nose buried in *The Code of The Woosters*. At the far end of Leon's aisle, a portly conductor swung open the carriage door and ambled inside. "Tickets! Get your tickets ready!" he boomed with a voice as wide as his barrel-chested torso.

Leon stood and reached for the overhead rack.

His heart sank—the duffel was gone.

"No, no, no…" he mumbled, hands beginning to shake as he pointlessly rummaged through the many bags, searching for something he knew was not there.

"What's the matter, son?" asked the old man, craning his neck up from the newspaper.

"My ticket," he said breathlessly. "I left my duffel on the last train."

The man offered him a sympathetic smile. Leon collapsed in his seat, frustration weighing on his limbs; that pressure, coupled with the humiliating defeat of forgetting something so vital to his journey—not only his ticket but all of his clothes—crushed him further where he sat. He chewed on the inside of his cheek as he waited for the inevitable arrival of the conductor.

"Tickets, please." The words caused a tremor to rise in his gut. The elderly woman shuffled through her purse and fetched two tickets, handing them to the conductor.

Two clicks of the hole puncher. Then he handed the tickets back to the elderly couple.

"Where's yours, boy?" asked the conductor gruffly. Leon couldn't meet his gaze. He turned slightly and saw his face was inches away from the conductor's potbelly. The gilded LMS Railway logo embroidered on his breast pocket gleamed annoyingly in his peripheral.

"Your *ticket*," he clarified coldly.

"When we switched trains," began Leon just above a whisper, "I left my duffel, and my ticket's in there. One way to Glasgow."

"These your parents?" He nodded to the elderly couple.

"No, sir."

Without looking up, Leon could feel the scrutinising gaze of the conductor. A wave of self-consciousness washed over him. He had showered yesterday, not today, only because he was in a rush to get to the station. His clothes were clean, but now, looking at their faded colours and weathered fabric, it was apparent that everything he wore was secondhand at best.

"I know the likes of you," said the conductor. He grabbed him firmly by his forearm. "Get up."

The old man croaked out against the conductor's decision but was met with a swift rebuke.

"We get at least a drifter a day," said the conductor, the amusement in his tone a sharp contrast to the annoyance etched into his furrowed, bushy brows. "On with you now." He gave Leon's shoulder a tug and eased him up from his seat. The conductor pushed him towards the end of the carriage; opened the door and instructed him to sit in the gangway connection.

"At the next stop, you're off. Understood?"

Leon nodded, too ashamed to fully meet his eyes.

"And go quietly," added the conductor. "Don't give me any hassle."

The conductor closed the carriage door and left Leon there. Wind whistled wildly around him, and the metallic groans of the train were earsplitting in the exposed gangway connection. He held onto a metal grab rail as every bump and shift in direction nearly sent him flying down toward the tracks.

He waited, sombre and alone. Waited to be kicked out, thrown out into the elements.

Without a pound to his name, without a fresh change of clothes, and without a home.

He had nothing and no one.

He'd been let off at Carlisle station. The downpour had calmed to little more than a dreary drizzle. Part of him was tempted to beg at the station—collect just enough cash to get to his destination. But the more powerful, prideful side of Leon was disgusted by the thought of having to resort to it. When Greta took him in, he'd vowed to never live on the streets again, where he was subject to the extremes of both scorn and sympathy innumerable times in a given day.

Yet here he was.

Back to square one.

He hadn't a map, but based on the flags at the station, he was still in England. He blindly headed north, walking along the shoulder of the A74 road, head hung low. Every car that zipped past, he swore he could feel the deprecating stares of the drivers burning into the side of his face.

But perhaps that was just his paranoia.

Hours had passed by the time he saw a Scottish flag, and he stopped in the first small town he could find—Gretna Green. Mouth thoroughly parched from the long walk, he meandered the streets in hopes of finding a fountain. He was unsuccessful but managed to sneak into a petrol station washroom and guzzle the cool water straight out of the tap.

As he made his way back toward the A74 road, he caught a whiff of cooked meats along with the distinct smell of fried potatoes. He turned to find a storefront whose shelves were filled with heaps of sandwiches, pasties, and fresh chips. He salivated at the sight. The sun was fast descending towards the horizon, and he hadn't eaten a thing since last night.

He stood in front of the encased display, nose nearly pressed to the glass, staring dreamily at the food with eyes that were beginning to glaze over. A middle-aged woman wearing a blue apron poked her head out from inside. She examined the tall, lanky young man who was nearly about to drool on the display.

"You can't eat it with your eyes, lad."

Hearing a Scottish accent for the first time almost made Leon chuckle. It was so different from what he grew up around. He stared at the woman blankly, struggling to form words.

She tilted her head, waiting for him to speak.

"See anything ye like?"

He nervously pointed to a ham and pickle sandwich.

She leaned forward to see his selection. "Ten shillings," she said.

Leon stared back at the woman, attempting to hide his shame. Even though it was the smallest interaction, he felt lousy for wasting her time. He shook his head, then let his eyes fall to the ground.

The woman studied Leon; she saw the lack of an umbrella, the moisture clinging to his ragtag clothes. She shot sidelong glances down the main street and fixed her gaze back on Leon.

"Ye alone?"

He nodded.

"From around these parts?"

"No, madam."

"*Madam*," she repeated with a snort. "Definitely not from around here."

He barely raised his head high enough to meet her eyes and attempted to produce a sad excuse of a smile.

"Where you comin' from?"

He wondered if he should lie but decided against it.

"London."

The woman's brow furrowed, and she stepped down the two steps to the street, wiping her hands on her apron, and stood next to Leon. "What brought you up here? You look too sad to have just gotten married." She grabbed his shoulder, eyes growing wide. "Did she leave you, lad?"

"What? No…" he gave her a confused look. "I'm heading north because I've got nowhere else to go. Starting fresh."

"And yer walking there?" she huffed a great big laugh of disbelief. When Leon didn't reciprocate the jest, the light wrinkles around her mouth and eyes scrunched up with concern.

"Saved up for a ticket to Glasgow, took me a whole month of work. Train broke down and we had to switch; I had my ticket in my duffel, and I left it on the train. Conductor kicked me off at Carlisle."

"What a dobber!" she exclaimed.

Leon gave her a confused look and watched her walk back inside, returning a few moments later with a ham and pickle sandwich wrapped in parchment paper. He glanced to the sandwich nervously, then back up to the woman.

"Dobber?" he repeated.

"Dobber, as in…a jerk. Arsehole. That conductor was an arsehole."

The woman smiled broadly and extended her hand that held the wrapped sandwich.

"I'm sorry, I can't—"

"Not a worry," she said, giving the sandwich a shake.

He hesitantly took it.

"Welcome to Scotland," she said warmly, gave him a rough pat on the back, then disappeared back inside her shop.

Shortly after leaving Gretna Green, he'd decided to switch to the A75 road and headed west to Dumfries instead of Lockerbie to the north. Much to his dismay, each time the distance to Dumfries sign reappeared, only a tiny fraction of the total miles remaining was shaved off. He continued wearily, wondering if this onerous trek would ever end.

The joy the shop owner's gesture had given him had long since faded. What it was replaced by were aches; his feet throbbed as if they had a pulse of their own, and his calves burned with every slight change of incline.

Upon arrival in Dumfries, torrential rain had soaked him down to his boxers. Whatever fuel the ham and pickle sandwich provided had been spent, and now his stomach spasmed violently every few minutes.

The small town abutted a river. The main drag of Glasgow Street was empty as could be. He found the first petrol station along the road he could duck into. He drank from the washroom tap and asked the clerk for the time. He discovered it was a quarter to ten, and then the clerk quickly shooed him back outside because he was dripping wet all over the floors.

The rain showed no signs of ceasing. Leon sat along the side of the petrol station, back against the wall, knees curled up to his chest in hopes of warming up. In this position, he could keep his limbs beneath the protection of the station's narrow roof overhang, but while being dry, it was no respite from the chilly night air.

As time passed, he began to shiver; the cold's intensity amplified by his waterlogged clothes. He fought hard to control the tremors. The icy wetness of the fabric would lick his exposed skin in a hundred different spots, and it proved so irksome he was tempted to strip down completely.

Leon let his head fall between his knees. He felt defeated, and he scoffed at how he'd become so well-acquainted with the sensation over the past few months. The wretched thing about defeat was it always brought along its friends, shame and regret. Those two partook in an agonising tug-of-war in his mind, feuding over who would reign supreme. When this turbulence occurred within Leon, his conscious mind dealt with a barrage of *shouldn'ts.*

Shouldn't have so carelessly killed all those animals. Shouldn't have murdered Prince Ernest. Shouldn't have left Greta in London.

Facing the bleakness of his new reality, his eyes began to well with tears.

But deep down, he knew he deserved the hopelessness he felt.

He had summoned all his misery into existence.

By the work of his own hand.

A throaty engine growled, followed by a series of loud metal clanks. From behind the thrumming rain, he heard what sounded like soft clucking. Leon raised his head, curiously peering up over his knees, and saw a rust-coloured pick-up park alongside the petrol pump. Attached to its hitch was a rectangular, open-air trailer lined with shelves of chickens. The man that emerged from the truck's cab looked to be in his sixties or seventies, yet he walked with youthful ease. He looked a good bit shorter than Leon, and scrawny; it seemed like the sun-weathered skin of his cheekbones and around his sunken eyes was barely hanging on. The hair on his head, his eyebrows, even his stubble were white as snow. And at the forefront of all his features was a stern, unwavering stare. He was gazing straight ahead, as if he were aiming through the sight of an invisible rifle. The man sported a thick field jacket and tattered denim overalls, and just before he entered the station, he turned to stare at Leon, piercing him with his pale grey eyes.

The intensity he felt from such a quick glance roused Leon, unknowingly distracting him from his sadness. When the man reappeared, he had a paper bag in hand, and he set it on the edge of the truck bed. He stuck the petrol pump into his truck, and Leon caught him watching the pump's litre and price counters clacking stridently as they spun, cutting through the sound of the rain. When the pump shut off, the man hung the metal nozzle back on its base and reached into his truck bed, retrieving the bag. He strode directly toward Leon, stopping in front of his feet, and stood exposed, being pelted by the fat rain droplets.

The man held out the bag and gave him a nod. Leon hesitantly opened it. Inside was a packet of crisps and a chocolate milkshake. Leon's manners were no match for his grumbling, empty stomach; he ripped open the bag and shoved the flaky, fried crisps into his mouth by the fistful, intermittently stopping to guzzle down some of the chocolate milkshake.

The man held still in the rain, silently watching him eat.

When Leon finished, the awkward silence between them became more apparent.

"Thank you," he said, attempting to garner the strength needed to meet the man's penetrating stare, but failed.

The prolonged silence began to agitate Leon, and he felt the sudden urge to say something, anything.

"I'm just travelling through," he blurted.

"Where to?" asked the man in a voice so gravelly it reminded Leon of the grumbling truck engine.

"North."

The rain filled the gaps of quiet, but the longer the man didn't speak, the more Leon wondered about his motivations, and despite the downpour, he decided to make his exit. "Thanks again," he said, giving the man a nod, then tossing the paper bag into the rubbish.

"Need a place to sleep for the night?" asked the man.

Leon turned around. Besides the man's unreadable expression, the offer also roused his suspicions. While he pondered a response, the rain began to freshly soak through his clothes again. "Where do you live?"

The man just stared at him, unfazed.

"All I need is a yes or a no."

Leon swallowed against a dry throat.

He gave a hesitant nod. Despite his leeriness about the man, he was beyond ready to get out of the elements. He hopped in the passenger seat of the truck cab. They drove out of the petrol station, neither saying a word to the other.

The dark night coupled with the rain made it difficult to discern their location, but from what Leon could gather, they were headed north. He had seen a few signs for a place called Cumnock. What intrigued Leon more than anything was that the man hadn't asked him a single question. They'd been driving for an hour in complete silence. In the same way Leon wasn't certain he could trust the man's intentions for offering him a place to sleep, wasn't the same true in reverse? How on Earth could the man trust *him?*

For all the man knew, he could be a thief. Or a junkie.

A *killer…*

Leon nearly laughed out loud at the thought.

When they finally pulled off the motorway, they passed what looked to be two small towns, eventually turning onto a dirt road. The truck's chassis groaned as they climbed the uneven terrain, and every sharp jostle of the trailer spurred a cacophony of startled clucks. The final stretch of dirt revealed a modest farmhouse. White face, red roof, and a few chimneys sticking out. To the far left of the property was a large wooden barn. Leon popped his door open and stepped out.

Without warning, the man began walking toward the barn.

"Hey!" Leon called out. "Wait up!"

He jogged to catch up with the man, each footstep squishing loudly into the soggy earth. The night was pungent with the smell of moss, moisture, and manure. When they reached the barn, the man slid one half of the tall, wooden door open and walked into the blackness within. Leon followed cautiously inside. The man struck a match and cupped the fragile flame with his hand, directing it into an oil lamp. The kerosene-soaked wick caught fire and illuminated the barn's interior with a soft orange glow. He grabbed the lamp's handle and set it on a small bedside table.

"You've got a cot with a wool blanket," said the man, tapping the cot's frame. "Outhouse is behind the barn. No heat or running water in here."

Leon watched as the man's eyes wandered around the space. "You can shower in the main house tomorrow. I'll bring ye a set of dry clothes."

"Thanks again," said Leon.

The man only nodded, hardly meeting his gaze. "Breakfast is at sunrise. Don't be late."

When the man left, Leon stripped out of his wet clothes, plopped onto the cot, and curled up beneath the wool blanket. The exhaustion that had been kept at bay from the stress of his journey crashed over him like a landslide. The barn itself was empty, only equipped with the basics. The side walls and rafters were filled with bales of hay. The scent of the old lumber mixed with the sharp, grassy scent of straw was oddly comforting. The rain slowed to a drizzle, and the pitter-patter on the barn's metal roof filled the space with the soothing sound.

He was fast asleep before the man returned with the clothes.

June 29th, 1964—present

Aniqa had thrice circled Buckingham Palace. From Spur Street to Constitution Hill, she inspected the full perimeter for every possible point of entry. The iron bars topped with the gilded fleurs-de-lis of the main gates rose high in the air, and behind them stood a line of guards—frozen like toy soldiers, the butt of the rifles resting in their right palms, red coats perfectly buttoned, and heads still, somehow balancing the enormous black bearskin caps, all while staring stoically straight ahead.

Although they would not divert their gaze, Aniqa knew better.

They were watching her.

The goal wasn't to slip in unnoticed, but to get close enough to a guard in a less trafficked area and use the letter as leverage to get in front of the Queen. But even that felt like a far cry from possible.

On her fourth loop, on a quiet section of Constitution Hill, she heard footsteps parallel to hers. She swivelled her head to get a quick pass of her surroundings. Being half past ten on a Monday morning, she was mostly alone.

The barrier on this side of the palace grounds was made of simple brick and far shorter than those of the main gates. Anyone with a decent bit of upper body strength could have hoisted themselves over, and then would have found themselves surrounded by the foliage of the palace gardens. To compensate for the lack of height, the walls were fortified with thousands of sharp spikes wrapped around a black metal bar. If one somehow survived the spikes, they would be met by a dozen rows of narrowly spaced barbed wire, all positioned at a steep incline, where its apex was far out of jumping distance.

Aniqa was trying to get back to her son in one piece.

Instead, she followed the sound of the guard's footsteps and waited until they grew louder. Once she imagined their positions were aligned, she used the bare strength of her hands to pull herself up high enough so that her head was level with the spikes; she feared a quick slip or muscle cramp might cause her to accidentally impale an eye, or worse, turn her face into Swiss cheese.

She just barely caught sight of the top edge of the guard's black fuzzy cap.

"Hey!" she called out in a strained whisper. "Psst!"

The guard whipped around and saw Aniqa's head just barely above the barrier. He slung his rifle around and aimed it at her. "Get down!"

She held the edge of the barrier with a white-knuckled grip, but her strength was slipping. "Please! I need to see the Queen." The guard cocked the rifle. "I—I have a letter…" she forced out shakily.

"Madam, *now!* Or I'll shoot."

Aniqa let herself drop to the ground. She caught her breath and brushed the dirt off her knees. The few passersby stared patronisingly as she slunk along Constitution Hill back toward the front of the palace. Her conscious mind told her with resounding certainty that she had failed. She wouldn't even as much as step foot on Buckingham Palace grounds, let alone get in front of the Queen. And now, a touch of fear crept into her psyche.

She may have just broken the law.

As she reached where Constitution Hill converged with The Mall, she saw a trio of guards outside the main palace gates.

"There she is!" one called out.

Her fight-or-flight instincts told her to run, but she fought against it. There was no point. The guard who had seen her along the barrier led the pack, with the two others flanking him, weapons drawn.

"You better tell me that bloody stupid stunt of yours meant nothing."

Aniqa's mouth was dry.

"I could have you arrested for trespassing. So speak. Now."

She wanted nothing more than to pull the letter from her purse and show them the wax seal, to tell them why she was really there, but a commanding voice in her head said *no*. It was three versus one, and if they decided to confiscate the letter, they would triumph. She had to protect it at all costs. The guard who had first spotted her studied her now, frowning. He was young, blond, face smooth and hairless.

An idea struck her. She began to flutter her eyelids; she outstretched a hand and began to rock side to side. "I feel woozy," she said, letting her eyes roll back in her head and then collapsing onto her side.

The two guards came to her aid, shouldering their weapons.

"I think I may have hit my head when I came down off the gate," she said. Then she flicked her gaze to the guard who had spotted her. "I swear, I just wanted to peek into the garden. Nothing more."

She feigned the most pitiful, pleading look she could muster.

The young guard sighed, shaking his head. His posture relaxed a bit.

"Help her up," he instructed. He still eyed her with a hint of suspicion, and then leaned in closely.

"If I see you around here again, I'll have you investigated. Understood?"

Aniqa nodded. The guard waved his hand. "Go on."

She thanked the men and quickly ran, grateful for freedom. As she walked, she tried to rein in her nerves and collect her thoughts. She wondered what her next move was. Minutes passed before she realised she'd unintentionally cut through St. James Park. And though the day was grey and dreary, the nature around her was bursting with life. Birds chirped, darting gayly from tree to tree. An elderly woman stood at the edge of a wooden footbridge, tossing pieces of bread at the swans who traced circles in the water delicately beneath her. The bright green foliage was still fresh from spring's bloom, not yet their darkest hue of summer.

Everything was alive.

And so am I, thought Aniqa.

She had failed miserably, but the day was still young. She wasn't ready to call it quits and return home.

There was another palace left to try.

John the Guardsman still had a few hours remaining of his morning shift. He'd never imagined that standing still—a task he had done successfully for nearly three decades—would ever become a nuisance. Yet here he was, wishing he could shake out his limbs and stretch, for his bones had begun to ache in old age.

The job was surely not for everyone, for although the pay was fair, most people weren't cut out to do mostly nothing. New guards had to be of sound mind because *that* would become their lone companion, day in and day out. Eight hours is a dreadfully long time to be alone with one's thoughts.

He would tell trainees to sing the lyrics of their favourite songs in their heads, imagine how life at home would play out when they departed—what their wives might cook, what their children might tell them about their day, or for the bachelors, he'd tell them to imagine their favourite drink at the pub or watching their football team win. But on the surface, guards had to uphold the straightest posture and maintain the blankest of canvasses. All while their eyes scanned the area, like a hawk waiting for something, anything, to wander into its territory.

Much to John's surprise, around an hour ago something had wandered into his.

A woman. She had dark, straight hair that fell past her shoulders and skin the colour of coffee with only a tiny splash of milk. She'd crisscrossed the gardens a half-dozen times and wandered along the southern side of the palace, lingering by its entrance too long for his liking.

What intrigued John the most was the fact she was alone.

A woman going for a stroll on her lunch break would walk through once or twice at most. If a woman came to the palace grounds to sightsee a bit of royal history, they were almost never alone. Always with a spouse, child, or acquaintance.

John wondered what brought the woman here. Even at a distance, he could see the nervous energy brimming from her. She fiddled with her purse strap, intermittently shifting her gaze to him. Almost as if, were she to stare hard and long enough, he might disappear.

The woman then pulled something white out of her purse. She suddenly began striding over to his post. He held still as she approached.

"Excuse me," she began. He saw her nervously chewing her bottom lip in his peripheral. "I need your help."

This woman was clearly in no immediate danger. He ignored her, for now.

"Sir, please," she said, and reached her arm out to touch him.

"Stand down from the guard!" He boomed the warning.

She took a step back, chewed her lower lip more intensely, then huffed.

He hadn't the slightest clue what could have vexed this woman, but even from the corner of his vision, he could tell there was a mental battle ensuing just beyond those dark eyes.

"My son and three others have been missing for two weeks," she said, through gritted teeth. "I have a letter from the Queen that was sent to a man named Albert Reid, who lives in my town. I am not here to cause a fuss. No one knows of this letter but me. I swear it." She swivelled her head upwards to meet his eyeline. "I just want to know why. *Why* did The Queen send this to Albert?"

The woman waved the envelope at him, and that was when he saw it.

A red wax seal.

His stomach sank to a depth previously unimaginable until this very moment. His muscles loosened, and he broke his post.

He watched shock fill the woman's eyes as he finally met her gaze.

"May I?" he asked softly. She gave an indiscernible nod, then handed him the letter. His heart thudded against his chest unbearably, and he held the weighty envelope, flipping it around to inspect it. He saw who it was addressed to. The lack of a return address. And of course, the Lancaster family crest impressed into the shiny blob of red wax. He sighed, shaking his head in disbelief as he held the exact same letter he had held just days earlier. The hundreds of letters he'd held over the past twenty years, same as this one, suddenly flashed before his eyes like a flip-book animation.

He stared at this woman in awe, and the intolerable guilt he'd carried for far too long began to make his eyes glisten. He hadn't an idea of the how, nor did he care to know. But whatever mystical force had summoned this rogue woman here with this letter, its power stemmed from both tragedy and miracle.

A confluence of destiny only God was powerful enough to see out.

And though the woman couldn't even begin to comprehend the barrage of emotions surging through John the Guardsman, she still saw the glimmer of recognition behind his tired eyes the moment he saw the letter. How it formed a crack in his unyielding exterior.

"Please," said the woman wearily. "Help me."

A sudden sense of calm began to slide over John; it started at his toes and worked its way up his burly frame like a warm blanket. He never imagined this day would come. Where he'd be forced to face the music. To stand eye-to-eye with the physical manifestation of the cosmic debt his deeds had helped aggregate. Suddenly, a sliver of sunlight slipped through the bruised clouds, and cast the edges of this woman's hair in an ethereal glow. She looked almost heavenly. *Perhaps that's what she is,* he thought. *An angel.* For a moment, he wasn't certain whether he was alive or dead. Awake or dreaming.

A guilty conscience plays many tricks.

He handed the woman the letter, and with it, allowed the peaceful feeling to fully saturate him.

He submitted.

Like all men must do when they meet their fate, they face a single decision.

Honour or dishonour.

His Adam's apple quivered as he swallowed, tears misting his eyes, and said softly and with earnest, "It's not the Queen you're looking for."

John the Guardsman asked if she had a pen. The woman lent him one, and he scribbled something on the back of the letter.

It wasn't until she had left the palace grounds that Aniqa saw the guardsman had written down an address.

20 Courtfield Gardens.

CHAPTER 21
THE PRINCESS AND THE PAUPER

March, 1940 – September, 1940—past

Breakfast was served at dawn, just as the man had instructed. A meal as plain as the house he dwelt in—beans, toast, porridge, and a boiled egg. When Leon had finished and was preparing to leave, the man asked him a single question:

"Can you work?"

He had never worked a day in his life. But he had lied before.

And despite trying to live on the straight and narrow, for the sake of his survival, he had chosen to lie. He justified this decision by telling himself it wasn't a *dark* lie. It wouldn't hurt the man in any way. He mused that maybe, if he were lucky, this lie would lead him to something good.

They would spend the mornings feeding the animals. The man owned chickens, cattle, and horses. They'd muck out coops, barn stalls, and feeding troughs. They filled the rest of the day with maintenance work— digging ditches, putting up or mending fences, restoring the barns or the farmhouse. They would take a tea break around noon, but didn't stop again until five, when the day's work was done.

In the evenings, the man would read on his verandah and smoke tobacco from a wooden pipe. Leon was never invited to join him, but after a few months working, he finally built up the courage to sit with him. The man took his new company much like he did everything else—silently and with little reaction. Leon would just sit quietly in the chair farthest from the man, enjoying the sounds and smells of the countryside. As the sun fell, the steady chirp of the crickets signalled the beginning of their nightly chorus. He'd hear the occasional moo from the cows, and the soft clucks of the chickens getting settled in their coops on the far side of the farm. He couldn't quite put his finger on it, but there was something about this new life that soothed his soul. The work was hard, but this was the time he cherished most.

The after.

Watching the dirt slide off his body and swirl around the drain when he showered, the dinner wholly crafted from the livestock they raised and the many gardens they kept. Quietly soaking in the surrounding nature from the verandah watching the sun fall over the lush green hills. All of it imbued a calm within Leon that he never knew existed. He even smiled in front of the mirror in the mornings because his face and arms had taken on a reddish hue from working in the sun. He imagined how much of a spectacle his new tone would have caused back home; the royals were expected to always remain fair-skinned.

So that became their routine.

They ate in silence, they worked in silence, and they rested in silence.

Day in and day out.

It baffled Leon how little the man spoke. Throughout the past year, only twice had the man broken his silence.

The first time was the week after Leon began joining the man on the verandah in the evenings, when he suddenly put down his pipe and motioned to Leon with his hand to follow him inside. He led Leon to the only door in the farmhouse that always stayed closed. Nestled between the kitchen and the man's bedroom, Leon felt his heart flutter as the man unlocked it with a brass key, for he had always wondered what lay inside.

A study.

There sat a tasteful wood-stained desk and chair, their glossy finishes gleaming slightly in the bit of light slipping in through the window. Two walls ran parallel from the room's entrance, each lined from floor to ceiling with books. Leon scanned the shelves in awe, but he didn't move forward. He glanced back at the man, who stood in the threshold of the room, lips pressed, eyes toward the floor.

Without looking up, the man must have noticed his pause.

"Go on," he said.

Leon tried to hold back his smile as he began combing through the many titles. Loads of fiction—classics, American and British literature. Plenty of non-fiction, too. Books on history, farming, Scottish lore, and mythology. This collection was sub-par compared to what he'd had at Kensington Palace, but it worked. Small but substantial.

As he continued his circle around the room, he kept glancing back at the man. The way his jaw muscles were taut, mouth contorted slightly, eyes not budging from the threshold floor—his countenance spurred a single word in Leon's mind.

Pain.

In these last few months, Leon had never seen the man's disposition change. He was always stoic. Always quiet. Unperturbed.

Like a pond without a single ripple. But now Leon wondered if that was just what the man wanted him to see. That beneath the still surface, an invisible current churned violently, drowning all the life within.

Leon glanced along the man's desk; a white picture frame caught his eye. It housed a photo of the man, a woman, and a newborn baby swaddled in a blanket. The man in this picture was beaming. A smile so wide and joyful that Leon quickly flicked his gaze from the photo to the man who stood before him at the threshold.

They appeared to be two different men entirely.

He grabbed the picture frame and turned it toward the man.

"Is this your family?" he asked.

The moment the words were uttered, Leon instantly regretted saying them. The man's vacant stare became charged with anger.

"Put that down." He ripped the picture frame from Leon's hand before he could set it down. "That was not for you to see," he scolded, then ushered him out of the study. The man hastily reinserted the key, and the door's lock clacked loudly as it slid into place. When he turned to face him, his lower lip began to quiver.

"Next time I let you in the study," he breathed out each word deliberately. "You will choose a book and leave. Then when you're finished, you may return it for a new one."

Leon responded with a meagre nod. The weight of the shame he felt pulled his gaze downwards, and he only saw the man's feet as he lumbered past him and returned to the verandah.

The man never spoke of the photo again. It took weeks for Leon to regain the courage to rejoin the man on the verandah and sheepishly ask for a book. He stringently avoided letting his gaze drift towards the desk, but even in his peripheral, he could see the picture frame was gone. And the whole time he searched for a new title, he could feel the man's piercing grey eyes burn into the back of his neck.

This must have been a special place.

A place that required an enormous amount of strength to even allow Leon to enter.

Though too ashamed to speak, he felt profoundly grateful, for the level of tranquility he experienced reading next to the man every evening was one he'd never come close to in Prince Alfred's salon. Back then, his solitude was tainted with the nagging anxiety of trying to ward off the quiet. But here, the pastoral sounds never ceased. The needle on mother nature's record never scratched, just kept spinning endlessly. And Leon loved that quality of his new home.

The second time the man spoke occurred a few months later.

Leon awoke in the barn and found a letter on his table. The man wrote that he was headed out to buy some calves and instructed Leon to do the day's work alone.

He felt a bit of pride swell in his chest when he realised that the man trusted him enough to leave him alone at the farm all day. He met the day's tasks with great enthusiasm because of the added boost of confidence the letter gave him. While he worked, there were a handful of times where he felt as if he was being watched. Each time the sensation tickled the back of his neck, he'd pause and sweep the area around him, but there was nothing except the gardens, trees in the distance, and the rolling hills. The last time the feeling arose, he swore he heard a car door slam. A sound so foreign these days it set alarm bells off in his mind. He dropped the garden hoe and headed in the direction the sound had come from. He crested the largest hill on the property and looked about the area. His eyes followed the long dirt driveway that snaked through the hills, and what he saw in the distance made his heart jump.

On the main road parked beneath the shade of an old sycamore tree was a black car. Its engine cranked the moment Leon laid eyes on it. It then pulled out, making a wide U-turn before driving off.

No one had ever parked so close to the man's property before, and their closest neighbours were a quarter of a mile away. Leon made a mental note of the occurrence and continued working.

He finished a full hour earlier than normal, and that was when Leon realised that while the man was spry for his old age, he was much slower in his work than him. He showered in the main house, and then retired to the verandah. The man was always the one to make dinner, and he was too fearful to meddle with the food in the kitchen, so instead, he passed the time until the man's return by reading. Since he was alone, he mindlessly chose the rocking chair closest to where the man normally sat. He soon found the stress of the day melting away as he got lost in the book.

He was so engrossed in the story that the loud clacking of the cattle trailer seemed muted. It wasn't until the man's truck door slammed that Leon flinched and looked up from his book.

The face that stared back at him through the wooden verandah railings was frighteningly familiar. It radiated the same look of pain and anger he'd seen that first day in the study. The man lumbered up the steps and pointed to him.

"*That* is not your chair. Get up."

Leon stood slowly to keep his tired legs from trembling, then let his head fall. He tried to circumvent the man but was met with a large, calloused palm on his chest.

"Look at me," he said. The man pointed over his shoulder, "That was my wife's chair. Ye will not sit there again."

Leon left the man on the verandah. He was too embarrassed to continue reading in his normal chair; he set his book down inside and returned to his barn room.

They ate in silence that night.

But not the happy kind.

June 10th, 1941—past

Leon found it amusing how quickly a day could become a year.

Outside of those two interactions, the man and Leon never spoke to one another. They co-existed peacefully, like the bee whose sharp stinger never harms the flower. Luckily, he had spent enough time with the man to learn his idiosyncrasies.

To learn what stings.

He'd seen the changes the four seasons brought, and with them, Leon grew to appreciate the ebb and flow of nature. Cycles of life and death; death and rebirth. The crispness of the air in autumn, the wetness of winter, and the fragrant smell of blossoms in the spring. While these shifts in scenery gave his eye something to marvel at, it was simply a backdrop.

What pricked his perception more sharply was how the work changed throughout the seasons. Tilling fields and sowing seeds in the spring, harvesting crops late in the summer, and digging ditches in the autumn to syphon water away during the rainy winters. That was what Leon truly grew to understand, for that knowledge was cemented by the lingering effects of the labour itself—his calloused hands, sore muscles, and aching bones. Long gone was the Leon whose face hardly saw the sun and had servants waiting on him hand and foot. His scrawny figure had filled in; the muscles on his back, arms, and shoulders had swelled in size.

The work they had done over the past year had inadvertently made Leon a man.

And the more time that passed, the more he felt *Duke* Leon dying. His old life was slowly fading away. It was a welcome change; one he did not resist in the slightest. He wasn't certain he'd ever forget the pain of losing Theodora, and there was a part of him that didn't want to. Because he was petrified that if he allowed that sensation to dull, the memories of her might fade too. Everything else was as good as dead in his mind. The many horrors of his childhood. The blows from his mother, being bullied by William, and the day outside the palace walls where he was forced to…

He couldn't garner the strength to think of *that* memory.

Yet here he was, in his new life. Alive and well.

He was no longer the black sheep of the family because he had left the herd. Not by his own will, but part of him was grateful, nevertheless. For that winter morning in Baden-Baden had somehow led him here. To his new life in the Scottish countryside. To his nameless friend of few words whose generosity he was beholden to.

Although he would never openly admit it, Leon knew the man was equally thankful for a companion. He witnessed it in his actions. How he would unlock the study just as Leon was finishing his current book. How he would sneakily watch how voraciously Leon ate certain dishes and would then cook that dish more often. How he began bringing him into town regularly. On Fridays, they'd stock the local convenience stores full of fresh milk. Saturdays, they sold eggs and produce at a local market in Catrine. Then on Sundays, the man took him to the Catrine High Kirk.

That was where they were headed now.

The chassis emitted metallic squeaks as the man manoeuvred the truck down the long dirt driveway. One of the right tyres hit a pothole and lurched Leon's side of the cabin violently, causing him to bounce in his seat, nearly hitting his head on the roof. Once the terrain smoothed on the paved town road, the man and Leon looked at each other, laughing at how ridiculously he had been jostled.

In his peripheral, Leon caught the man smiling. The expression was so seldom seen on the man that it caused Leon to smile too. He hadn't seen the man this light of heart in all the time they'd spent together over the past year. He had observed that when they went to church, the man seemed slightly more at ease, but nothing like this.

Last weekend they had made an unexpected trip into town, and the man bought him a pair of navy trousers and a white dress shirt.

"Happy birthday," the man had said.

Leon quickly looked out the passenger window, for recalling the moment made his eyes misty with tears. It was then that a memory from when they first met resurfaced; the man had asked him how old he was. Leon told him he turned nineteen on June 7th. Nearly a year later, on the day of his twentieth birthday, the man had remembered…

All of Leon's life, he'd only worn clothes made from the finest materials, received expensive gifts on his birthday, and was given anything he desired at the drop of a hat. Yet something as simple as a new set of church clothes brought him to tears. It was as if, without words, the man had validated his presence. All the arduous farm work. The silent days, weeks, and months. The man was telling him that he belonged.

"I want to move you into the main house."

The man's gravelly voice was so foreign, Leon thought he'd imagined him speaking.

"What?"

The man quickly glanced at him before looking back out onto the road. "It's time you leave the barn. Would ye like that?"

"Yes," blurted Leon without a second thought. He had to fight to contain his joy.

The man's gaze meandered about the dreary Scottish day in front of them. "If you're to live under my roof, I want ye to be a man of the Lord. I've arranged for you to be confirmed by the Kirk after the service ends."

Leon had no words. The man caught the disbelief and smiled.

"So, what'll it be?"

"Of course," said Leon, beaming.

Tucked away off the Chapel Brae stood the Catrine High Kirk, a handsome relic hidden behind a row of trees. Constructed of red brick, its original hue had long since faded. Churchgoers who didn't live in town would park along the Chapel Brae and walk the rest of the distance. Leon never minded; he enjoyed the cool morning breeze and how it carried the faint scent of moss and damp earth.

Leon still remembered the first time the man had toured him around to marvel at the full glory of the structure. Perched atop the roof was a belfry; its large bell tolled at the top of every hour and before service began. The eastern face was magnificent. There were four sets of arched cathedral windows. White metal traceries crisscrossed the glass. Leon found it interesting the glass was clear, not stained. There was a fifth set of arched windows, but they were cut horizontally in half. Beneath the arched half were two large doors that had been painted a deep shade of blue.

He remembered how pleased he had been to see *that* colour.

The man told him that the building itself had stood for close to 150 years. It had been built atop a hill overlooking the town; no homes surrounded the immediate property, but instead gravestones were peppered throughout. As if whomever created the structure wanted to keep the space sacred for all the people of their faith—both living and dead.

The choir's hymns bounced off the stone ceilings, reverberating with an amalgam of voices that seemed to transcend the boundaries of the Kirk itself. Leon mused that perhaps the blissful feeling the music gave him was the closest thing to Heaven he'd get to experience.

During the sermon, the man would gently nudge Leon with his elbow if he caught any delay in the turning of his bible's pages. He was always supposed to follow along with the minister, and normally, he did this with ease. But today, he buzzed with anticipation for his confirmation and was unable to focus on anything else.

When the sermon ended and the crowds began to disperse, Leon jumped up before the man could.

"Easy there," said the man with a chuckle; when he stood, he met eyes with the minister who waved them both over. Leon's throat parched as he approached the pulpit. Excitement reaching its apex, it seemed as if his very skin was vibrating with warmth.

Leon surmised that this place, this very moment, was the farthest from the darkness he had ever been. Soft light spilled in through the glass windows, eradicating even the most resilient of shadows. The churchgoers were all merry, chitchatting as they lingered in the pews. And the minister who awaited him had the kindest eyes he'd ever seen on another man. He reminded Leon a bit of Greta, with some crow's feet wrinkling his otherwise soft face—yet another pure soul.

The man followed Leon to the pulpit, and once there, the minister placed his bible on the podium in front of him. He then looked to the man, smile softer than before, and his expression steeled over a bit.

"Henry, who is this young lad ye have brought before me to take the rite of confirmation?"

Henry stared back at the minister and flinched slightly where he stood, as if he had been shocked by an invisible cattle prod. He turned his gaze toward Leon, the corners of his lips upturning as he realised the absurdity that he'd lived with the boy for over a year and never once asked his name. Henry was fighting not to laugh. The giddiness began to spread to Leon, for he hadn't learnt the man's name either.

"Do ye not know the lad's name?" The minister cocked his head toward Henry.

Mouth agape, he looked between Leon and the minister.

As Leon watched Henry freeze, he quickly wracked his brain. Turbulent memories crashed through his conscious mind; the ones he would have rather forgotten entirely. He could hear his mother's decree, his last conversation with Greta, the hearty laughter of Theodora as they played made-up progressions on the piano.

In a single moment, he felt all the joys and sorrows of his old life.

The pain that had pushed him *here*.

Just before the minister could chide Henry, Leon hushed the cacophony of voices from memories past.

He let it fully slip away, for good.

The darkness was a distant memory, and he felt the new spirit he'd become acquainted with over the past year bubble up in his chest.

Who do you want to be? a little voice asked him.

"Albert Reid," he answered.

Balmoral Castle
July 19th, 1941—past

Princess Edith found it eerie how Queen Eleanor's sitting room could be both warm and cold simultaneously. A fire burned regardless of the time of year, but no matter how close Princess Edith sat to its flames, a biting chill would slink around her. The oscillation between the two temperatures created a sharp contrast that wouldn't otherwise have existed if the room could just make up its damn mind. She would spend whatever time that remained of her visits in silence, peeved by overbearing heat and penetrating cold.

She always wondered if the phenomenon arose from the absurd size of the space or simply from her mother's presence. For no matter how hearty the fire, it seemed to pale in comparison to Queen Eleanor's potent chill.

Stop thinking such ridiculous thoughts, she chided herself, shifting uncomfortably in her seat.

Queen Eleanor lingered by a collection of family photos hanging on the far wall.

"I feel like I blinked and then they were grown," she said, brushing one of the gilded frames with her thumb. She sucked at her teeth. "How I'd love just another day when they were young, and we were all together."

Queen Eleanor turned, eyeing Princess Edith over her shoulder.

"Don't you feel the same?"

"I do," she said. The crackling fire was replaced by the pulse pounding in her ears. She bit the inside of her lip to distract from the boiling anger she felt. Princess Edith knew exactly what her mother was doing. Her statement was nothing more than bait.

She was neither a fool nor a novice to Queen Eleanor's tactics. She had learnt many years ago that conversations with her mother were but a perilous dance. One where the Queen would always take the lead, and while the ground felt sturdy enough for the swaying steps of the routine, only a seasoned eye could discern that it was all a ploy, and the path had already been predetermined.

This was why Princess Edith had to watch her tongue.

Queen Eleanor turned from the photos and slowly traipsed around the perimeter of the room.

"Was dinner to your liking?" she asked.

"Yes."

"Humph," she muttered. "An odd answer for someone who hardly ate."

Queen Eleanor circled to the hearth and grabbed the gilded fire iron. She began poking the logs; they collapsed and resettled with a myriad of crackling pops, a reinvigorated burst of flames.

Princess Edith couldn't take it any longer. She loathed this room and her mother's furtive glances, the intentional verbal tiptoeing—it all drove her mad. She would take the bait if it meant she could escape this godawful space more quickly.

"Forgive me for being forthright, but I find it hard to believe you summoned me here to ask what I thought of the food."

Queen Eleanor snorted, then began to smile. She hung the fire iron and slowly made her way to sit in the chaise across from Princess Edith.

There we go, thought Princess Edith. *Now she's on my level.*

Eye-to-eye.

"Oh, my rebellious one," said Queen Eleanor. "You're correct; I did not ask you here for something so trivial."

"Then, what?"

Queen Eleanor's gaze drifted toward the fire. She traced her thumbnail back and forth across her lower lip; it floored Princess Edith to see her mother visibly mulling over her words. Uncertainty was unlike her.

"I've found Leon."

Behind the electric shock those words carried, as the seconds passed, Princess Edith realised she had forgotten to breathe.

"I—I thought once you banished—"

Queen Eleanor looked up from the fire.

"I hired someone. He's been watching him from afar since he returned to Britain a year and a half ago."

"A year and a half!" exclaimed Princess Edith. "That long and…" She bit her tongue, glaring at her mother reprovingly. This new information caused a heaviness to sink in her gut, as if her stomach were being filled with lead.

Her son was out there, somewhere, all alone.

"How is he?" she blurted without a second thought.

"Surprisingly well," began Queen Eleanor with an air of nonchalance that poked at Edith's insides, much as if her mother were still wielding the glowing hot fire iron. "He's living in Scotland and working as a farmhand. According to my informant he goes by the name Albert Reid."

"He changed his name…" whispered Princess Edith. Her soul deflated. His last tie to the Royal Family, his *name*, had been taken from him.

"It was to be expected. Abandoning his name was part of the decree."

The logs in the fire toppled; a burst of flames exploded and illuminated Princess Edith's ghostly visage. Queen Eleanor had to fight flinching at seeing the full extent of her daughter's deterioration. Face gaunt, cheekbones protruding unflatteringly, and the bags beneath her eyes so pronounced, they looked like two crescent moons made of shadow.

"Why did you banish him, Mother?"

Princess Edith watched the Queen's eyes flicker in the orange-yellow light, as if she were replaying a film reel in her mind's eye.

"That I will never tell you, my dear. You haven't the heart to hear it."

The embers of anger within her suddenly turned into a raging inferno.

"This all began with you." Princess Edith forced out the words. "With the lie."

Queen Eleanor did not respond.

"Was it worth it?" she asked. "In protecting the reputation of our bloodline, which is all but intangible, you have lost so much that is real. Your daughter. Your sister. And now your grandson." Princess Edith's lip began to curl in disgust, eyes glistening with tears. "I pray every night that on the day you die, when your spirit leaves its vessel, you will not be released from the weight of your decision. I hope you feel it doubly so."

Queen Eleanor had let her gaze drift, fixing it on a pointless spot in the room. She breathed deliberately and evenly, unwilling to let her stony exterior crack.

Her mother's silence only stoked Edith's anger more. She stood, staring down at her as she began tracing her way to the far wall of the room. "Have you no heart?" She grabbed the family photo Queen Eleanor had been looking at earlier. "Does it not pain you that there's someone missing from these pictures?"

"Enough!" boomed the Queen.

Princess Edith released her white-knuckled grip on the picture frame and set it down.

"Sit," the Queen instructed.

Princess Edith returned to her seat.

"You must understand that I did not make that decision lightly."

"Then tell me why."

Queen Eleanor shook her head.

Princess Edith snorted, then stood. "I'm through with this," she said, headed for the long hall leading out of the chambers.

"Edith," said the Queen.

She stopped in her tracks, waited through an unbearable pause.

"If it helps you rest a bit easier, do know that the weight you speak of, I feel deeply. There's not a moment that goes by each day where I do not feel guilt."

Although the words did not suffice in quelling Princess Edith's deep-seated anger, she could not deny that they were soothing to her soul.

"And?" she asked, turning back to face her mother.

The Queen mustered the strength to look her daughter directly in the eyes.

"I've been thinking about sending Albert Reid a letter."

June 29ᵗʰ, 1964—present

It took five minutes for the taxi to drop Aniqa off in front of 20 Courtfield Gardens. It was a handsome terraced house constructed of champagne-coloured brick; its narrow face profuse with windows—over a dozen total covered the building's five storeys, each adorned with ornate white mouldings. Behind her was a large garden square, with all the houses of Courtfield Gardens encircling its lush greenery.

Aniqa noticed a peculiar detail about *this* house, though. All its many windows were shuttered. Her steps toward the door were measured, and she felt a subtle sense of wonderment that fate had brought her here. Curiosity would not let her leave until she saw this through.

Aniqa needed to know what lay behind that door.

And *who* would answer.

She reached the top of the steps and knocked.

No one answered. She gave the door a few more raps. A few seconds passed; still nothing seemed to stir inside. Just as Aniqa began to knock again, the sound of a latch sliding caused her heart to soar in anticipation.

Then, the door opened.

She recognised the woman who stood before her as Princess Edith, one of Queen Eleanor's daughters. She had light auburn hair, a good portion of which had faded to grey. Its texture poufy, cascading in waves but stopping just past her neckline. Her skin fair, with surprisingly few wrinkles for a woman of her age. She was of slender build, and she wore a conservative but tasteful dress. Aniqa could have sworn Princess Edith had on a bit of makeup. Almost as if she had been waiting for someone to arrive at her door.

Most notable were Princess Edith's piercing blue eyes.

I've seen those before, she thought.

Princess Edith studied Aniqa, equally as intrigued by this stranger at her door.

"May I help you?"

"I hope so," Aniqa said, rifling through her purse, riddled with nervous energy. She realised that she hadn't thought of what she would say when this moment finally came. "I was hoping you can tell me who wrote this letter."

Aniqa presented it to Princess Edith and watched her hand tremble slightly as she grasped it. Her mouth fell agape, and she looked up from the letter, eyes flicking across Aniqa as if she were staring at a ghost.

"How did you get this?"

"I stole it," said Aniqa. "And brought it to someone who identified the impression in that seal as your mother's family crest."

Princess Edith rubbed the red wax seal with her thumb, studying the letter as if questioning its validity, then gazed up at Aniqa the same way the guardsman had—with a look of pure bewilderment. "Who gave you this address?" she asked, a tinge of suspicion in her voice.

"A guardsman at Kensington Palace."

Princess Edith let out a raspy breath, and her head fell. Whatever defensiveness Aniqa had witnessed a moment prior had faded.

"Your Highness, I'm not looking to trouble you. My son has been missing for over two weeks. I drove all the way from Scotland, and I want to know who wrote this letter and why was it sent to Albert Reid."

Princess Edith's chest rose and fell with each shallow breath. "You're the boy's mother."

It surprised Aniqa how the words sounded more like a statement than a question.

"He's my only son."

Princess Edith's lower lip trembled wildly, and her ragged breathing reached its peak. She burst into tears and threw herself into Aniqa's arms.

Aniqa froze, but after a few seconds of blubbering, embraced Princess Edith, holding her close. The cries were so raw, it reminded her of the day she'd found out her father had been killed. Aniqa had not cried that way since. Not for her mum. Not even for Arun when he went missing. Because deep down, her gut clung tightly to the belief her boy was still alive.

As she consoled Princess Edith silently, the convulsive cries did not lessen. Aniqa knew that the type of pain on display in front of her could only arise from one thing.

I wonder who she lost, she thought solemnly.

"I'm sorry…I'm so sorry," whimpered Princess Edith.

Aniqa gently stroked her back, and although she wondered what the apology meant, she did not ask.

They just held each other.

Mother to mother.

CHAPTER 22
THE LONDON CHEQUE

August 1ˢᵗ, 1941—past

Princess Edith approached the eastern entrance of Kensington Palace once the sun had long been down. Due to the visit to her old stateroom earlier that day, she was able to wander around the staff quarters long enough to learn the times of John the Guardsman's shift. As one of the most loyal of the Queen's Guards, he rotated between Buckingham and Kensington Palace, even sometimes accompanying the Queen, Jean-Claude Marron, and the rest of the family to Balmoral Castle during the summer months.

The unbearably sticky night air made Princess Edith uncertain whether it was due to the lingering heat of the day or her prickly-hot nerves.

When John the Guardsman saw Princess Edith approach, he broke his post to give her a small bow. "Your Highness," he said.

"You know not to address me like that."

John swallowed dryly. "Edith," he corrected. "How may I be of service to you this evening?"

She gave him the most sober stare she could muster and said, "When you end your shift in half an hour, meet me at my residence, 20 Courtfield Gardens. Do not speak of this to any of the staff, and please, do not question my request. I will reimburse you for any fares you incur."

John pondered this bizarre request. After becoming the most revered of the Queen's Guard, he didn't want to jeopardise his position.

Princess Edith had moved just about all her belongings from her former apartment, 1A, in the palace, and she technically no longer lived there. But she was still the Queen's daughter.

"See you then," he said.

John the Guardsman arrived promptly at the door to 20 Courtfield Gardens just after eleven. Princess Edith let him in and turned the landing light off behind him. She offered him tea which he accepted. He moved awkwardly about the foyer, unable to make up his mind where to stand.

"Please." She waved her hand to an open seat. "Be my guest." She fetched the hot water and tea tray and added, "I don't have many of those these days."

John's eyes roamed the living room. In the far corner, clothes and other belongings were piled in a heap. He got the sense that Princess Edith had made a hasty attempt at cleaning the space before his arrival. He glanced at the end table beside him, then slid his index finger along its surface, carving a path through a thick layer of dust. He quickly brushed his finger off as Princess Edith reentered the room, then set the tea tray on the coffee table.

"Milk?" she asked, pouring the tea in his cup first.

"Sure."

Despite Princess Edith being the loveliest of Queen Eleanor's daughters, her warm demeanour, even now, wasn't enough to let him relax.

Nothing about this impromptu rendezvous felt right.

"You're no longer at your post," she chided. "Be at ease."

He loosened his posture a bit. Not because he wanted to. Only because she demanded it.

"If I remember correctly, you have a wife."

He nodded, and she took a long sip of her tea. She set the cup down, still holding her eyes on him.

"A son?"

"Yes," he answered. "Just turned eight a few weeks ago."

"How lovely."

John took another sip of his tea to hide his discomfort.

"What's his name?"

"Peter."

Princess Edith let out a tiny snort and stared at him through a thin smile. "May I be frank with you?"

"Of course."

"Let me present you a scenario." John watched her cheery demeanour sour. "Imagine that right after Peter was born, he was taken from you and your wife."

John grumbled at this asinine example, but Princess Edith held up a finger. "Please. Just listen."

He chewed the inside of his lower lip.

"Not to worry, John. Your Peter was not kidnapped. But instead claimed by a relative whom you lived with. And for reasons beyond your control, the boy was raised from the time he was an infant to believe your relative was their true parent. You, on the other hand, even though you spent an immeasurable amount of time around the child, were forced to do only that. Spectate. You watch Peter grow into a healthy young man and painfully observe how he forms closer bonds with other members of the family. You are merely a forgotten shadow on the wall. You might get a hug at Christmas or Easter. That is the only time you may embrace your beloved Peter."

John watched Princess Edith's eyes redden, fighting to keep her mouth from contorting as she spoke.

"Then, just as he's become a man, he's kicked out into the street. And he's barred from ever contacting you, or anyone else in the family for that matter." The look in her gaze was filled with so much pain. He'd never witnessed that kind of melancholy in a woman's eyes before.

"What would you do?" she asked flatly.

"I'd try to tell him the truth."

"You cannot!" A sadistic laugh escaped her lips. "Oh, and though it cannot be confirmed. The other parent. Let's say, your wife, who tried to tell Peter the truth a hundred times over, was killed for doing so. What then?"

"Well, I don't know. I haven't a sufficient answer. Might attempt to get as close as possible without getting caught. I'd try to support him, even from afar."

Princess Edith sighed, then looked up at John with an expectant smile.

"Just as I imagined you'd say. Because you love your son, as I do mine."

"You have *a...*" His voice trailed off, and the pieces began to click in his mind.

"John. Everything I am about to say must go with you to your grave. It is a secret whose full detail only you and I would share." She poised herself, swallowing. "If that is too great a burden, I shall speak no further, and you may dismiss yourself."

"My Lady," he began, pausing. If the imaginary circumstances she had just described were in fact real, that would explain the pain. That heartbreaking look of defeat behind her blue eyes. The air in Princess Edith's house was so still, tension so heavy, it reminded John of the moment before an orchestra plays the first note of a symphony, with the conductor holding his baton high above, a silent harbinger of all that's to come.

"Continue," said John.

Princess Edith began her story, all the way from the beginning.

"When I was sixteen, Queen Eleanor hired a tutor for my younger sister, Maud. The tutor, Sir Charles Stirling, was a handsome man in his twenties. At the time, I couldn't have fathomed in the slightest the utter misfortune my youthful lust for Sir Charles would bring into the world. We laid together, in secret, many a time. Just after my seventeenth birthday, my monthly visitor never arrived. Much to the Queen's horror, the morning nausea began not long after. Once a doctor confirmed I was pregnant, the Queen quickly carted me off to Osborne House, where I remained for the entirety of the pregnancy. I always knew my mother disapproved of my laying with a commoner tutor, but never to what extent. Looking back, I wonder if perhaps the Queen left me be so as to not stress me, because in all that time, Queen Eleanor never once visited, nor spoke of plans for after the baby was born. The balmy air and warmer weather of the Isle of Wight was a splendid place to carry the child, and I prayed he would be healthy and strong because of it. On the contrary, with the dreaded isolation I experienced in that house, I feared its effects might also be passed onto the baby.

"It was June 7th, 1921, on an oddly cold spring day when I went into labour. A brutal experience, but with the help of midwives, I delivered a healthy baby boy. I only got to hold him for a few minutes," she said through tears. "The Queen arrived to escort me back to London. She entered my quarters unannounced, and closed the French doors behind her, even going to such unnecessary lengths as to close the curtains. It was then that my entire world, my life, and the life of my son was crushed in just a few simple breaths."

"'The boy will be raised as mine,' said Queen Eleanor.

"I never felt such an all-consuming pain. She then informed me of the lie. Sir Charles had been fired, and to keep him quiet, given an indefinite annuity and paid residence at 20 Courtfield Gardens. The Queen said *she* had spent the entirety of my pregnancy at Balmoral Castle, hidden away from the public eye and the rest of the family. Only Prince Alfred was permitted to see her."

"'Tomorrow, I am staging the boy's birth at Buckingham Palace,' said the Queen.

"The maids at Osborne House later told me that they had to shut all the doors leading to my quarters to muffle the violent screams. But the Queen hadn't flinched in the face of my pleas, nor my shouting expletives.

She silenced me with a simple threat.

"'If you or Sir Charles reveal yourself as the true parents, the boy will be put up for adoption. Or worse.'

"All of this because a commoner tutor had infected her bloodline. Before we parted, Queen Eleanor uttered one last thing.

"*'You may name him.'*

"On the state boat back to the mainland and in the car ride to the palace, I vowed a thousand times over, that before I take my last breath on this earth, I will make sure my son knows his true mother's name.

"Before the staged birth, when the Queen had asked the boy's name, wholly out of spite for her monstrous lie, I gave him the name Leon. It was not a royal name, but rather one I had learnt from lingering around Sir Charles during Maud's lessons. Derived from the Latin—*leo*—it meant lion. I knew whatever life lay ahead for my son, he would have to be equally as brave.

"The public had bought the staging, although most of the family knew it was but a charade. They knew of my nine-month absence, and some were even privy to the furtive glances Sir Charles and I had exchanged in the palace before I became pregnant.

"Leon was to be raised in Kensington Palace. Queen Eleanor did not want him living at her residence. In the months that followed, I made the strategic decision to move into apartment 1A. If I couldn't be the boy's mother, then I would certainly try to be as close as possible during his upbringing.

"I would attempt to sneak into his nursery late at night, to hold my son, to rock him in my arms and sing him a soft lullaby. The first time after I was caught, they began keeping his door under lock and key. I watched how my sisters and his cousins would often treat him harshly. It was as if everyone in the Royal Household knew, yet no one dared say a word. To them, Leon was a permanent stain. But one that had a mouth to feed, a body to bathe, and spirit that needed nourishing.

"Yet no one stood ready to nourish him. To give him love.

"Princess Theodora noticed this and began spending more time with Leon. He took to her quickly, and though it pained me immensely to witness their bond budding, I knew it was what he needed. And I will forever be thankful for my late aunt's gesture.

"May God rest her sweet soul.

"As he grew older, Leon became more reclusive. He often isolated himself for long hours in his room or in Prince Alfred's study, who had passed away shortly after Leon's birth. I mused that God must have witnessed the Queen steal Leon's future, and therefore he robbed her of her beloved Alfred.

"A short but satisfying taste of retribution.

"I often lamented, lying awake through sleepless nights, that Leon was being punished for a mistake that wasn't his to begin with. Destined for a life of misery for something out of his control. I prayed night after night that this wouldn't be the case. But just like where we are now," said Princess Edith, wiping her wet eyes, "he began his life alone, and now he continues it that way. Banished from the kingdom. Never knowing his place in this world."

John the Guardsman hoped in the dim lighting she couldn't see that he had teared up too. "So, what's your plan?" he asked plainly.

"Queen Eleanor told me she has found Leon. He's apparently doing well. He goes by the name Albert Reid and is working as a farmhand in Scotland. She let me know that she plans to write him a letter."

"And?"

"I'm going to write to him as well."

"How will you manage that? Do you have his address?"

"No," she said, a smile tugging at her lips. "But that is something you can get me."

"Edith, I—"

"Would you not ask for help if it were for Peter?"

"Well, of course."

"Then, why can't you help me write my son?"

Suddenly, John's memories of the day outside the palace walls resurfaced. Seeing that poor dog splayed open like a lab experiment. How he had shakily held his rifle on Leon, afraid the Queen might demand he shoot the boy. Then, having to witness Queen Eleanor's grotesque form of punishment...

The youth who was capable of *that* was Princess Edith's son.

"Do you know why Theodora took him in?" he asked.

Princess Edith's brow furrowed.

"No," she said. "Queen Eleanor never mentioned it. But I've always wondered."

John opened his mouth to speak, but his gut was struck with a sudden qualm, stopping him in his tracks. After all Princess Edith had been through, did she really need to know the gruesome detail of what had happened that day? She had mentioned that the Queen reported Leon was doing quite well for himself in his new life. John tried to imagine himself in Princess Edith's shoes; would learning of a slain animal stop him from writing his Peter?

Not a chance. He believed her to be equally as resolute.

It's simply a letter, said his conscience. *What harm can come from that?*

"I was curious myself," he said, shelving his worry. "Thought you might know." He watched the slight tension in Princess Edith's body ease.

"So, will you help me?"

John pushed through the last bit of reserve he felt, smiled, and gave her a nod.

"I will, My Lady."

"Thank you," she gasped and kept her face down, as if not to let John see the degree of exuberance slipping through her growing smile. He could have sworn he saw happy tears in the corners of her eyes.

"Know that I am forever indebted to your kindness," she said.

Princess Edith began detailing her instructions to John. First, he had to begin aligning his shifts with whichever palace the Queen was staying in. Since he already rotated between Buckingham and Kensington, this wouldn't be a problem. He was to check the outgoing mail daily for any letters addressed to Albert Reid. Then, he would copy the address down and bring it to Princess Edith.

"What about the seal?" he asked.

She haughtily waved a brass wax stamp, revealing a sly smile.

"I stole the Queen's. She'll presume it's lost and get a new one made."

"One last question," began John softly. "Will you reveal yourself to him?"

Princess Edith's eyes flicked aimlessly around, as if she were recalling an elusive thought that she had had many times before, attempting to grab hold of its reins. To strike the delicate balance between the unfortunate truth of her circumstance with her maternal desire.

"No." She forced the word out. "For now, I just want to correspond with him. To be present in his new life, to hear how he passes his days—both pleasures I was never permitted in his old life. If I must pose as my mother, so be it. I pray that God will have mercy on me and one day allow my son to learn the truth. That the love I show him in these letters is not Eleanor's, but mine."

August 8th, 1941—past

Within a week, John had procured the address for Princess Edith. She spaced out her own letter so that it was sent a week after the Queen's, and felt her heart flutter when she began writing:

Dear Albert,

Halfway through writing the letter, the phone rang. The vibration of the shrill bell echoed wildly throughout her house. She walked slowly to the phone, surprised that anyone would call at this late an hour, then picked it up.

"Hello."

"Edith." Her mother's cold voice sprang from the receiver.

"Mother," she croaked. "Is everything all right?"

"Far from it."

"Why? What's wrong?"

"Don't say another word," she hissed. "I have good cause to believe you were the one who stole my wax stamp."

Princess Edith's heart sank to an unimaginable depth.

"What intrigues me is the timing," began Queen Eleanor. "A few days before I send the first letter to the boy, the stamp disappears from my study."

"I—I swear—"

"When I said I have *good cause* it's because I know for certain. I would not accuse you simply on conjecture. Now, are you going to return the stamp to me? Or will you deny what you've done?"

After a few seconds of silence, Queen Eleanor snorted.

"Very well then. I would like to think you wouldn't be foolish enough to write to him. But on the off-chance that that *was* your plan, consider it failed. I'm sure you likely made a sweet offer to one of the guards you're so friendly with to do your bidding, but the staff working in the mail room have already been alerted to watch out for any additional letters addressed to or from Albert Reid. They will shred all those outside the ones I send or receive in direct reply."

Princess Edith covered her mouth in an attempt to mute her cries.

Her mother let out a tiny, pitying laugh.

"Did you honestly believe that I would let you undo all the work we have done to keep this lie a secret?" Queen Eleanor clicked her tongue. "You might be sharper than your sisters, but do not forget that it was *I* who first whetted your blade."

The call was replaced with the droning dial tone. A lump formed in her throat, and as the seconds passed, the protruding feeling was too unbearable. Her limbs felt numb and foreign, and to avoid collapsing where she stood, she clumsily returned to her desk.

The moment she sat, she burst into tears.

In a single phone call, her mother had crushed a universe of future potential. What little hope she had left to form a connection with her son had been obliterated. There was so much she wanted to say, bottled up inside.

For the guilt, although not entirely hers, ate away at her soul.

She wanted to apologise—for everything.

For him being banished, for the lack of love Queen Eleanor showed him throughout his childhood. She wanted to atone for sins which her cowardice made her complicit in. She wanted to ask forgiveness for she knew the Queen had far too much pride to ever do the same.

But none of that would come to fruition.

Princess Edith had been forced back into silence. The state that had become all too familiar to her throughout the past two decades.

The gravity of her failure weighed on her like a ton of bricks, squeezing with a pressure so tremendous that her very spirit began to break apart. Bit by bit it dissolved away, until there was nothing left but an empty void.

And as she sobbed with her head down, the blackness behind her eyelids drew her attention to the nothingness expanding in the centre of her chest, whose edges seemed to lick at her insides with a seething, white-hot tongue.

In the darkness, in the silence, a single thought came to her mind:

If I cannot write to him, perhaps there is a way I can support my son.

The thought gave birth to an idea.

When it struck, the emptiness within her dissipated like smoke in the wind. She gently put down her pen and stationery and headed upstairs to the bedroom. There, she rifled through her desk until she found what she was looking for.

A royal chequebook.

She tore a single cheque off and returned to her study. She paused as she grabbed the pen, weighing her decision. Was money a suitable replacement for a mother's love? Certainly not. But the Queen barred her from writing to him. From ever telling him his mother's true name. She was unable to hold him in a tender embrace. And she would never get to hear the highs and lows his new life may bring.

This was the best she could do. For now.

She had loved Leon when he was still Leon.

And she would love *Albert* equally so.

Her son had endured a near-constant pruning of his spirit, and now with her help, he would finally be free to blossom.

Princess Edith wrote the cheque for a thousand pounds and made it out to Albert Reid.

She signed Queen Eleanor's name, then sealed the cheque in an envelope. She reached for the wax stick, whose flame flickered quietly, and gingerly positioned it above. A pitter-patter of the viscous red wax fell onto the envelope, and as it pooled into a blob, she stamped it forcefully. She blew gently on the seal, staring at the Lancaster family crest.

She loathed all it stood for.

Its power had at the very least given her a handsome yearly endowment. One which would never run dry. She would support her son from afar, giving him bit by bit what was rightfully his in the first place.

Princess Edith sat the sealed cheque on her desk and retired to her bed.

When the mailman picked up the cheque the next morning, it began its journey to the village of Catrine. The cheque was postmarked from London with no return address. And although the cheque would travel smoothly by both mail train and car, the essence of what lay behind the innocuous red wax seal could not be seen with the naked eye.

Only God knew the unspeakable power contained within.

A force carried solely by the winds of fate.

It blew the tiniest spark of destiny across the land. One which would catch fire and lead to an inferno that He, and *only* He, could extinguish.

CHAPTER 23
THE MOTH AND THE FLAME

October 21st, 1944—past

While the first letter from his mother had been a surprise, what confounded Al more was the cheque that arrived around a week later. No letter accompanied it, no return address—nothing. Just the Queen's red wax seal.

Henry always gave him the envelopes, never prying about their contents. Al had begun going into town alone more often, partly because he was feeling more comfortable in his new home of Catrine. He was no longer afraid of showing his face, no longer worried about his past coming back to haunt him. He was Albert Reid, and the village had welcomed him warmly. Plus, he'd read in *The Scotsman* a few years back that the Queen's youngest son, Duke Leon of Albemarle, had died at the age of eighteen from haemophilia. The photo they used was a portrait of him aged fifteen.

Very shrewd of you, Mother, he remembered thinking.

As the cheques continued arriving, Al worried what might happen if Henry saw one. Surely there'd be questions, the answers to which could not be explained without sabotaging his alias. For that reason, he began depositing the cheques to the Cumnock branch of the Bank of Scotland. There, he met Deborah. A fresh-faced brunette who appeared to be not much older than he. Alas, she didn't make much of a fuss—just assisted him with creating an account and depositing the money.

Throughout the past three years, he had deposited cheques that together totalled £27,000. With that kind of money, he could have bought a brand-new Jaguar SS and a gargantuan estate in the Scottish countryside, all while having plenty left over. But that was of no interest to him, for he had lived in palaces all his life.

More than anything, he just wanted a normal life. And he planned to do everything in his power to craft exactly that. He didn't spend too much too quickly because it would be a dead giveaway that he was anything but ordinary. So, he was prudent with his funds.

He withdrew a modest amount each week, and instead of buying anything, he gave it away.

On Sundays, he'd discreetly tithe once service was over. The minister sheepishly admitted that no one gave as generously as he. When he dined at a restaurant, he would tip handsomely. And whenever he saw a wee lad or lassie lingering outside a shop, he'd give them enough shillings to buy their favourite treat.

The townspeople who had shown him warmth were becoming even warmer. It gave Al such genuine happiness to do those acts of kindness. He imagined this feeling was as close to true contentment as he could get. The past three years at the farm had been a whirlwind, but one whose winds did not destroy, but gently picked up the ashes from his old life and settled them on new, fertile ground.

In a place where things could grow.

Now he was where he ended all his evenings, in his new room in the main house.

Each night when he lay down, he prayed. His prayers began with thanking God for his new life—the beautiful Scottish countryside he now called home, the kind townspeople that had welcomed a stranger into their community, and for God allowing Henry to find him at the petrol station that rainy night.

Al had never had the luxury of having a father. Queen Eleanor had told him that Prince Alfred died just after he was born. Suddenly, his mother's voice disrupted his peace, echoing in his mind, just as it had throughout the cavernous court room on New Year's Day.

"Your father tried to test me once, and it didn't end well for him."

"Alfred?"

"No, Leon. Your real father."

"Shut *up!*"

He sat upright in bed as he blurted the words. He hoped that Henry hadn't heard him, because Henry was the closest thing to a real father he had ever had. The last thing he wanted was to give him reason to think ill of him.

Al scolded himself for allowing his mother to interrupt his nightly prayer. When he finished, he turned off the small bedside lamp and was engulfed in darkness. As he tried to drift off into slumber, he began to hear something.

The sound was muted, but still distinct enough to recognise. The cries were hoarse, each sounding like a drawn-out groan.

Not again, thought Al. He tiptoed to the bedroom door and opened it to confirm his suspicions. He had heard the same cries from Henry the past few nights.

Over the last three years, Al had noticed that right around mid-October, Henry would lock himself in his study from the moment they finished their work until late at night, not even coming out to eat.

Al wished he had the courage to ask Henry what was wrong, but he knew he wouldn't be given an answer. For when he did finally emerge from his study, Henry acted as if he hadn't shed a single tear.

When Al returned to his bed, the last thought that surfaced before he met the blackness of slumber was the same one that had occurred every year when he heard Henry's sorrowful cries:

I wonder what happened in October.

One week later.

The scents pervading the air in the kitchen tickled Al's nose—pungent onions, sweet carrots, savoury gravy, and seasoned ground beef. They sizzled and simmered in their respective pots and pans; Al stirred the gravy every so often with a wooden spoon; the fragrant brown liquid caused his mouth to water. A steady *drip-drip-drip* came from Henry syphoning the excess grease from the meat into a glass jar beside the sink. When he finished, Henry retrieved a potato masher and offered it to him. Al spent the last few minutes of prepping the meal squishing the peeled and boiled spuds.

Cutlery clinked. Serving bowls and plates thudded softly on the table. Soon, the separate pieces were consolidated into the final dish:

Mince and tatties.

Outside of the spices, everything came from the farm—the meat, milk, butter, potatoes, carrots, and onions. The notion that he had cultivated his own nourishment, from sowing the seed to harvest, gave him a swelling sense of pride.

Henry spooned the steaming gravy over their bowls piled high with mash, veggies, and meat—in that order—and began scarfing it down. Filling their bellies after a long, wet day of labour.

Dinner always provided enough silence to allow his mind to wander. With every savoury morsel he bit into, Al was mentally chewing on something else entirely—an idea; one which had arisen months ago and that he'd grappled with every day since, all while attempting to garner enough courage to present it. He wasn't afraid of Henry; every year his pace of work had slowed more, his build becoming frailer. At his ripe old age, a violent gust might prove victorious in knocking him to the ground. On the contrary, he *was* afraid of Henry's reaction.

The temper whose short fuse required only the tiniest of sparks to light.

"Thank you," said Henry. His gravelly voice caused Al's fork to stop mid-motion while securing a piece of food; the tips of the tines scraped shrilly against the bowl.

He stared at Henry like a deer in the headlights.

"For what?"

"For not asking," he replied, shovelling another bite into his mouth. He chewed awkwardly, jaw jerking around as if it were being propelled by a rusted-out hand crank rather than ligament and bone. Al mirrored him, taking another bite. Each time he swallowed, he quickly filled his mouth again, for he hadn't a clue whether Henry expected a response, but he figured a mouthful of food was sufficient reason to stay quiet.

"I know you heard me this past week," said Henry in between bites, gobbling down the last of what remained in his bowl. He pushed it aside before looking up at him. His already grey-blue eyes had somehow faded more since they first met.

"Ye did hear me?" he croaked, smacking his tongue around his palate, sweeping away remnants of the mince and tatties. "In years past too, I assume."

Al nodded.

"Figured as much. But I don't want ye worryin' about me when you hear it again, 'cause you will. This year same as next. So, here goes nothing." Henry took a deep breath in and held it, lips pressed, eyes closed. The rigid flexion of his body made it seem like the air filling his lungs was as sharp as glass, but despite the pain, he didn't want to let the breath go.

"My wife…Helen, she was…" He paused, letting out a titter as his eyes gleamed wistfully. "…She was my light in this world, shining bright on the darkest of days. And for the village, too. There wasn't a soul who didn't love her." Henry's gaze drifted farther away from Al's. As if he wasn't looking *at* anything, but rather *through*—as if before him was an invisible window to memories past. "I reckon that God knew that a curmudgeon like me needed someone like her. You know I'm a man of few words—"

Al barked a laugh, then immediately reined in his amusement. Henry smiled as if to tell him: *it's okay, I know.*

"Helen did the speaking for me. At church, in town, and when we had friends over. She had a stockpile of charisma that seemed to never run dry, enough for the two of us."

"She sounds lovely," said Al.

Henry sniffled, eyes shimmering.

"She was, lad. It's why when we found out she was pregnant, I was over the moon. I thanked the Lord each night for giving us a bairn. Between Helen and I, we had all the bases covered. If she had a boy, I could teach them the lay of the land, the work, and how to one day become a good and honest man. I'd teach a lassie the same things in a different way, but more importantly, I knew in my heart they'd probably take after their mum, being blessed with all her kindness and grace..."

Henry's mouth contorted beneath a strained brow.

"When the local midwife delivered a healthy baby boy, that was the happiest moment in my life..." He choked back a cry. "But then she started yelling for a doctor, saying something about Helen's blood pressure. She was fading in and out; the midwife was scrambling to call for help. The happiest moment of my life began spiralling into a nightmare." Henry blubbered, unable to hold it back any longer.

"Then, she was gone. Just like that."

Al felt Henry's pain drift over to his side of the table. It was like an oil spill, whose inky black edges trapped him in the viscous sludge, suffocating the life out of him.

"I came home with an unnamed baby boy. Alone." He coughed, taking a sip of water before continuing. "Sure, the neighbours helped. Gave me swaddles, stitched me some diapers, and for Christ's sake, I had loads of dishes and desserts and flowers piled up on the verandah. Some probably knew how much of a shite cook I was, but it was also their way to mourn their own loss. Helen was a pillar that held up so much of Catrine. They knew I wasn't fit to shoulder that weight."

Henry streaked the tears into the grooves of his weathered, wrinkled skin with the back of his hand.

"Two weeks later, I found the boy cold in his bassinet. I don't remember much of the month that followed. It's all a blur of misery, a kind so painful I hadn't known it existed. I figured the boy knew I wouldn't be able to love him the same way his mother could, so he passed on—as a means to be with her."

"Don't say that," blurted Al. "You would have been a great father."

Henry huffed, baulking at the statement.

"Trust me. I never had a father, but if I did, I would have been lucky to have one like you."

A bit of sympathy emerged behind the quizzical stare on Henry's face. "What about your mother?" he asked.

"She's the reason you found me that night."

Henry shifted uncomfortably in his seat. "Anyhow, enough sad talk for tonight." He stood and began clearing the table. Al joined in helping, but once the all-too-familiar silence reclaimed the space between them, the anxiousness surrounding the idea he wanted to present to Henry resurfaced.

Not now, his mind chided.

He yielded to rational thought. He could wait. But he wasn't certain how long he'd be able to. For the proposition was so grand, it had caused an immense pressure to build up within him. And he feared at any moment, it might burst out.

The wind grew stronger as night fell over the farm; it whistled through the hills and hissed through the trees, the branches groaned with hollow *pop-pop-pops*, and the few vestigial leaves that had withstood the changing of the seasons crackled as they fell, blanketing the ground with a layer of rust-coloured death.

A wisp of spicy-sweet tobacco smoke tickled Al's nostrils, and he let out a delighted sigh. He found an odd comfort being present for Henry's nightly routine with the wood pipe. The piquant notes lingered on his clothes perpetually, but he didn't mind. The scent was yet another reminder that he was here—his new life, living with a new name, seeing beautiful new faces and even more beautiful surroundings. Sometimes, he had to pinch himself. Next March would be five whole years he'd lived with Henry.

Five years. After so long, Henry must see me as more than just—

He cut the thought short. Corked it, bottled it up, and sealed it away with all the others surrounding the idea.

What could a little more pressure hurt?

The soft scratching of Henry thumbing a page's corner pulled Al from his daze. He regained the sensation that he too was holding a book. Lightening his grip, he realised he'd created a sweat stain that perfectly outlined his clammy hands on the hardcover.

"You haven't turned a page since we sat down," said Henry without looking up from his book.

A chill raced down Al's neck. *Henry* had broken their silence. Not he.

"Did my story trouble you?"

"No," he said.

"Well, your face says otherwise. Ye look ill."

Al's windpipe constricted, and he sat frozen, unable to muster enough focus to turn a page despite having not read it.

"I know it's not my place, but for months something's been off." Henry took a long draw from his pipe. "Earlier you mentioned your mum. If you've got a story to tell, I'll listen."

A deep rumbling arose in the base of his gut; the vibration ricocheted violently up his spine, through his very spirit, atom slamming into atom, until a deadly chain reaction was set into motion, and once it began, there was no stopping it. The pressure he'd been harbouring reached a critical point of no return.

"I do have something that's been on my mind."

Henry slipped a bookmark between the pages before shutting it closed. "Go on."

Al's heart thudded against his sternum, his mouth began to parch, and the pores in his palms submitted wholly to the fear coursing through his veins, throwing open their tiny gates, allowing profuse sweat to seep through. Just before he spoke, Al was accosted by his imagination; the steady chirps of the crickets, the wind flitting through the trees, the faraway clucks and mewls of the animals—all came to an unsettling halt.

It was as if nature was saying without a single word:

We are waiting…

"I've been thinking," began Al, trying to steady his quivering voice. "If there comes a day when you can no longer work. I'd like to buy your farm."

The sounds of the countryside held silent, as if holding their collective breath. Beneath the dim porch light, fuzzy yellow indistinct from the blackness of night, he could just barely see those powdery grey eyes staring back at him, unblinking.

"Not—not now, of course…" Al stammered. But even this clarification didn't elicit a response from Henry. "I—I know the work, the land; I'd keep everything the same. I'd take care of it, you know. Like you taught me. And I have the money. Enough to fix up the barn, get a new outbuilding—"

"Al," said Henry.

The distinct downcast timbre in his voice caused Al to panic. "I'll pay double what it's worth. Really. This place means a lot to—"

"I don't pay ye," interjected Henry. "How could you afford it?"

"You know those letters I get once a month." He thought he could see Henry produce a nod. "They are cheques. I've been saving them up for years."

"Who sends them?"

That question caused Al's gut to clench.

The *who*…

"I can't say," he answered just above a whisper. There was a long, dreadful pause that was so unbearably drawn out it caused a bit of nausea to bubble up in the pit of his stomach.

"*This farm*," began Henry, enunciating each syllable as best he could through his ageing voice. "This farm was built with sweat and blood. *My* blood. My father built it before I was born. Once he passed, it was mine." He swallowed loudly, gripping the ends of the rocking chair's armrests tightly, steadying himself. "You are my friend, Albert. You are a good man. But you are *not* my blood. And you never will be."

The countryside had still not resumed its nightly chorus. And for the first time since he had arrived in Catrine, he came face to face with his old, familiar foe.

The empti—

Al didn't have the strength to even acknowledge it by name.

He could sense it, slinking and slithering in the periphery of his being, trying to slip into his spirit unnoticed, like a parasite searching for a weak piece of skin. He rejected it from entering immediately. But still, just a single moment in its icy presence catapulted him through a labyrinth of memories; the dinner where his family's gangling limbs were puppeteered, the grotesque squeals of Midnight after she'd birthed the gnarled stillborn, the day in front of the easel when his record player broke, the eerie calm after his mother instructed him to eat the flesh of the dog, and the hollow, empty air of the courtroom in Baden-Baden after he was banished from the kingdom.

It *all* came back.

"Your blood is dead," Al said so flatly and absent of emotion that it levelled Henry where he sat. "Your wife and son aren't coming back. So you'd rather leave this farm to no one—let the wood rot out with termites, pasture be claimed back by weeds, animals be taken, brother separated from brother, all because I'm not your blood—"

Henry shot up, the rocking chair juddering across the porch until it slammed against wood siding. "Quiet!" he shouted, a bulging vein in his temple catching a glimmer of the porch light. "'*Why should fools have money in hand to buy wisdom, when they are not able to understand it?*' Proverbs 17:16," he said through gritted teeth. "You have not earned a stake in this land. You laugh in the face of God! Ungrateful, when I clothe you, give you a place to sleep, and food to eat."

Al snorted, marinating in the pain from this freshly acquired wound.

"Peter answered: '*May your money perish with you, because you thought you could buy the gift of God with money.*' Acts: 8:20." Al stood, towering over Henry, his anger reaching its apex. "'*Do not withhold good from those whom it is due, when it is in your power to do it!*' Proverbs 3:27!"

"Get out!" bellowed Henry. His crooked index finger tremored wildly as he pointed off the porch. "Ye will sleep in the barn tonight, and every night thereafter till you learn to be grateful for what you have," he sputtered. "Learn not to covet thy neighbour's land." He ushered Al down the porch steps and continued shouting as he trudged toward the barn. "How dare ye speak of my late wife and son like that! I hope you never know such a pain…"

Henry's grumbling faded as Al entered the barn. Head hung low, he plopped down on the edge of the cot, its stiff springs squeaking sharply as they settled his weight. The familiarity of his old cot added to the uneasiness swimming through his chest by reminding him of when he first arrived at Henry's and the long year he spent here before moving to the main house.

Back when he was stranger and not friend.

The pungent, grassy fragrance of the freshly-baled hay filling the barn stung his nose, and he loathed how even this scent, which normally comforted him—as it signalled the harvest months—seemed unpleasant. And now, Al couldn't help but interpret it as a harbinger of the death that winter would bring.

He sighed. Without his book, there was nothing for him to fill the time with. He lit the wick of the kerosene lamp on his bedside table, then lay down, slipping under the covers of the cot. He stared blankly at the ceiling, listening to the wooden bones of the barn groan beneath the wind.

Al tossed and turned for what felt like hours, floating in the liminal space between awake and asleep. Where it was impossible to discern between the darkness behind his eyelids and the blackness of night filling the barn.

An aberrant thought prodded his mind—the light of dawn may never come. But surely, morning had to be around the corner.

Right?

If time was indeed passing, its linear nature seemed to have dissolved away in the face of this dark, silent night. Time had become more of an amorphous blob than its standard, intricately woven fabric, whose every second pushed the universe forward into the future. Not now. Something had broken. Like a clock whose gears kept turning, yet the hands had snapped off. Unable to tell between past and present. Then and now.

Within this tenuous space, where time and space had split, where the dream and the waking were one, a pestilent malaise began to slither around Al's being. It bubbled through his gut, prickled his skin, and slammed against his chest. He could hardly feel the beating of his heart, or the scratchiness of the wool blanket that had enveloped him earlier.

The darkness of night cradled him in its icy grip, lulling him with its silent tongue, and nourishing him through an invisible tether—one which pumped the emptiness back into his veins, bit by bit, until every last drop of blood was infused with all-consuming nothingness.

Al felt an intense wave of vertigo crash over him; he fell, stomach lurching as this invisible gravity drew him deeper into the abyss. He steadily plunged farther and farther into this void blacker and more desolate than any he could have imagined existing. He feared the freefall would never end. Just as the sensation became too much to bear before he was about to cry out in agony—it stopped.

The darkness snickered soundlessly, then cut the umbilical cord that connected them together. It knew that now was the time. For it had watched Al with its omniscient gaze, day after day. It amused the darkness how Al had assumed that throughout these past years, they had been separated. The truth was quite the contrary. The darkness had held Al within its black, hollow womb. While the gestation was much prolonged, it made this moment all the sweeter.

The rebirth bound by fate.

The darkness dissolved away, and left Al suspended in the void.

While he was still comprised of blood and bone, the fusion the darkness had performed was finally complete. Death attached to the living. Void tied to matter.

The two were now one.

Al was reunited with the one sensation he had avoided for far too long.

The emptiness.

It permeated through every cell in his body, radiating outward, gobbling up what was left of his soul.

Then, a voice materialised. And it spoke not *to* him, but *through*:

"You know what to do."

The abyss collapsed like a dying star; the supernova that followed catapulted him the incalculable distance he had fallen, until he pierced the membrane of the liminal space.

Al jolted up, gasping for air, clutching at the gaping hole in his chest, only to realise that it wasn't there. He threw back the wool blanket, sweat peppering his skin, and sprung from the bed. The absence of feeling the emptiness had summoned caused his heart to skip a beat, and he paced the floor of the barn to distract his mind from its arrival.

No, no, no, he thought, and as the soft scuttling of his bare feet on the dirt floor filled the space, he realised that it was the only sound he could hear.

The sheer and utter silence floored him. The wooden framework of the barn had settled. Not even the slightest breath of breeze whispered by. It was as if the creatures of the night had not only stopped their chirping and clucking and bleating but disappeared entirely. They'd scattered like ants, running away from a malevolence so potent, its energy radiated not like the rays of the sun, but with a prolific blackness thicker than shadow.

All stemming from the emptiness within Al.

It swallowed him up like a black hole with its vacuous, greedy mouth. It continued outward, consuming every last speck of matter, never stopping, never satiated.

"You are not my blood. And you never will be."

The echo of Henry's hoarse voice entered his mind. But not like before, on the porch. There was a menacing tinge to his tone. A snide mockery of *who* Henry saw him to be, a figurative wad of spit hocked on his face, a punch to the gut that said: *you are not worthy.* All the years of gruelling work. Caring for the farm as if it were his own. Looking up to Henry like a *father.*

"You are not my blood. And you never will be."

"You are not my blood. And you never will be."

"You are not my blood. And you never will be."

The phrase repeated in his mind in an endless, agonising loop.

"You are not my blood. And you never will be."

"You are not my blood. And you never will be."

"You are not my blood. And you never will be."

The cacophony of sneering Henrys made him cry out in the night, shouting at the top of his lungs, "Stop! Please…please make it stop!"

Another voice entered his mind. But it wasn't his, nor Henry's.

It belonged solely to the emptiness. It said:

"You know what to do."

"I do," he replied mentally.

Al surrendered wholly to the emptiness. Henry's voice disappeared, washed away by an invisible black wave on the shore of his soul. He caught sight of the toolsets stored on the far side of the barn. He walked over, grabbed a hammer and a fistful of steel nails, and left.

The night outside held perfectly still, like a placid lake without a single ripple. Al extended one foot and held it above the ground, lowering it gingerly, inch by inch, until foot met soil.

Nothing stirred.

He had to fight the urge to chuckle, because it pleased him enormously how the night seemed to welcome him in with open arms. He tiptoed across the grass and arrived at the farmhouse window closest to him. He held a steel nail in one hand, perpendicular to its ledge, then with the other, readied the hammer in his grip. Adjusting its metal head just a hair above the nail, he delicately met it; the *tap-tap-tap* so faint, Al felt confident Henry's eroding hearing wouldn't be able to pick up the sound, especially mid-slumber.

Having to be so gentle with each tap, it took a countless number to drive the nail fully into the window's ledge. Then, Al moved to the next one, repeating the process. He continued circling the farmhouse until all the windows had been staked with the long, steel nails. He then returned to the barn, where he pulled two 2x4s from a pile of unused lumber. Not a single thought crossed his mind as he trudged back to the farmhouse. The emptiness held the reins of Al's soul, barring all emotions from entering, refusing to let go until the moment was right. He leaned one 2x4 on the front door and the other at the back, but didn't nail them in yet. This wood was far thicker than the window ledges, and it would be impossible to nail those soundlessly.

As he began his final trip to the barn, something tried to penetrate the emptiness, like a drowning swimmer in the depths of his soul, struggling to race up to the surface to take a breath. It came as a distant echo, a whisper so faint he could hardly hear it, but he recognised who the voice belonged to—Al.

The boy he'd met on the ferry.

The one whose name he stole.

"The darkness only defines us if we let it."

Just as the words were uttered, they dissolved away. For the voice that had carried them, the tiny fragment of the Al who had existed here these past five years, the piece of him that had swum from the depths of his soul, was suffocated the moment it surfaced. The emptiness snuffed out his light, flung him back into the periphery, and repaired the puncture that had been made.

Al trudged thoughtlessly into the barn, stopping in front of the bedside table. He hoisted the flickering kerosene lamp into his hand and approached the bale of hay closest to him. He took a fistful of straw and stuck the ends into the lamp's flame. The fire raced along the dried straw so quickly he had to throw it to keep from being burned. It landed atop the bale of hay he had taken it from, and the flames began eating away at it with incredible speed. The smell of smoke began to tickle his nose, and he hastily hopped around the perimeter of the barn, igniting the bales haphazardly, until a misshapen ring of fire emerged. The flames began to jump at the dirt floor and lick at the wood rafters high above. As Al neared the door, he stuffed his trouser pockets full of straw, then slipped outside, kerosene lamp still jangling in hand.

He ran to the farthest building on the property, unable to feel the beating of his heart, the icy emptiness permeating his body from head to toe, fully engrossed at the task at hand. Time was of the essence. He entered the building and torched the hay there too. The cows began to groan and bump against their stalls as they sensed the heat, unable to escape the approaching flames. Al wouldn't meet their eyes as he finished the loop, slamming the big wooden latch behind him as he exited. As he approached the chicken coop, he could hear the pleading behind him—undulating, high-pitched moos of cows whose flesh began to burn as the building went up in flames. He quickly threw some burning straw beneath the coop, which was built off the ground, and a cacophony of concerned clucks began as it grew hotter.

Al pivoted and then broke into a sprint toward his final destination.

The farmhouse.

He quietly scaled the steps, opening the door as smoothly as possible. He torched the curtains, the couch—anything with fabric. He threw handfuls of burning straw in random spots by the edges of walls, into the kitchen, into the guest room, in front of Henry's bedroom door. Then, he quickly left and—throwing caution to the wind—furiously pounded the 2x4 across the front door. He sprinted to the back door, slamming the nails clean into the board with just a few strikes.

Job completed, he ambled to the front, and secured a spot closest to Henry's bedroom window. His eyes glimmered in the orange light of the growing flames contained within. A sinister smile emerged the moment he heard the thudding footsteps. He watched as the front door shook so violently it threatened to rip off its frame, but the nailed board would not budge. More footsteps, and a moment later, he saw Henry struggling to push up the nailed-shut window, thick black smoke licking at the glass.

The once quiet night was now filled with a symphony of horrors—howls of the dying animals, hisses of singeing skin, and pops of the bubbling gristle melting beneath the searing, white-hot flames.

Death and destruction surrounded Al, yet he relished it. Savoured every moment watching Henry's frail figure frantically trying to heave the window open, the violent coughing spasms as he inhaled the fumes, and the look of pure, unadulterated fear written clearly on his weathered face.

Al smiled; his spirit amidst a rapture unlike he'd ever known. The highest of highs. This euphoria reared up, reaching its apex. It coursed through his veins with a blistering heat, perfectly in parallel with the roaring fire all around him. He gave Henry a haughty wave and watched as the flames caused the window to be obscured by an opaque, yellow-orange shimmer.

Henry was gone.

Al snorted, then turned away from the house.

An ear-splitting burst of glass shattered behind him, followed by a clipped thud. He whipped around to see Henry on all fours, scrambling to stand to his feet. He stared at Al with eyes as wide as saucers, mouth agape, half his face charred red. Flecks of flame dotted the bits of intact fabric between the patchwork of raw, blistering skin along his limbs.

Al dawdled, flipping the hammer in a circle before gripping it once more. He let Henry crawl a few feet away, watching deadpan as he slapped wildly at his burning clothes and wincing sharply as he hit exposed skin.

Henry caught Al's approach in the periphery of his vision, and his heart mustered a last pump of adrenaline to his old, tired body. He raised up onto his haunches, floundering about in a zigzag pattern, but failing to pick up any tangible speed. Al bounded toward him in a few long strides and pushed him to the ground.

He leapt atop him, and Henry wailed out in agony as his freshly charred skin was squished, pieces sliding clean off as he gave one final push of resistance; he flipped over, now eye-to-eye with Al. Man to man. Elder to youth.

Al straddled him, pinning him between his legs as he squirmed. The tears in Henry's eyes turned to steam as they slid out onto his red, enflamed cheek. Al raised the hammer, cocked back above his head.

Henry stared up at Al, his powdery blue eyes flickering with the glare of the orange flames towering all around them, and it was then

Henry accepted his fate.

Lips trembling, he croaked out a single word:

"Why?"

Al slammed the hammer against Henry's face repeatedly, a wet, bony *thwack, thwack, thwack*. Blood spatter speckled Al's face, and even as Henry's skull began to collapse, the rage that had built up made him continue. *Thwack, thwack, thw—*

Al awoke drenched in a cold sweat, peppering his body head to toe. His muscles spasmed and he flinched upright, frantically patting the wool blanket and edges of the cot. He touched his face, neck, hair. Just to ensure—

Thwack, thwack, thwack.

Al turned to see the wooden barn door gently hitting the edge of its frame as it closed and opened. He coughed out a great big sigh of relief and positioned himself on the edge of the cot, bare feet against the cool dirt of the barn floor. He tried to steady his breathing; *in and out*, he guided himself, deliberately filling his lungs, holding the breath, and then releasing it in an elongated exhalation. The surging wave of nausea he felt upon waking began to subside, but only slightly.

As the seconds passed, all his senses switched back on, returning from dream to waking. It was then he noticed that the night was not silent; it instead teemed with the sounds of the countryside. A gust of wind hissed through the rafters of the barn, and it sent the door flying, and when it swung back, it hit the frame again with a thundering *thwack*. The sound sent an electric shock up his spine, so he continued breathing, soothing his frayed nerves. He reminded himself that the reality in front of him could be simply and easily explained.

He had fallen asleep with the barn door slightly ajar, and the kerosene lamp still burning by his bedside.

That was it.

But the longer he repeated this explanation, the more mental energy he spent clutching onto the idea that *this* was all that was real. The physical, material world. The more it began to slip out of his grasp.

Other sensations began to scratch at the back of his being. Although the emptiness wasn't within him, he could still feel a lingering chill in the centre of his chest, as if it had just been there. He remembered tossing and turning, the liminal space, and the endless freefall in the abyss. He heard the faint echo of the darkness' snickering laughter, and the umbilical cord that had tethered them being cut.

Lastly, he heard the hollow, inhuman voice of the emptiness which said: *"You know what to do."*

The cascade of sights and sounds and emotions from the dream caused his mind to go haywire. Reliving it proved too much to bear. Now wide awake, he looked around the barn, and his eyes settled on the flickering kerosene lamp. He gazed into its soft yellow light, watching as the soot-covered edge slipped down, eating away the soaked fabric. Like a moth to a flame, Al hoisted the lamp into his grip, and exited the barn.

He walked into the night in the hopes of clearing his mind.

CHAPTER 24
THE WITNESS

The droning hum of the car tyres had fully benumbed Aniqa. There were numerous other sensations on the A1 her mind chose to ignore. Cars whizzing past, the occasional honk, and even the murmurs of the radio— all muffled, muted. Her hand gripped the wheel firmly as she sped along, easily staying within the confines of the white lane lines.

But she wasn't really there.

Not consciously at least.

Mentally, she was still two hundred miles away, sitting across from Princess Edith, cradling a cup of tea that had long gone cold. She had begun this journey alone, and now she was returning to Catrine with an invisible passenger.

A secret never meant to be hers.

Aniqa wasn't sure why Princess Edith had told her the story. She'd gushed for hours, like a poorly built flood barrier that had finally broken, having held back the immense weight of the waters far longer than anyone expected. The lie that poured out of her seemed unfathomable. She couldn't imagine having Arun ripped from her arms the moment he was born. Being raised by her *mother.* That thought alone caused such an ire within her that an acidy bile began lapping at her insides.

I would have killed her.

She wondered if Princess Edith had grappled with the same impulse. Aniqa felt a twinge of the horror the princess must have felt the past forty-something years. Trapped in a nightmare she couldn't wake from.

What could she have done?

That question made her realise the stark difference between the two of them. Her own mother was just another immigrant worker, among the many who made the long journey to Britain for a better life, hailing from Bangladesh, Pakistan, India—all leaving for similar reasons, whether war or poverty. She, like the rest, had left her home behind and arrived in a foreign land where they knew not a soul. All to live in a tiny London flat, making hardly enough money to get by. She grew more bitter by the year, but unlike a wine that was once sweet and rich, her mother had always been sour. When the cancer came, it ate her up swiftly. A harsh end for a harsh spirit. Once she passed, the world went on. No one cared. Not even Aniqa. Her mother's life but a cosmic blink.

But Princess Edith's mother was the Queen. How on earth could she undo a lie concocted by the most powerful and longest reigning monarch the world had ever known?

Aniqa knew the answer.

The tragedy wrapped up in *that* truth pushed down like a ton of bricks on Aniqa's chest.

The weight of her invisible passenger.

She rolled down her windows to let in a smidge of fresh air. The longer she thought of Princess Edith's dilemma, the more she felt she couldn't breathe. Her airway was clamping down in the face of her pain. The immeasurable agony she saw etched in the grooves of Princess Edith's skin as she sat in her house; wrinkles not borne out of natural ageing but from the eroding mixture of shame and guilt. She was maybe fifteen or so years Aniqa's senior. Yet the soul that sat across from her seemed far older and exceedingly more tired.

Aniqa realised she had seen that same look before—when her mother was lying on her deathbed. When the cancer proved too strong a foe.

She wondered whether Princess Edith was still fighting her own battle. Or had she too surrendered? Perhaps she thought it was too late. That at this point, it would do more harm than good. Or on the other hand, maybe there was a little dark voice inside her that feared what her son had become in her absence.

Perhaps she wanted to tell the truth to *Leon*, but not Al.

That notion seemed likely enough.

Princess Edith did not acknowledge in the slightest that her son may have been responsible for Arun and the lads being missing. Aniqa didn't press her, because she discerned from her body language that the right amount of pressure would break the poor woman to pieces. Even so, there was a part of Aniqa that believed Princess Edith *did* suspect his involvement. She wouldn't utter the words, but her countenance told another story.

Then, she remembered the letter.

Inside wasn't a letter at all, but instead a cheque.

The moment Aniqa presented it, Princess Edith tore it to shreds. Bit by bit, until she tossed it into the rubbish. As if the very paper the cheque was printed on was tainted. Destined to fuel a fire she hadn't started. Yet here she fanned its flames.

Despite this, Aniqa wasn't sure what to make of her trip. Of her new passenger.

She did get what she sought after, it seemed—the truth about Al.

Margaret couldn't remember the last time she'd taken this byway. The Chapel Brae was a single lane road that snaked through the countryside, connecting the two towns. It was so narrow that, if a car was heading in the opposite direction, someone would have to pull on the shoulder to let it pass. There wasn't much out here besides rolling green pasture and the occasional farm.

"You know these people?" asked Gordon as he looked between the road and her.

"Colin, aye. He's been in the drunk tank more times than I can count. But not the family."

The Clark residence sat at the periphery of both Catrine and the minds of the townspeople. Once on the property, you could throw a stone and it would be a toss-up as to whether it landed in Catrine or Sorn. Margaret squinted as she rotated the parcel map, tracing her finger along the route, counting the street numbers—

"Here," she said, pointing over the dashboard to a dirt road jutting off the Chapel Brae. Gordon whipped his patrol car onto it, fishtailing due to a recent rain. As he straightened out and continued up the path, the tyres ricocheted clods of mud, barraging the undercarriage with a staccato of brassy smacking sounds that filled the cabin.

The word around town was that the Clarks were poor. When the dilapidated farmhouse came into view, she could see why. Much of its painted faces had chipped away, the edges of some of the wood siding severely rotted from moisture penetration and no apparent upkeep, and the rest of the property seemed equally in disarray. Profuse, knee-high weeds spanned as far as the eye could see and a miscellany of defunct items were strewn about the garden—a bicycle missing a wheel, corroded cuts of unused piping, and an Atco mower that had rusted out to the point where the fans, motor, and chains seemed to have fused together in a tawny twist of metal.

"Looks like a nice piece of land," said Gordon, stepping over some litter to get to the house steps. "Shame they don't take care of it."

"I've heard about this place from locals, but never seen it. Eyesore is an understatement."

Gordon chuckled as they ascended the rickety wooden steps. As he knocked, a thought crossed Margaret's mind; the Clarks *seemed* poor, but this house, as derelict as it was, sat on one of the largest plots in town.

It made her wonder how they came into the land. If they had money, why did they choose to live this way? Maybe something had happened to cause them to spiral. Perhaps the drug and alcohol use were a shared vice, not just Colin's.

A portly woman flung open the door, built like a sack of potatoes. The screen door gave Margaret a clear enough vantage point to inspect her. The woman's grey hair was in an unkempt bun, flyaway strands fanning out into frizzy corkscrews and, judging by the grease, it had been in that same bun for quite some time. Her cheeks and the bridge of her nose were splotched with rosacea. Before she said a word, she lit a fag, taking in a long draw, eyes flicking between them, without a hint of fear nor real interest.

"I didn't call ye," she huffed, tendrils of smoke escaping her lips.

"We're here to see Colin," said Margaret.

"See him!" she muffled a laugh. "You'd be lucky. Haven't seen him in weeks."

The woman took another long drag, blowing the smoke indiscriminately, and the fume cloud engulfed them. Margaret and Gordon exchanged a glance.

"He hasn't been home at all?" asked Margaret.

"Nae."

"When was the last time ye saw him?" added Gordon, leaning closer to her as a way to discreetly peer inside.

"Hell if I know." She shifted her weight, returning to the comfort of the cigarette beneath the prying eyes of the detectives. "What's he done this time? The bastard stole me best bottle of Macallan before he left."

"So ye don't know where he might have gone off to?" asked Margaret.

She snorted. "If he did tell me, I was probably too tanked up to remember."

The apathy of her answer prodded Margaret's gut. She watched as the last of the woman's fag disintegrated to ash. She flicked the butt; it landed at their feet with a *hissssss* as it fizzled out on the wet landing.

"Aren't you Colin's mum?"

"Aye, I am," said Ms. Clark, brow furrowing, then shifted to where her shoulders were squared with Margaret's. "I don't care for ye're tone, officer. What, you trying to say I'm a bad mum for not knowin' where he is? He made it to nineteen alive because of *me*. None of ye fed or clothed him, that was—"

"My colleague wasn't being cross with ye, Ms. Clark," interjected Gordon. "We just need to know if you are his mum for our paperwork. We're here because we believe your son may have some information that can help us find those missing lads."

"Huh," she said, resting her hand against her flabby hip. "Ye say some lads gone missing?"

"Four, actually," replied Gordon solemnly.

She opened the screen door to face them. "Makes *five* if you consider Colin," she mumbled through a clenched jaw. "But no one in this town's ever considered him, have they?"

She gestured with an arm inside. "Have at it, then. Just don't break anything."

Margaret nearly laughed at Ms. Clark's stipulation after she entered. The condition of the inside mirrored the home's exterior. One of the sofa arm's stuffing was spilling from a broken seam. The television balanced on a stack of three upturned milk crates. And the whole place smelt like a mix of mildew, cat piss, and cigarette smoke.

"Where's Colin's room?" asked Gordon.

"End of the hall, last door on the left," instructed Ms. Clark without breaking her gaze from the television set as she plopped into a stained brown plaid armchair.

Margaret followed Gordon's lead, and as she passed through the dining room and began down the hall, she saw only one picture hanging—albeit off-kilter—on the wall. She used her sleeve to wipe the dust from the glass, revealing the family posing in the photo. A much younger and thinner

Ms. Clark stood next to a rather plain looking fellow who she assumed to be the father, and in front of them were three lads. Two were taller and around the same height, but the third seemed to be the youngest, and even in his youth, Margaret recognised the face that would grow to be the Colin she remembered from that morning at the station.

"Where are the older lads?" shouted Margaret.

"Went off to uni and never came back!" Ms. Clark barked the answer over the staticky mutterings of the television programme.

So, his brothers left him, thought Margaret. *No wonder he had so much time on his hands.*

"Nothing to see here," said Gordon, thumbs hooked through his belt loops as he rejoined her in the hall. He gestured with a sweeping motion of his hand.

She entered Colin's room to see that it looked like Ms. Clark hadn't even cared enough to change the sheets since he'd been gone. The covers were half-thrown back, a glass of mouldy water sat on his bedside table, and dirty clothes were strewn about. Tacked to the wall was a Beatles poster.

Definitely a teenager's habitat.

Margaret milled around the room. She knelt in front of two separate chests of drawers. One larger, one smaller. The larger contained clothes, undergarments. The smaller, knick-knacks. Football cards, pocket-knives, tools. A few empty packets of cigarettes and crumpled, half-eaten chocolate bars. But nothing stuck out. She moved to the wardrobe, where she found a boneyard of empties—mostly Jameson and Glen Logie, but there were a few vodkas and rums. As she perused, she gained a clearer picture of the young man who had once occupied the space.

This was an addict's room.

She dug around in the empties but found nothing of importance.

"Any luck?" called Gordon from behind her.

"Nae. I've checked every nook and cranny. Nothing."

Gordon dropped down into a push-up position, craning his head to peer under the bed. "Judging by Stu's reports, seems like Colin was spying on Al. You'd think he'd have kept a journal of some kind."

"My thoughts exactly," added Margaret.

They both returned to the hall empty-handed.

"Let's check these," said Gordon just above a whisper, pointing to another hall door. They proceeded to search that room, then another. Both yielded nothing.

A bit of defeat stuck to their heels and slowed their traipse to the living room. Ms. Clark didn't acknowledge their return, just shooed Gordon with a flabby wave of her arm when he blocked her view of the TV. "Is there anything else you can think of?" he asked, patiently waiting for her to break her gaze on the boisterous programme blaring through the TV's tinny speakers. "Is there anything Colin said when you last saw him that sticks out? Did he ever mention a journal, or do you know where he might have kept one?"

"Nae," she said, not looking up. "Nothin' of the sort."

Margaret decided to wander a bit more while Gordon peppered Ms. Clark with questions, probing for the right one. She quietly circled the dining room, tapping her hand along the tops of the wooden chairs she passed, and even with that tiny bit of pressure a few of them creaked. The stench of rotting food struck her nose as she entered the kitchen; calcified remnants of unrecognisable meals past adhered to the white ceramic plates in the sink. She pinched her nose, and after finding more of nothing, a cracked door at the end of the kitchen beckoned her.

Upon entering, she stood in a boot room—an entryway of sorts— and in the distance through the window, she saw a clothesline; a few garments swayed to and fro in the gentle breeze. To her left was a brand-new Hoover washing machine, and boxes overflowing with junk encircled the perimeter of the space.

She proceeded carefully, feeling that if she were to take too heavy a step, the piles of clutter would come crashing down. A sudden flash of light caught her eye. She looked in the direction it came from but couldn't find it. She took a step backwards, positioning her eyes toward the side of the room it came from, and saw the flash again.

A shattered circle of glass glinted the grey light of the day at a specific angle. Its tiny, shimmering disc barely protruded from the pile it sat in. Margaret bent over, then cupped her hands, parted the sea of rubbish, and from it retrieved a camera.

She gingerly tapped the shattered lens; it produced a high-pitched *ting-ting* against her nail. Flipping the black camera body around, on its bottom was a worn label. She squinted and saw a faint name written in pen:

C. Clark

A surge of electricity raced down the camera along the circuitry of Margaret's nerves, arriving at the growing warmth in her chest, tickling her spirit. She scrambled back the way she came, barrelling toward the living room where Gordon stood in front of an apathetic Ms. Clark.

"Why's Colin's camera in a pile of rubbish?" asked Margaret, breathless.

Gordon stared at the camera body; a shimmer of hope slid across his widening eyes.

Without the slightest swivel of her head, Ms. Clark glanced at the camera. As if she'd only heard Margaret's question as a delayed echo. God forbid someone interrupt her programme. She squinted, then resettled her gaze on the TV screen.

"Are ye blind?" she coughed a chortle. "It's broken. *Rubbish*."

Margaret had expended every last bit of her patience.

"Your *son* might be dead. And ye care more to piddle around watching a talk show than you do him. So tell me, Ms. Clark, did he put that camera back there when it broke?"

The strip of rosacea across Ms. Clark's face enflamed as she blushed. She clicked off the TV and glowered at Margaret.

"Nae. Some hen brought it here a few weeks ago. Said she found it in the grass walking the path by the river."

"Did ye not think twice to—" Margaret cut her castigation short as she saw Gordon nod in the direction of the door. She reeled in the frustration trying to slip out and took a steadying breath. "Thank ye for your time. We're taking this as evidence."

Ms. Clark turned the TV on again with a forceful click, ignoring their exit out of spite.

"Tell Colin he owes me if you find him," she spat through a trembling jaw. She took a swig of some brownish concoction in an unlabelled bottle, then shooed them with a wave of her arm.

The algae-tinged wooden steps groaned raucously as they descended, and in their hasty walk back to Gordon's patrol car, Margaret's breath hitched as she slid back the locking mechanism on the camera body, and a spring-loaded door popped open.

Please, Lord. Please…

A roll of film fell into her palm.

The basement reeked of stale sweat. Pungent body odour wafted from the boys' armpits—and musky other parts—but those scents were overpowered by the putrid, stomach-turning smell of drying vomit. The acid-tinged air burned the children's noses, and they all positioned themselves as far as possible from the person responsible—James.

The sound of retching echoed across the stone walls as James emptied his stomach again. He was hunched over on all fours, drool and sweat sliding off his chin into the fresh vomit. He choked back a breath after he was finished, sitting back on his knees, panting heavily. A few seconds passed before he started fingering the puke, like he was drawing invisible patterns, or searching for something that wasn't there.

"It's all bile," said Gavin. "There's nothing in there for you."

"But I'm…I'm *so* hungry," squawked James, followed by a painful groan vibrating in his throat.

"Don't," said Gavin, without looking over to witness whether his brother took the advice or not. "It'll make you sicker."

Arun's best guess was that James had caught some sort of bug from drinking the water from the toilet cistern. All their stomachs panged and gurgled incessantly, but none of them had gotten sick.

Today was day seven without food. Arun, Gavin, and Fiona huddled in a corner, bodies arranged like eaves of a roof, one on top of the other, to preserve their warmth. The ceramic shards they had fashioned from the cistern cover lay beside them at arm's length.

They waited patiently, hour after hour, for the brick wall to open. Without meals, they had lost all sense of time, unable to discern day from night. Sleep was the only respite from this waking nightmare, but even this they did in a rotation. There was always someone eyeing the door. Waiting for the moment they'd been craving so ravenously—the opportunity to attack.

Arun wondered if it would ever come.

He even began to doubt whether they would have the stamina required to overpower Al. His limbs were growing heavier at an alarming rate. Simply walking across the room to cup some water into his hands from the cistern made his trembling legs ache, as if he'd just scaled a steep hill.

Although he wouldn't admit it consciously, Arun's mind was growing weaker, too. He caught himself imagining the frozen children, floating peacefully on their ice blocks. They possessed no beating heart longing to see the light of day. No muscles to ache. No stomach for the emptiness to gnaw at.

At least they can rest…

He'd flinch, jolting his whole body to centre his drifting thoughts. He had to stay rooted in reality. But was reality worth it? He much preferred sleep, or the wandering imagination of his mind, compared to the dismal circumstance they had fallen prey to.

Arun knew that if nothing changed, they would die down here. Al wouldn't think twice to let them rot away if he had to. James had lost his mind, and there was a part of Arun that didn't blame him.

Fiona stirred, eyelids fluttering as she woke. A squeeze of her warm hand reminded him that she had been holding his own the whole time she slept. He wasn't exactly sure about the origin of the habit, but not long after Craig was killed, Fiona began slipping her cupped hand into his. He welcomed her soft touch—looked forward to it.

"It's my turn, isn't it?" she asked in a whispering half-yawn.

Arun nodded.

She extended her arms, wriggling around in a full-body stretch, then raised herself up, resting her weight on her forearm.

"I had a dream he came down," she said. "We got him."

"Sounds like a good dream." His smile must have seemed lukewarm, because Fiona studied his countenance carefully, brow furrowing.

"He *will* come—won't he?"

"I'm sure he will." He pushed out the words with as much conviction as he could muster. "And when he does…" He grasped the ceramic shard lying next to him, giving it a wave. The tension in Fiona's body eased; she let out the breath she'd been holding with a long exhale through her nose. She smiled, and though they weren't touching, Arun felt that same warmth in the space between them. He reached out and cupped her hand.

"You still look tired. Why don't you rest some more before we switch?"

"You sure?" she asked with a loving squeeze of his hand.

"Aye. I'm fine."

Fiona removed her weight from her forearm, lying down. What little meat she had on her bicep served as a fleshy pillow between the cold concrete of the basement and her head. As she squirmed a bit in an attempt to get comfortable, a blonde curl slipped down onto her face.

Before she could use her free hand—the one cupping Arun's—he pushed away the grimy lock, tucking it behind her ear. Her eyes held his gaze, with a warmth so intense they felt like two miniature suns beaming up at him. The heat produced by that earnest look of fondness spread throughout his chest, and it was then he realised that the sensation was one of the last things keeping his spirit from withering completely, like a houseplant locked away in a room with only a single sliver of light.

Soon her breathing shifted into the rhythm distinct to slumber. He stared up blankly at the ceiling, searching for patterns in the worn brick. When that failed to keep him alert, he tried creating a mental calendar, counting back the days to when they first arrived here. But time and time again, he always hit that empty space. The black void of nothingness that spanned the days following Craig's death.

He couldn't account for that. Nor did he ever want to. He figured his brain had erased that gap of time, boring a hole into the grey matter and coiled nerve fibres, singeing the ends of the synapses which housed the memory. All for his own good. Just so he could survive a little longer.

"You're a good liar," said Gavin.

The words ripped Arun from his mental musings, pulling him back to the present. He turned to Gavin and shot him a confused look.

"You said you are sure Al will come." There wasn't a hint of grievance in Gavin's tone. It was more sombre than that. An *I-would-do-the-same* expectance. "But you aren't sure we are ever getting out of here, are you?"

"No," he said.

Uttering that word stung like a drop of acid on his tongue.

Al gingerly aligned the record above the centre spindle before letting it rest on the platter. He turned the power dial, then adjusted the arm to the farthest edge of the vinyl. The faint crackling sound produced as the record began to spin gave him an anticipatory burst of joy. The relief he craved was moments away. His longtime foe hung in the air throughout his home, oppressive and thick. It felt as if every step he took, he was wading through quicksand, fighting to keep his neck above the invisible, viscous sludge, trying to avoid the inevitable suffocation, struggling to take a good breath.

But then, the operatic chorus faded in, and their voices eviscerated the silence in an instant.

His favourite—Gustav Holst.

Once the music filled the space, his house returned to normal. He could breathe. But still, in the farthest reaches of his being, a tinge of unease scratched at the base of his soul.

It was precisely the same sensation he'd felt that fateful morning.

That inkling of intuition that brought him to find Theodora's lifeless body.

His soul knew then just as it knew now.

There was no escaping fate. Margaret wouldn't rest until he was carted off in handcuffs. Even in the event she didn't succeed, with as many eyes there were on his house, he'd never be able to dispose of their bodies. One day, when he passed away, they'd find a pile of bones in the corner of the basement room.

They'd find his art.

The darkness he had hidden away would be unearthed, cast into the light for all to see. He wondered what would happen to the *good* he was able to do. Would Kissinger Grounds be left to rot? At the mercy of the elements, year after year, until it disintegrated into an unrecognisable pile of rubble? Where would the children go? Would the church be renamed? Or would they burn it, in conclusion that the unhallowed owner's presence could never be expunged from its stone walls? Would they shutter TLC? Would his employees be able to put food on the table?

All these questions needed no answer. For in the span of one generation, all Albert Reid would be remembered for was the evil he brought into the world. The good he'd created would be destroyed out of vengeance. While he accepted this inevitability, it tortured him, nonetheless.

Gustav Holst's orchestra reached its peak; the brasses blared triumphantly, the strings holding the highest notes, and the chorus harmonised in an angelic crescendo.

Suddenly, his mind landed on the name of this composition—*Ode to Death*.

As the track finished, the needle continued its subtle sway along the grooved path, steadily and silently heading toward the first notes of the next piece. Al pondered the spinning of the record. How the electric motor propelling it could not be stopped, save for smashing the whole thing to bits. The needle waited patiently, turn after turn, each empty ridge of the vinyl heightening the anticipation for the one containing song.

This disc would keep spinning. And the music would keep playing, long after he left the room. Even without an ear to listen. Spinning, spinning, until the record reached its predetermined end. The destiny that had already been inscribed long before the first note ever played.

His *own* record was reaching its end. Riding along the last of its ridges. He could feel it in his bones; a sort of knowingness of the final track to come. Powerless, he would be forced to let it play.

But who's to say I can't enjoy the music?

A bittersweet feeling arose in his chest. In these last grooves, these last moments in this life he created, he planned to push the needle just a little while longer. Baulk at the ugliness of fate's face, just as he had since he was a boy.

Al walked to his desk, sat in the cushioned leather chair. He retrieved some stationery from a drawer, licking the tip of his pen before he met paper:

Dear Mother,

As he wrote the two words, the needle caught, and the music resumed. Gustav Holst's orchestra heralding the end.

Margaret's pulse thudded in her ears. Blood scalding and effervescent, it caused everything from her head to toes to surge with heat. Luckily, the safe lights of the dark room cast a red, alien glow that camouflaged her flushing cheeks. But that didn't stop the energy from escaping. It spilled out, manifesting in the form of a nervous tapping of her foot.

"Stop that," said Gordon in a scolding whisper. "You're making him more nervous than he needs to be."

She stopped the tapping and watched the scrawny lad, who looked young enough to be just a day out of uni, shakily place the undeveloped photos in small bins filled with a mixture of liquid chemicals, one by one, giving them a little shake as he went down the long row he had created.

"How long will it take?" she asked.

"Fifteen minutes. Ten if we're lucky."

There it is again, thought Margaret. That god-awful silence. As they waited, it seemed to dilate time. How could she wait *fifteen goddamn minutes*?

Sorry, Lord, she added to the thought for taking His name in vain.

She wanted to tap her foot so badly she began to feel an imaginary burning sensation, like she'd stuck it over an open fire. *If I could just do something—*

"Ye said you're from the Cumnock station?" asked the lad, glancing at Margaret for a second before returning his attention to another undeveloped photo he placed into the liquid.

"Aye."

The lad tried to suppress it, but Margaret could see the slight twinkle of excitement clear as day, even behind the unnatural glow of his red eyes.

"You're here for those missing lads, aren't you?"

Margaret and Gordon exchanged a glance.

"Ye can say no," said the lad with a snort. "But I know better. Me mum told me growing up there's always answer in a pause."

Gordon shook his head and gave an *I'm-fine-with-it-if-you-are* shrug of his shoulders. She acquiesced with a sigh. "We are. But if nothing comes of this, don't go running 'round the station telling them what you were working on."

"Understood," he said.

Margaret watched as he went down the line of the bins of liquids, giving each of them a shake to keep the liquid moving. His hands still trembled.

"You're doing a fine job, lad," she said. "You can relax."

"I'm not worried what you think of my work. It's those kids," he said with a great big breath of pent-up air. "They're on the news every night. I'm worried for them."

"You and me both," said Gordon. "You and me both…"

Margaret fixated on the subtle shaking of his hands. This nervous energy. The same one agitating her, pushing her to *just tap that damn foot of yours*. The lad felt it too.

They each stood shoulder-to-shoulder, necks craned over their respective bins, studying the images that had partially developed and were fading in more by the minute.

"This one's just a house," said the lad.

Margaret peered over into his bin and saw what he was referring to; the outline of a house coming into view, its face oddly familiar.

Don't jump the gun. Just wait.

She didn't have to wait long.

"Is it?" asked the lad.

"Al's," she answered, eyes flicking anxiously at the other developing photos. Her own bin housed a photo that looked like…the inside of a shed, maybe? Or a small room, a corridor, with a door.

"Uh, guys…" said Gordon, voice jumping in pitch. "I think it's them."

"Are you—"

The question stopped short the moment she saw the photo that lay in his bin. The four lads stood on the side of Al's house. The patterns of their clothes, the strands of moppy teenage hair, and curious looks on their faces—all faded in.

"They're in front of his storage shed," said Margaret, pointing a finger just above the liquid.

"But we cleared the whole thing out and found nothing."

"Still, this is proof the four lads were together, and that the last time they were seen before disappearing was outside of Al's house."

Gordon chewed the inside of his lower lip. The lab worker lad slipped around the two of them and checked more bins down the line.

"What's this?" he asked.

Margaret and Gordon shuffled to his side, glanced at the picture, and then looked up at each other, wide-eyed.

"We are all seeing the same thing, right?" asked Margaret.

"It's an open door and a flight of stairs leading down," said the lad. "Can you make out what's at the bottom?"

The three of them squinted. Margaret realised the gradient in this black and white photo was produced because the flash bulb had illuminated the surfaces closest to the camera lens more brightly, and those distant to it were more obscured by shadow.

"It looks like…" said Gordon through a tensed jaw, gruff voice slipping with a tinge of frustration. "A new room. A hall or something. Definitely not a dead end."

An idea struck Margaret. She swivelled her head down the line of photos and her heart fluttered in her chest the moment she realised the glaring pattern right under their noses. She hurried down to the bin at the far end.

"If these pictures are from Colin's last moments…a roll of film is chronological. *So*, what's the final photo of?"

As she reached the bin, with Gordon and the lad at her heels, her mouth dropped. She extended her hand—

"Let me," said the lad, dropping a pair of tongs into the chemicals, grasping the fully developed photo at its edge. He pulled it out, letting the liquid drip off, giving it a light wave in the air. He brought the photo close to their faces, and in the flooded red light of the darkroom, the three of them saw the unimaginable.

"Oh my God," said Margaret breathlessly, heart pounding with a fresh wave of adrenaline. Arun, Craig, Gavin, and James stood interspersed in a long hallway made of stone brick. In the distance, two double doors sat ajar, and inside looked to be…water? *How is that possible?* There was also a wooden dock and floating ice sculptures. The look of fear on the lads' faces was palpable. Closest to the camera, back facing the lens, was a grown man wearing a long black wig, whose wavy curls fell past his shoulders. The bright flash must have given Colin away, because the man's head in the photo was frozen mid-swivel, turning back to see who was behind him. Just half his face was visible, like a blurry, illuminated crescent moon. But even with just half his features on display, the icy, pale colour of the eye caught in the camera's dazzling flash was all she needed to recognise its owner—

"Al," whispered Gordon breathlessly.

Margaret turned to the lad, adrenaline buoying her spirit, creating a crispness and clarity of mind that could only emerge from a mission whose end was in sight.

"Do you have a patrol car?" she asked.

"Nae, but I have my own," said the lad.

The shakiness returned to his hands. The energy they all felt grew more intense by the second, infusing the air with an invisible electricity.

"I want you to do everything I am about to say exactly as I say it," began Margaret, fixing her gaze on the lad, resting her hand on his shoulder. "Take this photo and go straight to the Cumnock police station. When you get there, ask for my sergeant, Stu. Give him this picture and call the magistrate. If he gives you any lip, you get the office clerk to call the magistrate for you. Understand?"

The lad nodded continuously as she spoke.

"Tell him Detective Gordon Ross has requested a second warrant for Albert Reid's home."

Gordon glanced at Margaret as she said this last instruction but didn't challenge her.

"We have no time to waste. I'm not breaking my promise," she said turning to Gordon, chest rising and falling with ragged breath. "We are going straight to Al's. *Now*."

Stu sat at his desk, massaging the skin above his brow bones with his middle finger and thumb. In and out, slowly and with firm pressure, pleading internally that it might ease the migraine that felt like someone had plunged a pickaxe into his skull, attempting to split it in two.

The blinds to his office were shuttered. Beyond the glass windows, the steady hum of mutterings amongst the officers and the occasional ring of the rotary phones were all muted. He thanked God at least those sounds were hushed. Much to his displeasure, they paled in comparison to the loudness of his own mind. The dates, the numbers, the faces over the years crashing in a culmination of calamity that he stood in the centre of.

The eye of the storm.

One he'd walked into willingly.

Yet never understanding its trajectory, even now.

As he sat in the grips of a vortex, a whirlwind of uncertainty and regret, he prayed it would just pass. That he'd open his eyes to see clear skies.

But the pit in his gut told him the contrary.

He would stay fixed in the centre of it all, the maelstrom that had ripped away his spirit bit by bit with every violent revolution. Even from within the winds of this storm, he had managed to clean up as much debris as possible. He had successfully retrieved the donation records, but still. Had he left any stones unturned? He couldn't be sure.

Now, all he could do was pray. Pray for Margaret's hunch to be wrong. Because if she was *right*...

Please, let this all be over soon. I can't take it any longer.

Just as he finished that wee thought between him and the Lord, a sudden flurry of footsteps overshadowed the office monotony, oscillating in intensity from softer to louder until they stopped just outside his office door. Stu's eyes bulged as a lad barged in, panting heavily, sweat clinging to his windblown locks. He threw down a photograph and with his other hand, a police ID from the Ayr station.

"Detective Gordon Ross sent me," he said, catching his breath. He pointed a shaky finger at the picture.

"He said to call the magistrate. To get another warrant for Albert Reid's home."

Stu held the photo up, and the beating of his heart seemed to stop the moment he saw the four lads. The look of fear on their faces. The hallway that looked eerily similar to the blueprint Margaret had provided to get the first warrant.

And then there was the man. The half of a face beneath tousles of black hair that didn't seem to match the head they sat on.

A wig.

His heart was still beating; he was alive. Wasn't he? But his chest had gone numb.

"If you don't call him, I will," threatened the lad.

Stu rested the photo back on the desk, his motions smooth and dreamlike, and through trembling lips mustered one word. "Aye."

The lad let out a big breath of relief.

As the clock ticked, and the rest of the office held silent, waiting to hear what news this lad had brought, Stu knew what this photo signified.

The hour of fate had arrived.

The music stopped.

The Gustav Holst record had played its final note, and the vinyl now spun silently, stylus dragging along the empty ridge closest to the centre.

Silence reclaimed Al's home. A moment later, the arrival of a new sound stymied its suffocating presence—

A car engine.

His steps to the front window were measured as the sound grew louder. The grey light of day slipped through the crack in the curtains, and as he reached them, he felt his nerves fray. The unspooling of his psyche. The subsequent fear that crept through his chest was unlike any kind he'd felt in his entire life. Its bite carried a bit of anaesthetic—a numbness that seemed to seep through his bones as if they were being filled with concrete. An inconceivable heaviness weighing him down where he stood.

It was the same irrevocable knowingness he'd felt earlier.

That his track was reaching its end.

The eyes of his soul had witnessed what was to come, long before he could ever take a first glimpse. He drew back the curtains and saw a black patrol car pulling into his drive.

Margaret and Detective Ross hopped out and began approaching the house.

Al took a deep breath, and that numbness reached its peak. It tried to keep him rooted there, but he fought against it, peeling his feet from the floor, backing away from where he stood.

He walked over to the record player, pinched the arm, and moved it back to the middle of the disc. The song immediately jumped from the speaker, and with a flick of his fingers, he turned the volume dial to its maximum. The angelic orchestra blared, echoing raucously throughout the house.

With a hurried swoop of his hand, he grabbed a newspaper lying on an armchair and lumbered into the kitchen. He turned the gas burner on with a *click-click-click-click*—a flame caught.

Behind the music, pounding knocks sounded at the door.

He stuck the newspaper into the flame, letting it catch.

Al made his decision.

This life that he had built, from the ashes of fire and fury, would end just as it had begun.

A patrol car spun out of the Cumnock station. Aniqa slammed on her brakes to avoid hitting the officer, and he gave a red-faced wave of his hand, peeling out onto the main road.

She collected her breath and drove into the car park.

Just as she killed the engine, two more officers barrelled out of the station door, sprinting to their patrol cars. Her brow furrowed as she watched them peel away just as the first officer had, and as she began her approach to the station, her heart began beating with an unpleasant hardness. Each percussive thud sent a wave of adrenaline spiderwebbing through her arteries and capillaries and veins.

She climbed the steps to the station and when she opened the door, the commotion that met her was dizzying. Officers zigzagged the main hall and all the adjoining offices. Dozens of phones were ringing off their hooks. Endless shouting, desk clerks handing out batons, utility belts, and weapons.

Pure chaos.

An officer bumped into her shoulder as he pushed toward the exit, nearly slamming her back against the wall.

"Sorry!" he called out before lumbering down the steps.

A baby-faced officer appeared out of the reception doorway; since he was the only person she'd seen so far *walking*, she grabbed his arm before he crossed the hall.

"Hey, what's going on?"

He whipped around, and the moment he recognised who was holding him, a panicked expression spread across his face. "Stu!" he shouted, craning his head to face the long hall. "Aniqa's here!"

She gave a hard tug at his arm, clamping down with as much strength as she could put into her grip, and as he turned back to face her, she saw in her peripheral vision the dozens of people standing from their desks and peeping their heads into the hallway to ogle at her presence.

"You tell me what's going on right now. I'm not waiting for Stu."

The lad's eyes lit up, a nervous energy brimming from every ounce of his being.

"The magistrate gave us a second warrant for Al's house."

"How?" she nearly shouted the word.

"Detective Ross found a picture of Al in his basement…"

Before he could even finish his sentence, and even with seeing Stu approach from down the long hall out of the corner of her eye, she darted out the station exit.

She didn't need to see the picture.

She didn't need to hear someone tell her the details.

Because she already *knew*.

Hands shaking uncontrollably, she steeled her nerves just enough to slide the key in the ignition. She floored the accelerator, engine roaring to life as she careened out onto the main road. The dreary countryside became a passing blur of green and grey. An exhilarant mixture of fear and euphoria percolated through her, every cell in her body riding on the wave of adrenaline that soared to unimaginable heights. Tears glistened in her eyes, and she gripped the steering wheel, jaw clenched, steadying her breath as she attempted to hold a visualisation in her mind's eye. To manifest the moment that she'd been so desperately praying to God for throughout the past two weeks.

To see Arun's face.

To hold her son in her arms again.

Alive.

CHAPTER 25
THE RED DOOR

A crashing thud came from the stone ceiling of the basement, and the whole room, including the floor which they sat upon, rippled with a violent vibration. Gavin and Fiona looked at Arun, chests rising and falling, *waiting…*

I guess I'm the leader now, thought Arun. A painful reminder of Craig's absence. The only problem was, he wasn't Craig. Nor could he ever be.

More thunderous bangs echoed from up above. They all flinched in unison, and James covered his ears, tucking his head between his knees.

Fiona glared at Arun. *Do something! What are you waiting for?* He could hear her high-pitched voice just through the intensity of her stare.

Arun popped up onto his feet, and surprisingly, didn't sway or topple over; his legs seemed to be buttressed by something other than muscle alone, because the last seven days without food had robbed him of every last ounce of strength. He eyed the ceramic shards. More thuds, cracks, and crashes came from the ceiling. It sounded like furniture was being thrown about.

Something is going on…but what do we do?

"Do you hear that?" asked Gavin, holding out his hand.

With a momentary lapse in the chaos above, far behind the cement brick and woodwork of the house which contained them, two faint voices emerged.

"What are they saying?" asked Arun.

"Al," blurted Fiona. "Someone's yelling his name."

A rush of energy surged up through Arun's spirit, it pushed outward at his chest, upward at his shoulders, counteracting the oppressive weight of this prison. The mourning of his dear friend. The lack of nourishment. It all faded away in the light of this newfound realisation.

Someone was up there. They weren't politely ringing the doorbell, but *shouting* for Al.

"It's time," said Arun.

The three of them grabbed their ceramic shards and readied themselves at the invisible, recessed wall. And at the right moment, they would ignite the last bit of stamina their tired bodies had held onto, day after day, knowing that this moment may come. One final push.

The fight that would give them back their freedom.

They would either live to see the light of day.

Or die trying.

"Do you smell smoke?" asked Margaret with a twitch of her nose.

Gordon sniffed the crack of Al's front door.

"Christ that's strong!" he shouted, choking back a cough.

Margaret made her way along the perimeter of the house, attempting to sneak a peek through a crack in the blinds, but none allowed a glimpse in. She continued around the right side of the house, and the burning smell grew stronger. She held a mental image of the house's layout in her mind's eye, which she had done her best to keep sharp since the day of the first search.

I'm nearing the kitchen…

She ducked her head beneath the first set of the drapes and—

Flames.

The edges of what had been the curtains were singed with black soot.

The entirety of Al's kitchen was engulfed in an inferno.

"Gordon!" she shouted, and he nearly barrelled into her side a moment later.

"He knows he's guilty," he said breathlessly, eyes growing wider.

Desperate not to be too late, Margaret ran to the one place where she'd gotten too close for Al's comfort.

The shed.

Gordon bounded next to her as they ran up the drive. She'd believed since the beginning this was where the children were, but she'd never been able to prove it. But now was not the time for a self-righteous pat on one's own back. The path that lay directly in front of them was the opportunity she'd been waiting for all along.

To keep her promise.

The splintering thuds of Gordon's kicks to the shed door drew her back to reality, and once the hole was large enough to fit his hand through, he unlocked it. A collection of tools lined the walls, and Margaret grabbed a sledgehammer she saw, handing it to Gordon.

"There," she said, pointing with a trembling finger toward the handful of discoloured bricks on the back wall of the shed. The one she'd popped out of place before she was arrested had already been replaced and recaulked.

A guttural huff caught in Gordon's throat as he swung the sledgehammer over his shoulder, letting it come down on the back wall, causing the bricks to buckle. They didn't fall, but with two more heaving swings, a hole formed. Gordon continued crashing the sledgehammer down on the crumbling bricks until the rest of the false wall began to crumble. She'd never seen such a determined rage in his eyes. As the last of it collapsed, the straining of his face muscles from the repetitive blows eased, and his mouth fell agape.

"Look," said Gordon.

Margaret took a step closer and turned to see what had transfixed him. Just a few feet beyond the pile of rubble, she saw it.

A red door.

"Ow!" winced Fiona, cradling her hand to her chest. "The wall's hot." She flicked her gaze uncertainly between Arun and Gavin.

Those three words caused the prickly fingers of panic to flick and flitter across Arun's skin. A maelstrom of opposing forces tugged at his body, each fighting for their hold of the reins, crashing into one another like ocean waves beneath a violent squall.

Exhaustion. Adrenaline. The will to survive.

A thundering crash came from outside the room, followed by a burst of sizzling pops and a crackling *whoosh.*

"Is that fire?" asked Gavin shakily.

The storm of competing sensations within Arun settled, and his conscious mind resurfaced as it processed Gavin's question. His gaze drifted to Fiona nursing her stinging hand.

Then, it clicked.

"Now," he said, too quietly for his heart's liking. Urgency pounded with its invisible fist at his breastbone, forcing a burst of air out of his lungs.

"*Now!*" he bellowed.

Fiona and Gavin flinched, then readied themselves, shards in hand.

"On the count of three, we push the door with all we've got!" He pointed at Fiona's hand. "It might burn us, but that's better than burning alive down here."

"One…Two…"

Fiona, Gavin, and Arun gave each other a final nod of recognition.

A shared thought:

This is it.

"Three!"

They slammed their shoulders into the wall, pushing with their forearms against the stinging hot stone. "Aghhh!" Gavin cried out, fighting against the urge to pull away from the burning sensation.

"Keep going!" shouted Arun.

The concealed wall just barely began scraping the floor as it slid back from its closed position. "I can't! I can't…" whimpered Fiona as she pulled back.

Gavin and Arun followed suit—a momentary reprieve from the burning stone.

Do something, scolded his lizard brain. The part of his DNA that had kept his ancestors going for millennia. The fight or flight reflex.

Do something! Now, or you'll die! it roared.

He whipped around, eyeing James in the corner of the basement.

"We were only able to open it when we had four people. When Craig was still alive," said Arun. Al never meant for this door to be opened. It was only because there were enough of us. It's how we studied the lock. It's how I almost escaped."

He couldn't believe whether they lived or died was reliant on the strength of *one* more person. Resting in the hands of the person who had foiled their escape plan. The person who had lost his mind long before they ever went hungry.

James.

"We need your help," said Arun. "If you don't push with us, we're all going to die."

"Please!" begged Fiona, trying to hold back her tears.

No response. Head still cradled between his knees.

"Starving is bad…but imagine your flesh burning to a crisp. The black smoke filling your lungs. Charring it until you can't even take your last breath. The flames licking you, blistering and bubbling until you're a pile of mushy flesh and burnt bones."

"Stop!" James cried out, clamping his cupped hands more tightly against his ears.

"We won't ever get adopted," said Gavin, his tone flat. "You won't get to see that action flick you've been talking about for months. Your whole life will have meant nothing if you die here."

"Shut up!" He hiccupped back a cry. "Da is coming, I know it. He won't let us die."

Arun watched a steely gaze slide across Gavin's face.

"He's probably already dead by now."

Fiona and Arun turned to Gavin, surprised by this verbal pivot.

The Gavin that stood before them was so far removed from the one who had entered the basement two weeks ago that they seemed to be two different people entirely. Something had changed him down here. He stared disdainfully at his cowering brother; in the darkness behind his eyes, the unflinching countenance framing his tired, grimy face, Arun knew that Gavin, *this* Gavin—would pull at every string necessary to get through to James.

"I bet the fire outside these walls has already torn through the whole upstairs, Al included. And we're next."

James' head slowly rose from between his knees. Arun flinched from how severely James had deteriorated; this was the first time he'd taken a good look at him since before Craig died. This starving shell of James that sat knees-to-chest across the room from them was a mere remnant of the outgoing—albeit awkward—lad he had met on the football field that fateful day. His pasty white face proved a disturbing contrast to the dark circles beneath his sunken eyes.

"He might be dying as we speak," said Gavin. "You might be able to save him. Then everything will go back to normal."

James' disposition shifted suddenly—a shimmer of hope, a shock to the right synapse within his brain that had completely unravelled in the past week and a half.

He stood up, and Arun and Fiona watched dumbfounded as James approached their line of three. He slipped in at the end, giving them a miniscule nod of his head.

Here we go, Arun thought. *It's now or never.*

"On the count of three!"

Arun counted, and when he reached three, the four children gave one final push. Teeth gritted, wincing as their skin met hot stone, a mixture of pent-up tears and sweat soaked their grimy faces. They pushed because their lives depended on it. They pushed because death's presence had become more prominent by the day, impossible to ignore. It stole their breath. Squelched their hope. Echoed in their empty stomachs. Radiated through their aching bones.

Arun pushed with the immeasurable weight of the loss of his only friend.

Fiona, to see her parents again.

Gavin, with an anger so potent, it blazed inside his little body like a vortex of fire.

And James pushed with misguided hope.

The quartet gave it their all. They became so engrossed in the effort, they no longer felt the straining of their weary muscles, the scorching of their skin, or even heard the guttural groans that escaped as they heaved with the fullest extent of their strength.

They didn't realise that the door had opened.

The moment they came to, they were met with something far deadlier than the isolation of the basement room.

Fire.

Al sat at the beginning of the dock. The frosty air of the frozen room tickled his exposed skin. The waters holding his weight were tranquil, and he swore he'd never seen his art so perfectly still on their ice blocks.

Calm. At peace.

Almost like they knew what was to come.

His day of reckoning.

He could have sworn he caught a few of the sculptures' cold blue lips slightly upturned in the beginnings of a smile.

My imagination's getting the better of me, he thought.

The fire roared behind him in the hallway.

He still wasn't sure why he'd settled on his last moments as a free man to be spent in the frozen room. Perhaps because he found a bit of irony in the symbolic parallel of the spot where he sat. Around him, wood cracked, exploding in bursts of sparks. Metal warped under the heat. His home was being destroyed. And yet, he faced another version of destruction. One that was icy cold. Innocent blood spilled, frozen skin chipped with a chisel and sculpted into art. The destruction crafted from his own hands.

The children whose souls he spared, before they were soiled by the wickedness of this cruel world. A painless death. A truly pure spirit. One who would never have to face abuse, rejection, and the immeasurable hurt that stained us year after year, until children grow into adults, bitter and tainted, each layer of pain like a coat of black that grows thicker as time passes.

From within the fire, he heard footsteps.

"Al!" a shout came from behind him.

Margaret.

Then, a flurry of softer footsteps arose. A throng of youthful battle cries.

Before he could turn around, he felt the sharp pinch of a blade going into his back.

Margaret bounded down the long basement hall, bobbing and weaving around burning piles of debris. As she moved, she covered her nose with the sleeve of her arm, so as to not let the smoke incapacitate her.

Her jaw dropped as she emerged from a thick cloud of smoke.

The kids were attacking him.

Al swatted a ceramic shard from Gavin's hand; it went flying against the wall and shattered.

A blonde girl shrieked at the top of her lungs in a valiant war cry, and stabbed Al just above his Achilles tendon, along his calf. Arun jumped behind Al, trying to kick at his backside to propel his body high enough to retrieve the ceramic shard impaled into Al's shoulder blade. The third boy, James, stood off to the side and held the shard against his chest, hands trembling.

Gordon reached for his baton from his belt loop, handcuffs unlocked and readied in his other hand. The two hastened their approach toward the chaos.

"Stop!" commanded Gordon. The children paid no attention. "Albert Reid, you're under arrest!"

Al flailed his limbs, trying to knock the kids off like they were a colony of angry fire ants scaling his tall frame. His calf seeped blood, and there was a misshapen maroon stain around his back wound.

"Cover me," said Gordon.

She nodded, staying within a few feet of him.

A crashing explosion of sparks came from above, and Margaret ducked reflexively as a pile of fiery debris fell in front of her.

"I'm all right!" called Gordon from the other side of the billowing smoke ascending from the debris. "Stop!" he shouted. "He's under arrest! Stop attacking!"

As the smoke began to thin, she heard a wet, choking cough.

"James!" someone screamed. "What are you doing?"

"Get off him!" echoed the girl.

Him…

The word made Margaret's heart flutter. A moment ago, everyone had been attacking Al with no cries of contest.

She jumped around the pile of burning debris, and as she regained her footing, her mind flashed to the one child who *hadn't* attacked—

A loud *thump* echoed in the basement as Arun body-slammed James. He ripped the bloodstained ceramic shard from his hand, tossing it and letting it shatter, then he squeezed his legs together, pinning James down beneath his knees. Arun punched him repeatedly, over and over, until his swelling eyes began to roll back in his head.

"Stop!" Margaret called out. Arun's raised fist froze, and he looked back at her, a tidal wave of red-hot anger flushing his dark skin. "We have to get out of here!" she said, choking back a cough. The black, arid smoke stinging her lungs was beginning to make her lightheaded.

Gavin looked at his brother James as if he'd just seen a ghost. His gaze was wide-eyed, hollow. Al was nursing his wounds, and Gordon lay at her feet, coughing wetly. She calculated the precise order of all she had to attend to. Whipping out her handcuffs, she used the entirety of her strength to hop over Gordon's body and pounce on Al.

"Tackle him!" she called, and within a split-second, the children threw themselves at Al, helping her pull him to his knees. He didn't even put up much of a fight. With a tinny *cl-cl-cl-cl-clack*, the first handcuff locked into place around his wrist. She bent his other arm around his back, twisting it with disregard for the pain, and locked the other.

Another loud crash—more burning rubble fell through the ceiling farther down the hall.

"Don't let me burn to death," said Al, then coughed violently, struggling to steady his breath. "Please."

Margaret moved over to assess Gordon. She held a wavering hand above the wounds, too afraid to touch, uncertain how to proceed. He coughed and blood-tinged spittle flew from his lips. She grimaced as she took a hard look at his stomach. Attempting not to react as his friend, but as a cop. Blood had seeped through both his undershirt and uniform, forming a large circular stain that spanned from his solar plexus to his beltline.

More disintegrating chunks of Al's home fell through to the basement.

For a split-second, panic petrified her where she knelt. Gordon's olive skin, which flickered in the orange light of the flames, had already lost a few shades of colour, and his green eyes that normally shimmered, seemed duller.

"Get out," he croaked.

"No. I'm not leaving ye here."

Gordon reached up, grabbing her arm. The crashing farther down the hall was so loud, she didn't even notice Al shimmying away. Her dear friend was fading fast, and that grasped her attention with a white-knuckled grip.

"Go," he said. "Keep your promise."

Like a searing-hot blade being plunged into her soul, those three words galvanised her. The panic evaporated, and like a slow-motion film racing back up to normal speed, she let go of Gordon's hand.

Keep. Your. Promise.

A splash came from the frozen room. Al had thrown himself into the water, and now he was bobbing up and down, trying to keep his head above its surface.

"I can't breathe," whimpered the blonde girl, hot tears rolling down her face. Arun still had James pinned under him. Gavin covered his nose with his shirt, staring at Margaret with those dead, empty eyes.

Margaret climbed to her feet and turned to see the fiery obstacle course that stood between them and the stairwell leading to safety.

She whipped around; seeing Al floating in the frozen room sparked a thought.

That's it!

"All of you, jump in the water. Wet yourself from head to toe. It's the only way we'll make it without burning alive."

She led the way, jumping off the edge of the dock into the frigid water. It sharpened her senses more acutely than even the strongest cup of the station's shite coffee. One after another, they jumped. Arun, Gavin, and the blonde girl. James hadn't budged.

"You too," she said. "I'm not letting you die."

She felt a pair of eyes on her as she said this, but she couldn't tell who they belonged to.

"Now!"

He listened, sitting on the edge of the dock and sliding into the water.

"Dunk yourselves under," said Margaret as she trod water, looking around at the children. "Once we are soaked, we jump out, and run to the stairs. Got it?"

They all nodded, save for James.

"We can't stop, or the fire will burn this water off and we won't make it."

There was uncertainty in the face of the blonde girl.

"I'll lead the way, okay?" Margaret added. The girl nodded.

"All right, we are going to go under in three…two…one. Now!"

They all submerged themselves, and the moment they resurfaced, Margaret pulled herself up onto the dock. She hoisted each of the children out, and once they'd made it to the edge of the basement, dripping from head to toe, she looked down at Gordon. The light in his eyes seemed half-faded.

I'll come back for you, she thought, then gave the signal to the children to go.

"Stay right next to me!"

And with that, they ran. They jumped over the first pile of burning rubble closest to Gordon. No one tripped, and they manoeuvred around the second unscathed. A loud crash came from above, and the blonde girl screamed as she jumped out of the way of another falling pile of debris. "I can't!" she hollered, throat raw from the smoke, hacking up a lung. "I can't do it."

Without asking, Margaret scooped her into her arms.

"Come on!" called Arun in front of them. "We have to go under this one."

A burning determination radiated outward from the lad's black eyes. She'd seen the same look in Aniqa before. But this was even more intense.

A look that said *I will get out of here alive.*

They each crawled carefully beneath a charred support beam that had fallen, leaning diagonally across the width of the hall that was being licked by flames. Margaret did a quick scan for a headcount.

We're all still here.

They were halfway down the hall. The last few piles of burning debris were larger. They had to jump and shimmy, pray their feet or bodies wouldn't fail them in a moment like this. It was then she realised the children were barefoot, as she heard a few yelps from Gavin and James. "Keep going!" she rasped, choking back a cough.

When they finally reached the bottom of the stairs, her heart sank as she looked up.

The entirety of it was engulfed in flames. An inferno.

The stairway to Hell.

But you have to get them out. Keep your promise!

The voice of her conscience was shrill. Determined, but wavering.

"What do we do?" asked the blonde girl. The air around them was thick with smoke and boiling hot. The icing on the cake was that their soaked clothes were already half-dry.

If you do nothing, you die.

If you try and fail, you still die.

But if you do nothing, you will certainly die.

Her subconscious mind pestered her, pricking her with instinct.

"We might burn," said Margaret, voice trembling. She gulped dryly, summoning as much confidence as she could muster. "But we can't stop. It might hurt. But we can't stop. You understand? We run up there as fast as we can, and we don't look back!"

"On the count of three," said Arun with a solemn nod.

She returned it.

"One, two, three!"

With the blonde girl in her arms, she ran. The three lads were in front of her, and they bounded up the stone stairwell with blazing speed. She winced as she heard the sizzling of the soft, wet skin of their feet, the excruciating yelps as they fought to propel themselves toward the light at the end of the tunnel.

It looked *so* far, like a pinhole obscured by noxious black plumes of smoke. She smelt the distinct putrid smell of burning hair and felt the squishy *gush* of her shoes beginning to melt on the hot stone. The children cried out, and she fought the urge to scream from the flames jumping at her heels. Her instinct pushed her forward, adrenaline masking the pain, but the heat was equally as powerful—it scorched her lungs, and the flames tried to eat away at her damp shell of clothes bit by bit. It was as if the fire were a sinister siren; it valiantly tried to call her back, to drag her down into the basement with its blazing tendrils and crush her in its deadly embrace.

The smoke became thicker the higher they went. But her legs kept pushing. The blonde girl's pinching grip around her neck reminded her, *I am alive.*

There was only one thing crossing her mind, over and over, as the rest of her physical sensations began to dissolve away:

Keep your promise.

Arun burst through the red door and nearly faceplanted as he tripped over the pile of rubble from the destroyed false shed wall. He rolled around on the floor, slapping himself wildly to put out the flames that clung to his clothes. He scrambled to his feet, saw Gavin and James hit the floor, then Margaret, who held Fiona. She collapsed to her knees in exhaustion, Fiona crawling out of her grip, and Arun smacked at her hair, which still smouldered and sizzled.

The door to the shed was already open.

Behind the smoke, he smelt it—*fresh air.*

Then, he heard police sirens.

His heart soared, and he barrelled out of the shed and down Al's drive. The grey light of the Scottish day blinded him, but he didn't slow. He prayed God wouldn't let him smash into Al's car or let him trip and sprain another ankle.

He didn't know where he was headed. He just ran. The cool, dewy grass soothed his scorched feet. And though his exposed skin was singed and throbbed, the exuberance of this moment—escape—the *real* escape, filled him with such bliss he couldn't feel any of it.

He saw the cops swarming Al's house, and as his vision finally adjusted to the light of day, tears filling his eyes, he just ran, he kept running.

The undulating whine of the police sirens frayed her nerves, as if a razor blade was peeling them back fibre by fibre. As Aniqa crested the hill on Holm Farm Road, her heart caught in her throat.

A gargantuan column of black smoke rose above what was left of Al's house. The roof had collapsed, exposed beams and the wooden framework looked like charred toothpicks from a distance. A great fireball had engulfed everything.

The many patrol cars eclipsed her view of both the drive and the garden.

She slammed her brakes along the street, gave her handbrake a forceful pull, and jumped out of her car.

Run, a little voice told her. What bristled the hairs on the back of her neck was that it wasn't her mother's voice.

It was *Arun's.*

And so she ran.

She ran around the slew of officers and patrol cars, ran along the gravel in search of green grass, feet slipping in the mud from the recent rain. Her heart pounded, and she kept hearing his sweet voice.

Run. Run. Run.

"I'm coming, I'm coming," she said, breath shaky, eyes filling with tears. "Mum!"

When she heard *that* voice, her soul jumped. An electric shiver slipped down her spine, and her own voice, this time, reminded her of the truth she knew in the farthest flung reaches of her being.

From the part of her soul that was *Mother.*

That voice wasn't in your head.

She turned in the direction the voice came from, praying during the fleeting second mid-motion that she wasn't imagining things.

But her intuition hadn't lied.

Arun was in a full-on sprint toward her.

"Mum!" he shouted, chest heaving, arms pumping at his side.

"Arun!"

She ran with all her might, skidding across the wet grass, opening her arms as they neared each other. As he got closer, she saw his lower lip trembling wildly, and then saw how skinny he was. The thick layer of soot and grime and sweat on his skin. The tattered, stained clothes, singe-marks on his hair and the enflamed patchwork of puffy skin across his body.

Arun barrelled into her arms, his *mother's* arms, and began sobbing.

"My baby…my baby," she said over and over, holding him tightly, smoothing his hair with her hand.

His cries were unlike anything she'd ever heard. Not like the night of the nightmare. She pulled back, taking a good look at him up and down, wiping his tears away with her thumb, as a flood of her own poured down her face. His physique had changed. Scrawnier. Weaker.

But that wasn't it.

It was something else.

"Your eyes," she said breathlessly. He looked at her, brow furrowing, but when she saw how his eyes had changed, she pulled him close again, a fresh wave of sobs rocking her chest. Because the boy she remembered before he went missing wasn't there anymore.

The youthful shimmer in his dark eyes had disappeared.

Before her stood a different person.

Not quite a man, but not the son she remembered either.

She felt a weight to the way he held her, a heaviness to his spirit.

What happened down there?

A storm of police officers crisscrossed Al's garden and drive, and none seemed daring enough to interrupt their reunion.

"I have to go back! *Please!*" a voice screamed; throat hoarse with desperation.

"Is that—?"

Arun nodded. "The lady who saved us."

Margaret.

She glanced up the drive to see Margaret pushing against three officers, clamouring to re-enter the raging inferno that had completely engulfed Al's house.

Aniqa's eyes began to dart around the garden. There was a blonde girl, the smaller missing boy she knew as Gavin, and his brother, James. Each had a handful of cops and paramedics surrounding them, dabbing their skin with cotton balls, poking and prodding their limbs in rough examinations. She could see their little heads nod as they were peppered with questions.

Her eyes kept darting, looking for—

She broke her gaze and looked at Arun. "Where's Craig?"

He shook his head, face contorting, then was rocked with violent sobs. He threw himself into her arms again, and her son's groans of agony caused a hole to form in the centre of her chest.

"Craig! Craig!"

Hearing Elaine Robertson's voice from a distance caused a shiver to slide down Aniqa's spine. She turned to see Elaine tramping in circles around the garden, pushing officers aside, shouting her lad's name. Her ghastly complexion exacerbated the frazzled look on her face, bug-eyed stare, and hair that looked like she'd stuck a fork in an electrical socket. George followed behind, with sunken eyes and dark circles the colour of soft bruises.

At the sight of Arun, Elaine beelined toward them.

"I can't," said Arun, pressing his face deeper into her shoulder. "I can't do it."

Elaine took one look at the sombre stare Aniqa gave her, and it was as if without words, the two friends communicated.

"No, no, no…" She mumbled the word endlessly. "No! No, it can't be. *Craaa-ig!*"

The way Elaine howled her son's name caused Aniqa to shudder; her grip on Arun tightened. She didn't try to console him. Just let him blubber, let him pour out his pain, let him grieve this loss in the safety of his mother's arms.

She felt the edges of Elaine's pain drift over. It cast an icy blanket around them and continued spreading across Al's property. A grief like that has its own gravity. It swallows up everything in its vicinity, capturing everyone's attention within its black net of misery. The children looked up at her, then the paramedics, then the officers—one by one, they each paused to bear witness to this raw display of pain.

To give her space to mourn.

Elaine's guttural cries were replaced by the droning horns of the fire engines. It was eerie to see her bawl, mouth wide-open, George at her side, yet the sound was gone.

Dozens of firemen spilled from the two trucks, racing up the garden with their hoses, and those who stayed back connected them to the tanks. The firemen began spraying Al's house with two roaring jets of water. A few sets spurted past Margaret, disappearing into a side entrance. Aniqa could faintly hear Margaret's rasped pleas—a frantic set of directions.

Gordon—she heard his name.

Then, it began to rain.

The fat droplets hissed and sizzled as they fell onto the burning structure. The once most beautiful house in Catrine was now an unrecognisable pile of rubble.

As Aniqa held Arun in her arms, the rain picked up into a downpour.

For one final time, the Lord cried for Catrine.

He cried as he faced the duality of His creation. The delicate balance which all life hangs upon. Good and evil. Happiness and misery. These teetering extremes pop in and out of existence, every second of every moment, in the brightest of days and in the darkest of nights. A family celebrates the birth of a child. Another mourns the death of theirs.

But how could God cry, when even He knew that this was simply the balance of things?

Wasn't His plan perfect and righteous?

The ebb and flow that allows a burbling brook to provide water to drink is the same force that produces a violent torrent that sweeps away an entire village.

To the Lord, it was all the same. What was important to Him was the sum of the parts.

The balance.

Yet even now, He cried. Although Craig was safe in His Heavenly Kingdom, and the balance was close to being restored, His creation could not grasp the true nature of this pattern.

The why.

So, He cried. The Lord's tears fell on Catrine.

They put out the fire that had been burning for far too long.

The one He had needed help to extinguish.

He looked down upon his children with such boundless love.

He cherished the relief in Aniqa's soul.
He lamented the grief radiating from Elaine's equally so.
But that was simply the nature of God's work.
And that's why He wept.
Striking perfect balance in an imperfect world.

CHAPTER 26
THE QUIET

It took the firemen over an hour to extinguish the flames. All that was left were steaming piles of charred wood, broken glass, disintegrated remnants of furniture—a mutilated shell of the house that had once stood. The clean-up crew, comprised of volunteers, were wading in the River Ayr; a fair portion of the debris had toppled into its tranquil waters. They tossed piece after piece onto the riverbank, then carted it off in wheelbarrows.

The only section of Al's home that wasn't destroyed was the frozen room. The fire captain chalked it up to the water that filled it in tandem with the refrigeration. The system itself was two-pronged; the air being pumped in was well below freezing, but along the circumference of the room, beneath the water's surface, was a heating coil. It kept the water close enough to freezing that it wouldn't ice over.

To ensure what Al kept down there would *float.*

Margaret listened to the fire captain's explanation, the mechanics of it all. But she believed there was a deeper meaning as to why that room, and only that room, still stood.

Perhaps the Lord had barred the flames from reaching it, sapping their oxygen before they could destroy what lay there. It was as if He protected it, waiting until precisely the right moment to give a big wave of His all-powerful hand, presenting the room, with all its contents perfectly intact.

As if to say:

Look what he has done.

Although every cell in Margaret's body screamed for her to stop, for her to rest, she couldn't. She burned the midnight oil, clinging to the adrenaline—bolstered by the euphoria of keeping her promise. That relief was soon overshadowed by the horror of having to face the work of Al's hand.

His creations.

All it took was a hammer and chisel to break the frozen ropes tethering them to the dock. Groups of officers hoisted them into their grip—ice blocks and all—and carried them up the stairs, placing them one after another along the edge of the garden closest to the house.

By now, the whole of Al's property had been cordoned off, keeping nosy neighbours and headline-hungry reporters at bay. The crime photographer snapped photos of each of the sculptures—

Children. They're frozen children, Margaret, her mind chided.

She had to constantly tell herself that they were real. A close look at the flower-like patterns of skin protruding from their arms, or their grey-blue lips which were once rosy, were the only ways to discern that they were at one point in time living, breathing, children.

"They look peaceful," said the photographer as he snapped another picture.

He didn't say it to anyone in particular. But Margaret was within earshot to hear the comment. As she digested it, taking a good look at all the children...he was right. There was something meditative about the way they sat on their ice blocks. No fear in their faces. No pain. Just peace.

The thought sent a shiver up her spine.

In total, thirteen frozen children were recovered from Al's basement. And despite the temperate summer weather, it took until close to midnight for them to fully thaw. The ice blocks melted away, and their petrified limbs could finally outstretch, bodies laid out side-by-side on the grass.

Their skin had lost its former blue hue and was replaced by an ashen, bloodless grey.

What would be burned in her memory was Al's look of horror as he was carted out in handcuffs and came face to face with Elaine. She cursed him, shrieking as spittle flew from her lips, bucking against the handful of officers who strained to hold her back like a rabid animal. Eyes red with rage. Hands swatting and striking, fists grasping at empty air. Trying to inflict pain back onto Al. If she did happen to best the officers' strength and land a punch, whatever damage she caused would have been only the tiniest sliver of the pain she felt.

Stu gave the boot of the patrol car two swift pats, drawing Margaret from her thoughts. She turned and watched as the officer drove off with Al in the back seat.

Just like that, he was gone.

The moment she had been waiting for throughout the past two weeks.

She turned back around, letting out a long, weary sigh as the photographer finished snapping pictures of the last child.

Perhaps it was just Margaret's imagination, but now that Al was no longer on his property, she could have sworn the faces of the children shifted. Like the thawing ligaments and muscles were now truly at ease once their captor, their killer, had disappeared.

They could finally rest.

But then, her mind began to spiral.

Would their spirits find the rest they sought, given the way they were taken out of this world?

Would the town?

Would Elaine?

Would she?

Questions without answers.

What Margaret feared more was the alternative. Already having the answer but hiding from the blinding light of its truth, ignoring the scratching presence at her mind's gates.

A voice that said coldly and unequivocally:

No. They wouldn't.

The rhythmic clanking of chains stirred Elder Louise from her already fitful slumber. The sounds came in sets of two; the first—tinnier, lighter. The second—cumbersome rattles, metallic scraping along the concrete floor.

One, two. One, two.

As she sat up in bed and her mind flickered awake, a flash of memory caused her to recognise the noises.

Shackles.

It threw her back to the day of her own transport. The double shackles, one belly chain around her waist, cinching her wrists, and the other at her ankles, dragging across the ground. This remembrance pricked at her senses, expelling whatever drowsiness lingered, because throughout the past nine days as a prisoner, she was the only inmate who had been brought in this way.

With so many chains.

The drunks, the bastard fathers; they were bound only by a simple pair of handcuffs.

Not her. Not after disappearing four children.

So, who was this—?

Al appeared, framed by the black iron bars of her own cell. A towering figure sticking out from shadow. A flickering yellow bulb struggled to illuminate the hall. The officer escorting him fished through a jangly ring of keys, then with a metallic *click* opened the lock. The cell door squealed shrilly as it swung open.

Elder Louise imagined its tenor almost as sing-song—happy to have someone new within its iron mouth, but even more ecstatic was who it welcomed in.

Albert Reid.

A devil among men.

She snuck furtive glances as he settled into his cell, patiently waiting for him to turn and see her. Head hung low, he shifted on the bed's edge, but kept his gaze on the floor.

Look at me, Al, she thought. *Look at me!*

As if hearing the faint, telepathic echo of an old friend skitter across the stone walls, Al looked up. His face blanched, icy blue eyes bulging out from a backdrop of clammy white canvas. The bewilderment of his expression was priceless. He popped up, throwing himself into the iron bars, and the officer jumped back before Al could grab him.

"Hey! Please, I beg you. Move me to another cell."

The officer ignored him, and instead, approached her own.

Elder Louise's breath hitched as she watched the silver key slide into the lock.

The officer swung her cell door open, took a step back, then gave her a nod of his head. "You're free to go."

She choked back a cough. "What?"

"I said yer free to go. All charges have been dropped."

She didn't look back at her cell. That cramped space was the last thing she wanted housed as a memory. When she was arrested, she had made amends with the fact this cell may have been home for the next forty-odd years. Sure, the bed riddled her ageing back with knots, sheets that robbed warmth they were so thin, and air profuse with must like that of an abandoned cellar. But she knew better. It had all been a test. For within that 6x8 cell, her only comfort had lain in her faith. The knowledge that the Lord had a bigger plan.

Now, Al gawked at her, each wide eye intersected by the black iron bar resting against his nose. The shame and shock oozing out of every pore of his being was so unlike the man she'd known. The one whose word was never questioned. The one who had built his life on kindness, compassion, and generosity, although it had all been a façade.

Was this the man behind the mask? The *real* Al?

If so, there was a part of her that pitied him.

Pitied the man staring up at her like a ghost from his past.

"Can I have a moment alone with him?"

The officer barked a laugh, then reined in his surprise, mustering as much respect as he could for his Elder.

She caught his reticence. "Don't worry. Just wait at the end of the hall where you can still see me."

Another half-second of reluctance. "Aye."

He turned and walked a few lengths away, out of earshot.

She faced Al and held his frightened gaze, then bridged the gap between them in one bound.

"Keep your distance!"

"Don't worry," said Elder Louise. "He won't lay a hand on me."

This assuaged the officer just enough for him to stay put.

She eyed him sombrely. As she looked *down* on the man she had looked *up* to for much of her tenure with the Kirk, a flurry of questions zipped through her mind, but only one came out: "Why did you do it?"

Al stayed silent.

"You had everything. A beautiful life. The love of the town." She paused, corking the emotion she felt trying to escape. "You framed me for kidnapping, made a fool of me, and used my own faith—corrupted it—to fulfill your wicked bidding. So, the least you can do is tell me, Al. Why?"

"It was an accident," he said, then looked up from the floor to meet her gaze. A twinkle of awe shimmered behind the icy blue of his irises. An air of bittersweet wonderment. "It was an accident, Louise." His chest rose and fell with desperate, tired breath. "I didn't kidnap them. They snuck into my basement, and I had no other choice…I had no other choice but to keep them there."

Elder Louise let out a snort, holding her old friend's gaze. "If you hadn't known before, now you surely do."

"Know what?" he asked, eyes flicking across her face fearfully, as if she alone held the key to Pandora's box, housing a magical answer that would alleviate his unrest.

"God makes no accidents."

Her words squelched whatever measly flame of hope Al had left, and she turned, leaving him in his cell without a goodbye.

Arun felt like a fish thrown into a new aquarium.

He knew it was *his* room, the same room he'd been in just two weeks before, but the space seemed to have lost its old familiarity—bedsheets unnaturally soft, air tinged with a boyish scent he didn't recognise as his own, and furniture that baulked at this stranger who had returned in place of the old Arun.

"You can sleep in my room if you'd like."

His mum stood in the doorway, eyes glassy and wistful. As if, were she to look away or even blink, he might disappear.

"I'll be all right," he said.

She dropped her chin.

"Really. I can hardly keep my eyes open I'm so knackered."

"Light on or off?"

"Off."

She paused before flicking the switch, reluctant to leave him alone, but conceded with a sigh.

"Love you."

"Love you too, Mum."

She left the door slightly ajar, and when the lights went out, Arun's eyes fought to adjust to the sudden change. The dingy halide lamps of Al's basement always stayed on. He noticed the tiniest bit of dark-blue twilight slipping in around the curtains' edges, along with a faint band of yellow from the hallway as his vision faded in.

The shadows in the fuzzy transition from light to dark, although fleeting, sent a barrage of the day's memories to his mind's eye, each one a distinct iridescent flash. Watching these flashbulb memories rip through his consciousness one after another was dizzying; it also exacerbated his wounds. The skin of his feet throbbed. A scratch in his trachea sent him into a coughing fit. And although he had eaten, he still felt an emptiness in his stomach. It was the same feeling he'd had since Craig was murdered, and a part of him imagined it may remain there for the rest of his life.

A hollow place carved out by his departed friend.

Against the advice of the doctors, his mum had taken him home from Ballochmyle Hospital. His wounds were apparently minor; mainly a lack of nourishment and a handful of first and second-degree burns. He said goodbye to Gavin, not James, and then spent a few minutes by Fiona's bedside. He found it difficult to leave her.

What is this feeling? he remembered thinking.

After they clasped hands, Arun could hear an exchange between Fiona's parents and his mum, though he didn't pay attention to what was said.

His mum glanced over at him every few seconds on the quiet ride home; her stare was loving, but he could tell this was a nervous tic—making sure he was still there. He glimpsed this same anxiety as she had said goodnight just moments ago. The worry that if she diverted her gaze for too long, or let him out of her grasp, she might lose him again.

He figured he'd do the same if the roles were reversed.

The thought brought up a memory.

One time, he had asked his mum how she managed without her mother.

The way she uttered her answer stuck out in his mind all these years later. The coolness of it, almost stoic: *"People find their own ways to survive."*

Their *own* ways. Distinct to each person. He knew that's what was going on now, in the aftermath. His mother's nervousness, the neurotic glances.

That was how she was choosing to survive—trying to live with the knowledge that her son had gone through Hell and back and came out of it alive.

Arun's ways to survive would develop over the years to come, but tonight's was simple.

He lied.

Twice, actually.

He lied when he told her he would be all right, and he lied again when he said he was so tired he could hardly keep his eyes open.

The truth was that he was wide awake, and as he lay in his too-soft sheets and even softer bed, he grew uncomfortable. Squirming, tossing, and turning until he finally gave up. He slid one leg off the bed, then inched his body down, abandoning both his pillow and blanket.

The cold wooden floor was not the concrete basement, but it blunted the worst of the shock from trying to sleep in a real bed. A place where he'd drift off to a lazy dream or an unwelcome nightmare. A place where the memory of what happened might fade, might slip from his grasp like a slick, slithering eel.

He was afraid he might forget.

This is how I survive, he thought.

He lay on the floor, eyes wide open, staring into the otherworldly eyes of Craig, lying parallel to him across the room.

The two friends stayed like that for hours. One passed, one living—yet the bond between them was as strong as it had ever been.

Arun didn't remember falling asleep.

Across town, Margaret was back home.

The bed seemed to welcome her with open arms; a congratulatory embrace for a job well done. *Keeping my promise*, she thought. Though the house wasn't empty, she felt very much alone—Walter hadn't joined her in bed. He sat in his favourite leather recliner, rocking it slightly, a drink in his hand and an antsy disposition she couldn't put her finger on. She could hear the muted mumblings of whatever mindless programme he was watching through the wall.

Sleep beckoned her, pulling her deeper within its tender grip, and as she felt herself drifting, she flinched violently awake.

You've done all you can do, her mind chided. It was right. The bodies of the thirteen frozen children had been moved to the coroner's office for identification. Arun, Gavin, James, and Fiona were safe. There was only one who hadn't made it out alive—Craig Robertson. She hadn't yet found the strength to face Elaine and George. A small nagging voice at the back of her mind scathingly said: *If you'd found them sooner, Craig would be alive.*

She tried to push the thought away, and by dodging it, she fell back into slumber's grasp. The clock on her bedside table read 3:45 in the morning—she'd been up for close to twenty-four hours. Her eyelids grew leaden, and as they fluttered closed, for the first time in sixteen years, she didn't see the little girl cowering in the corner of her room, transmitting a silent plea to Margaret, not to leave her alone.

Every night since the girl's death, Margaret would see her, sitting across the bedroom floor, casting an unblinking stare. Never saying a word but haunting her, nonetheless. An obstinate reminder of her decision to do nothing.

But she was gone.

Margaret wasn't certain if the girl's disappearance stemmed from today's deed. She wasn't sure if the cosmic scales of karma were finally balanced. But she quietly thanked the Lord, over and over until she met the first lull of slumber.

Thanked Him because for the first night in sixteen years, all she saw was darkness.

Judge Alexander Mackay rolled a pen back and forth between his forefinger and thumb. He normally wasn't one for mindless tics, but he was fighting hard to stomach the two dozen photos splayed across his bench.

He took a quick gulp of the bitter, tepid coffee that his aide had poured when he first arrived. *Tick-tock, tick-tock, tick-tock.* The hands of the large clock on the far wall crept towards midnight, producing the only audible sounds in the large space. Even the handful of people seemed to be holding their breath.

Waiting for him.

The Judge had been awoken just before eleven, informed of the arrest of Albert Reid. The officer on the other line asked him a slew of questions, attempting to schedule an arraignment for the following day. He refused, pulling his old, achy body out of bed, and told the officer the arraignment would take place within the hour in the Kilmarnock Court. He'd been waiting anxiously for the past two weeks, watching the coverage of the missing lads day after day.

This ad hoc midnight hearing had come together just as smoothly as Judge Mackay planned. No reporters. No nosy passersby crowding the seats. Just a few officers, Sergeant Stu from Cumnock, his aide, the court stenographer…

…and Albert Reid.

He sat across from him in shackles, head down.

The Judge returned his attention to the photos. Thirteen were of the naked bodies of the children, skin grey and ashen, eyes closed. One mangled corpse of Craig Robertson. A photo of the frozen room. Four photos of the charred, badly burnt holding rooms within Al's basement. The remaining photos were of equipment—cleavers, knives, and scalpels. Syringes and a cocktail of anaesthetic drugs.

"Sheriff, please have the defendant rise," he began, clearing his throat. "I'm not certain it matters, but for the record. On the fourteen counts of kidnapping and murder, Albert Reid, how do you plead?"

The court held its collective breath.

Al, now standing, did not raise his head to meet Judge Mackay's eyes.

"Guilty," he said.

No one uttered a word. The clacking of the stenographer's keys filled the room.

The plea did not placate the Judge's restless soul, because after thirty years serving as East Ayrshire's highest-ranking judicial official, he knew better. Righting one wrong wouldn't bring back the fourteen lives robbed.

Nothing could.

He gathered the photos with a sweep of his hand.

"The evidence before me is beyond damning. These crimes are unprecedented in this court of law and will forever be a stain on East Ayrshire's history. Murders that had no motive other than to kill, a reckless disregard for these innocent lives whose futures were stolen from them."

Judge Mackay took a steadying breath and noticed the sweeping silence of the room. The stenographer's fingers rested just above the metal keys of the typewriter, waiting.

"There will be no trial. Your confession and the physical evidence warrant my immediate verdict. Albert Reid, you are to be sentenced to death by hanging tomorrow at 15:00."

He pounded the gavel.

Its fateful echo travelled far across the dim Scottish night.

A droning voice trickled into Princess Edith's dream space, like a TV with wavering signal, staticky and intermittent. The bright light of a midsummer morning beat against the thin skin of her eyelids. She blinked; the tears on her face had evaporated overnight, leaving behind a fine, brackish dust. As her conscious mind came to, physical sensations switched on like a series of electric circuits. The pain in her back from falling asleep halfway between the floor and a chaise. Her throat felt tight with every breath, aching and raw.

She propped herself up against the chaise. Her arm tingled with a flurry of invisible ants; she realised she'd fallen asleep with her arm folded against her, clutching the photo of her and Leon at Osborne House that Easter morning. She shook out the sensation and placed the frame next to her.

"…In an ad hoc midnight ruling, Judge Alexander Mackay of the Kilmarnock Sherriff's Court sentenced Albert Reid to be executed by hanging at 15:00 today…"

The words that followed were garbled, unintelligible. She whipped around, eyes settling on the hands of the grandfather clock—

05:35.

She rose to her feet and began the trek upstairs to her study. The permeating cold radiating from the centre of her chest pruned each and every nerve in her body, sapping them of sensation. She felt like a walking corpse headed to a date with destiny. The voices of the newscast were now soft murmurs as she reached the second floor.

The path to her desk elongated, a supernatural stretching of time and space. She waded through the room, air thick with gloom, each forceful step a deliberate effort to reach her destination. The polished serpentine mahogany desk baulked at her cold fingers as she traced them upwards, pulling a jewellery box sitting in the back corner toward her.

Opening it was dreamlike; seeing the ornate silver key lying within caused her heart to flutter. She never imagined this dreaded moment would come. She knelt in front of the desk drawers, slipping the key into the grooved orifice. The sound of the lock catching as she turned it numbed her soul even further.

She pulled the drawer open.

It was empty, save for two sealed letters.

She held them to her chest as she left the room, ran her thumb across the textured paper of the envelope—another grisly reminder that this nightmare was real, that she was indeed awake.

As Princess Edith reached the foyer, she grabbed the doorknob, already knowing precisely where she was headed.

When she swung the door open, she jumped at what she saw.

It was *her*.

Except the Princess Edith who stood at the bottom of the steps was thirty years younger. A long-forgotten memory. A cruel apparition intent on torment. The ghost of herself held her gaze, emanating a sombre reminder from her blue eyes.

"You have always known. You knew then, and you know now."

Hearing the delicate tenor of her younger voice caused her skin to prickle with gooseflesh.

She then noticed that the look this past version of herself gave wasn't quite square with where she stood.

As if she was looking *through* her—at something else.

Princess Edith glanced around and saw that housed within the slight reflection cast off the protruding bay windows was another ghost of her past.

Sir Charles' spectral form, a wispy outline of the man she remembered, stood exactly where she was standing. In the same spot; the ghost and the living converged in an overlapping, invisible border. She flicked her gaze back down to younger Princess Edith, and then it hit her.

She was staring up at *Sir Charles*.

This scene she'd stumbled onto wasn't supernatural in origin, but a memory.

A final barbed jab from the heavens, a malicious, physical manifestation of the moment she had tried to bury in the recesses of her mind, avoiding it at all costs.

She watched as the reflection of Sir Charles mouthed the words she'd heard echoing in her mind since the news of Leon's arrest yesterday, like a record whose needle was caught endlessly on the same sadistic lyric. The words from that memory, thirty years ago, were uttered from the top of these steps to a Princess Edith who was more naïve but equally as miserable.

"I hope for the sake of our son that your decision to do nothing never comes back to haunt you."

Princess Edith's steps synchronised with the faint echo of the grandfather clock's metronomic ticking. She held the sound in the forefront of her mind—a poignant reminder of passing time.

The fleeting nature of the moment at hand.

It was a little over a mile to Kensington Palace, and she'd run practically the entire way. Pushing past strangers, illegally crossing busy intersections, and ignoring the gawking passersby who recognised her. Commoners weren't used to seeing a royal share their pavement.

But she hadn't time to sit in London traffic. She only trusted her two feet.

Her breath was ragged as she reached the palace gardens, cutting through the manicured greenery, legs burning as she sped up in the final stretch to her destination.

John the Guardsman saw her before she saw him. He caught the flitting of her dress fabric zipping through the hedges.

Princess Edith watched John's shoulders sink the moment they met eyes. After all these years, she knew that her arrival heralded nothing but misfortune for her old friend.

She bounded up the steps, still hearing the ticking metronome in her head, attempting to outrun the rhythm of passing seconds.

Hurry, her mind prodded. *You're running out of time.*

As she reached John the Guardsman, a swell of emotion billowed through her spirit, threatening to escape in the form of tears.

"John," she croaked. "It's Leon, he—"

"I know." He cut her off and kept his eyes fixed on the rifle he held with a white-knuckled grip. "I heard, Edith…"

She choked back a cry. It took all her strength just to breathe steadily, to not blubber when she had to get this message out.

"I have one final favour to ask of you."

John did not look up.

She saw a twinge of regret flicker behind his tired countenance, then rested a gentle hand on his forearm.

"Please," she rasped. "I need my son to know his mother's name."

It may have been from the glare of the morning rays, but she swore she saw tears glistening in his eyes.

"John…" She retrieved the two letters from her handbag and extended them toward him. "I beg of you. Get these to Leon."

"I can't leave my post—"

"I'll handle it. Just go, now."

"Why don't you?"

His question had a sharp edge that stung.

"I haven't the strength to make the drive, and I can't let the public…"

"Edith, even now?" snorted John. "On the dawn of his death you're still thinking like the Queen."

She grimaced before shooting him a stern look.

"The world needn't know my mistakes. I just need *him* to know. He must, before..."

She dropped her gaze in an attempt to shield him from seeing tears.

John stared down at this ageing Princess with a broken soul the same way he had since the night she'd informed him of her dilemma twenty years prior. With pity.

He reached out and took the two letters from her wavering hand.

"I'll go," he said. "Not as a final favour to you or Leon. But because it's the right thing to do. Because since the news yesterday I can't help but think about the cheques. About the horrors you inadvertently funded—"

"Stop," she said, wincing. "Just go."

He let out a long, troubled sigh. "I pray the Lord forgives me for my hand in this mess." He gave one last formal bow to the Princess. "And I hope for your sake he does the same for you."

John the Guardsman left her side, breaking his post for the first time in his career. As he made the trek back to his residence to fetch his car, he had a little word with God.

He prayed that he would never see Princess Edith again.

Neither in this life or the next.

Aniqa joined Arun in the dining room. They sat at a cramped end sliver of the table because she hadn't made time to clean. Instead, she'd pushed all the clutter that had accumulated throughout the past two weeks over to make just enough space to eat. She filled Arun's teacup, then hers. She dipped a piece of toast into the fried eggs to break the yolk.

After the first few bites of her breakfast, she looked over at Arun.

Aniqa watched him fiddle with the tomato on his plate, pushing it around with his fork. He'd made a dent in his eggs, beans—her brow furrowed when she noticed he had slipped the sausage links and black pudding off his plate entirely. They sat uneaten, wrapped in a napkin.

"Why haven't you touched those?" she asked, mouth full, pointing with her fork. "Black pudding is your favourite."

"Not now." He chewed the inside of his cheek, averting her gaze. "I can't even look at them."

A part of her wanted to press for a *why*, but she decided against it.

Aniqa continued eating. Arun shovelled a few more bites of beans into his mouth. He even swallowed begrudgingly, as if each additional bite was only meant to placate her prying stare.

"You can stop if you're full."

He pushed the plate forward, dropping his utensils as if they were coated in an invisible grime. In the bit of silence that followed, she realised that though they had been reunited, there was an emptiness in the house that had never been present before. Perhaps she was sensing another iteration of what she'd felt yesterday when looking into her son's eyes.

That Arun was back.

But not the Arun she remembered.

"Can I go lie down? My stomach hurts."

"Just rinse your plate first."

He grabbed his half-eaten breakfast, and hesitated when he reached toward the black pudding and sausage.

"I'll get that for you."

He produced a tepid smile—a silent thanks. A moment later she heard the tap running. When he'd finished, he passed through the dining room to get to his room.

"So," she said.

He stopped before he reached the hallway, turned back. "What?"

"About today. At 15:00…Al's execution."

"I know."

"Do you want to…" Her voice trailed up at the end, the tiniest inflection hinting at a half-finished question.

Arun's expression shifted.

There it is again, she thought. *The new Arun.*

Older, wiser, and undoubtedly damaged.

"I planned on it," he said. The certainty in his voice floored her. Hardly even a teenager, planning on going to an execution with a nonchalance as if it were going to play football with his friends. "Are you?"

"If you want to," she said. "I'll be there with you."

"Okay."

He turned back around, and just as he was about to walk away, a sudden maternal fear coursed through her. She blurted without thinking: "As long as you understand that we'll be watching him die."

Arun froze where he stood. He took a steadying breath. "He killed Craig right in front of me, Mum."

Her soul winced. A twisting, wrenching knot in her gut.

"And now I want to watch him die too," he said flatly, then disappeared down the hall.

John the Guardsman smacked the car horn with an open fist.

"Christ! C'mon, move it, will ya?"

Fast approaching three, he was belly-deep in Edinburgh traffic. First, congestion came from construction. Then, a simple bump between two cars caused other motorists to slow down, ogling at the accident before speeding back up.

He had to make it out of here quickly because he was losing precious time.

John swerved onto the shoulder and floored it.

Once he got through Edinburgh, it was a straight shot to his destination.

As he circumvented the stopped cars, eventually making it to open road, he shot a nervous glance at the two letters resting on the passenger seat.

Hang on, you bloody bastard, he thought. *Don't die just yet.*

The prison came into view through the patrol car's window. Its austere face was speckled with russet-coloured brick that spanned from the ground all the way up to the chimney stacks. The roof was a faded cobalt, and above the entrance were metal letters of the same colour which read: B A R L I N N I E

As the patrol car reached the prison entrance gate, realisation finally hit Al. In a few hours' time, he'd be dead. A series of *lasts* zipped through his mind one after another. *Last building I'll set foot in. Last drive. Last faces I'll see. Last breaths. Last meal. Last day. Last hour. Last minute.*

Despite these frantic thoughts, a peculiar calm permeated through him. A sense of relief from yielding to fate's hand. Perhaps the feeling was bolstered by the presence of music. Rock and Roll sprung from the tinny patrol car radio, and while Al loathed the genre, it was better than nothing.

A prison guard ushered the car forward with a broad wave of his arm, and a loud buzz sounded. As the gate inched open with a mechanical *clack-clack-clack*, another sound emerged.

A surge of muted voices.

"Quite a decent turn out ye got," croaked the officer, without looking in the rearview.

Al straightened his posture and saw a sea of people being split by the patrol car crawling forward. He felt like he was being carted on a conveyor belt, with the onlookers' gawking faces slowly slipping past his window, one by one. They each projected slightly different versions of the same negative energy—scorn, hate, disgust. All aimed at him.

His gut ratcheted tighter as he remembered the last time he'd seen a stare so caustic. The day outside the palace gates when the Queen caught him slaying the dog. A look infused so wholly with revulsion it was as if his mother had etched it into his memory with a sharp chisel.

A bright light tore through the cabin, causing shimmering stars to ripple through Al's vision. Not even a second later, another blinding flash. Reporters congregated at the front of the dense crowd, strategically waiting at the mouth of the prison's entrance. The photographers' flashbulbs burst in quick succession, a dizzying line of white. The squeal of the patrol car's brakes was eclipsed by the discordant roar of the crowd.

"Keep yer head down," said the officer before he stepped out. He pushed against the crowd as he shimmied to the back door. A handful of prison guards appeared; they wedged themselves between the line of onlookers closest to the car. The officer gave Al a nod, then popped open the door.

A tsunami of sensations crashed over him as he stepped out. Hundreds of voices coalesced into an ear-splitting cacophony of heckling hoots and hollers. The flashes intensified as the photographers caught sight of him; a spray of dazzling sunbursts pockmarked his vision with burning halos, and the slow fading of green-white afterglows rendered him blind. The officer tugged at his chains, and as he moved, the guards followed, flanking both sides and corralling him toward the entrance. Just before he made it inside, a wad of spit hit the ground in front of his feet. He turned to find the spitter—a mother standing with her son. She cursed him at the top of her lungs, red in the face, unintentionally squeezing her lad's hand with a vice grip, causing him to wince.

The lad's expression piqued his interest. It wasn't like the others. No unbridled anger or bubbling contempt. Just pure sadness. They held each other's gaze for a split-second, and as the lad attempted to squirm away from his mother's grip, Al heard the words his look conveyed: *Why am I here?*

He knew the question all too well. Every thunderous slap from his mother. The patronising glances from his cousins, their callous jeers reminding him that *you are the black sheep of the family.* The hushed whispers of the staff when he'd enter a room. Alleviating the emptiness when he started killing animals. But truthfully, the question had haunted him long before those incidents. When he noticed the queerness of his own mind. The constant need for background noise. The fact he was always surrounded by people but still felt terribly alone.

The lad slipped out of view as the guards pushed him inside the prison.

Why am I here?

At just eight years old, Al remembered the sordid thought that accompanied the question.

I wish I was never born.

The guards ushered him through the concrete labyrinth of HMP Barlinnie. Al let out a faint titter as he remembered what the three-letter prefix stood for: *Her Majesty's Prison.*

Even in the hour of his death, he couldn't escape his mother's almighty presence.

Aniqa and Arun didn't exchange a word during the fifty-minute drive from Catrine to HMP Barlinnie. Arun was grateful because he hadn't the tiniest shred of desire to talk. He knew *she* certainly could have. Since he'd returned home, the number of furtive glances he caught in his peripheral were growing with every passing hour. She had good reason to be concerned. This morning, she'd found him sleeping on the floor. He could also tell by the tremble in her voice that it shocked her how candidly he had admitted that he wanted to watch Al die.

Wanting to see Al die wasn't rooted in vengeance. He didn't yearn to see him suffer. *An eye for an eye* wouldn't bring Craig back.

Arun wanted to watch Al die because he hoped it would mark the physical end to this nightmare. To all the horrors he wished he could unsee. He prayed that what began with the man with no skin would end after Al took his last breath.

"Look at all these people," said his mum, drawing him from his thoughts.

Arun peered out of the window. A massive crowd stretched from the prison entrance, wrapped around the building, and only tapered off at the edges of the car park. "It's moving," he said. Those waiting were in an amorphous queue, and as people entered the prison, it slunk forward like an accordion. His head bobbed forward as the car came to a stop.

"You ready?" asked his mum as she pulled the hand brake.

He responded with a nod. They left the car and began their trek through the thickening crowd. A chill crept through Arun's chest, and he zipped his jacket closed. Yesterday's mild weather was but a long-lost memory and had been replaced by an unusual cold for the time of year. Thick grey clouds hung low, their wispy tendrils tickling the chimney tops of the prison.

His mum tightened her grip on his hand as they carved a path through the people. Before they could fall into the queue, a man with a cigarette pinched between his moustachioed lips went bug-eyed at the sight of him.

"The lad!" cried the man, hoisting the bulky camera at his side, and the metallic disc atop it suddenly emitted a bright white flash. Other cameramen rushed them, and a few stuck microphones right in front of his mother's face. They bombarded her with questions, and she ignored them, just pulled him along more aggressively, keeping him close. The crowd parted as more people caught notice of the commotion, inadvertently pushing them ahead of the queue. Once the prison guards recognised them, they mobilised to disperse the media and usher them safely inside.

The height of the adults around him eclipsed most of Arun's view. What he could see was lots of concrete. Jail cells lining the walls. The edges of one side of the ceiling were lined with concave glass windows, filling the interior of this gathering space with soft grey light.

"Where will it be?" he asked.

"I don't know, love."

A round, elderly woman adjacent to them caught this interaction. Her face lit up just as the cameraman's had when she saw who he was.

"Ye ought to have a better view than this." The woman cleaved the people in front of her with a stubby arm. "Get outta the way! This laddie made it out with his life, he gets a front row seat."

"You don't have to—"

"Nae danger." The woman pushed them along gently. "Go on."

She kept shouting about who they were, and the crowd slowly split in two, allowing them to the front.

Now, Arun could see.

"Is that—"

"The gallows," said his mum, a solemn tinge to her voice.

In front of them was a raised offshoot from the large room where they waited. The entirety of it was painted stark white. In the centre, a thick rope hung down, a circular opening at its bottom. His eyes wandered to the floor, and he noticed a distinct rectangular border directly beneath the rope. The rectangle was split in half, and it reminded him of the swinging saloon doors from the American westerns that sometimes came on TV, except they were flat on the floor.

If those doors swing open—

The realisation knocked the breath clean from his lungs.

He felt two taps on his shoulder, and when he turned around—

"Fiona!"

He embraced her in a bear hug, and they held each other for what felt like an eternity. When he finally pulled away, he paused to take a good look at her. Cleaned of the dirt and grime, her hair was not sandy, but a bright, straw-coloured blonde. Her shiny face had a rosy hue to it—she must have rested and eaten her fill. Her blue eyes shimmered with excitement, and he wondered if she saw him reciprocate the same. Hidden beneath that was the pain they shared, like a dark shadow in their souls only the two could see.

"You made it," he said.

"I had to convince my parents. They didn't think it was a good idea."

He grabbed her hand. "I'm at least glad I got to see you again."

A heavy *clank* wiped Fiona's broadening smile off her face and made them jump. Silence unfurled its invisible petals until it fully bloomed across the space. In the stillness, the faint rattle of chains echoed from down the long hall lined with cell blocks.

Fiona turned and pointed at the clock on the far wall.

The minute hand hovered just before 15:00.

"It's time," she said.

John the Guardsman raced west along Edinburgh Road, slaloming through the lackadaisical traffic, pleading to the heavens for God to have mercy on his soul just long enough to carry out Princess Edith's final wish. Spittle flew from his lips as he bargained with the Lord, muttering like a madman; in exchange for delivering him safely to the prison, he'd be willing to accept any punishment for the naïve hand he'd had in Al's heinous acts—even damnation.

John knew better. He remembered how the old saying went:

Man plans, and God laughs.

He couldn't alter fate's permanent ink. For what would transpire in the here and now had already been written.

The tachometer needle bounced against the redline, emitting an aspirated whine as he pushed the Mercedes engine to its limit.

"No, no, no—c'mon now!" He punched the dashboard, frustrated.

The fog grew thicker by the second. His visibility of the cars on the road shrunk from three, two…until he could hardly see the bumper in front of him.

There was no choice—he had to slow down.

He scanned the street signs frantically zipping past on his right. Instinct tickled at his neck from having studied the route a dozen times over when he filled the car with petrol.

Any second now…it's coming…it must be…

Cumbernauld Road.

Now!

He jammed his brakes, whipped the wheel right, and careened through the intersection in a smokey vortex of burnt rubber and exhaust fumes as the oncoming cars screeched to a halt to avoid crashing. He locked his elbows, braced his body against the centrifugal force of the drift, and went skittering down Cumbernauld Road before regaining control of the steering.

Within seconds, his destination came into view.

HMP Barlinnie.

He swerved into the car park, made no attempt to find a spot, and pulled up half on a kerb, leaping out from the driver's seat with the letters in hand. He sprinted toward the prison entrance, pulse pounding at his ears, and tried to take a quick glance at his wristwatch. Stinging sweat blurred his vision, and he couldn't make out the precise time, but he was close.

There weren't any stragglers outside the building, and the sight made his heart flutter. He bounded through the entrance and was met with the indistinct edge of the crowd. He pushed through them, and the sickly realisation that not a single person uttered a word slunk down his spine with an electric chill.

It was *far* too quiet.

Three minutes earlier

It's an odd thing, Al mused, *knowing that every step I take is another step closer to death.* He kept his pace even, straightened his spine, elongated his posture. He knew that to the crowd, he was nothing but a vile monster, so at the very least, he intended to die with a bit of dignity. Let those present from the village see a bit of the Al they remembered. The one who stood tall, was even tempered, and looked people in the eye when he spoke.

He made sure to do that now, too, as the prison guard pushed him toward the gallows, and he caught first sight of the crowd.

Look them in the eyes, his mind prodded.

It took strength to hold their gazes, and truthfully, he hadn't much left. He was a tired soul desperate to rest.

The looks they cast were imbued with such scorn and abhorrence and downright rage that every cell in his body begged for him to drop his gaze. To stare at his feet until he walked up those stone steps. He had to remind himself of the truth to remain resolute:

They don't understand. They never had, and they never would. His family hadn't. Even he couldn't fully comprehend it.

He had often wondered if he was born this way, with the darkness lying latent inside, like a black, malignant egg waiting for the right moment to hatch. Or rather, had this cruel world moulded him into who he became? Carving his soul with its sharp claws, rendering him empty and forever bearing the scars.

If there was an afterlife, perhaps he might get an answer.

Alas, he figured God wouldn't grant him the satisfaction of knowing.

Better yet, he wondered if he could ask a question of his own. The one that had crossed his mind an infinite number of times. From the very first night when he gutted Midnight, to the more recent mornings he would spend marvelling at his frozen works of art. Despite being cogently aware of his guilt, and having accepted that the darkness radiating through him couldn't be wrung from the fibres of his soul, this still was the question that kept him up, night after night:

If God was truly all-knowing and all-powerful, why did he let me set foot on this earth?

His own foot hitting the first step drew him back to the present.

The thirteen steps to the top of the gallows seemed to shrink as he scaled them. Each subsequent raise of his leg felt heavier, as if the muscles themselves could sense the impending doom that awaited him. He became acutely aware of his breath and realised these were the last minutes with air in his lungs.

As Al reached the platform, his eyes drifted to the noose hanging from the ceiling. Flanking it were the chaplain and the executioner, who stared stoically, watching him approach. Unconsciously, he must have slowed— the prison guard nudged him forward.

This is it, he thought, and his heart began to thud percussively in his chest.

The executioner slipped out a pocket watch from the breast of his fashionable grey tweed suit. He glanced at the time, then shut its metal lid with a quick flick of his wrist. He gave the chaplain a nod.

As the chaplain began his prayer, Al found himself studying the executioner. He had rather round cheeks for a thin fellow, large earlobes that stuck out, and heavy brows that sat above sparkling blue eyes. An air of gentleness exuded from him; a quality Al found peculiar for the man who was about to lead him to death.

The executioner pulled the black hood from his pocket, ruffling it out.

"First time I've had the guilty share my name," he said, a bittersweet titter escaping his lips. There wasn't a hint of mockery in his tone. Only remorse.

"Turn forward."

Al listened to the instructions, then felt a hand on the small of his back push him to where he stood beneath the noose. The executioner reached up, took a portion of the rope in each hand, and guided the opening to rest around his neck. He walked around, pulling at the knot to ensure it was snug against his chin.

Now, Al faced the crowd. The last faces he'd ever see.

He saw those closest to him—Aniqa, Arun, Fiona, her parents, Craig's parents—Elaine being the one who glowered with the most animosity. Amidst the mass of people, he spotted a black pulpit robe—*Louise.* His gut panged at the thought that even she had come to witness his death.

As he surveyed the crowd, a sudden shift of movement at the back of the room caught his eye. Someone was running, pushing past the thickening crowd, carving a path deeper toward the gallows. Al couldn't get a good look at their face because they bounced off people, one after another, with an unusual foolhardiness, like a pinball ricocheting with no goal other than to keep its momentum.

As the person reached the centre of the crowd, he stopped and looked up, meeting Al's gaze.

The face staring back at him was one he hadn't seen in decades, but he remembered it all the same. It belonged to his old friend—John the Guardsman.

Even from afar, Al could see the vein bulging on his weathered forehead, his neck muscles taut, chest heaving in rapid breath. His lips trembled as if he were holding back, like he wanted to say something—

With a *whooshing* black blur, the hood was thrown over Al's head.

Beneath the thick cloth, only the faintest light slipped in. A thread of panic began to unspool within him, beginning at his gut and spiralling outward through his limbs.

Why is John here? The thought zipped through his mind, followed by a frantic flurry of others. *Someone from my past. To the world I was already dead. Why would he come?*

There was no turning back; no conceivable way to get his questions answered. He stood there, awaiting each passing moment with dread, wondering which breath would be his last.

Then, the floor gave out.

His stomach dropped for a split-second as he fell, and the entirety of his weight caught at his neck with a loud *snap*. The coarse fibres of the thick manila rope tightened as he swung to and fro, cinching the arteries in his neck, crushing his windpipe. He could feel the tiny capillaries popping in his eyes from the building pressure. His lungs flexed inwards as they became starved of oxygen, heart racing at an unbearable pace. And much to his horror, he realised the fright induced by John's arrival had been accompanied by something else.

The emptiness.

A terror unlike anything he'd ever known plunged its invisible fist into his chest, grasping his floundering heart with a white-hot grip, squeezing it tight, sending electric shockwaves of agony along his nerves. But soon, an icy numbness spread from the centre of his chest, and his thoughts felt fuzzy. Behind the fading pain and the dulling sensations of imminent death, he couldn't help but fixate on the overwhelming silence.

Cloaked by the black hood, the pounding of his heart fell to the wayside, and it was as if the entire room held its collective breath. Not a whisper. Not a shuffle. Just pure, soul-crushing silence. He imagined that the hundreds of people were leveraging the quiet hanging in the air, like a membrane they could press their ears against, a conduit for the *one* sound they were desperately waiting to emerge.

Al's final breath.

His life flashed before his eyes, a maelstrom of scarce joy and abundant horror, memories he'd tried so hard to forget, the darkness he'd attempted to keep locked away. As his body went limp, the irony of his final moment flittered through his failing mind.

The emptiness was his lone companion in death. He had spent his entire life avoiding it, and now it welcomed him into its suffocating embrace. No tunnel of light. Just its icy cold touch, extinguishing the last of his life spark, calling him back into the black womb from whence he came.

"Time of death, 15:03," said the executioner, flicking his pocket watch closed.

The chitter-chatter of the crowd resumed. Those who had watched couldn't understand the significance of what they'd just witnessed; the truth only known to Aniqa and John the Guardsman. That despite there being only one body hanging from the noose, two people had been sentenced to death today.

Albert Reid *and* Duke Leon of Albemarle.

CHAPTER 27
THE SHADOWS THE DEVIL CAST

Aniqa squeezed Arun's hand tighter as Al's body went limp. A sudden realisation hit her like a freight train: *I gained my son back, and Princess Edith just lost hers.*

Her mind went hazy as the guards pulled Al down from the noose. She waited for something within her to shift; a palpable change in the air after Al died, a clear delineation between the horrors of the past two weeks and the after.

But the shift never came. She was forced to grapple with the idea that the normal life she'd once led may never return. The reality that Al's death wasn't an end at all. But rather a beginning, and those left in the wake of his black shadow were forced to pick up the pieces. Forced to try and mould the broken remnants until a new life took shape.

"You're hurting my hand," said Arun, wincing.

Her conscious mind came back online, and she turned to see Fiona's parents staring at her with a mild look of concern. She released her grip.

"Ye all right?" asked Fiona's father.

"Of course. Just a bit shocked is all."

Someone bumped into Aniqa's back, nearly knocking her off-kilter. The massive crowd was shuffling towards the exit.

"Let's follow them before we get trampled," said Fiona's mum.

Aniqa kept Arun at her side. It warmed her heart seeing how overjoyed he was to be with Fiona. How gently he held her hand. The way the two looked at each other. Fiona's mum must have caught this interaction, because the two mothers met eyes and exchanged a tickled smile.

The crowd thinned as they neared the exit, and Aniqa saw the profile of a man's face slipping out the prison doors. Weathered skin, bushy brows, and a thousand-yard stare that screamed exhaustion.

I've seen him before, she thought.

John the Guardsman.

Go after him, another voice prodded. But it wasn't hers.

It was Princess Edith's.

Now! she bellowed, echoing like thunder in her mind.

Her voice jolted her spirit, and she turned to Fiona's parents.

"Watch Arun for a moment."

They obliged with a bewildered nod.

She leaned down to her son. "Stay with Fiona, all right?"

"Okay."

Aniqa felt a grotesque pulling sensation in the centre of her chest. As if John had his own gravity, drawn to him by an unknown force too strong to ignore.

"Pardon me," she said repeatedly as she pushed through the exit, trying to lay eyes on John again. As she neared the car park, she caught sight of the wispy hairs atop his balding head.

"John!" she shouted, pleading internally that her instinct hadn't lied.

He turned around, and his jaw dropped.

"It's you."

John the Guardsman knew there was a wistfulness to his words, a disbelief she could read clearly.

"What are you doing here?"

Shamefaced, he clicked his tongue, dropping his gaze to the ground.

He reached into his jacket pocket and felt the edges of the letters.

"I…"

"What is it?"

He didn't know what to say. Then, something Princess Edith had said this morning resurfaced.

"I told her everything. She knows, John. She knows the truth."

A shiver crept up his spine.

Why did Edith tell me that?

"John?" Aniqa's voice broke into his thoughts.

Pins and needles prickled his skin from head to toe, and the edges of his body felt indistinct—almost like an invisible, staticky border rippled around where he stood. His hand grasped the letters and pulled them from his pocket.

John lowered his voice, leaning in. "Princess Edith's final wish. She wanted…" He glanced around, checking for eavesdroppers. "…*him* to know the truth before he died." A defeated snort escaped his lips. "I didn't make it in time…"

Aniqa broke her spellbound stare at the letters and looked up at him. "What will you do with them?"

Her question prodded his soul, stoking the embers he'd attempted to smother in years past. A resurgent wave of memories crashed over his mind, drowning him in a black, soupy mixture of regret—the first night Leon had returned to the palace with a bloody fist in his pocket, keeping mum about the boy's midnight ventures in the gardens, and not telling Princess Edith the truth about her son the night she told him the story of the lie. Those decisions seemed so miniscule at the time, but now, John the Guardsman could see they were but the toppling of dominos, spurring an endless chain reaction whose path of destruction had ultimately led to this.

He felt her hand grip his forearm, snapping him out of the daze.

"Well, you are a mother too," he said pensively, looking over her shoulder at Arun, approaching with the blonde girl and her family.

My time's running out, he thought.

In the farthest reaches of his gut, he craved nothing more than to sever the connection, rip free from the rotted cord tying him to the lie. The dark legacy he'd helped create.

"Take them." He pushed the letters into her hands.

"I can't—I… I don't—" she said, dithering.

"Do with them as you please. She told me that you know the truth."

"Then why don't you destroy them?"

He smothered a laugh.

"I've had a hand in this mess for far too long, my dear. I'm partly responsible for it, you know. The cheques. The lie." He gently grabbed her hands, pressing her palm over the letters. "She told you for a reason, Aniqa. I may not know it, and you neither. But I've known her since she was a child, and I'm certain of it."

"Wh—what on earth should I do with them?" she stammered.

John the Guardsman smiled. "Burn them, publish them for the world to see, what have you. Nevertheless, they are yours now, and that's your decision to make. Not mine."

He dipped away just before her family arrived at her side. As he slipped through the crowd, he could hear the faint voice of her son asking, "Who was that man?"

"Just someone I know from work, love," she said. A slight scrunch of Arun's brow informed her she hadn't sold him on the answer.

"I'll ring you soon so these two can meet up," said Aniqa with a smile to Fiona's mum. She watched the two children embrace as they said their goodbyes.

A warm sensation tickled the side of Aniqa's cheek. She raised her hand, touching the source of the peculiar sensation, and then noticed her hand warming too. Her eyes squinted as the faces of Arun and Fiona's family grew brighter, trying to adjust to the shifting exposure.

She turned and looked toward the sky.

Rays of light poked through the thick grey clouds. They multiplied by the second, revealing little pockets of blue, and she watched in awe as the last of the shadow disintegrated before her eyes.

Soon, all the heads in the crowd peered upward.

For the first time in as long as any of them could remember, the sun came out.

Margaret cupped her face with her hands, shielding her eyes from the bright fluorescents of Stu's office. She gently rubbed the skin of her browbone in hopes that it would soothe the stress running rampant through her. Last night she had rested. The little girl who haunted her dreams was gone. But she also realised that Al's arrest wasn't a cure-all. She couldn't wave a magic wand and erase the trauma of what she'd seen throughout the past two weeks.

Because today was a new day, but she was still Margaret.

The same Margaret who two weeks ago had prayed to the Lord for her life to be worth living, just for a little while.

Her wish had come true.

But at what cost?

She gulped, her throat dry, wincing at the thought.

You can go home now, her mind prodded.

She rubbed her eyes a final time, rousing herself back to baseline. She pocketed her patrol car keys—a nagging reminder of Al's lie, the fact

Stu had believed it, and the incredible lengths she had gone to prove her theory right. She was officially back on as an officer.

You're tired, her mind butted in again. *Go home.*

She ambled to the door more like the living dead than an actual human being. Stu was partly to blame. He had questioned her all morning, forcing her to retell the events that transpired in Al's house from beginning to end a hundred times over. An inspector from the National Police was in critical condition after being stabbed by the orphan, James. Which technically happened on her watch.

As she stepped out into the hall, she came face to face with someone she hadn't spoken to in ages—Annie Stewart.

She revealed an anxious, gummy smile. Arms crossed, she kept glancing between the floor and Margaret, as if she had to amass a plethora of courage just to maintain eye contact. "Can we speak for a moment, in my office?"

"Aye. Is everything all right?"

Annie simply gestured with a wave for her to follow, and they began the quick walk to the admin office. "I don't want to answer that question out here," she muttered under her breath.

It was during those handful of steps following Annie that Margaret realised that all morning she had been with Stu. The moment after he left the station, Annie appeared.

Was she waiting for me this whole time?

Once inside the office, she slanted the shades shut, then with just a silent look, both of Annie's assistants left the room, as if this moment had been carefully rehearsed.

"What's going on, Annie?"

Annie fanned out a half-dozen manila folders on her desk, letting out a shuddering sigh.

"These are our donation records," she began shakily, clicking her tongue with self-reproach. "Well, these are the records since I've been keeping them. The past twenty years to be exact."

"And?"

"Before you open this, I wanted to say…I'm sorry."

She slid a manila folder to Margaret. Then she stood, and continued the nervous babbling: "Sorry, 'cause if it weren't for the fact that I spend most of my time watching the lot of you, I wouldn't have noticed."

"What am I looking at here?" Margaret thumbed through the paperwork.

Annie pulled a few pages out of their folders, pointing to a handful of dates and numbers that had been underlined. "Albert Reid has been donating to the station in the amount of £500 every month for the past ten years."

"Tell me yer pulling me leg."

"Nae," she said, fidgeting with the edges of another folder. "He's consistently been the largest donor—" Margaret was about to speak, but Annie cut her off. "Which, on its face isn't a problem, is it? I would have left it at that if it weren't for the way Stu was actin'. Right before the magistrate gave the first warrant for the search of Al's house, he looked sicker than I've ever seen him."

Margaret felt dizzy, reading the countless dates; '63, '62, '61, on and on, every month, year after year.

"—That's why I made copies," continued Annie. "Found scratches around the keyhole of the donation records filing cabinet, too."

"What's all this have to do with Stu?"

"Well…" Annie dropped her gaze.

The prolonged pause made Margaret's stomach swim with nausea. "Out with it already."

"I wondered the same thing. After he asked me for copies of the records—made up some dodgy excuse about needing them for the National Police's records—I went to pay a visit to Deborah. Our representative at the bank. She manages the station's account…"

There it was again, thought Margaret, growing impatient. *That reserve.* As if every word the poor woman pushed out stung like she was chewing on broken glass.

"…I sat with her and compared our donation records to the physical deposits to the account. And they don't match. Twenty percent was missing from the final deposit. It took Deborah a while to figure out why, but that's when she discovered her manager had been the one to alter the deposit slips. Making them all match, so the twenty percent seemed to disappear into thin air."

"Her *manager*…" Margaret's voice trailed off, eyes glazing over.

"Walter made it disappear."

"No, it can't—he wouldn't—"

Margaret fought the urge to retch, her world spinning, cold sweat beading along her temples.

"Deborah discovered a single account shared by Stu and Walter. They each withdrew their ten percent share, keeping the account bare, so as to not attract attention."

"I can't…" murmured Margaret, grabbing onto the desk to hold herself steady.

"They each pocketed fifty pounds a month for the past ten years. Which by my calculations amounts to," she paused, glancing down at her paperwork, "£6,000 apiece."

Margaret began seeing old memories in a new light. The hefty down payment they put on the house. His truck, that he'd purchased outright in cash. The fact he never mentioned any money troubles, though they seldom received raises. She had never thought twice about Walter managing their finances, and now she regretted being so naïve, especially when their neighbours all around them were struggling to make ends meet.

"I'm sure they didn't know…" began Annie, carefully mulling her words. "What Al was really up to."

Margaret stood, taking a moment as she drifted woozily off-centre.

"That's the thing I don't get," continued Annie. "Al has the restaurant, but you'd think he'd be pouring most of his cash into the Kirk and Kissinger Grounds. There shouldn't be much left over. She couldn't give me the exact number, but Deborah told me Al was loaded. Might have one of the biggest accounts in all of Scotland, she says…"

"Doesn't matter where he got the money," said Margaret, bracing herself with the desk. "Look what he did with it. The museum of nightmares in that basement." She slid the manila folder back to Annie. "Not only is it blood money, but it's illegal to steal donations. Even if that was what the three of them arranged."

"Aye, it is."

"Annie. I want you to take the documents and head to Ayr. Stu's boss works there. Take Deborah if you can."

"I was hoping you'd join me," said Annie.

"I will," she said, heading for the door. "But first I have to pay a visit to Walter."

Margaret stewed with revulsion as she tramped down the hall. Now that the truth had been revealed, she could finally see clearly. The way Stu was reluctant in every step of the investigation. How he believed the lie Al crafted with the false statement. The many hoops the department had to jump through for a warrant. The way he piddled around Al's house during the first search.

Sergeant Stuart wasn't an evil man, but he was a greedy coward. It was the possibility that petrified him—that the man who had lined his pockets for the past ten years was someone other than who he made himself out to be.

That fear was imbued in every action. A willful ignorance that may have cost Craig his life.

As Margaret cranked her patrol car and raced home, she went numb. She had to mentally detach from her soon-to-be former boss and her husband. Because no matter how much pain it caused her thinking about her own life being bolstered by Al's funds, it wasn't her fault.

Walter and Stu had chosen to make those decisions.

Now they would have to face the consequences of their actions.

Two days later

Craig's funeral was held at midday in the Catrine Cemetery. The gentle pitter-patter of a sun shower proved a jarring contrast to Elaine's shuddering sobs. Dappled light shone on those in the crowd, and the surrounding hills glistened with a fresh coat of moisture, heightening the deep verdant hues of summer.

Arun found it peculiar how nature's paintbrush chose to make such a dismal day colourful.

Elder Louise read a passage from Matthew as the pallbearers lowered an empty pine casket into the ground. He'd heard rumours that what was left of Craig's body was so badly mangled that the Robertsons chose to cremate the remains. But due to their strong Christian faith, they went through all the motions to give themselves and the community a proper chance to mourn. Instead, they placed memorabilia of their son inside the coffin. Photos, toys, his favourite sweets—Arun suggested they put in a Bobby Lennox jersey he always wore.

Fiona squeezed his hand as the casket hit the bottom with a soft thud. Her parents had allowed her to attend. He wondered what they thought of their daughter's fondness for him. Not that it really mattered in the end, because they would never understand it. The time they spent in that basement had formed an unbreakable bond between them.

Arun and Fiona were sandwiched between his mum, Craig's parents, and Fiona's parents. His mum nestled next to Elaine, who held onto George and her whilst crying. All the eyes in the crowd were on them—the people directly affected by Al's sins.

But there was someone he knew their eyes looked past. Nor could anyone else see.

The ghost of Craig stood adjacent to Arun, watching the pallbearers heave dirt onto his own casket. Much like the first night he'd slept back at home, he wondered if the Craig he saw now was just a figment of his imagination.

Even if that were the case, he was grateful.

Because every day since his best mate died, the world around him seemed darker.

Buckingham Palace

Two quick raps came at Queen Eleanor's chamber doors.

"A letter arrived."

She recognised Jean Claude's muffled voice.

"Come in," she said, not glancing up from the newspaper as Jean Claude entered. She was skimming yet another front-page story about Albert Reid's execution with such astounding aloofness that it gave her goosepimples. Reading about her son's death as if it were a column about sports or politics or the weather. She had no other choice. *Keep your emotions at bay, Eleanor*, she reminded herself constantly. *You cannot let them see it troubling you.*

She finally looked up at Jean Claude when he arrived at the foot of her chaise. The face that stared back at her was emotionless—as if he too were detaching mentally from what had transpired these past few days.

He handed her the letter. "I believe this is his last."

She produced a thin smile. "Very well then. Please leave me be."

Jean Claude gave a quick bow and turned for the door.

Queen Eleanor crossed the sitting room and retrieved a gilded paper knife from her desk. A sense of melancholy spread through her chest as she realised this was the final correspondence. The last letter she would ever open. She slipped the knife through the envelope and began reading where she stood.

Dear Mother,

I write this knowing that the police will be beating down my door any second. It's only now that I am realising the truth at hand. That in building this life for myself, I gave Albert Reid great freedom. But in exchange for that liberation, I kept Duke Leon locked away. His spirit became slave to the charade. He did slip out at times, but even in those instances, I kept his presence hidden below. Throughout my life, I wished for nothing more than to be good. A good son, a good friend, a good man. Fate had another trajectory in mind. Though, I often wonder who gave me that initial push towards the tracks of darkness. On the contrary, this sickness could very well have been in my veins from the day I was born. We do share the blood of tyrants. Conquerors. People who will lie just to keep their power.

My evil deeds are soon to be revealed to the world. But do not fret, as my real identity will die along with me. Queen Eleanor of Lancaster's legacy is safe and sound. I do regret that I must admit a few things before I go. In all these letters over the years, I have erred in addressing each with Dear Mother. You may have reared me. Clothed me. Fed me. But you never once showed me love as a mother should. I loathe giving you the satisfaction of knowing, but I still to this day wonder why. Why strike me but not embrace? Why stare like I am more a nuisance than a mere child whose fragile heart pumps the same blood running through your veins?

I may not know the reason behind your cruelty, but I do remember. I remember the day you made me eat the piece of dog. I remember when you banished me in Baden-Baden. I remember that your last words hinted at the fact you killed my real father.

I remember that you laughed.

I did not share in your amusement.

But perhaps you will find this next bit as amusing as I do.

For the last ten years throughout your visits, when you dined at TLC, I've been feeding you the flesh of Scotland's vilest. Addicts, bastards, rapists. All while I watched you savour every morsel in your gluttonous mouth.

You always said that you wished I'd tell you one day.

Now you know the secret.

Surely by the time you are reading this, you will have seen what was unearthed from my basement. I'll never understand why you began sending the cheques, but at least you can finally see where your money went.

Your son,

Duke Leon of Albemarle

A tremor arose in the Queen's gut; it rippled violently outward, amplified by the pounding of her heart. She darted toward the master bathroom, teetering with every step as she broke into profuse sweat. The reflection she caught in the mirror was a sickly shade of green. She lurched forward, catching the porcelain rim with her clammy hands just in time before retching the contents of her stomach into the toilet.

The putrid smell of the half-digested eggs and haddock she'd had for breakfast made her gag, spurring another wave of vomit. Once her stomach was empty, and acidy yellow bile was all that was left, she still felt ill. She was confronted by the notion that no amount of retching would rid her of the knowledge of what she'd been eating twice a year for the past decade.

Queen Eleanor trembled as she pulled herself to her feet and wiped her mouth with a washcloth. She took a moment to steady herself, let the blood return to her head, then lumbered across her chambers to the telephone.

Jean Claude flinched as he heard the shrill shattering of glass. The teacup and carafe on the silver serving tray he held juddered as thundering knocks of falling furniture came from inside the Queen's quarters.

Although the thick wooden doors dampened the sound, he could hear the rasped screams of Queen Eleanor clear as day: "You sent him *money*?!"

Osborne House, Isle of Wight

Princess Edith set the telephone down whilst Queen Eleanor's tinny screams could still be heard from the receiver. She walked listlessly from her state room, down the marble staircase, through the grand parlour, and out onto the sandstone mezzanine.

The balmy air's typical gentle lilt was gone; she instead was met with salty gusts whose intensity waxed and waned carelessly, stinging her nose and making her eyes water. Despite the weather's fickle temperament, the vista from atop the mezzanine was still marvellous. Beyond the tree line, the inky indigo waters of the Solent lapped rhythmically at the shoreline, and the sun had just disappeared beneath the horizon, leaving traces of its departure in the display of colours streaked across the sky—a luminous mixture of red, magenta, and violet.

"Red skies at night, shepherd's delight," muttered Princess Edith amusingly. She hadn't seen the sky so brilliant in years.

It must be a good omen, she thought.

She descended the stone steps onto the lower terrace and circled the fountain, passing the statue that stood at its centre. She'd seen it countless times throughout her life, and even as a little girl, she remembered being perplexed not by the bronze woman's naked body, but how her hands were tied behind her back in chains.

"Andromeda," her mother had called it.

The poor woman statue simply having a name didn't placate young Princess Edith, as she remembered it. She wanted to know why her hands were chained. The Queen explained that Andromeda was the daughter of an Ethiopian King who had been chained to a rock as a sacrifice to a sea-monster, but was saved by the audacious Perseus.

Princess Edith continued walking down the garden path, letting Andromeda and her chains disappear in the dim twilight behind her. A titter escaped her lips at the irony—the statue that had piqued her interest the most as a child was but a prescient warning of the life that would await her.

The invisible chains bound at her wrists the moment she was born a royal.

Yet she had never broken free, despite having always held the key. Sir Charles had come close to pushing her over that edge. The leap of faith that would have led to freedom. But even he failed. She instead shrank away, pouring her miserable spirit into her art. The countless paintings and sculptures that were no remedy for the pain but sufficed just enough for her to survive.

If only she had known that her decision to do nothing would ultimately lead to not only her son's death, but the death of over a dozen others.

Children.

She winced at the thought. *What if I had raised him? What if he had known me as his mother?* But now, these nagging questions were futile. Too late to contemplate what could have been.

Princess Edith staggered as a squall knocked her forward, as if the wind itself were attempting to hasten the inevitable. She continued down the path and reached the swatch of trees closest to the water. She'd cut through them many a time, whether it be playing with Princess Maud or even alone. They surrounded the Swiss Cottage: a brown, Alpine-style chalet—whose interior had been constructed at three-quarters size—so the royal children could practice cooking and gardening. But she hadn't wandered to the Swiss Cottage to reminisce of the days of yesteryear.

She instead searched for something among the trees, squinting through the fast-fading twilight in the hopes that she'd see its face. A memory burned in her mind's eye; the umbrella-shaped clusters of tiny white flowers, wavering atop stems that rose above her head as a child. But what had prickled the hairs on the back of her neck was how the groundskeepers reacted when she picked the flowers as a child. They cut the lot of them down and ripped out the roots.

Still, she knew they spread like weeds. Every summer they returned, hidden by the trees at the water's edge. She just prayed that they hadn't been cut down yet this season.

Where are you…?

She saw it fluttering about in the wind.

Hemlock.

Its tiny white petals caught the last of the dying light. Twigs snapped beneath her feet as she trudged through the brambles, and when she reached the hemlock, she plucked a few flower clusters from their stems without hesitation.

The gentle incline of the terrain back to Osborne House was enough for Princess Edith to feel her age. The bones in her knees ached, her breath grew short and laboured. Though still slim in figure, she knew the acceleration of her physical decline had been exacerbated by the exhaustion in her soul. A tiredness that she had long ago accepted would only be relieved by death. Ever since the first day she'd gone along with the lie, she'd began slowly rotting from the inside out.

Today that rancid fruit would finally fall.

As she reached the top of the mezzanine, she turned to take one final, sweeping look over the grounds. The lush green foliage was but a misshapen blur of dark silhouettes, and the waters of the Solent a blanket of shimmering black, reflecting the light of the rising moon. The faint chill of night tickled her skin as wind whipped around her. She drew in a deep breath of the salt-tinged air, and choked back a sob as she recalled John the Guardsman's last words with excruciating clarity:

"I didn't make it in time, Edith..."

She turned away and went inside, uttering a mental *goodbye* to the woman in chains, for she knew that soon she, too, would be freed of her own. The walk upstairs was smooth—not hurried but not dragging, either—a graceful, steady gait that could only come from a heart at peace with its destiny.

In the privacy of her stateroom, she plugged in the silver kettle. It felt like an eternity for her to hear its distinct, whining whistle. She casually tossed the hemlock flowers into a teacup. As she began pouring the boiling water, she caught her ghastly reflection in the mirror. She didn't recognise the woman staring back. The woman who hadn't eaten or slept in days. The woman whose cowardice had foisted unnecessary evil upon the world.

Her entire life she'd been petrified to make a move. To defy her mother, to buck the Crown and do what was right—for herself and for Leon.

That Princess Edith, the rotten one, hidden behind the ageing shell of the woman staring back at her, had given up her entire world just to protect a lie.

A blissful calm permeated through her chest, and as she stared eye-to-eye with her reflection, she delivered one final blow to the woman that she loathed in the mirror.

She made a decision:

It's time to be with my son.

Princess Edith raised the steaming hemlock brew to her lips and gulped it down.

Gavin walked down the dormant hospital hallway, but he couldn't feel his feet. It seemed as if each step taken landed on a predetermined floor tile. He could move forward, but only in this narrow, endless pattern. It reminded him of the dodgem cars at the fair.

The silence of Ballochmyle House at just nine in the evening baffled him. Outside of the flickering hum of the fluorescents and distant murmurs of nurses, not a sound could be heard.

Or perhaps it was the other way around—his mind playing tricks. The percussive thumping of his heart, the pulse pounding at his ears. The hospital very well may have been bustling, filled with an untold number of sounds, but he simply couldn't hear them.

One, two. One, two.

He continued down the hallway, placing each foot on their designated tiles, reading out the numbers of the rooms under his breath.

"...Forty-seven, forty-eight..."

He felt guilty. He had lied to the helpful old hen working the reception desk. He figured the story he wove was both simple and clever enough; that Elder Louise was fetching James some biscuits from the cafeteria and would be right up behind him.

It did happen to work, but that was hardly the extent of his wrongdoing tonight.

He'd snuck out from Kissinger Grounds just as the midsummer twilight dimmed to its standard shade of dark blue. The only time when there was enough darkness to hide amongst the shadows, darting from the dormitory, past the playground, using trees and hedges as cover to escape the sprawling property undetected. When he reached the pavement of the main street, he ripped a handful of daisies he found along its edge, snapping off their roots with a twist of his wrist.

All according to plan, he thought.

He wasn't sure what he was expecting, but surely it shouldn't have been this easy. Maybe a hiccup at reception, or a nosy nurse asking where his mum was. On the other hand, being that he was James' only brother, it made sense that he would visit.

Gavin had been released two days earlier, but James had to stay. He had contracted some sort of stomach bug from the toilet water that required a cocktail of medicines to rid him of it.

The daisies shook slightly in his trembling hand as he neared the room he was looking for.

"Fifty-three."

A second wind coursed through him like electricity. He glanced around, checking for any passersby, and silently slipped into the room. His eyes went wide the moment he saw James, and he watched his chest slowly rise and fall, adrift in a medicated slumber.

He gingerly set the flowers in a conspicuous spot on the counter in case a nurse walked in, then inched toward his brother's hospital bed. Despite his heart racing with newfound energy, a heaviness burdened his soul. Insomnia's jagged nail scratched at what was left of his rational mind, throwing reason to the wayside, and inserting hysterical thoughts of its own.

Gavin couldn't remember when he'd slept last. Maybe a fitful thirty minutes here and there since they escaped the fire. But even before then, he hadn't slept properly. When he'd slip from the waking world, all he could hear were Craig's screams. Those blood-curdling, agonising shrieks that stretched from when Craig was dragged down the hall to the bone-crushing thuds which had made them cease. He couldn't get them out of his head, like a TV set stuck on full volume that wouldn't shut off.

Now, he was a few feet away from the person responsible.

Craig would be alive right now if it weren't for James. I wouldn't have heard the screams. That officer wouldn't have been stabbed. I can't listen to those God-awful screams any longer…

His eyes glistened, lower lip trembling as he reached James' bedside. With a careful hand, he began slipping the pillow out from beneath his neck. Once it was almost off the bed, Gavin continued to smoothly pull it with his free hand, then quickly cradled his brother's head, steadily letting down its weight without jarring him.

James did not stir.

Gavin threw himself atop his brother and pressed the pillow down with as much force as possible.

"I'm sorry…" he whispered. "I need to sleep."

Three minutes earlier

"You hang in there," said Margaret, placing an uncertain hand on Gordon's forearm.

"Aye. I am."

"Ye got banged up so bad they're bound to give you another promotion when you get back."

Gordon laughed, then coughed, clutching his side with a wince.

"Sorry," she said.

"Nae. I need a good laugh after the shite we have been through."

We. Gordon using *that* word caused a warm flutter in her chest.

She watched him wince again as he propped himself up in the hospital bed. Even in pain, she still found him attractive; his green eyes shimmered, his strong jawline defined beneath the thickening stubble of a three-day five o'clock shadow. She admired the casual air about him, despite having lost a quarter of his blood and nearly dying on the operating table just a few days earlier.

"After what you just told me, I bet you're about to get a promotion yourself. There's not a chance the department doesn't terminate him," he said.

"I guess so…" She shifted uncomfortably, trying to avoid thinking of the weight of that responsibility when she was still having difficulty processing all that had happened to her quiet life in her quiet town.

"You deserve it."

She lowered her head, shrugging in a bit of insecurity.

"I mean it, Margaret. Those kids wouldn't have been saved if it weren't for you."

A growing smile emerged on Gordon's face; he hadn't the straightest set of teeth, but they seemed to gleam white from the contrast of his olive skin.

There it is again, she thought as the warm fluttering resumed. "Thank you. Really," she said. "Well, anyhow, I'll let you rest."

She hugged him carefully, then headed for the door.

"Margaret," he said.

She turned back, raised a brow.

"What are ye going to do about Walter?"

A sound tried to escape her open mouth as she paused, mulling her answer. "I honestly don't know."

There was a twinge of disappointment in Gordon's countenance, and though this reaction pleased her, she wouldn't allow him to see it. He mustered a friendly nod. "I'm sure ye will figure it out. Goodnight, Margaret."

She said goodbye and began down the hall towards the stairwell. As she neared it, something moving in an adjacent room caught her attention. A pair of flailing arms jutted out from beneath a pillow. It took a split-second for her eyes to adjust, but she recognised the lad crouched atop the hospital bed, smothering someone beneath his grip.

Gavin! She blocked the air in her throat before she screamed, not wanting to warn him of her approach. She bolted into the hospital room and lunged at Gavin, pulling him back by his shoulders. The pure fury pouring out of such a small laddie frightened even a seasoned officer like her, and as she tried to peel him off completely, he jerked back, elbowing her in the mouth. Margaret tasted blood and saw stars in her vision as the muffled screams of the struggle beneath the pillow filled the room. She staggered, then rebounded, pouncing on him again, using her strength to heave Gavin to the ground.

The wind was knocked clean from his lungs, and his eyes bulged, staring up at Margaret in shock. The rage she'd seen just a moment ago began to fade. Perhaps the fall knocked this from his spirit, too.

"Doctor!" she shouted.

Once the pillow slipped off, she realised the person beneath it was James. *His own brother…*

The skin of James' forehead and cheeks scrunched up tightly as he began to bawl.

"I'm sorry," he blubbered, hiccupping violently. "It was my fault he died…I'm sorry…"

Gavin slid up with his back against the wall as he began to sob too. A nurse skidded into the room, running to James' bedside. Moments later, another. Then the doctor came. A cacophony of chatter echoed from all corners of the room. Margaret's lip stung as a nurse's aide dabbed some alcohol on the wound to clean it. She could tell by the way the nurse's lips moved that she was being spoken to.

Asking her something, but the voice that emerged was muted.

The two brothers' undulating, pent-up cries filled her ears to the point of ringing. What haunted Margaret the most was that those agonising sobs were coming from children. Not an old man who'd seen a lifetime of horrors, or a soldier coming back from the war.

She realised that the children who went into Al's basement had died down there.

The two lads in front of her were merely what was left of them.

CHAPTER 28
THE EVER AFTER

1969

Five years later

"Do I look silly?" asked Arun in a hushed voice.

Aniqa set down the camera and walked over to him. "You look like a Scotsman," she said whilst gently fixing his crooked shirt collar. She held his gaze lovingly, cupping his cheek. "A handsome one at that."

He blushed as he pushed away her hand. "We've got to get going or we'll be late," he said.

Fiona responded with a nod, then hugged both her parents.

Aniqa scurried back to grab the camera. "Just a few more before you go."

"Mum…" griped Arun.

Fiona's mum registered his hurry. "Why not get these last ones outside? It's beautiful out." She gave him a discreet wink, ushering Fiona to the door.

"Brilliant!" echoed Aniqa. She followed them outside, winding up the camera with a mechanical *click-click-click.*

The day that met them in the garden of Fiona's home was picture perfect. A deep blue sky stretched from horizon to horizon, with only a handful of wispy cirrus clouds floating high above. It was then that Arun was reminded of how gorgeous Fiona was. Her blonde curls seemed to glow in the sunlight; they cascaded in tight ringlets past her shoulders, resting at her collarbone. The thin, girlish figure he remembered from years ago was no more. She'd blossomed into a woman. Her blue eyes twinkled as she caught him admiring her, and then she revealed Arun's favourite feature—her beaming smile. She gestured for him to stand close, and he wrapped an arm around her side as they posed for the last of Aniqa's photos.

They had been dating for a few years now, and he couldn't imagine his life without her. He thanked God often that at least one good thing came out of that basement. They never spoke of their time down there, because just like it had been from day one after they were rescued, they didn't have to.

Arun and Fiona saw it in each other's eyes.

The faint shadow only the two could see.

Aniqa approached; she gave Fiona a hug, then turned her attention to him. Her eyes glistened as she looked him up and down. "I'm so proud of the man you've become," she said, just quietly enough that only he heard it.

"I love you, Mum."

He gave her a long, tender embrace. Wrapped in his mother's arms, he caught himself welling up too. For he was reminded of her sacrifice. The fact she'd raised him alone on a single wage, how she'd finished her degree with no help but her own, and most importantly…that during the two weeks he was missing, she never gave up hope.

"I love you more," she said, straightening out his vest a final time.

He smoothed out his ruffled kilt and said his goodbyes, taking Fiona by the hand and heading to his car.

The first few minutes of the drive were silent. Fiona kept glancing furtively at him, and he noticed how she was mindlessly picking at the fabric of her dress in her lap.

"What's wrong?"

"Well…" She paused. "I remember you saying not to mention it, but are ye sure you're okay with this? I know this will be the first year you miss it, and I don't want to be the reason—"

"Fiona, *please*." He steeled himself, grip tightening on the wheel. "I swear I'm fine."

"But we still can make time if ye want—"

"Nae. I'm not going to miss the dance, and it's a good lesson. What if I join the military or I'm off on holiday? I can't plan my life around a single day forever. Just let it be already."

Fiona turned her head to watch the rolling green hills of Cathkin slowly give way to the city. They were headed to the Year Six dance at Hutchenson's Grammar School in Glasgow, which she attended.

Arun felt bad for being harsh. It wasn't her fault that she could read him like a book. She could see the truth—that he wasn't okay. That he was mentally beating himself up for working late last night, for oversleeping, for almost missing lunch with Fiona's family, and for having to make a last-minute alteration on his kilt that ate up the rest of the afternoon. His anger lay in two places; the first with his countless blunders throughout the day, but the other was his constant bending to superstition. The dark thoughts that coursed through his wild imagination about what might happen if he missed it. The fear that he might never see him again.

For the past four years, on the 31ˢᵗ of May, he would spend a few hours at the graveyard talking with his old friend.

It crushed him that today was the first birthday he'd miss.

The last of twilight had faded away. They'd eaten and drunk their fill and danced to the lively tunes for hours on end. Though Arun already knew a few of them, he enjoyed meeting the rest of Fiona's mates.

The clock struck eleven, and by now, most of them were covered in sweat. The body heat produced from the swinging and frolicking of many at the Cèilidh had made the room unbearably stuffy.

Fiona pulled at his hand. "Let's get some fresh air."

She led him out onto the terrace. To Arun's surprise, they were completely alone. The flickering yellow glow of the streetlights became fuzzy halos as the fog began to roll in. Besides a passing car here and there, they could hear nothing but the sound of their breath.

Arun heard an acoustic melody slip through the cracked terrace door. He recognised the song: *Ae Fond Kiss* by The Corries.

"Ae fond kiss and then we sever,

Ae fareweel, alas for ever…"

Fiona extended an open hand to him. "Would you give me this dance?"

He met her cupped hand with his, pressing himself to her. He could smell the sweetness of her perfume as she tucked her neck against his chest. They both began a slow swaying to the bittersweet ballad.

"Who shall say that fortune grieves him,

while the star of hope she leaves him"

As the thick fog enveloped the terrace, for a fleeting moment, it felt like they were the only two people left in the world. The sounds of their peers and the city had disappeared, and this song, this dance—was theirs alone to share.

"Thank you," said Fiona, just above a whisper. "For coming tonight."

"I wouldn't have missed it for the world." He tried not to show it, but those words had stung. Because there was something else he was missing…

They continued their dance, the warmth of their shared embrace insulating them from the tickling chill of the fog.

"Had we never loved sae kindly

Had we never loved sae blindly

Nor never met, nor never parted

We would never have been so broken-hearted"

Fiona pulled back, wiping away tears from her glistening blue eyes. "You should go," she said. "It's not right."

"Fiona, I told ye—"

"*No,*" she pushed out the word. "He was your best mate. I—I didn't know him long, but I do know how much he meant to you. And today is his birthday." Fiona choked back a cry. "I won't be able to bear looking at you if ye don't go."

Her eyes flickered wistfully as they held his gaze. He pulled her into his arms in a tight embrace, then leaned back just enough to give her a kiss. "Did I ever tell ye how much I love you?"

"A time or two," she said. They exchanged a teary-eyed, hiccupping laugh.

As the song finished, he placed his hands on her shoulders. "I want you to go with me."

"But my house is here, you'd have to drive me all the way back—"

"Fiona," he said, ducking his head to level with her. "I want you there."

"We can make it before midnight if we leave now," she said.

They slipped out a side stairwell, forgoing goodbyes to save time. Once in Arun's car, he sped onto the A77, overjoyed that Fiona was by his side.

I'm coming, don't you worry, he thought.

He had to hop the gate to the Catrine Cemetery. Once in, he positioned his torso atop the gate's edge, extending a hand to Fiona. She grabbed it, and he hoisted her up and over, the rough texture of the brick snagging at the fibres of her dress.

They began their careful traipse around the headstones, and a familiar sensation swept over Arun. Every time he came here, he felt like he'd slipped into an old, long-forgotten dream. As if he were staring through a looking glass, seeing the ghost of his former self, and all the stains still clinging to his soul.

As they neared Craig's grave, Fiona stopped in her tracks.

"What is it?" he asked.

She shook her head. "You go. I'll wait here."

They communicated with just a look:

I understand, she said.

He nodded.

Every step closer to the spot, he could feel the darkness resurfacing. The pain they'd all shared those two weeks. When he reached it, he plopped down cross-legged in front of the headstone. In the dim moonlight, it was hardly readable.

Craig Michael Robertson

1951 – 1964

"Happy 18th birthday, mate…" he said, voice wavering. The cries that poured out of him were just as raw as they had been the first night it truly hit him, when he realised Craig was gone and never coming back.

Once he was able to steady himself, he began talking, just as he always did. He got Craig up to speed. Told him about the dance tonight, his good marks in Year Six, and how he and Fiona were both headed to the same uni in the autumn.

He would also ask questions.

After each one he uttered, he stayed silent, leaving room for an answer.

But no response ever came. He trembled at the thought he may never hear his old friend speak again.

The memory of how Craig had begun fading painfully pricked his mind as it returned.

For the first few weeks after they were rescued, Arun saw him—or perhaps the ghost of him—alive in his imagination. He would sleep on his hard floor each night, still unable to handle the softness of the bed, staring into his friend's spectral eyes, talking to him until he drifted off to slumber.

One morning, the ghost of Craig disappeared and never came back.

Those weeks turned into months. Seasons passed, and the sun kept coming out. His mum finished her degree. Craig's parents sold their house and moved South. Time continued to pass. As he grew older, Fiona and he started dating. He found himself caught up in his schoolwork, trying to make his mum proud. But even years later, he'd still end his nights talking to the voice of his old friend.

Thanking him for the gift of life.

That was the part that always summoned the tears.

For deep down, he had always known it was his fault. That was why he still couldn't reconcile Craig's sacrifice.

Why? he thought. I led us there. *It should have been me.*

When certain details of Craig started to become hazy, like the distinct varieties of his laugh, or the sharpness of his green eyes, Arun panicked, and started taking weekly trips to his grave to talk to him there. But at that point, the voice Arun spoke to with Craig was much deeper, and the voice that spoke back was still boyish. The Craig who lived only in his memory. The more the realness of Craig continued to fade, the more frightened Arun became.

Because both in life and in death, Craig was the only real friend he'd ever had in this town.

How can I go on living if I let the person who saved me fade away?

He grappled with that thought daily now that so many years had passed, and he was on the cusp of adulthood. He noticed something else, too. As the sharpness of his memory of Craig faded, so did the rawness of the pain. The wound still tender, but healing.

Perhaps that was why he sat next to Craig's grave, still talking to his dead friend half a decade later. Because holding onto the pain was the only way to keep the memory of him alive a little longer. To let go of the pain was to let go of Craig, and it hurt Arun too much to do that.

But now, it had been close to two years since he'd last heard his voice.

In the hopes of eliciting a response, he grasped onto the pain, digging it up from the depths of his soul.

He remembered the summer with no sun. The man with no skin. The nightmares. The frozen children. The day Margaret saved him. And most poignantly, he remembered Craig's enduring friendship.

"*Please,*" he said through tears. "Say something…"

But nothing. Just pure, agonising silence.

He turned to glance at Fiona. She mustered a tepid smile, as if to let him know she was all right.

Arun thought back to what he'd told her earlier, in the car.

"*I can't plan my life around a single day forever.*"

The reality of those words was almost too much to bear, and he choked back a sob.

"I'm sorry, Craig…I'm sorry it wasn't me."

He stood and said his goodbyes to his old friend's grave. In the first few steps toward Fiona, he felt an icy jolt on the small of his back. The sensation sent shivers racing along his skin.

Arun turned around slowly, and there he was.

Craig.

He looked exactly as he remembered him. Thirteen years old, shimmering green eyes, with a smug smirk that was years older.

"Where'd you go?" Arun asked breathlessly.

Craig snorted, shaking his head. "I figured it would be easier to let go this way."

He mulled Craig's simple answer.

"She's waiting on you, mate."

Arun glanced over his shoulder at Fiona. He turned back, still speechless.

"Go live your life. I'll be waiting for ye up there."

Craig pointed to the sky.

"But——"

"No buts."

Then, Craig took a step forward and wrapped his arms around Arun. He held the outlines of his cold form; it made Arun's eyes misty how Craig's head barely came up to his chest.

He pulled back. "Now go," said Craig.

Arun streaked tears across his cheeks as he wiped them away.

Craig let him go and smiled, nodding in Fiona's direction.

The walk back to the car was silent. There was a noticeable shift in the night air as they exited the cemetery, and he wondered if Fiona could sense it too. Every breath he took seemed fuller, and he wasn't certain if what he had just witnessed was real, but with every passing second, he realised that something had changed.

As if Craig's cold touch had said without words: *It's okay to let me go.*

Once he cranked the car and began the drive back to Glasgow, Fiona reached over and grabbed his hand. Her soft touch made his heart swell.

Finally, she broke the silence. "Who were you talking to back there?"

Arun didn't answer.

He just revealed the beginnings of a smile.

"How simple a thing it seems to me that to know ourselves as we are, we must know our mothers' names."

—Alice Walker

CHAPTER 29
THE DAY OF REST

June 30ᵗʰ, 1984

If Aniqa could do it all over again, she wouldn't have taken them.

When John the Guardsman handed her the two letters that day, it was like she had been pricked by an invisible thorn. Just an imperceptible twinge at first, so faint she hardly noticed. What she didn't realise at the time, was that each passing day she kept those letters tucked away behind a dusty desk drawer in a forgotten corner of her house, the thorn inched deeper. That was what frightened her the most—the idea that her skin had fully healed, and the thorn had become a permanent part of her.

Perhaps that's why she gave them to me.

The thought crossed her mind often. Almost like Princess Edith knew that if the letters didn't reach her son in time, she had to at the very least safeguard her final words in the hands of someone who knew the truth of her secret.

Two decades later, Aniqa still felt the pesky pinch of the thorn. The nagging reminder that the darkness imbued in what was given to her that day was never meant to be hers. Its presence was most noticeable each time she embraced Arun. A sharp, stabbing pain deep within her right hand. It was almost as if Princess Edith's spirit would materialise for a split-second, channelling the intensity of her rage into a single, focused spot.

A shrieking hiss from the afterlife that said:

You still have your son!

Aniqa always tried to bury the wince beneath her firm grip, praying Arun wouldn't notice. She knew better. A residue had been building up in her soul, slowly accumulating year after year, and with each added layer it became harder to hide from those around her. Carrying the weight of sins that were not her own had aged her beyond her years. Sometimes when she was alone, she would curse the late princess. For Aniqa imagined that she'd had an epiphany the morning she learned her son would be sentenced to death.

That her pain was only real if she left a piece of it behind.

A long caterpillar of cigarette ash disintegrated, falling onto her wrist with a singeing tickle. Aniqa flicked the butt instinctively. An ember jumped out; she watched its red glow fizzle, burning a little scar into the armoire.

Aniqa had lost track of how long she'd been standing here, catatonic, staring at her reflection in the mirror. Hours, maybe. It had become a cumbersome part of her routine. Chewing on the fact that the woman staring back at her was the spitting image of her mother. Aniqa's hallucinations of her had long since disappeared. She snorted, reminding herself of the final act of retribution conjured up by her mother's Machiavellian mind; she had discovered the one place where she could still surface that Aniqa couldn't avoid—her face.

Her greatest fear had come true. Physically, she was becoming the woman she had spent most of her life hating. She just prayed that she had broken the cycle; that she had severed the generational tether of trauma once and for all. That each time she held her son, he felt only her love, and that none of the stains within her soul passed over.

Arun and Fiona were expecting their first child—a boy. The thought that she would soon be *Grandmother* always sent her mind spiralling. If she feared holding her fully grown son, how could she ever muster the courage to cradle an innocent newborn? The tiniest bit of darkness might blemish their spirit. Despite how stringently she tried to avoid acknowledging it, the thorn's prick was still there. Deep down, she knew she'd never be able to touch her grandson if she didn't rip it out entirely and allow herself to bleed.

Leaching out the poison given to her that fateful day.

That was why she kept the letters out of sight.

Aniqa had tortured herself throughout the last twenty years, debating what to do with them. She'd already run through a laundry list of options: burning them still enclosed, tearing them to pieces, burying them in a random patch of dirt. She even once tried returning them to John the Guardsman, and that was when she'd learnt of his passing. That day was the first instance she'd felt it—a clap of thunder in her chest that petrified her where she stood. When she'd failed to find John at the palace, a violent tugging within her spirit seemed to pull her away, guiding her feet back to her car, accompanied by a booming, internal voice that said:

Don't!

That was the last time she touched them.

Aniqa never told Margaret of Al's true identity. Nor anyone else for that matter. It had dawned on her a few years ago that she was the only one left alive who knew the secret. Queen Eleanor, Princess Edith, and John the Guardsman had all departed this world.

She figured some things were better left with the dead.

A large part of her pondered why she hadn't. A few times she had been close to leaping off that cliff, taking the letters to a journalist. She imagined the press would have had a frenzy, but the world would finally know the truth.

At least then the burden would be shared.

But she couldn't.

Aniqa had long been at an impasse. There was a piece of her that wanted to let the letters rot until the ink bled out into the page, the message written on them fading away, indecipherable. Purely out of spite. Princess Edith's son had wrought nothing but death and destruction in this world.

Any time those ideas surfaced, she felt that peculiar sensation return. The clap of thunder in her chest. The tug-of-war in her soul.

Princess Edith held one end of the rope, and Aniqa the other.

This morning, Princess Edith pulled back.

Aniqa had been awoken by a coarse, scraping sound.

Short and sharp, but loud enough to pull her from a deep sleep. There was a tickle at the nape of her neck as she searched the house for its source. She slowly went through each room, but in the farthest reaches of her gut, she knew exactly where to look.

Her breath hitched the moment she reached the threshold.

The desk drawer was extended fully out of its wooden slot.

She let out a titter as she stared at the two dust-covered letters within. A smile tugged at her lips, and she reached down, picking them up for the first time in years. Princess Edith had forced her hand. Above her desk, she noticed the date on the wall calendar.

June 30th.

Twenty years to the day since Al's execution.

In that moment, everything clicked.

Aniqa finally knew how to rip out the thorn.

As she drove down the long, straight run of Naver Street, it came into view.

BARLINNIE

The cobalt letters caused an upwelling of emotions tied to the memory of that day—anger, sorrow, and surprisingly, gratitude. While she'd been thankful for getting her son back alive, the most piercing memories of what she'd felt crashed back into her mind with vivid clarity, like a meteor blazing across a sky that had long been dark.

The desire for vengeance.

She remembered its distinct bitter taste. How she'd fantasised countless times about the moment the gallows floor would open, watching Al drop as the noose tightened around his neck, forcing him to pay for his crimes with his life. Once justice had been served, she was reminded of the hard truth she'd had to face in the aftermath. That Al's death hadn't brought back her son—the child who would forever be trapped in that basement.

As she made her way from the car to the prison entrance, she felt the chilly air creep through her clothes, and it drew her attention to how unnaturally cold it was for midsummer. Thick grey clouds hung low, tickling the chimney tops with their wispy tendrils. The eerie sensation of déjà vu swept over her, like she was walking through a replica of that day. Twenty years separated the two dates, yet she couldn't tell the difference. It was as if Al's death had made an imprint in this place, a scar of sorts, and the world had captured its blueprint perfectly, right down to the very last detail.

The clerk that met her inside didn't look up from her paperwork, just adjusted her bifocals hanging from the edge of her crooked nose.

"What can I do for ye?" she asked in a raspy monotone, still scribbling away.

"I need to visit the grave of someone who was executed here."

"Name of the deceased?"

"…Albert Reid."

The woman's pen stopped. She pushed her glasses up the bridge of her nose, eyes squinting as she studied Aniqa with a sharp gaze. The woman's sagging jowls seemed to sink with reproach as she gave a tiny, bewildered shake of her head.

"Why?"

"I'm the mother of one of the missing children, and there's something I have to do."

The old woman sighed. "I remember ye from the news." She hoisted herself up from her chair with a slight groan, pausing to cast a solemn look. "I'll grab someone."

A few moments later, a prison guard appeared. He was middle-aged with a bushy handlebar moustache. His tired eyes only met hers for a split-second when they looked up from the floor and he gave her a polite nod. He didn't say a word, just waved for her to follow.

The guard led Aniqa to a plot of grass in a far-flung corner of the prison grounds. They stood over a tiny, nameless plaque made of stone.

"Are you sure it's his?"

The guard snorted. "You don't forget where someone like him lies."

He left her be. As she sat down in front of the grave, she tried to steady her ragged breathing. The sad truth was that the man beneath her wasn't deserving of what she was about to do, but she had no other choice.

It was time to bury the pain.

Aniqa slipped the letters from her pocket, feeling the worn texture of the paper between her fingers. Each envelope had a name written plainly in pen. She broke the red wax seal of the first, pulled out the letter within, and began reading aloud:

Albert,

I never had the opportunity of meeting you, but after seeing the horrific work of your hand, I am grateful that I didn't. Though I was aware of your existence from afar, I only saw the good—what you made visible on the surface. I hadn't the faintest idea that hidden within you, something else existed. The darkness festering within your soul. But I am afraid that even the deepest wounds cannot begin to justify your actions. Murdering innocent children, stealing them away from their parents, and robbing them of lives unlived.

The permanence of that pain is unlike any other.

I regret to admit that in a way, you and I are the same. My actions also caused countless lives to be stolen. And for that, I will have to face the consequences on my day of reckoning. Upon discovering the truth of who you truly are, Albert Reid, I can now say one thing with complete and utter certainty.

You are not my son.

Your flesh may have been borne of my own, but the evil spirit it housed was not. I do not know that man. Yet, there will always be a part of me that wonders whether my choices created you. But I have made peace with the fact I may never know that answer.

I must pay this debt with my life, and you will soon do the same.

Princess Edith

Aniqa set the letter down and grabbed the next. She slipped her finger through to break the seal, and as she unfolded the letter within, a chill spread from her trembling hands, up her arms, and settled in her chest, prickling her skin with gooseflesh. There was a presence to the cold, a fuzzy outline to the periphery of her being that seemed to grow stronger by the second. As she opened her mouth to read, Aniqa's own voice sounded as if it were infused with the spirit of someone else entirely.

My Dearest Leon,

I apologise that you are reading this in the hour of your death. Learning the truth after a lifetime of lies. For the sin I committed is impossible to atone, nor do I expect you to forgive me.

Queen Eleanor took you from my arms the day you were born. I was eighteen years old, and if I had known then what I know now, I would have done it all differently.

I would have raised you with your father by my side. His name was Sir Charles Stirling; he was a scholar, a wonderful man with a heart of gold, and he loved you dearly. He tried hundreds of times to write to you, and ultimately, he paid the price with his life.

And I'm afraid the lie I helped protect cost you yours.

I do not know how you became that other man, or if he was simply the dark side of a damaged soul split in two. But I will go to my grave steadfast in the belief that within you, the precocious boy I remember still exists. The one who took after my love of painting, who learnt the piano faster than all his cousins, and the one who, despite being marked from the day he was born, still sought the love he deserved. I deeply regret that I was not there to give it to you.

I cannot turn back the hands of time, but I pray God has mercy on our souls. For I dream of the day we can be together, and I can hold you in my arms for the very first time as my son.

The pain I have carried throughout this life is immeasurable. The sheer power behind it will ensure these letters reach your hands, and I shall not rest until you know the truth within them.

That you, Duke Leon of Albemarle—my son—are loved. I have loved you from the first moment I held you, and I still love you now as you face death.

Nothing will ever change that.

Your Mother,

Edith

Amber rays of sunlight spilled through the thick clouds, spreading their warmth across the broken land. Aniqa pulled a box of matches from her coat pocket, slipped one out, and struck it with a steady hand. She held the flame to the edge of the letters and watched the fire slowly crawl across, mesmerised as faded ink evaporated word by word until there was nothing left but ash.

The gentle breeze whisked away the last of the black smoke, and she felt the darkness within her dissolve away. The thorn was gone. She smiled as the earth seemed to shift upwards and then settle, as if it had taken one last tired breath before coming to rest.

Arriving as a soft whisper to her soul, in a voice all too familiar, Aniqa was given a second chance. To listen with a heart made tender by life's hardships. It was then she understood the beautiful weight of the words she'd heard countless times—the promise that begins at birth and knows no bounds.

"A mother's love never dies."

THE END

ACKNOWLEDGEMENTS

Thank you to my mother, father, and brother. I don't know where I'd be today without your love and support, and I'm eternally grateful for all that you have given me in this life.

Many thanks to my skilled editor across the pond, Marie O'Regan, whose keen eye helped weed out any lingering Americanisms and sharpen up my prose. To my cover designer, Nuno Moreira, thank you for crafting such a beautiful representation of the symbolism present within the novel.

To my closest friends:

Alexander, I'm incredibly grateful for your unwavering support of my writing over the years. You've read each of my manuscripts and provided me invaluable feedback. I am honored to be your friend, and it still amazes me how the universe managed to have us attend elementary, middle, and high school together, then community college, and ultimately, transfer to the same university. There's nobody I'd rather share a drink with and shoot the shit about life, science, and the wild stories of our youth than you. I can't thank you enough for taking my art and my work seriously long before anyone else our age gave a damn.

Cameron, thank you for always taking the time out of your day for our (many) phone calls. As a writer, it's a difficult position to put someone in—revealing the entirety of a story's plot years in advance before they ever get to read it. You have no idea how much I appreciate you serving as the sounding board for much of what happened in this story. Any book is a lot to keep bottled up in one's mind, and having you there to parse out certain plot points helped me immensely. You are as sharp as they come, and I believe I'm a better writer, but more importantly, a better person because of your friendship.

Shelby, my Aquarius twin spirit. You have been in my life since we were in the second grade as little bobcats at Blackburn, and I'm grateful our friendship has blossomed over the past few years. As a fellow artist, I admire you so much because with art, I can tell we are one and the same. Thank you for supporting me no matter where in the world I am, for celebrating the highs and comforting me during the lows. I cannot wait for the day we get to work together on a project.

For better or worse, I'm not sure I'll write another book quite like this again in my literary career. *The London Cheque* took a lot out of me. The place I had to go mentally to write this book is not somewhere I want to revisit, nor do I take the effect it had on me lightly. I didn't expect the internal wear and tear to happen since I've never experienced it before while writing, but as the story evolved, so too did the energy required to do it justice. After spending what began as days and quickly became months and years in the dark place I needed to go to capture what I hope comes across to the reader, it became exhausting. While I was relieved when it was finished, I knew deep down that I had left a piece of my soul behind, losing a bit of myself to the act of creation.

How the idea for this novel came about is still a bit beyond my grasp. It happened during my junior year of college at UNC in March of 2017. I was on spring break with a good friend (who, ironically, was a British exchange student) and we happened to visit my dad for a few days before heading to Miami. Little did I know, I would go to bed one of those nights and have a nightmare so vivid that to this very day, every nightmare I've had since pales in comparison.

I dreamt about the man with no skin. The basement room filled with frozen children sitting on the ice blocks, and the skin of their arms carved out into intricate flower patterns. I felt like I was awake for a few days, trapped in that cold basement, and when I finally escaped by swimming, I'll never forget the visceral anguish I felt from seeing the black van coming after me, knowing that recapture was imminent.

I awoke in a cold sweat, and three words came to me: *The London Cheque*. I remembered that I even said the words aloud.

I've had a fair number of dreams where upon waking, I scratch my chin a bit and say, "That might be an interesting plot." Then, I write whatever I can remember down before I lose it completely, stow it away, and move on. But I have never—before or after that dream—awoken with the title of a book on the tip of my tongue. And in the furthest reaches of my being, I knew that was special. The title was given to me, from God knows where.

Roughly two years after the nightmare, I shelved the manuscript I had been working on throughout college to begin writing this book— my debut horror. All I had were the title and the imagery from the nightmare. What came after were months of planning and research to connect all the dots. The culmination of that effort is what made it into this book. I want to thank author and historian Lucinda Hawksley, whose book *Queen Victoria's Rebellious Daughter: A Biography of Princess Louise* helped inspire certain scenes and orchestrate the family dynamics for the fictionalized version of Queen Eleanor's Royal Family in *The London Cheque*. I was so intrigued when I discovered this historical rumor—that Princess Louise may have gotten pregnant and given birth out of wedlock—that its speculation became the catalyst for the story's plot and served as the perfect throughline to shoulder the overarching theme. Remember, dear reader, this book is purely a work of fiction. There is no Duke Leon, no banished-royal-serial-killer in existence. The inspiration gleaned from Hawksley's biography solely includes the bits I find important to critique through literature: the Crown's tendency for secrecy, the power dynamics, and the lengths they may hypothetically go to protect their status and reputation.

To the residents of Catrine:

I apologize that your village had to be the setting for such a sad story, but I hope the research and care I put into learning about Catrine's history shows. I spent an untold number of hours walking every street (albeit virtually) and devouring any bit of historical information I could get my hands on to paint as realistic a picture as possible. From what I gathered about present-day Catrine, locals have been involved in campaigns to save buildings associated with its heritage, to benefit the community, and to build tourism. I truly hope to be able to spend some time in person and get to know the proud and kind people of Catrine.

Outside of the nightmare being the inspiration for the book, I feel like I have to tip my hat to honor those who came before me and are innovators in the genre. Stephen King, of course. I'm not sure how you write a fat manuscript in three months, but I hope one day to find out. I've counted, and there are fifty-one named characters in *The London Cheque*. I can only hope that I made them jump off the page and seem authentic to the reader even a shred as masterfully as you do. Catriona Ward, Neil Gaiman, Victor LaValle, James Hannaham, Robert McCammon, Nick Cutter, and Blake Crouch are also some of my favorite writers of dark tales.

Film-wise, Ari Aster is consistently putting out original, psychological horror. I also admire the late genre-jumping Stanley Kubrick, Yorgos Lanthimos, Darren Aronofsky, Damien Chazelle, Bong Joon-Ho, Paul Thomas Anderson, Charlie Kaufman, Luca Guadagnino, Wong Kar-wai, Peter Weir, Alexander Payne, Greta Gerwig, Lulu Wang, and many others. In the final scene of this book, I included a deliberate nod to one of my all-time favorite directors, Denis Villeneuve, as a tribute to his masterpiece of a film, *Incendies*.

I was twenty-two when I first watched Robert Eggers' *The Witch* in theatres. It was the first horror movie I can recall where the moment the credits rolled in the theatre, I thought:

Damn. I feel like I just watched something that I wasn't supposed to see.

When I started writing this book, I was inspired by that macabre sensation. I sought to create a story that, when someone turns the final page, they say to themselves: "I feel like I just finished reading something that I wasn't supposed to read." Maybe the story made you a little queasy at times, or perhaps it left you feeling angry, forlorn, or shocked. Maybe I even tugged on your heartstrings a little—or a lot. If *The London Cheque* has evoked any one of these reactions in just a single reader, then I will consider my goal as the writer accomplished.